The Last Conversation with Anna

The Last Conversation with Anna

-An Emotional Story of Emotions-

UDAY MAN SINGH

PARTRIDGE

A Penguin Random House Company

To order additional copies of this book, contact
Partridge India
000 800 10062 62
orders.india@partridgepublishing.com

www.partridgepublishing.com/india

Contents

About the author

Uday Man Singh

Uday Man Singh is currently working as software professional with NVIDIA Corporation since April 2013. He hails from a small town Orai from Uttar Pradesh. In his first organization he met few best friends for lifetime and this novel which is also his first novel revolves around those friends life.

(Email-id: udayman.s@gmail.com)

Dedicated to the person I love the most: My mother

All mothers in the world –

(A mother's job is the toughest of all)

my friends

and

Anna

This journey was not possible at all without constant support and guidance from my friends and family.

Special mention to Arundhati Bhabhi, she has helped me a lot in reviewing my work.

Thanks to Shantanu who helped in designing the cover page.

My friends Upendra, Vineet, Shailendra are the first guys with whom I shared the idea of writing and I thank them for not laughing at me and this idea. Thanks buddies.

Thanks to my great friends Nivedita, Vishal, Udita, Taruna, Arun, Shikha, Saumya, Jyoti, Pooja, Lavanya and Divya. I bugged them constantly with snippet of novel, which they read with patience and provided valuable suggestions.

Thanks to my friend Prateek and Akhilesh for constantly giving suggestions on the room, Prateek is one who suggested writing novel on MS-word to minimize spelling's error.

Thanks to MS-Office.

Finally thanks to my family friend Rani.

Thanks to my one great and special friend and inspiration Anna, for being with me in my good and bad times.

Thanks to my colleagues from Newgen and Nvidia, they always encouraged me.

I am sorry, if I forgot to mention any person who has helped me in this journey.

And my greatest apologies if any content of this work hurt anyone in any manner.

Uday Man Singh

Prologue

Anna – When I entered **teenage years**, I had fallen in love with one guy, I told my mother about it when I realized my condition and I was surprised to hear her response "Anna this will never be accepted in our family, hence I warn you to behave and also advise you to never indulge in such a thing ever in future". I don't know how and what those words did to me but it transformed my heart in to a stone and engraved those words in there forever. Later so many boys tried to come close to me in school, college and office but no one ever succeeded in converting that stone into heart. I know that no one can ever change me.

Rayman – My first encounter with any female friend happened when I was in **class fifth**. Her name was Savita, she was very beautiful and she was my best friend. We use to play together and eat together in recess time, go for opening prayer together. Until I played a prank on a girl using some other boy's name but that prank went wrong and messed up everything. Next thing I remember after that prank that I was being beaten in the principal's office and that is reason for breakup in my first friendship with any girl. We never spoke to each other afterwards and I know I was on fault and I didn't even try to clear misunderstanding as well.

When I was in **class ten** I have another great friend in Neha and I really want to marry her at that time. This is first time I felt love, I tried to tell her many times but she didn't get my feeling and she never expressed her emotions. I waited for two and half year for her and during this time I heard that she loved one of my fiend so I decided to move on and find someone else as that is the time of life when almost everyone experiencing same thing. I thought that I should also try like Mr. Edison for love until I get success (which I later realized that love doesn't work that way) and in **class twelve** I found Neeti and proposed her, she accepted my proposal. My story with Neeti continued for next one year and I informed her brother about my love for her because I am really serious, but this time I forgot who will marry her sister to a guy who is studying in class twelve and he played like Bollywood villain in my story and I wasn't able to see her for next few years.

When I was **nineteen years** old I cheated Neeti and one more beautiful girl Sadhna came in my life. I backed off one more time in front of Sadhna giving her excuse that I love Neeti and that is reason behind one more breakup and I know that this is also my fault that I fall for a girl though I was committed to someone else. Neeti also called me one day to confirm whether I flirt with other girls and I said yes and I can guess she must be thinking of saying fuck off to me but instead she said "be happy with them and forget and forgive me forever", I haven't tried to even convince her that I would change because I can't lie. Like all other times, I was at fault and I had cheated. I don't know if someone is going to change me and my attitude.

Let's party begin

An evening of winter of November 2008, climate is quite cold outside. Wind is colder in night on Delhi roads to even freeze blood inside veins. Visibility is also very less due to fog; it is hard to see even for few meters distance, no sign of any person not even security personals on traffic signals.

Suddenly noise from an auto rickshaw is start coming from distance on Siri-fort auditorium road. Who can dare to go out in this cold? This must be something very urgent or critical. Two guys talking to each other on passenger seat, they are very well dressed and appearing ready to attend wedding party and as this is wedding season hence it is possible that they are going to attend some wedding and Siri fort area have few marriage hall which makes it even obvious option.

Auto rickshaw comes to halt few meters before Siri fort auditorium. Opposite to that deserted road few hundred meters before auditorium this place have lots of people enjoying and having fun in open around Siri fort auditorium. Many cars, auto rickshaws, cabs moving in every direction, life is in full swing here. Siri fort auditorium is all decorated from outside, a program of live music from famous ghazal singer Jagjit Singh is going on in one open air hall of auditorium. Few people formed queue and others are fighting to make their way inside the hall some way or other. This place has no sign of cold, crowd making this place hotter than rest of the Delhi.

When auto rickshaw come to halt those two guys come out, only who can't afford to travel in car or cab will go in auto in this cold. One guy is taller and other is shorter from their dress it is quite visible that they are going for some party. Shorter guy walked past Jagjit Singh concert hall with fast pace and approached back side hall while the taller is still standing near rickshaw and paying fare. After paying taller guy also followed shorter guy walking even faster and in few seconds he matched mark with him. Both guys together made entry in one hall and it seems that party is already started in this hall when they reached inside and from decoration and crowd it is quite obvious that it is one corporate party. One stage is set up in one corner of that open-air hall, stage must be set up for employee performances, on right side of stage D. J. floor set up with D.J. ready to play music as soon he instructed to start the show, floor is big enough to occupy at least hundred people at a time, but most of the guys not seeming interested in any of the set up made around stage. In front of stage at distance of around twenty or twenty five meters few rows of chairs set up for accommodating guests of party and after those rows of chairs few meters area kept open and then few meters area covered with lighting and artificial ceiling of clothing, everything is glittering with colorful lighting. One side of lawn is laden with arrangement of food, where two stall of golgappa followed by few stalls of non-vegetarian starter than few stalls of vegetarian starter dishes followed by at least ten types of veg and non-veg salads and then same number of counter for veg curries followed by even more non-veg curries with all possible options followed by stall of Indian breads coming out of clay oven. People are at every stall, at least three long queues on golgappa stall and few people are around starter's stalls, but no one is looking interested in main course so early in the evening and that make those stall deserted.

At the end of lawn on right corner a group of at least hundred people are fighting for something and noise of their struggle can be heard even from long distance. It is not visible from outside what is being served on that counter but from fight it look like something similar to nectar being served from that counter. But when few guys came out of that counter they looking like as if they just survived some war and coming with glasses of colorful drinks in their hands and that made clear about this stall, alcohol is being served on this counter and most of the guys coming out with glasses of whisky, wine or beer in their hands. This counter is installed in the similar area of at least three other counters. After concentrating very hard to see behind crowd five or six bartenders are busy in making drinking as per crowd wish. Very few people looking interested in soft drinks or juices even girls are making entry at the counter in but in lesser number.

Those two guys are visible more clearly in brighter light now; taller guy is in blue denim jean and a stylish red and blue checked shirt with white color collar and shorter guy is wearing black trouser with printed red color shining shirt and both were standing after rows of chairs in open area and scanning whole hall with searching eyes, they are looking for their other friends now.

"I think Toni hasn't reached yet, have you called him or not?" Shorter guy said to taller guy.

"Yeah I called him before leaving for here; but I also feel that he hasn't reached yet. Let's go and have drinks in mean time while we are waiting for others."

Taller guy's name is Vishu and other one is Rayman, they both work in same company and it's their company annual party going on in this hall and they are waiting for their friends.

"What he said when you called him? Where were he and Vicky and any news about Praveen or Utsav? I think Tanu, Lavanya and Deepali must have already reached here and must be rehearsing behind the stage." Rayman asked Vishu in return.

"Hmm, he said that he will be leaving just after hanging my call and one of his cousins also coming with him. It might be that he is picking him from someplace out of route to here and got late. I don't have any update from Vicky, Utsav and Praveen. Utsav must have reached here and surely be on drink stall let's check him there."

"Let's eat something first, I am feeling little hungry and by the way I am not in mood of drinking too much."

"I somehow know that this is coming but I also know that as usual you start once then wouldn't stop till drink last." Both laughed on Vishu's comment on Rayman.

"I think Toni will be coming with his girlfriend this time and that must be reason for him getting late. I doubt his girlfriend's name is cousin that is why he is always busy with his cousin. What you say?" Rayman asked to Vishu with puzzled face.

"You are an idiot that is what I think but you are right this time." he burst out in laughter after this and Rayman also followed him in this act.

Vishu went to meet his some other friends standing few steps away and Rayman now paying attention toward stage but nothing interesting is going on there, Few guys are on the stage on formal suites and one gentleman is having microphone in his hand and addressing people sitting on chairs. Speaker is hidden behind a wooden podium making only upper half of speaker visible to audience. The person who is addressing audience is in his forties, having nice moustache with few grey hair, and wearing steal blue colored formal suite.

One girl of medium height is also standing in one corner at back of stage. She has her ears on his speech, and she is wearing flower printed Salwar Kameez suite. Speaker cracked some joke on stage which make everyone burst out in laughter in front rows, people on back rows followed the laugh riot without hearing anything as they all are busy in discussing something.

Rayman felt someone's hand on his shoulder and turned back after hearing "Hey man, how are you? When did you come? You must be looking for girls on the stage, there is still some time for girls to come on stage, and it's time for boring speeches. Have you seen anyone else?" It is Utsav. He is a little chubby, jolly guy in formal trouser and shirt. He is already looking like two or three pegs down.

"No, just time-pass, I and Vishu came few minutes ago, Vishu is with his flat mates I guess or may be with girls from their teams or may be with Tanu and her friend. Toni still not came; other girls might be behind stage. When did you come? You are looking like two three pegs down, How much you drank? Party is yet to start but you looking on the edge of passing out." Both started laughing after this comment of Rayman. Vishu joins them by this time and Praveen and Vicky are also with Vishu. Vishu has come in party mood by now and had one glass of large peg of whisky in his one hand.

Praveen appears techie geek from his face and appearance, He has frame less glasses on his eyes and wearing formal trouser and shirt. Praveen came with one of his friend from his college. Vicky is very thin and tall guy with hair style from his child hood, side partition with lots of oil in them. He also appears techie geek in his thick framed glasses and black trouser and round neck t-shirt of off-white color.

Praveen greeted and asked to everyone "Hello guys, when did you all came?"

Praveen's friend noticed Rayman and he greeted him as they three are from same college "Hi Rayman"

"Hey Akram How are you, I have heard from Praveen that you became some scientist."

"Yeah kind of"

"Hey guys who is that girl on the stage holding mic and wearing specs. I think I am falling in love with her." Utsav interrupted conversation in between and brought everyone to stage. Everyone shifted their focus from food and drink to stage to notice that beautiful and tall girl. She is appearing like some celebrity on the stage. She is in skirt top of dark red color and thick framed specs like Vicky. She is taller than average girls and beautiful with very nice figure. We all have our ears on the stage to hear her words clearly and then she spoke.

"Ladies and Gentlemen" Her voice echoed for at least thirty seconds in these guys' ears. She continued "Or rather I should say my dear colleagues, seniors and family members. It is my pleasure to call our Managing Director sir on the stage. Please put your hand together to welcome him on the stage.

"No, not again" Vishu and Utsav said in one voice.

A guy in late forties came on stage in navy blue color suite with contrast colored tie in between noise from claps from audience.

"Hey Akram, that is managing director of my company, let's come closure to stage, I want to hear his words." Praveen said to Akram and started walking toward the stage and Akram followed him.

"There they are, I said to you naah that they all will be together either drinking or feeding their eyes." Voice came from distance from someone coming toward these guys. Two tall and smart guys were coming with quick steps. Both guys are very fit and both are in formal clothes. The guy who said about them is wearing striped shirt and black trouser and shiny black shoes.

"Hi Toni" Rayman greets new guy.

"Hello" Toni greeted in return and he also greeted others as well. "This is my cousin Sanjeev and Sanjeev these are my buddies from office. Rayman, Vishu, Vicky and Utsav" Toni continued after introduction. "What is going on? Where are others, Tanu, Deepali and Lavanya?" Toni is not one of the guys who go after girls but Tanu, Lavanya and Deepali are close friends of this group. He further asked Rayman "What happened? Why aren't you drinking? What is this! guys, no food, no drink and no girls, this is how you are enjoying the party?"

"Hey Sanjeev, he is the one I told you about." Toni said to Sanjeev about Rayman.

"Oh, so he is the one. I heard a lot about you."

"Really" Rayman asked in surprise. Toni and Rayman with Tanu are in same team and Toni must have shared about the fun and gossips they are having in the office.

This conversation ended with the noise of claps and laughter which is coming from first few rows of audience which is indication that speech is over and that guy is leaving stage now.

"Hi guys" voice came from very beautiful, fair girl. "Oh-ho, Look at the Toni, have you come for some wedding or so?" Tanu made taunt on Toni

"Yes off course, of yours. Where is that Donkey you going to marry?" Toni responded very quickly.

"I'm not talking to you, don't you dare to talk to me again." She is very furious on Toni's remark.

"You guys started once again, it's not office bro it is party. What is problem with you guys? You start each and every place." Rayman said to both of them, he knows their habit of arguing very well as he witnesses all this couple of time every day.

"Hi Vishu, have you come alone? Where is Diya, hasn't she come with you?" Tanu asked Vishu.

"No, she had some work. Where were you and where are Deepali and Lavanya?"

"I was with them only they are preparing for their fashion show event behind the stage."

"Aren't you doing giddha or bhangra (folk dances from Punjab)?" Toni once again made taunt.

"I am not talking to you and I am not doing any giddha or bhangra, you do your salsa or whatever you can, I don't care." Tanu is still very furious.

"Hey Tanu, its ok yaar, leave this naah. We came here to enjoy why are you two fighting? Why you always have higher temper?" Rayman said to Tanu.

"It is his fault entirely, he always starts it. Idiot" She murmured under her breathe. Rayman hinted him to stop and winked and Toni replied with mischievous smile.

Tanu is appearing a bit upset after all this fight her face turned red with anger.

"Hey Tanu come here, what you doing there? Let me introduce you to my team mates." A well-built guy called her from the distance who doesn't cared to come near them.

"Hi" Tanu appearing happy once again after interaction with him and moved in that direction. Few minutes later she returned with him.

"Hey guys this is George from other group in our building. He is good friend of mine." Tanu introduced him to everyone. George doesn't know many of us but he knows Vicky and Toni very well. He greeted Toni first followed by greeting to everyone else.

"Hey Tanu, you enjoy with them, I am going with my team. See you around."

"I am also coming with you." Tanu followed him.

"Let's go and have some drinks yaar." Vishu said to Utsav and Rayman. Vishu and Utsav left to bring drinks. Rayman, Toni and Vicky stayed back there and talking about events in the party, Vicky still has his eyes and focus on anchor on the stage, Toni and Rayman are eyeing girls in the party. Sanjeev is enjoying snacks and drinks.

Their conversation broke with sweet voice from anchor "Hello friends. I hope you all are enjoying the evening. What else once can ask for? Music, food and drink and no tension of work" She is waiting for audience response now but audience is quite busy in food, drink and gossip, when no response came from audience even after two or three minutes she announced "Everybody seems to be very busy in enjoying delicious food and drink. But I want attention from all of you on the stage. Can you guys guess what is next attraction coming your way? Yes your guess is exactly right; please welcome our colleagues from our own office as models in fashion show organized by our cultural committee." After this announcement light dimmed on stage and anchor moved back of the stage, nothing is for next few minutes, slowly light came in center of stage in various color with smokes and fumes and one beautiful girl in some stupid clothes also visible in the center of that light, a very beautiful, sexy girl with extra makeup and wearing Salwar Kameez suit. A very fancy salwar kameez suit with dupatta draped from one shoulder to other side on waist. She roamed on the stage for twenty odd seconds and then a boy joined her on the stage and stood at one side of stage and few feet behind the girl who is standing in the center of stage near the front edge. Girl moved toward back of the stage after making three or four poses followed by same poses from the boy and then he also went back of stage.

Audience is also giving proper response to this event; every eye is glued on the stage by now. Crowd which was gathered around drink and snacks stalls, is now came forward near stage. One after another at least twelve to fifteen couples entered stage. Most of the couples are in same traditional Indian wear like first couple with little modification in design or color except one couple in which girl came in green colored shining saaree, her saaree is really disaster in this event, and that too shiny green with golden thin border, she is looking one odd in that group but somehow girl is looking very simple and extremely beautiful but looking really odd and hence no one noticed that girl, but really who cares about who is wearing what? It is fashion show of company annual function no guideline or specification is given about who can wear what.

"That girl is looking very sexy." Vishu pointed toward tallest girl on the stage, she is a dusky beauty with very beautiful eyes, slim and sexy with curly hair.

"Yes" Rayman and Toni also looking at that girl.

"Who" Utsav asked to confirm the girl and said yes after noticing that girl, he is still busy in drinks. Vicky on the other hand is still searching for anchor.

"There are lots of new faces in this party? Who is that girl, have you seen her before?" Rayman asked Vishu about tall girl.

"No but why? Do you like her? She is at least two feet taller than you." Vishu replied to Rayman.

"Hmm, and have you noticed that girl in saaree? She is looking so odd but she is so fair." Rayman further asked but this time no one noticed his question everyone is too busy in the event on the stage.

"We will go to D.J. floor after this fashion show." Fashion show ended as Vishu completed this sentence and stage once again filled with light and anchor is in the center of the stage.

"She is also very good naah" Vishu made remark on anchor.

"Yeah" Utsav and Rayman also nodded.

"She should have also come for fashion show, she is better than most of the girls in fashion show." While they were busy in their conversation anchor announced next event "Please welcome from my own team Jay and his team with their play on life of a software engineer."

"No. I can't take it" Toni, Vishu and other said in one voice.

"Let's have some more drink" Rayman said and Vishu and Utsav followed him, Vicky stayed there waiting for anchor to come again. Rayman, Utsav and Vishu had hard drink in their hands and rests are having soft drinks in their hands. Toni is holding snacks in his one hand and Rayman also carrying some snacks in one hand and rest of the guys eating from plates of these two gentlemen. By this time two others girls came and joined them, both girls looking really beautiful, one of them have slim figure like models is Deepali and other who is little chubby is Lavanya.

"Vishu, I was sure about you that you and Utsav must be drinking, Toni what happened to you, you are not drinking anything." Lavanya asked Vishu and Toni, Deepali is talking to Vicky and Rayman.

"How come you guys left stage, Is all your drama done there, it is good by the way. We can watch people dancing on dance floor now, especially our Vishu with his hanky on his for head." Rayman said to Deepali and Lavanya.

"Hey, it wasn't drama, it is fashion show and one more round will be coming later, but we are waiting for this play to end, what these guys doing on the stage, they are not ending their pathetic play." Deepali replied to Rayman.

"How long they going to take with this shit." Vishu enquired.

"I think one or two hours." Lavanya replied "Only they said to us to have some snacks as they will take around this much time so I guess they will definitely take said time."

"Shit" All boys said in union.

"Yes, that is the reason we came here to have something." Deepali and Lavanya are also looking upset with the play.

"Take this and we will bring other." Rayman and Vishu handed what they had in their hand and went to bring other snacks.

"Toni, where is Tanu, I though she must be with you guys." Lavanya asked.

"Who knows and who really care?"

"Hey what happened? Vishu what happened here?" Lavanya asked Vishu to confirm the reason behind being him so rude.

"I guess fashion show just ended and then they started some bull shit." Vishu is by now at least four or five pegs down.

"Leave it and you enjoy your drink."

"Oh God! they argued on something as usual." Vishu replied this little seriously and continued further. "Hey Lavanya, the news of transfer from our group to Delhi office, is it true? I heard few guys will be going to Delhi office."

"What I haven't heard any of this shit." Rayman cut conversation.

"Yes, I heard someone from other floor already transferred and one guy from our group will also be going there." Lavanya confirmed the news.

"I guess they will throw someone whom they think of no use." Toni made comment.

"In that case I must be on their list" Rayman taunted on his this remark.

"I guess it must be me, I am going to miss you all."

"Hey guys, what's up? Lavanya fashion show was awesome, how much this play will take? We want to dance now, it's already ten, and then they will start saying that there is no time for D.J." Tanu asked the same question to Lavanya, she is back in group now.

"So go and dance, who is stopping you?" Toni replied first.

"Are you mad? Yes you are mad. We can go to dance floor once D.J. start paying music, but not until they stop this non sense on the stage."

Play ended after one more hour and by that time everyone is exhausted, anchor once again came on the stage and this give satisfaction to people that they still have around one hour to enjoy dance. This time anchor appearing even more beautiful and this must be due to alcohol effect. She said something but Vishu and Rayman could not hear anything and that too probably due to alcohol.

"Hey Toni, what she said? Why isn't D.J. floor opened for us?" Vishu asked Toni.

"Dance is on the cards dear but not from you but somebody coming on stage and she said that fashion show next round will be followed by this dance performance." Vicky replied instead who is hearing anchor with concentration.

"I will kill them all. Phew" Vishu is quite angry "Let's go and eat something, I am feeling hungry. Is anybody up for food?"

"Yeah" Everybody followed Vishu to food stall.

"I am not eating now. I am going to take one more peg. Rayman are you coming?" Utsav said to Rayman.

"Yeah, I am also not hungry" Rayman and Utsav went to drink's stall and rests to food's stalls.

Few girls and boys came on the stage for dance performance some of them are already performed in fashion show, they must be fresh graduate, who must have joined company this year, this happens every time and everywhere, they make fresher to perform in school, colleges and companies. After twenty minutes dance performance ended and once again anchor popped out on the stage, and these special effects are only visible to drunken guys. She announced fashion shows next round a she already said in her previous announcement too.

Lavanya and Deepali went behind the stage after this announcement, Rest of guys sitting in a circle around two tables, Toni, Vicky, Vishu and Tanu are eating and Utsav and Rayman drinking, Rayman had two glasses of beer on the table and Utsav is having whisky.

"Why two glasses?" Toni asked Rayman.

"Ohh, when I went to bring beer last time they are saying that beer stock is finished so I took two glasses at once."

Fashion show started once again and this time theme is western opposite to traditional in first round and girls appearing sexier and guys dumber.

"Have you noticed that tall girl with curly hairs? Isn't she sexy?" Utsav made expert comment.

"Yeah" Vishu and Rayman supported.

"Control" Vicky said to them.

"Hmm" they just nodded but nothing is going to change in their behavior for sure.

"She is so skinny, she would be better if she would have little extra fat." It is from Vicky now.

"I love her like this" Rayman is also not far behind.

"Will you guys stop this non sense?" Tanu interrupted.

"What, you can also look at boys." Toni replied to Tanu.

"There is not even single boy, I can look at."

"This is problem with you girls; you always have some or other problem."

"I am serious; they are not even close to you guys."

"Hmm"

"Let's go home"

"How are you going home?" Toni and Tanu talking to each other and rest are busy in fashion show.

"I am going in office cab with Lavanya and Deepali. Why?"

"Nothing, just making sure that you are ok."

"OK" Utsav, Vishu and Rayman left Toni, Vicky and Tanu on that table and went to drink's stall to refill their glasses.

"I think Praveen left for home, people started leaving, and we should also look for cabs for home." Vicky said to Tanu and Toni.

"I want to dance." Tanu said sadly.

"OK, let this fashion show end and then we will decide what to do next. Let Deepali and Lavanya come."

By this time Utsav, Vishu and Rayman also came but surprisingly not with glasses but plates of food in their hands."

"Look there, they already started eating. I am going to take ice cream" Vicky said to Toni.

"We brought food for you also." Vishu said to Vicky.

"No thanks we are done with food, I want little ice cream, Tanu, Toni you guys want ice cream."

"Yeah" and they left to take ice cream.

D.J. chances are getting dimmed as time approaching mid night but fashion show in still going on at the stage. It is around ten forty when Lavanya and Deepali also joined them on the table and they also started eating from their plates.

"What happened? Fashion show is still going on, what you guys doing here?" Vishu asked Lavanya.

"It is about to end in five minutes. I am very hungry now."

As Lavanya said fashion show ended in ten minutes and anchor once again came on stage to announce that D.J. is on and people can enjoy dance and also warned them not to come on the main stage while dancing. Vishu handed his plate to Deepali and approached D.J. with Utsav and Lavanya. Tanu also followed them and so Toni and Rayman. In next five minutes everybody is on the floor, Vishu has his handkerchief tied on his forehead and this is not something new, it is his own style of dancing after tying handkerchief on the forehead. Vishu, Deepali, Utsav, Tanu and Lavanya are dancing in a circle near the D.J. floor as floor is already very crowded and Vicky, Rayman, Toni are standing by one side of this circle and clapping for them. Tanu's friend George is dancing on dance floor with his team mates and he called Tanu also over there after he noticed her. Tanu bumped into one girl on the way to D.J. floor, she was dancing with her team. They are the guys from boring play.

"Sorry" Tanu's friend said to that girl.

"Can't you see? Cheap people" One of her friend said back to them.

"I have already apologized then what is the need of arguing?"

Vishu is still dancing by the side of dance floor, Toni asked Tanu and her friend to come down the D.J, floor and turned toward that guy who is shouting on Tanu and her friend, he is one guy in mid thirty and a little fatter. He was dancing with his team before argument and then we noticed that beautiful anchor is also dancing with them.

"Sorry we didn't do it intentionally." Toni apologized to them once again and then they all left D.J. floor. That guy didn't noticed any word from Toni and turned back to dance with his team.

"This is last song of the evening, it is ten fifty five and as per police regulation we are not allowed to play music beyond eleven in the night." D.J. announced and this announcement made everyone furious. Everyone left for their home in cab or their own vehicle after this last song. Vishu is still angry as they got just two songs for dancing.

"Let's meet on Monday in the office, good night" They left for home after bidding good night to each other.

First glimpse

*R*ayman is at his seat in his office. A week passed after annual party, everything is back to his or her normal work routine in this last week in the office. They all work in Software Company and like any other software firm this is also extended and luxurious version of cyber café, where everybody is busy doing something on his or her computer. The office's interior made of glass work and wooden work, outer wall made of toughened glass and two glass cabin located in the center of office.

Office is divided in few rectangular shaped cubicle capable to contain eight people, Vishu and Vicky sit in first cubicle, Toni, Tanu and Rayman in second, Praveen, Deepali in third cubicle and Lavanya sits on other floor. Rayman, Toni and Tanu report to Ram who also sit in their cubicle behind Lokesh who is other guy in this team and one other senior guy sitting in this cubicle and leaving few seats empty in their cubicle. Vishu and Vicky's boss sits in their cubicle, one girl and four more guys making all of the seats occupied in their cubicle. Both the bosses are in their mid-thirty, Vishu's boss wears frame-less spectacles and both usually comes in formal wears. Vishu's boss has his eyes on other team mate's computer screen rather than on his own. Vishu is reading mail and Vicky already started his work.

A guy with at least twenty cup of tea in a tray walked past Vishu cubicle after putting one cup at his boss's seat. Vishu followed that guy to Rayman's seat and took one cup from tray, Toni, Tanu and Rayman also took one cup each, Rayman's boss also took one cup and turn toward his computer screen.

"Hi Tanu, Toni, Vishu and Rayman" Lavanya greeted everyone she also joined them in morning tea at their desk. "Hey guys, annual party's pics have come, they are with support guys and they will probably share by today second half." She broadcasted news which she got from some of her sources.

"These pictures will reveal many secrets, now we can see who was doing what at the party." Tanu commented with her gaze fixed on Rayman and Vishu.

"How was weekend? Has anyone watched any movie?" Toni asked everyone cutting Tanu's comment.

"I was here in office whole weekend; major release is due in next week." Rayman replied first.

"I went home." Vishu is second.

"You guys are so boring naah, let's go to some movie this weekend." Tanu taunted and Lavanya supported her with a smile.

"You don't have any work in office naah, whole day gossiping and that is the reason you can plan for movie." As usual Toni cut her comment.

"Gossip and me? We have left gossiping for you and Rayman, you both gossip all the day like girls."

Few guys already started working in the cubicles, Tanu calls Deepali for breakfast and Deepali joined them in their cubicle after few minutes followed by Praveen.

"Vicky, Let's go for breakfast, there is enough time for work." Toni asked Vicky for breakfast.

"You guys carryon and I will join you guys in five minutes, I have to reply this mail urgently and by the way if anybody brought anything special for breakfast, please left little for me too."

"We are having everything from cafeteria only, but come quick" Toni said and left behind others, who are already out of the gate toward cafeteria which is located on terrace, cafeteria half open air and half covered with shed. A small kitchen is located in one corner of cafeteria where small items like Maggie, omelet and tea can be prepared, lunch and dinner food is outsourced. The guy who served tea is cooking something inside that kitchen. That guy is lean and very quick in serving people. Plastic's table and chairs are arranged on terrace for employees to have their food or gossip in both open area and under the shed. Rayman and Vishu reached first in the group and they occupied chairs and two tables under shed for their group. Few guys are already sitting in cafeteria; they had finished their breakfast and but still gossiping there.

"Anybody wants tea?" Toni asked.

"We already had on our desks." Tanu replied first.

"I" Vishu and Rayman said in one voice.

"I too" Vicky and Lavanya also said yes.

"And you Deepali?" Toni asked to her as well.

"No"

"I will also have" Tanu said after everybody's response.

Toni ordered tea and come back on his seat, in this time everyone decided their breakfast.

"I will have sandwich" Tanu said to Toni.

"Me too" Lavanya followed Tanu.

"I will have Maggie" Rayman and Vishu once again ordered same thing.

"Is anybody up for Maggie-omelet" Toni again asked everyone.

"No" response from most the guys.

"I will have Maggie" Deepali is also with Vishu and Rayman.

"Hey Lavanya what is update on transfer news? I heard someone from our team is going Delhi office?" Vishu asked Lavanya as she always has all information about everybody.

"No idea"

"Send me there, at least I will be free from Baba" Vishu is talking about his boss. "And I will get chance to meet new girls. Here is no good girl in this office." Vishu added further.

"Everyone seems same when you start working with them." Deepali commented on his remark.

"Yeah, you are right." Toni supported Deepali remark "and you guys are also good." He added further with smile on his face.

"What?" Tanu is furious on Toni's smile.

"What you mean by what?" Toni responded and his remark created tensed situation but at that very moment tea came and avoided further trouble as everyone got busy in tea.

"I don't see any chance of my transfer. I have critical release next week. I am only men working in my team and I guess no chances of Lavanya as she is my counterpart in QA team." Rayman commented on transfer issue.

"I am doing nothing productive since last project, just few prototype and Tanu I guess not done anything since she joined." Toni commented with cunning smile.

"You might not have any work but I have lot to do. Excuse me" This response is expected from Tanu.

Toni placed breakfast order for everyone. Everyone is pulling each other's leg while taking sips of tea, breakfast arrived in fifteen minutes, after finishing breakfast they gossiped for fifteen more minutes and then back to their seats. Guys who were sitting in cafeteria in open area are still gossiping and enjoying sunshine.

Everyone got emerged in their work after reaching to their seats. Lavanya is still in Rayman's cubicle discussing about release next week. A guy in his forty comes in their cubicle from glass cabin in front of their cubicle. It is Nitin, the boss of office.

"Has Ram come yet or not?" He asked them.

"No sir, he hasn't come yet." Toni replied.

"Tell him that I am looking for him as soon he comes in office" he said without looking at anybody and went inside cubicle once again and everybody in the cubicle once again went to their work. Ram is manager of every person sitting in this cubicle. Ram is in early thirty, with average height and good personality and he is very smart guy.

"Good morning sir, Nitin is looking for you." Toni said to Ram when he entered cubicle after around fifteen minutes after his conversation with Nitin.

"Has he said anything else?" he asked in response while settling his hair with both of his hands and turned on his system after taking his seat and turned his chair toward Toni and Rayman with expectation of answer to his question, Toni and Rayman also looking at his seat and Tanu is looking at her system but her ears are on this conversation only.

"No sir, he hadn't said anything else."

"OK, let me see." And he left his chair and went inside cubicle.

"Good morning" Ram greeted Nitin.

"Good morning Ram, come in." No word came out the cabin after that, Ram closed the gate after going inside. Now two meeting were going on there, one is inside the cabin and second outside cabin in Rayman and Toni's cubicle. Vishu and Tanu joined them in the conversation.

"I guess we got some new client or project" Vishu said with confused expression on his face.

"May be early appraisals" Tanu commented with cunning smile on her face, she is one greedy girl like all others.

"Hmm, they will promote you as well in board of directors." Toni taunted and this made Vishu and Rayman laugh. At that moment Ram came out of the cabin. Rayman and Toni looking toward him to get something from his expression but he went directly to Vishu cubicle and asked Vishu's boss Shyam to join him in the meeting, he asked what is going on but he signaled to come inside, he then called Deepali's boss also for this meeting and after that cabin's door closed once again and both meetings continued.

"No problem, I'll handle." Ram saying coming out of cabin after some fifteen minutes meeting, Vishu's and Deepali's boss also following him out of the cabin and they all went to their seats, by now everyone went to their work, but this phrase from Ram once again pull their attention.

"Some bad news, I guess" Toni said to Tanu and Rayman.

"Let's discuss on lunch table." Rayman said and everyone is working but thinking about meeting all the time.

"Ram, coming for lunch" Vishu boss asked Ram in lunch time.

"Yeah, you go upstairs I will be coming in five minutes." Ram replied.

"Hey, let's go for lunch" Tanu asked everyone from breakfast.

"Rayman, listen, I need to talk to you for five minutes." Ram said to Rayman as he started walking for lunch.

"Sure" Rayman said to Ram and he stayed back while everyone went out of main gate but stayed in corridor waiting for Rayman to come out.

Lavanya in mean time went back to her seat to finish work she was doing before coming upstairs and asked Toni to call her when they go upstairs. Vishu and Toni stayed at exit gate and everyone else except Lavanya went upstairs.

"You have friends in main office too." Ram asked Rayman with worried expression on his face.

"No, you know me very well. I don't interact with anyone outside of the team in the office." He paused for a moment "Why? What happened? Do we have any work with them?"

"No" Ram sank in his though and didn't said anything for few seconds and neither Rayman. Then he continued. "We make friends when we got to work with anyone. You didn't have any friends here either when you came here." He paused for a moment and then continued "I guess even today you didn't have many friends here." Rayman is looking a bit concerned now and trying to connect the dots from what Ram said to him till now.

"No sir, I do have many friends, actually good friends in Vishu, Toni, Tanu, Lavanya, Deepali, Vicky, Lokesh and Praveen and others. But what is the point of discussion?"

"Nothing, just asking, let's go for lunch. We will sit together later." Both walked out of cubicle's area out of exit gate. Ram went upstairs and Rayman stayed near Vishu and Toni, Toni called Lavanya from phone placed at reception.

"What happened?" Vishu asked Rayman.

"I haven't got anything. He wanted to tell something but he said that he will discuss after lunch. I don't know what is going in his mind, he is asking whether I have any friend in Delhi office and then in this office too." He paused for few moments "Leave it and let's go for lunch, will see later."

"Yeah, Lavanya is also coming from downstairs." Toni replied, and Lavanya joined them in few minutes and then they went upstairs to cafeteria.

"What happened sir? What was the topic of meeting with boss?" Toni asked Ram in the evening when everyone is facing each other in the cubicle rather than looking at their system.

"Nothing, we are figuring who is good at C++ in our team. We have one good opportunity for C++, everyone was suggesting Rayman's name in meeting."

"What is it?" Tanu asked in response.

"Rayman might be transferred to Delhi office."

"I don't want to go anywhere without my team. I don't want to leave my friends. Why don't you send someone else, here is so many C++ guys in our group, please send someone who is willing to go there." Rayman replied to Ram with expression of anger on his face. "And I am working on this release also which is planned for next week. How can I be transferred at this time?"

"Well, Nitin was saying that transfer date will be decided after completion of this release." Ram replied.

"As you wish, if everyone wants me to go then I will go." Rayman said to Ram with disbelief in his voice, he continued with anger in his voice "Whatever is good for company, I am OK with that." Rayman controlled his emotions with this statement but his body language is not supporting him.

"Can't we send someone else in place of Rayman?" Toni asked to Ram.

"No, Nitin and other management guys had already decided on it, but if you guys want it, I will try from my side. But believe me it will be good for him, he will get a lot to learn there."

"It is ok sir, I am ok with it." Rayman responded and turned toward his system to continue his work with heavy heart.

In the evening everyone is boarding office bus to back home. Toni and Vishu are sitting on the last seat and Tanu and Lavanya on seat before their seat and Rayman on a single seat parallel to Lavanya seat.

"Why don't you talk to Ram if you don't want to go Delhi office." Vishu said to Rayman, he also got news from Toni and Tanu about transfer.

"I am Ok with it yaar. I will not be talking to anybody about it, if they really think that I am not good enough to work here than it's better I go." Rayman said with moist eyes.

"It's not like that yaar. I heard that they picked one random name and you are the lucky one to go and meet girls from that office."

"But I don't want to go away from my friends."

"You are forgetting Utsav, he is one scoundrel who can beat us all combined. You will get his company in Delhi office." This comment of Vishu made everyone laugh.

It is weekend after two days on transfer news Rayman is on his seat and Ram is giving him company, Lavanya came from her floor to Rayman seat, these three guys came on weekend for release on Monday.

"Is that issue resolved Rayman? Let's go home. You have wasted my whole Saturday yaar at least let me relax on Sunday." Lavanya is getting furious on this stay.

"Let me see what is the issue" Ram said to Rayman and joined him on his seat.

Rayman gave him background of the issue and they discuss for few minutes and both done some changes to fix the issue and it started working in few attempts.

"Lavanya, I am giving you release in ten minutes, just verify once at your end and we leave after that."

"OK"

"I know you can do it" Ram acknowledged Rayman "We can leave in half an hour now." It's only Ram who gives credit of his work to his juniors.

Lavanya is verifying release on her system after few minutes and they released it after that. Ram and Rayman are discussing on Rayman's seat in the meantime.

"We have released one more project on time and even more important you released it before moving to Delhi office, now you can join that office from Monday. I will talk to H.R. to expedite your transfer process now and don't worry yaar, everything will be good and if you don't like it just let me know and I will try to call you back. You may not like it for initial days that happens with everyone but have patience and faith in yourself. I think it's better for you as now you can start your career once again with new beginning, you have experience which will guide you in this beginning." Rayman is not showing any reaction, Lavanya is also with them and listening to them, they are not looking at each other, both are sitting head down, Ram is saying and Rayman is listening. They left for home after few minutes' discussion.

Tuesday lunch time, everyone went out for farewell lunch for Rayman arranged by team mates. Everyone from Vishu's, Rayman's and Deepali's teams is sitting together on lunch table. On Monday he had gone to attend some training which delayed his transfer for one day.

"I have never seen anything which I can say that this is bad thing about Rayman. I like to say only one thing which I think he should improve, I think he should be little more demanding toward his life, he is very content, always satisfied with whatever he gets." Toni said about Rayman when he is asked to say something about him, others also supported Toni's comment about Rayman. "One more thing, keep in touch."

"I will" Rayman acknowledged with a simple nod.

"Don't stare at girls in mew office." Tanu said with naughty smile on her face and continued. "We are your friends and understand you but in new office people will take time to become your friend and understand you, so take little precaution in the beginning."

"I have got a great friend in Rayman and I am sure that this transfer will not make any difference in this equation. We have shared a lot of memories here." Vishu is next to comment on Rayman.

"My wishes are always with you, keep in touch" Vicky commented next. Everyone else also said same or similar to this and finally it's Rayman's turn to share his thoughts before leaving for Delhi office. He started thanking everyone.

"Thanks everyone, this is my first ever farewell, I have never got any chance to witness farewell in school or college. I am really very much touched with this; I promise that I will always remain in touch with you all and at the same time I am also expecting same from you all too. All the best to you all" Rayman completes with this. It's Ram's turn to share his thought and also give him some advice for coming days.

"I know that you don't want to go away from us and this team. But at the same time I am sure that very soon you will make good friends in that office too and I hope you will feel the same there also. Time has given you one more chance to start your career and you can avoid the mistakes which you might have made first time. All the best" Ram paused for few moments and continued few seconds later "You have proved yourself so many times and I am sure that you will definitely shine this time also and finally remain the way you are and keep in touch."

"Sure sir, I will always remain in touch with everyone and I will always remember what you said." As Rayman concluded, everyone started moving out of the cafeteria. In the evening in office H.R. representative comes to Rayman and said him to go to Delhi office next day.

"You need to go Delhi office tomorrow and I will be there to introduce you with your new manager and your new team. I am H.R. representative for that team also, so if you have any concern or query you can come to me at any time." Evening was emotional for Rayman and his friends also, they all discussing about Rayman's transfer all the way to their homes in office bus.

Next morning Rayman went to Delhi, he has seen this office in past also in trainings and meetings. Office is an old looking four stories building with company name's logo visible on main gate. Building's surrounding is no so great, bad and torn roads and lots of dust. Few cars and bikes parked in parking area outside the building, a small cabin for security personal located on right side of company entrance.

"Excuse me sir, what is the purpose of your visit?" Security personal stopped Rayman on entrance. He normally knows people from the office but he is from Noida office and hence he doesn't know him.

"I am from this office."

"Sir, may I see your identity card?"

"Sure" Rayman shows him identity card.

"Have you joined recently? I have never seen you before."

"I am transferred from Noida office, and it is my first day in this office."

"OK sir, you can go inside."

Rayman moved inside and called H.R. representative from reception, reception area have big company logo on front wall and couches for guests.

"Hey Rayman" It is H.R. rep who just came inside the reception area from the office other building in front of this building. "Sorry, I am a little late"

"Hi, it is OK"

"OK, just give me five more minutes; let me check with your new manager." She went inside toward dev area through a glass gate.

Rayman is looking at the door from where H.R. rep went inside for next ten minutes; she came out with a guy following her and talking to her with broad smile on his face. This man is in his early thirty or so with thick mustache and has thinner body frame. He appears techie geek from his appearance; he is in torn jean and lining shirt and had little messed hair.

"Rayman this is Samarth. Actually Jay is your new manager but he is not in the office so you will be reporting to Samarth until Jay comes back."

"OK"

"Hi Rayman" Samarth greeted Rayman.

"Samarth now Rayman is all yours" H.R. rep handed over responsibility of Rayman to Samarth.

"Thanks"

"All the best" H.R. rep leaves after this comment.

"Thanks"

"Come with me and I will introduce you to your new team." Samarth went inside glass door and Rayman followed him.

A narrow passage followed after glass door, right side of that passage is small glass cabin followed by cubicle's area with the capacity of around twenty people and on the left side of the passage is a room made of glass walls for around fifteen people, Samarth entered left side area and Rayman followed him. Most of the people are sitting on their seats and working, few guys are discussing in group. There is one small meeting room inside that area, Samarth asked Rayman to wait inside that meeting room.

"Have a seat" Samarth asked Rayman indicating toward a chair. Meeting room can hardly hold six people. Samarth sat on the chair opposite to Rayman. "Tell me about yourself." Samarth asked further, and Rayman replied with telling him about his old team and technologies he was working on there followed by Samarth telling him about himself and then his team and his work, and then about the project and products he will be working on.

"So you can see that work is not completely different from your existing work, only difference is that you have to work harder and need to show a little more commitment. You need to give more of your time and dedication in here." Samarth is telling about his work, team and products with pride. "That doesn't mean at all that we work all the time, we party a lot too." Samarth keep telling about his team to Rayman. "Well Jay was not here for last two weeks now and we are expecting him next or next to next week to join us back and your actual work allocation and alignment with new job will be done only after his return and till then I will try to get you understand what work we are doing here but first let me introduce you to our team. In the mean time you also get to know them." Samarth is trying to make Rayman comfortable in the new environment.

"Sure"

"What kind of environment you have in your previous team in Noida?" Samarth asked to Rayman.

"We are not just a team but more a family with lots of friends, who are always there whenever we need each other."

"In that case you will enjoy here as well, we are also works like a family. Let's see how soon you will be able to adapt in new family?" Samarth stand up from his chair after this statement "Come, let me introduce you to your new team's member."

After this both Samarth and Rayman moved out of the meeting room to big cabin where all the people having their eyes on the door of meeting room waiting for Samarth and new guy to come out.

First meeting

$\mathcal{R}$ayman is stepping into new life following Samarth with mixed expression of anxiety and nervousness on his face.

"Hello Everyone" Samarth brought everyone's attention "I need few minutes from all of you from your busy schedule. Let me introduce him to you all, he is Rayman and he is joining our team from today. He has been working with other group in our Noida office since last three years." Samarth introduced Rayman to everyone in one go.

Rayman now looking at people in that room, around ten people are sitting in that area while rest of seats are empty.

"Hello everyone" Rayman said with expression of nervousness on his face.

"Hi, Jiten" A smart guy with average height and build greeted Rayman extending his hand toward him.

"Hello"

"Hi, I am Alan" A very beautiful and taller girl greeted him next.

"Hello"

"Hello, I am Abhi" This hello is from a very young boy, he is looking like that he didn't even completed his study. Everyone else from team exchanged greeted one after other. Samarth provided Rayman a seat and now Rayman is passing his time with emails or reading something on internet. In lunch time Jiten and Alan asked him to come with them for lunch at the cafeteria on terrace. This building's cafeteria is not much different from Noida office cafeteria, main difference is that this cafeteria fully under shed. Crowd is little dense compared to Noida office as this office have more than ten teams compared to only two teams at Noida office.

"So, how are you finding this office and people here?" Jiten asked Rayman, who is sitting with Rayman and all other team members on the same table.

"It is nearly same as old group, just missing my friends."

"Hey Rayman, how come you are in this office?" Utsav tapped on Rayman's shoulder. "Is some training?"

"No man, I am transferred to this office, in this team." Rayman replied with smile on his face for first time since morning and this is because of seeing his one friend Utsav.

"What? No one told me about it. It's surprise for me. I have heard that someone is coming from Noida office but I don't know that it is you. Well I am happy to see you here, I am sure you will enjoy here. See you around. Bye for now" Utsav went to his team mates sitting on other table.

"How do you know Utsav? He is really good at dancing. I have seen him performing in every event." Samarth asked Rayman.

"We were in the same team earlier. He was also transferred in some team here few months back." Rayman replied to Samarth.

Rayman and Utsav are having tea at Ashoka café outside of his office building in the evening around 4 o'clock.

"What happened yaar? How are you transferred here?" Utsav asked Rayman taking a sip of tea and puff of cigarette.

"I have no idea about it. They said to me that this team needs someone having my skills. So they sent me here."

"It is all bullshit. My boss was thinking that I was worth of nothing so he threw me here. Not sure if story is different in your case." Utsav said with anger in his voice and on his face too. "But I think it turned out good for me, and I hope same for you. Enjoy yaar. I have to leave now, let's meet at lunch tomorrow. Bye for now" Utsav said to Rayman after they finished their tea, and both left for their offices, Utsav sits in other building in front of Rayman's office building.

"Rayman, are you coming for lunch?" Alan asked him in lunch time next afternoon, she is standing on the door of that area. Rayman raises his head and meets his eyes with her eyes to reply and start thinking. 'I have seen her somewhere earlier for sure, but I couldn't recall where?'

"Rayman" Alan called his name once again.

"Oh sorry, I was thinking something, I am not coming you guys carry on. Actually I will go with Utsav today. Thanks by the way."

"Crazy" Alan murmured under her breathe and she left that cabin after Jiten, Abhi and Samarth.

Rayman is on the stairs and going to cafeteria with Utsav, two girls are going around six to seven steps ahead of them. The girl on the right side is little chubby and of average height with little curly hair of dark brown color, she is wearing blue jeans and cream white round neck t-shirt with blue strips on it, while other girl is little skinny and a little taller she is wearing salwar suite, both have long hair. Their face are partially visible to them when they talk to each other, from that glimpse it is clear that girl on the left one is dusky while other have little extra fair complexion. Both girls are beautiful. Rayman and Utsav are staring those girls for few steps.

"How are you finding girls here?" Utsav asked Rayman.

"All the same here or there, I haven't seen any girl from fashion show or specially that anchor girl."

"What are you saying man? Have you gone crazy?" Utsav asked with surprise. "Why?"

"Anchor, I mean you haven't seen anchor. Really" Utsav asked.

"No" and he continued "Why? Where is she?"

"She is in your team buddy and she was having lunch with you yesterday on your table."

"You mean Alan. Ok, that is the reason I always thinks that I have seen her somewhere."

"Leave her for now; tell me which girl you like in these girls" Utsav asked pointing toward those two girls ahead of them. He continued further "Don't you like slimmer girl on left. Isn't she sexy?"

"No, I think other girl on right side is better. I like her she is fairer and more beautiful."

"She is just six or seven on our scale buddy."

"For me she is perfect ten." He paused for a moment "May be nine but not less than that."

"I think other one is nine and she is just six."

"Well whatever you think about them, I like girl on right side. Why are we fighting? You like left one and I right one so there shouldn't be any fight."

Rayman has got an old looking system and sitting in inner cubicle on the left side of Abhi, no one is sitting on other side of Rayman. Few seats are vacant in that cubicle having some piles of paper on those seats. It is around five in the evening, everyone is busy in their work, and one phone started ringing on Alan's desk.

"Rayman, call for you." Alan called him for the call.

"Coming"

'Who will call me on landline, must be from H.R.' Rayman picked the call thinking these words and responded "Hello"

"Hello, Toni here. How are you? How is your new team? We got your extension from reception."

"Hi, I am good yaar. It is really good that you called. Team is also good yaar. Work is not started yet. I am missing you all very badly."

"We too missing you here, once you get work you will start enjoying there."

"How is everyone else there? Lavanya, Tanu, Vicky, Vishu, Deepali, is everyone fine?"

"Yeah, everyone is fine yaar; I am missing you a lot. Tanu fights all day as usual and Lavanya doesn't come that often since that project is completed."

"I am also alone without my all friends. I remember gossiping with you and Tanu all day."

"Don't be so emotional, tell me how are girls there?"

"Same as there, I feel even Tanu is more beautiful than these girls or it is maybe because I am not liking this place at all."

"What are you saying, Tanu and beautiful."

"What you guys are discussing about me, are you guys talking about me?" Tanu's voice is coming from background.

"But I have seen one beautiful girl yesterday but couldn't see her face completely. I have seen her on stairs when going for lunch with Utsav." Rayman paused for a moment and added further "You remember that anchor from annual party! She is in my team." He said later sentence with little excitement in his voice.

"What" Toni asked with excitement and this took everyone's attention toward the call.

"What happened?" This is Vishu who asked this to Toni.

"Nothing, he said that anchor from annual party is in his team."

"What?" Vicky and Vishu asked together.

"Which anchor? Are you talking about one from annual party? She doesn't even have dressing sense and you guys are dying for her." Tanu is looking jealous with that anchor.

"Yeah, she lacks dressing sense, especially this dirty sense you got." Toni replied with quirky comment.

"What happened?" Rayman asked after hearing Toni voice.

"Nothing, Tanu is saying something non sense."

"I am not talking anything to you, and even you haven't got any sense." Tanu left cubicle angrily.

"Hey Bro, Let me talk to that anchor." Vishu said to Rayman after snatching receiver from Toni's hand.

"Sure, do you really want me to give her receiver?"

"No yaar, I am just kidding, how are you?" how is work and everything?"

"But I am really serious you really want to talk to anchor? By the way I am good and work too but missing you all very badly."

"And how is that other girl, you are talking about earlier." Toni asked this time after snatching receiver back from Vishu.

"I don't' exactly knows about her, couldn't see her face completely that day."

"What? And you are saying that she was beautiful." He paused for a moment and continued "She must have got very sexy figure than."

"Hold on brother, you are taking it wrong. It is not like that at all. I just liked her n first view that's it."

"Leave her in that case. I, Tanu and Vikas will be coming to your office next week for training, see you then."

"Oh, it's great news. We will have tea and bread pakoras at outside at Ashoka's stall."

"Sure, bye for now."

"OK, bye" Rayman placed receiver back on cradle and then he noticed the same girl outside glass cabin while going back to his seat from Alan's seat whom he noticed on stair case earlier. She is talking to some girl. It is appears from their body language that she is working under other girl. She kept her hair free and her hair coming in front of her face and blocking her face from Rayman's sight. She turned to leave and at the same time she cared her hairs which are coming in front of her face behind her ear with her left hand and once again she blocked her face with her hand. Rayman is still standing on Alan's seat to see her face but his luck hasn't favored him. Alan is looking upon at Rayman's face to check why is he still standing at her desk? Rayman finally left Alan's desk when that girl settled on her seat. 'OK dear, next time' Rayman thinking while walking back to his seat and with his eyes still out of glass wall on her seat.

Time passing day by day and Rayman is trying to adjust in new team and environment at the same time missing his old mates.

"Sir, I don't want to stay here. Please call me back there, I love working with you all, I am missing you all very much." Saturday evening Rayman is talking on his cell phone to his old team's manager Ram.

"Rayman, it will take some time to get to know new team and work, have some patience and try and wait for at least one or two months and if you feel the same even after that then let me know I will try for your transfer back to here or I will refer your resume to my friends in some other companies, don't worry and enjoy, think like you are at onsite and will come back after completion of assignment in one or two months. OK, tell me one thing have you got work?" Ram is trying to convince him from his side.

"No sir, no work assigned yet, and I am sure I will never be able to settle here."

"OK, I will talk to Nitin and try from my side to call you back but I still think you should give at least two months there and I think once you get work you will start enjoying there. Or I will myself refer your resume, don't worry and enjoy."

"OK, as you say." He disconnected call. It is small garden where people walking in a circular path on perimeter of that garden, few people are sitting on the grass in the garden. Rayman is sitting on a bench with a girl on the side of that walking track. This girl is very good family friend of Rayman, they also studied together whole life. He is discussing about the transfer and told her that he is missing his friends in new team very much. She also said the same thing which everyone said to him that he will get new friends in new team as well.

"I don't like anything here. I want to go back to my old group."

"But they send you here naah, when they don't want you than why you want go back to them."

"You will not understand."

"Sure, I will not understand and I don't think anyone else also can understand except you. It is just you who is working and left friends and family, rest of the world enjoying everything."

"It is getting late yaar, I am going back to my home, and you also go inside otherwise your P.G. owner will get angry."

"Isn't any beautiful girl here? You got few girls in your old team, is it because of them, are you missing anyone from them?"

"Hey Riya, it is not like that, you are getting it all wrong, by the way all girls look the same when you work with them. I miss my friends." Rayman and Riya both left with these words to their homes.

"Hi Toni, Tanu and Vishu" Utsav greeted everyone after entering food court at 3Cs to join party in progress. They have joined two tables together to accommodate all at one place. Vishu and his friend Diya sitting on one side, Lavanya and Tanu on other side on table one, while Toni, Riya and Rayman sitting on other table.

"Hi Utsav" Riya greeted Utsav when he sat by her side. "Hey Utsav, you are also in Delhi office, Rayman is getting so frustrated in that office, isn't that office really good?"

"No, I like Delhi office even more that Noida one. I have no clue why doesn't he like this office?"

"Leave this topic yaar, how are you guys, Diya how are you and how is your work going?" Rayman cut Utsav and Riya conversation.

"I am good, but want to change job, I am getting bored in this job. I want to do something else." Diya is Tanu's flat mate and met Vishu through Tanu and they have come closure with time and became very good friends.

"Why? Vishu told me that your job and company both are cool. What is the issue?"

"Nothing, just want change." Vishu by that time brought honey chilly potatoes, which is his favorite in this food court. Utsav and Toni brought food from various counters according to everyone's choice.

"By the way guys, Rayman got very beautiful girls in his team and around." Toni made comment while eating fries.

"Why don't you go there?" Tanu cut his comment on girl.

"Sure, I love to. I got bored seeing you daily." Tanu didn't respond anything but Lavanya signaled Toni to stay quiet and that make him change tone of his voice. "I am just kidding yaar, I am not going anywhere. I love working with you all guys."

Party ended around ten in between gossip and food and then everyone left for their home. Vishu left with Diya to drop her first at her place and Toni agreed to drop Tanu and Lavanya and Utsav left alone, Rayman left with Riya to drop her at her PG on the way home.

Around three weeks passed after transfer and now Rayman got some work and also get to know team mates a little. It is Wednesday and time is around twelve when a guy in mid or late thirties dressed in blazer and trouser entered the area where Rayman and team sit. He has average look with average height and dusky complexion with broad smile on his face. His entry in the cabin brought everyone on their toes except Rayman as he is not familiar with him.

"Hello guys, how is everyone? I am sure you all must have missed me a lot." He said with that broad smile.

"Hi sir" Samarth replied and Alan, Jiten and other team mates followed, Rayman still sitting on his seat but his eyes are on this guy.

"Who is that new guy in our team?" he enquired Samarth pointing toward Rayman after greeted them all.

"He is Rayman. He has come from Noida office to work with our team."

"How is he doing?" He asked Samarth while approaching Rayman's seat at the same time without listening his reply.

"Hi, I am Jay. You must have heard about me, I am your new manager and you will be working with me with direct coordination. How have you found this place? Well now I have come you will definitely enjoy here."

"Hello" only words from Rayman in response.

"OK, let's meet in few minutes." He moved out of the cabin with these words to team members.

'Oh shit, he is the same guy with whom we had argument on D.J. floor in annual party. I will be screwed here for sure.' Rayman is thinking after seeing Jay.

"Rayman, your cell is ringing" Abhi asked Rayman who is still in his thought.

"Hello" Rayman greeted after taking the call. But thoughts are still coming in his mind. 'I am fucked, god send me back to Noida before he recognizes me'

"Hello Rayman" Its Ram, his boss from old team. "How are you? How is your work going?"

"Everything is fine at my end. How are you and have you talked to boss for my return?"

"I am also good, Rayman I tried for it but you have to stay there for few months at least, because we have to send someone from team and if we decide to send someone else than whole process need to be done once again. It is just for few months and you will be back after that."

At this time Rayman looked outside of cabin through glass wall and noticed that Jay is talking to same girl he noticed on stairs but girl has her back toward Rayman and Jay is facing Rayman, he tried sneaking a peak of her face but could not get any and in this effort he forgot that he is talking to Ram.

"Are you there Rayman? Don't be upset yaar. You see everything will be all right with time."

"Hmm yup, I am listening."

"OK, let's talk later; I have to go for lunch. Everyone is waiting for me. Bye"

"Hmm bye"

"Let's go for lunch" Jay asked team member after returning to their room.

"I will go with my friend Utsav. You guys carry on." Rayman replied to his invitation.

"Have lunch with team once in a while, or how else will you make friends in team?" Jay again asked Rayman. "Let's come with us."

"OK" Rayman following Jay now out of the cabin thinking. 'What he thinks of himself, we can't even go for lunch with friends.'

"Are you enjoying here? Or still adjusting in new environment?" Jay asked to Rayman entering cafeteria.

"Honestly, I am missing my friends very badly."

"Don't worry yaar you will make friends here as well, consider me as your friend." Rayman and Jay sat on the table where rest of the team sitting together except Samarth. Rayman located Samarth standing near other table talking to two girls Samarth hiding one girl and other girl is dusky girl from stairs he noticed one day. Other girl must be the same he liked and noticed two other instances but not able to see this time as well.

"Samarth as usual talking to girls, he was like this all the time. He is never going to be mature." Jay commented on Samarth.

"So, have you started liking here or not?" Alan asked Rayman.

"Little bit"

"Well, you speak very less otherwise you will make friends here as well." Her voice is so sweet and calming.

"Yeah, I usually make friends first than I talk a lot."

"How can you make friends if you don't talk to them at first place?"

"You got good sense of humor. Well do you know someone who goes toward Maharani Bagh? I have to take office bus for that route."

"Really, where you live in that area? Actually I live near that area and I commute by office bus." Alan replied his query.

"I live nearby Ashram's crossing"

"OK"

"You can come with me"

Rayman is getting comfortable with Alan, Abhi, and Jiten and for some reason with Jay also, even it is his first encounter with him. Samarth is back to their table and Rayman once again looking toward the table where Samarth is standing but those girls are not at that table now.

'Who is that girl and why am I so much eagerly wanted to see her face? She is like ghost, never coming in my sight. What is so special in her why is she pulling me toward her?' Rayman is lost in his thought once again. Everyone finished their lunch in between conversation and went back to their desk. Rayman tried several times sneaking a peak toward the desk of that girl during the day but couldn't find her.

"Tell us about yourself a little, what you liked here except work?" Alan asked Rayman when both walking toward their bus for home in the evening. But before Rayman could answer Alan screamed at higher voice. "Run Rayman. That is our bus. Our driver is real scoundrel he will not stop bus for us." Alan started running slowly as bus picking speed and Rayman also following her with the same speed. They both caught bus after few meters running behind the bus.

"Can't you stop bus for two more minutes?" she asked driver boarding the bus. They sat on a seat at back rows and had conversation all the way back home; this conversation is beginning of a new journey of a possible friendship.

"I usually boards bus at eight fifteen in the morning from opposite side of road, let's meet tomorrow morning. Bye" Alan said to Rayman when they got off the bus at reaching their stop.

"OK, bye"

"Hey Abhi, want to have tea from outside café, office tea sucks" Rayman asked Abhi next day around ten in the morning.

"Yeah sure"

"Alan, are you coming for tea at outside café?" Abhi asked Alan.

"Yup coming" She followed Abhi and Rayman to Ashoka tea stall.

"Hello man" Utsav greeted Rayman; he is already smoking at the café. He further asked "How are you? Looks like you started liking here."

"I am good, yeah liking a little now."

"Hey bro, you haven't introduced her."

"Come" Rayman and Utsav approached Alan and Abhi, Abhi is ordering tea for them by that time.

"Alan, Abhi this is Utsav." Rayman introduced Utsav first to his team mates and then them to Utsav.

"We already know him. We have seen him in various events in annual party." Abhi said to Rayman.

"Hi Utsav" Alan acknowledged Utsav.

"Hello guys" Utsav greeted both of them in response.

"How is work in your team? Rayman doesn't seem enjoying here too much."

"I usually take time to adjust" Rayman cut their conversation to reply Utsav's query. "By the way I started liking this team as well."

"Really, it's good then. OK bye for now, I am out for quite some time now. See you at lunch." Rayman also went back to his seat with Abhi and Alan after finishing their tea.

Three months passed since transfer of Rayman and now he quite settled in new team with the support from his friends from old team and from his new made friends Alan, Abhi, Jiten, Samarth and Utsav. Rayman is doing good in new team and helping time to time members in new team and this the reason he made everyone his friends.

On the other hand people are missing Rayman in his old team too. In conversation during breakfast and lunch and especially when Toni, Tanu, Vicky and Vishu go out for evening tea at road side vendors.

"Hey guys has any one talked to Rayman lately, he hasn't called in last two weeks at least, in his early days after transfer he used to call daily." Toni asked Vishu about Rayman.

"I think he has settled in new team, he must have found new friends or maybe girl friend." Tanu cuts their conversation in between.

"Yes, that office's girls are not like you. Girls in our office neither good at work and nor at their looks" Toni as usual teased her.

"Again" Tanu frowned at Toni. "How many times I need to teach you how to behave in public?"

"This is the result of your teaching." Toni responded and everyone laughed.

"I don't remember anchor's face, I have foggy image of taller girl from fashion show, and I can't remember anything else from party." Vishu commented.

"I also have foggy image of anchor in my mind" Vicky responded on Vishu's comment.

"Do you guys know Rayman's manager is the guy who had argument with us in party at D.J. floor? It is Rayman's good luck that he doesn't remember that incidence." Vishu told them about Rayman's new boss.

"Let's go back, we are out for an hour now I guess." Toni reminded them about the time and they went back inside after having tea and gossiping at tea shop for an hour.

Back in the Delhi office everyone is on their seats either doing their work or checking mails, some reading and some doing something related to their work.

"I have completed that assignment and checked with Samarth also. He also verified." Rayan is talking to Jay about his work assigned by Jay.

"Great, I will verify and let you know." Jay seems busy and responded as usual in filmy style.

"OK, let me know if anything else needs to be done."

"Wait, I have something else for you. It is very urgent and critical too. Management guys directly looking into it and it have involvement from other team also." Jay stopped Rayman to tell him about his new assignment. He continued "One more team is working on this project from our group. They are working on one module and we have to work on one particular module. I will further share information and mail related to this project. Come with me I will introduce you to other team's member working with you on this project. You can also take help from them if required." Jay went outside their cabin and signaled Rayman to follow him, he stopped on one seat in the cubicle where that girl from stairs incidence sit, Jay started conversation with someone and Rayman is standing behind Jay and couldn't see that person from behind of Jay. He turned to his right to introduce him to that person.

"Rayman, this is …." Rayman couldn't hear anything further after seeing the face of that person.

Let's be friends

"*R*ayman, Rayman, Are you listening to me or not? I said this is Anna." Jay repeated but no response from Rayman.

"Hi, I am Anna." This is the same girl whom Rayman noticed on stairs while going for lunch with Utsav few days ago, and couldn't see her face completely in last few encounters, now when she came in front of him he is so busy to memorize her face that he forgot to respond to Jay or Anna.

"Hi I am" he paused for few moments "Rayman." He completed thinking 'I guess'

"Where is Ruchi?" Jay asked her about her manager.

"She has gone out for some work or may be in some call in conference room."

"Who is working on that new project on SAP?"

"I am working on it with Ruchi." She responded with sense of pride and smile on her face.

"Actually he will also work on that project on one module and he needs some information to start on it. Who can help him on it?"

"Ruchi knows about it better, I have just started so I think it is better if you ask her."

"OK, thanks. We shall talk to her.

Jay and Rayman started walking back to their seat and then she spoke again to Rayman this time. "But if you need any help you can discuss with me any time."

"Sure thanks." Rayman replied but his mind saying something else altogether. 'I think Utsav was right, she is just six or seven pointer, but she has something which attracts me toward her. She is extremely fair and little chubby with very attractive face with not so sharp features, her eyes behind those spectacles doing the talking and her smile has some magic in it. No one can take his or her eyes off from her face after seeing her eyes or her smile.'

"Bye for now, we will come later to trouble you." Jay bid good bye going away from her seat.

"Bye" She bid bye to both of them with smile.

'Wow, what a smile. Even dying person can get second life after seeing her smile.' Rayman is thinking about Anna all the way to his seat.

Two weeks passed after that first meeting between Rayman and Anna, in mean time Rayman met her manager Ruchi once to get understanding about the technology and work. Ruchi is really a very nice girl. She is in early thirties, but looks like in twenties due to her soft and sweet voice and charming face. Rayman also got one chance to interact with Anna. She usually talks very less and works all the day, she talks with her friends openly but Rayman is not a good friend of her so her conversation with Rayman limited to discussion about work or responses to his queries. One evening Rayman and Alan are going back toward their bus.

"Do you have idea about project I am working these days?" Rayman asked Alan.

"How can I know about your project?"

"Yeah you are right, it is basically kind of integration of our product with some third party tools and you know I am working with a girl from Ruchi's team. Do you know her?"

"Yes. I know her. She is from my batch only. You are talking about Anna naah as she is only girl in her team. I have seen you talking to her few times. So what? What is so special working with her?"

"Nothing, I just likes her, she is so sincere and so fair also." Alan didn't respond anything after his comment; Rayman added further "She looks very innocent and very beautiful."

"Beautiful, what make you say that she is beautiful? She is fair I agree but that is because she is Kashmiri. I don't find her any beautiful and her attitude, may god save from her attitude." Alan doesn't seem on good term with her. It is obvious that no girl like praise of other girl but this is something else.

"Why? What about her attitude? What is wrong with her attitude, she seems good to me."

"OK, in that case you are lucky. I haven't seen her made any friend in office." Alan started walking fast toward bus and Rayman following her with quick steps. By now Rayman got hint that she doesn't want to talk about Anna.

"You didn't tell me, what is the issue with her attitude?" Rayman once again asked Alan after sitting on the same seat in the bus.

"Why are you so interested in her?"

"Nothing, just want to know about her, she didn't talk too much to me except related to work."

"That's it, this is the problem with her, this is exactly problem with her attitude, she thinks as she is princess of somewhere."

"So what is the issue in it? I also talk very less in initial days with you guys; some people take some time in socializing with others. That is not attitude but nature of person."

"She doesn't interact with people so easily. You know she had argument with everyone in our team. She argued with Jiten very badly in one trip over some silly topic." Alan paused for few moments and continued "You know she is from Abhi's college, but I have never seen them having any conversation, have you seen them talking ever?" Alan is in no mood of talking about Anna and Rayman changed topic of conversation to discussion about work and his old team mates for rest of journey.

Next morning on breakfast table Jiten, Alan, Abhi, Rayman and Samarth are having breakfast together in cafeteria, Samarth and Jiten pulling legs of other guys together.

"Hi Anna, come here, you can join us for breakfast." Samarth called Anna when she entered cafeteria for breakfast.

"Sure sir, good morning guys." Anna came and sat on their table and greeted everyone with her trademark pretty smile.

"What are you having in breakfast?" Samarth asked her.

"Parathas"

"Do you cook yourself or you have maid who cook for you?" he further enquired.

"I cook for myself" she responded with pride.

"You know cooking, I really doubt." Jiten also joined the conversation with this comment.

"Yes, I know cooking very well, I live alone and I do lot of things before coming office every morning, I clean my home, do dishes, then cook my breakfast and lunch and in evening I cook dinner after returning from office."

Alan and Abhi are having breakfast quietly. Rayman is talking to Alan and Abhi but his attention is on the conversation between Anna, Samarth and Jiten. He sometimes stared at Anna in between when no one observing him.

"Look Alan, learn something from Anna." Samarth dragged Alan too in the conversation.

"Why should I learn something from anybody else, I know cooking very well. I can cook many things like cakes, Maggie." Alan is looking angry when replying to Samarth's comment.

"Do you know cooking?" Anna asked Samarth.

"Yes, every kind of fish curries, crabs, and few other non-veg dishes. I also live alone and cook often. You guys can come to my home someday then I will cook for you."

"And you?" Anna asked Rayman.

"Yes, many things or almost every normal north Indian curry."

"Then bring something for us someday."

They finished their breakfast in between conversation and everyone is back to their seats. Few weeks passed without any major event in their teams, Anna joined them sometimes on breakfast table and also sometimes on their seats for gossip. One random day Rayman is at Anna seat around twelve in the day.

"How is your work going?" Rayman asked Anna.

"Completed, Haven't you seen my mail yesterday, you are also there in the recipient."

"Oh yes, I have seen that"

"Then why are you asking? Where is your mind these days?"

"Hmm, I forgot. How is everything else?"

"Fine and I have started my previous work after this project."

"On which technology are you working?"

"Java, do you know Java? On which you are working?"

"Java, I too want to learn Java, I work on C++. I worked on Java for one or two times but not good at it."

"It is same like C++" She left her work and now turned toward Rayman talking to him with all her concentration on the conversation. Her expression is suggesting that she is guessing the purpose of his visit to her seat and Rayman also got the feeling about it so he bid her bye and left her seat, and she once again dived in her work. Back on the seat he is having conversation with Jiten about Anna.

"Anna doesn't seem kind of normal sometimes, what do you think?" Rayman asked Jiten, they both are sitting on Rayman seat and Jiten is talking about work and Rayman dragged topic of conversation to Anna.

"I can't say for sure but my experience is also same, she is psycho, we once had argument on Agra trip."

"What? Really"

"Yeah, that over some straw"

"What"

"Leave it. But why are so interested? What is the matter? Hmm" Jiten asked with mischievous smile on his face.

"Nothing yaar, I am working with her these days naah. By the way she is strange for me too." Samarth came inside the cabin from somewhere and he made one announcement after entering the cabin.

"Hey guys, we are planning to go out for trip, what you says guys? It is so hot in Delhi these days. Let's go on some hill station on weekend."

"Wow, this is great idea" Alan shows her joy very first.

"I am in" Abhi responded after Alan.

"I can't join. I have lot of work here and at home as well." Jiten responded after Abhi.

"I too can't join. I too have lot of work on this new project. I have still not completed and I have to complete by this week end." Rayman also denied for trip.

"Don't worry guys. We can plan one or two week later." Samarth consoled them.

"We don't have any other girl in our team. We have to ask someone else." Alan raised one more concern.

"Why do you need some other girl?" Samarth asked to Alan.

"What you mean by why? It will not look good if I go alone with all boys." She expressed anger in that response. She asked further. "Doesn't anyone of you have girl friend?"

"No" most of them replied in one voice.

"What sir, you are playboy of our team and you don't have a girl friend?" Jiten said to Samarth.

"Leave it, you bring yours, Rayman don't you have girl friend?" Samarth changed topic cleverly.

"No sir, but I can ask one of my friend."

"Then ask naah please, or how can I come?" Alan requested Rayman.

"I can't say for sure whether she will come or not but I will definitely ask her and update you."

"OK, I will also try if I can get someone from our office" Samarth also gave one other option to Alan.

Jay also came in cabin and asked Jiten what is going on? Why is this ruckus? Why you all are gathered in group, doesn't anyone have any work? Jiten told him about trip plan.

"So what is the problem in it? Let's go this weekend but plan for somewhere near so that we can return on Sunday night and can join office on Monday morning." Jay instructed Samarth and others.

"No sir, we are not going this weekend. We are planning for two weeks later. We all are busy in something or other this weekend and we also need to arrange one girl's company for Alan." Samarth replied to Jay and everyone went back to their seat after discussion for few more minutes except Jay and Samarth.

"May be I will not be in town after next weekend, you guys doing it purposefully so that I can't join you all." Jay left the conversation with this statement and went to his seat and added further from his seat. "You guys will definitely miss me."

"Off course but your bullshit not you." Jiten, Alan and Abhi said under breathe.

"Sir we can plan further one or two weeks later." Jiten suggested an alternative.

"No yaar, you guys carry on, I am not sure about my return date." Jay ended conversation with this statement.

Trip plan is almost final and now everyone is thinking about whom can they invite for the trip to give company to Alan? Jiten is very secretive in this case and he hasn't told anyone about whom he is going to ask. Abhi and Alan have no one to ask, Samarth is planning to ask friends and colleagues from office and Rayman can ask only Riya.

"Hey Anna, how are you and how is your work?" Samarth is at Anna seat talking to her for a change.

"Everything is all right sir, how are you? You were seen with H.R. girls very often these days, is something cooking?"

"I am good too and I met her for interviews, we have to select few guys for our team." Samarth paused after that and continued after few moments "by the way would you like to join us for the trip to some hill station near Delhi?"

"It would be very tough for me, I love to come, and there was no outing in so many days. But I have too much work and I also have to ask to my parents. Who else is going?"

"We have two weeks to complete work and you are going with your colleagues so I don't think your parents will have any object and it's just my team so you will definitely enjoy."

"I don't have any friend in your team, how can I enjoy, I am not coming."

"Well, then it's your chance to make new friends."

"I am not interested in your team by the way, but I will ask some of my friend and I will let you know if I can join you."

Samarth tried convincing her with few more attempts but she denied with same response. It is evening or better to say late evening Rayman is in the park with Riya in front of her PG.

"Riya, my team is going on trip to some nearby hill station, would you like to join me. It will be fun."

"Hmm, I guess so. Some girl from your team must be going with you. I know that is where your fun lies. I know you very well you flirt."

"You are wrong."

"Then go and enjoy. When are you going?"

"Two weeks later, I am asking you too."

"Why and what I will do with your team? I don't know anyone of them?"

"It is fun trip yaar. You will enjoy and you will get to know people, and maybe you will be able to make new friends also."

"OK, let me see and I will let you know. Just ask about it one or two days before you go. Let's leave now it is getting late now." And by this statement they both left for their homes.

One weekend evening Toni and Tanu sitting at 3Cs food court and discussing something.

"I told you to pick Lavanya on the way. I know that they all will take time so that at least she would have been with us, now wait for everyone." Toni seems angry on Tanu while saying this.

"Who was stopping you from picking her? It is only Lavanya who wants to go back home, I haven't told her to go home and Vishu is coming in ten minutes. I have talked to Diya and she said that they will be here in ten minutes."

"Hi Tanu, Hi Toni, How are you guys? And what is the plan? Where is everyone else?" Rayman asked them after entering food court followed by Riya.

"Vicky said that he will not come, he has some work at office. Lavanya left for home and might come in few minutes. Vishu and Diya will be here any minute." Toni replied.

"How are you guys?" Tanu asked them.

"I am good, how are you?" Riya asked in response.

"I am also good but I guess Toni is not that good, he is missing Lavanya."

"Why! What has happened to you?" Rayman asked Toni.

"Nothing yaar, I am also good, I guess she lost her mind."

"OK, hey guys by the way my team is going on trip to some hill station. Anyone interested?" but before anyone could answer his query, Vishu voice came from behind.

"Where are you going?" He greeted everyone after asking question to Rayman and Diya also greeted everyone.

"Some hill station, exact destination is not decided yet. Why? Are you interested in joining us for the trip?"

"No, who is going by the way?"

"Not too many people, just five six guys from my team and maybe one or two from other teams and do you remember anchor from party, She will also be coming."

"OK, Now I see why you are so much excited about this trip. Leave this trip and let's all go to some place maybe over the weekend."

"We are not going anywhere. You guys can never plan anything at all." Tanu responded with her usual frowning voice.

"Then you plan naah, we will all join you on that trip." Toni replied or rather taunted on her remark.

"Sure" Tanu hit him on shoulder while replied his comment. Lavanya joined them around half an hour later, they gossiped till ten or eleven and left for their home after having their dinner.

Monday morning Rayman is at the cafeteria having breakfast with everyone from his team. Samarth and Jiten are discussing about the trip, Alan and Abhi are discussing about weekend and Rayman eating quietly. One other member from other team is also having breakfast with them and it's Anna.

"Anna, come naah please. You are not going alone you will get company of Alan, I am not sure about Ruchi but I guess she might also come. It will be great fun." Samarth is still trying to convince her.

"But sir, what will I do with you guys? You guys are going on team trip, I will get bore there."

"You can also ask any of your friends and you can also ask your boyfriend." Jiten smiled on the remark of boyfriend and this also took everyone's attention toward the conversation.

"I don't have any boyfriend. I don't think I have found any boy who can be my boyfriend, but I will ask one of my friends and let you know" She replied with straight face and finished her breakfast without any other word.

"I have some work, I need to go. Bye sir." She left without saying anything else.

"Alan, why don't you ask any of your friends from your school or college? It would be great if she can join us." Samarth suggested one more option.

"No one is in Delhi, every single person moved out of Delhi and if anybody is in Delhi then I am not in touch with them for last few months at least, and hence can't ask them."

"Then cancel the trip, we are not going anywhere."

"You guys can carry on; I don't want you guys to cancel the trip because of me."

"We will not be leaving anybody else behind from the team. Jiten and Jay are already not coming and now you too aren't coming then who is left for the trip, me, Abhi and Rayman. Let's cancel it."

"I will ask Riya if she can join us." Rayman said to Alan and Abhi while Samarth is moving out of cafeteria with anger and everyone else following him to their seats.

"Why don't you ask Anna, you are a girl, you can understand each other, she can't say no to you." Rayman suggested Alan on the way downstairs.

"Why will she listen to me? She is not my friend yaar? Why don't you ask her? You were working with her and you seem closer to her than me. You go and ask her, who knows she might say yes to you."

It is lunch time and Rayman is at Anna seat, Anna is looking busy in her work. She is kind of workaholic and she usually found emerged in her work. She didn't notice that Rayman is standing near her seat while he sat on a chair by the side of her seat.

"Anna" her friend who is going for lunch called her to tell about Rayman and winked about his presence.

"Oh, hi Rayman, how are you, I haven't noticed you. What is it?" She asked to Rayman as usual with excitement's expression on her face.

'How the hell can I ask her for the trip? Why is she so scary? Why she always stare with this killer look? Dear, come out of work some time, it is so beautiful around.' Rayman is in his thoughts.

"Need some help?" Anna asks once again but with anxious expression in her eyes and face. She makes these faces when someone wastes her time.

"No, No, I am not looking for any help."

"What is it then?" She shot another one. Rayman is not expecting this and his face went pale with this cross question. His heart racing around four hundred beats per minutes.

"Nothing, it is lunch time so I came to know your where about." Sweat's droplets came on his forehead, He seems very nervous with his comment. Nervousness is visible on his face, Anna also got this feeling and she decided to pull his leg.

"What happened to your team? Where are they? Do you want to come with us for lunch?" Anna fired one more question but before he could answer anything Anna's one friend rescued him from the situation when she asked Anna for the lunch. "Anna, let's go for lunch. You can continue your conversation on lunch or after lunch."

Alan also came out the cubicle at the same time and asked Rayman for the lunch and this gave him chance to save his neck from this situation.

"Yes coming. Wait for two minutes for me." Rayman said to Alan and at the same time bid good bye to Anna. Anna and her friend went to cafeteria and Alan and Rayman with their team following her toward cafeteria.

"What were you doing at her seat?" Alan asked Rayman.

"Nothing, it is related to work." Rayman responded but his mind is thinking something else. 'What people were saying about her is correct. She is really weird some times. She nearly killed me. She can never be a good friend of mine.' Rayman took a sigh of relief.

When they reached cafeteria Rayman's team took different table than Anna's team. Jay is accompanied by his one friend Harry who is the same girl for whom he fought with Rayman's old team's mates in annual party. They are also sitting with them. Samarth started conversation about the trip.

"Ruchi is possibly coming for the trip, she need to confirm from her husband and possibly he will also join us. So no need to worry now." he said last statement to Alan. Everyone is looking relaxed now as trip will not be cancelled after confirmation from Anna's boss Ruchi.

"Why don't you also join us with your wife and kid?" Samarth asked Jay.

"You guys purposefully planned trip at this time when I am going outstation so that I can't come with you and no one can have an eye on you."

"No sir, we can post pone trip till you come back." Jiten and Alan also supported this statement of Samarth with nod.

"You guys carry on now, with so much effort you got yes from Ruchi, I don't think she can plan again. We will go somewhere else next time together."

Finally trip is taking some firm shape and with so hot in Delhi they will be definitely enjoying in hill station's cooler environment and this is the reason that everyone seems happy when trip's plan got finalized.

One Wednesday evening Rayman is sitting in the park in front of Riya's PG with Riya. They are also discussing about the Rayman's team trip.

"I am leaving this Friday for the trip with my team." Rayman informed her about the trip.

"How is whether in Shimla? Is it really cold there?"

"Yes, why don't you come and see yourself."

"What will I do there? I don't even know anybody in your team except you." Riya seems upset with this remark and she raised one more concern "Will your boss allow me?"

"Yes, why will not he allow you? I already asked you to come. Do you want to come?"

"Yes" she replied with her head down in dull voice.

"Then be ready on Friday evening. I will pick you from here and don't forget to take some warm clothes. You will need them."

"Sure, but need to go now. Bye for now."

Thursday morning Rayman is at cafeteria for breakfast and everyone from his team also with him on that table. Anna, her boss and her friend from her cubicle are also sitting with them on their tables. Ruchi is discussing with Samarth about trip and seems very excited.

"Everyone is ready now, I asked my husband about the trip and Avi is also coming with us."

"Anna, why aren't you coming with us? What will you do here by the way? You will enjoy there with us." Ruchi asked Anna.

"Hmm" Anna nodded, she couldn't say no to Ruchi. Anna is discussing something secretively with her friend after that.

"We both are coming for the trip." Anna and her friend confirmed in one voice after few minutes.

"Sir, one of my friend also coming for the trip, can she join us?" Rayman also asked about Riya at that moment however he already talked about her with Samarth but he confirmed again.

"Sure, I will be booking hotel in the evening and till that time anyone can join us for the trip."

"I guess we are ten people in all by now and a small sized bus will be enough for us." Jiten said to Samarth, as Jiten will be booking bus for the trip.

"No, we are eleven, my one friend from H.R. also joining us." Samarth corrected Jiten.

"Even then small sized bus will be enough."

By the next afternoon everything is done as per the plan, Samarth booked hotel and Jiten managed travel and collected information about route and decided about stop on the way. Now everyone is discussing about the final preparation. Most of the guys came with their bags packed to office. They will be picking Ruchi's husband on the way and Rayman, Riya and Alan also boarding bus on the way as their home is on the way.

"Is your friend coming?" Alan asked Rayman.

"Yes, I will be leaving early to pick her from her home and board bus from your stop with you."

"What is her name?"

"Riya"

"OK, I will be coming with you when you leave for home."

"No issue"

Rayman and Alan left for their homes around five in the evening and it is around nine now Rayman, Riya and Alan waiting for the bus at their pickup point. This is Alan and Rayman bus stop for their office bus too.

"Ask them why are they taking so much time?" Alan said to Rayman.

"I talked to Abhi few minutes ago and he said that they will be here any minute."

Around ten minutes past nine a bus with capacity of around twelve people stopped in front of them, a boy stepped out of the bus. They boarded bus and noticed that last row is empty and one seat with Abhi and one front seat with driver are also vacant. Alan decided to sit with Abhi and Rayman and Riya sat on last row. Bus has two columns of seats, one column have one person seat and other two persons seats. Anna is sitting in the row before last row on single seat. Rayman is sitting just behind him and Riya took the seat behind two person seat. Last row seat is joined and has capacity for four person and hence providing lot of space. Ruchi and her husband sitting on seat behind driver seat on two person seat, by their side sitting Jiten on single seat. Samarth and her friend are sitting behind Ruchi's seat. Abhi and Alan are sitting behind Samarth's seat. Anna's friend is sitting between Anna and Jiten's seat on single seat.

"Leave your bags in the alley, we will arrange them in baggage are when we stop for dinner." Samarth said to Rayman and Alan. Rayman introduced Riya to everyone after settling down. Ruchi introduced her husband to Rayman and Alan. Bus kept moving for next two hours without stopping and as it moving wind getting cooler with night. Very dim light is illuminated inside bus. Everyone is almost slept except Jiten and Samarth.

"Driver Ji, please stop bus on the restaurant in that big old building." Jiten asked the driver pointing toward a restaurant inside a big and old building with large gates.

"Sir, we will get good food here and also interior is awesome." Jiten said to Samarth.

Bus stopped at that road side restaurant (Dhaba) and light illuminated inside bus with full intensity and this woke up everyone from their sleep. Jiten and Samarth announced that everyone needs to come out for dinner. In next fifteen minutes everyone is out of the bus and most of guys want to freshen up so they started searching for wash rooms. Everyone is at dinner table after fifteen minutes except girls and little strange but driver is also missing. Samarth and Jiten are discussing why girls haven't come back even after fifteen minutes.

Tour de Narkanda

*R*ayman Samarth and Avi went into search for girls after waiting for thirty minutes and found that everyone is standing outside of ladies washroom and washroom door locked from inside. They started gossiping there and after few minutes their driver gave shock to everyone when he came out of ladies washroom and this finally provided chance to girls to freshen up before dinner.

"Can you hold my wallet for few minutes? I need to use washroom." Riya asked Alan.

"Sorry, but I can't." Alan's response is surprising for Riya.

"Hey, give it to me." Anna asked Riya for wallet.

Riya handed her wallet to Anna and after fifteen minutes everyone is back on dinner table. Jiten asked everyone about what they want to have in dinner and ordered dinner. Riya and Anna sat side by side and talking all the time. This is probably beginning of new friendship.

It's almost midnight when they again started their journey. It is going to take another eight to ten more hours to them to reach their destination Narkanda, which is even few kilometers ahead of Shimla. Everyone is sitting on the seat for the next part of journey. Rayman's legs spread in alley in between of Anna and Abhi seat but nearer to Anna seat. After few minutes everyone fallen asleep and it's very quiet in the bus except slow music playing on bus stereo. It must be around two or three in next morning when Rayman felt sudden pain in his leg which is stretched in alley. His leg is feeling very heavy. He lifts his head to enquire the matter and sees that Anna sleeping with her head on his thigh and clutching his leg like a pillow with one of her hand. She is in very deep sleep. Her hairs are over half of her face. Rayman tried to pull the leg and at this moment Anna make her grip on his leg even tighter. All lights are switched off inside the bus and only light coming of moon through creaks of curtains over glass windows. Her face is partially visible in between hairs, her eyes are closed, and her lips appear very pretty. He wants to wake her up but he couldn't due to fear of breaking her dreams, so he fall back again trying to sleep and closed his eyes but it take him some time to sleep in between the pain.

It is around seven in the morning and we are few kilometers away from Shimla. Rayman is awake and could not sleep anymore due to pain which is increased even more now and Anna is still sleeping like earlier in the night having grip on his leg, he noticed that Alan is also awake now and looking at Anna and his leg and before Alan could look at his face to say anything he closed his eyes to imitate that he is in sleep to avoid any conversation. After half an hour they entered Shimla and driver halted bus at one road side restaurant after few kilometers entering Shimla and this broke everyone's sleep. Anna is also awake now and she looked at Rayman but he is still closing his eyes. Everyone moved out of the bus in next few minutes and standing outside of washrooms in the queue to freshen up everyone is tired after whole night journey. Girls are still in problem as their bus driver once again occupied girl's washroom.

"What happened to you, why are you limping?" Abhi asked to Rayman who coming toward him, Abhi is sitting on one mile stone by road side and Rayman is returning from men's washroom.

"I don't know, I think it is cold of Shimla which caused this." Rayman lied as it is hard to tell that Anna was sleeping with her head on his leg.

"You seem very sensitive to cold." Abhi make taunt and took his camera out of his bag and start taking picture of surrounding. Ruchi and her husband are at the restaurant and looking at options for breakfast. After fifteen minutes everyone is at table and deciding what to have in breakfast.

"I will have bread omelet." Rayman decided about his choice.

"Maggie" Abhi and Riya choose Maggie.

After that Jiten, Ruchi opted for Parathas, Samarth and her friend chose omelet and Anna decided to have Maggie. Once again they are back in the bus to start for journey to their destination after one hour. After two hour's drive Samarth instructed driver to take bus on a diversion toward a narrow road going upward on a hill. Driver parked bus after climbing hill for five hundred meters in front of a hotel and everyone come out of the bus. Hotel's signboard reads 'Hotel Hatu Peaks'

"Awesome" is Ruchi's comment after seeing the hotel and surrounding.

"Let's get fresh and eat something, we have one hour and then we will leave for sightseeing." Samarth announced to everyone. Jiten and Samarth are in one room, Rayman is with Abhi and Ruchi and her husband in one room, Alan sharing room with Samarth's friend and rest three Anna, Riya and Anna's friend sharing one room.

"You go and get ready first, I will have tea first." Rayman said to Abhi lying on the bed and he ordered tea on intercom.

After thirty or forty minutes everyone is in the dining hall of the hotel, Ruchi and her husband reached first and enjoying their tea.

"Would you like butter toast with tea? It is our specialty." waiter asked them.

"Then bring few plates." Rayman confirmed the order.

He brought toast in five minutes and everyone liked the toast. It is around twelve o'clock when everyone started walking after Samarth to start their journey for sightseeing, Samarth already visited Narkanda twice so he knows everything in surrounding. They went to small market placed on the bottom of that small hill where their hotel is situated. They visited temple situated in middle of market. Everyone is visiting small shops after temple visit to buy something as a memento of the trip. Abhi bought a cap from a shop which local guys wear to prevent them from cold. It is quite hot in Delhi in these days of June and July while they are enjoying cold weather in Narkanda and this is the reason they wrapped themselves in warm clothes to prevent them from falling sick.

"Do you want to buy something?" Rayman asked Riya.

"No, I don't need anything."

"OK, as you wish. I asked as I asked you to come on trip."

"Well, you haven't forced me, I wanted to come."

"Riya, what are you buying?" Anna also asked Riya coming closure.

"Nothing, have you bought anything or liked anything?"

"No, I think everything is available in Delhi."

It is around two thirty and they by then visited market very well and surrounding in the town. By now everyone seems little hungry. Samarth asked everyone for food.

"I am feeling hungry, is anybody else also feeling for the food? I think it will be better to have food in the market before moving to hill area. I am thinking of going to Hatu Peak Mountain after lunch. We can either track there or can take cab. I don't think our bus can go there."

"Let's have lunch before tracking to the hill. I am also very much hungry. Riya, aren't you hungry?" Anna asked Riya, she appears very eager to taste new food from this place. Jiten and Samarth inspected at least two or three restaurants before settling down in one small restaurant finally.

"This one is looking a bit cleaner than others and food is also looking good to me." Jiten said to Samarth.

"OK, we can have lunch here. Ask them to arrange tables for us. I am calling these guys."

Abhi and Jiten told restaurant owner about their requirement for seating arrangements, Riya is gossiping with Anna and her friend. Ruchi and her husband are talking to Alan, Samarth and her friend and Rayman approaching Jiten and Abhi to give them hand in seating arrangements.

"I will have something from north Indian dishes." Rayman said to Samarth after taking seats.

"I will have something from local dishes." Samarth replied.

"I will also have something from local dishes" Alan supported Samarth's option.

"I want to see menu first." Anna always has different view.

"I can eat anything from north Indian dishes, Rayman order the same thing for me what you are ordering for you." Riya said to Rayman. Abhi asked waiter to come and take order for lunch. Rayman, Riya, Samarth and Jiten ordered non-veg dishes while other ordered veg dishes. After finishing their lunch around three thirty they started journey for Hatu peak. Hatu peak is around at one mile's distance from main market. Ruchi and Avi decided to track and Rayman also joined them. Rest guys going via cab they took from local taxi stand.

"We will reach first, they have to travel at least three four times than us around the hill. We have to walk around half kilometer only." Avi said to Ruchi and Rayman to provide them motivation for tracking. After walking for around twenty or thirty minutes they reached at top of Hatu peak while other coming via cab still not reached there and they also reached around five minutes later except Anna and Abhi. Anna and Abhi de-boarded few hundred meters before and they also tracking to top, they reached at last even five minutes after of cab guys.

"Haven't you got tired after tracking so much?" Riya asked Rayman when they meet on top.

"No, it was fun. You should have also come with us."

"No way, you can even go back tracking if you liked so much but I will go by cab only."

Samarth is taking pictures of trees, clouds and nature in surrounding after adjusting lenses on his camera. Abhi and Jiten taking pictures while girls taking pictures of each other and making various poses.

"This place is better than Shimla. There is no crowd at here. It is so quiet and peaceful." Ruchi said with joy.

"I love this place. It is really cooler than Delhi. Wish if I can work from here." H.R. girl said to Samarth.

"Weather is same as Jammu. Jammu is even more beautiful than this place." Anna made remark.

"I agree Jammu is more beautiful and I think Kashmir is even more beautiful than Jammu." Rayman supported Anna remark.

"Yeah, you are right. Kashmir is even more beautiful." Riya said in support of Rayman's remark. "But this place is safer than Kashmir." She further added.

"Have you guys been to Kashmir?" Anna asked them.

"Yes, we were there for one week." Riya responded.

"Why?" Anna asked in response to Riya.

"We were gone on a trip just like this one. We both went on that trip too with few of our friends." Riya paused and continued further. "I heard you are Kashmiri, you must have visited Kashmir many times."

"NO, I was born in Kashmir but then we migrated to Jammu during riots." She said blankly but there was so much to say in those few words.

Samarth is still taking pictures of surrounding and these guys one by one. Ruchi and Avi are discussing and enjoying the nature in surrounding. Jiten, Abhi and Alan are making poses for pictures for Samarth standing together. Anna and her friend Shilpa are discussing something while adjusting their pose for picture, Rayman and Riya standing a little far from them.

"Hey let's go to that temple there. Let's see who is idol in that temple?" Abhi says pointing toward an under construction temple at one side on the hill and he started walking after saying this and Jiten also following him, everyone else also following them except Samarth and her friend who were still taking pictures of surrounding but he also shifted his and his camera's focus toward temple.

"It's lord Shiva's temple." Anna screamed with joy after entering the temple ahead of everyone.

"Hello brother, is it new temple under construction or renovation of some old temple in progress?" Jiten asked one of the workers working on the site.

"This is very old temple. We are renovating and expanding temple." By the time Samarth and his friend also reached there and they offered their prayer there. They wander in every direction on that small area at top of hill and they decided to go back to hotel after spending around three and half hour as it is started getting dark.

"Hey Samarth, ask the hotel manager if he can arrange bone fire after dinner or with the dinner in the lawn area." Ruchi gave very good suggestion to spend time together.

"Oh yes, this is really good suggestion, we will definitely ask manager to arrange bone fire here." Jiten and Abhi are also supporting Ruchi. Around eight in the evening they are back to the hotel and Samarth started working with manager for arrangement of bone fire and Jiten is also helping him in this and rest of the guys are back in their rooms to freshen up themselves after day long wandering in the woods. After all the arrangements Jiten is having tea with Rayman and Abhi in the dining area with butter toast and Alan also joined them after fifteen minutes.

"Want tea?" Abhi asked her.

"No, I will have dinner after some time." Anna, Riya and Shilpa also joined them at the same time when Alan responded.

"Tea" Rayman asked them.

"Yup" Anna and Riya replied together, while Shilpa denied.

"You are having toast too, please ask for us also."

"Sure"

Samarth also came in the dining hall from outside with Ruchi and her husband after making all arrangement for bone fire.

"Guys, arrangements are done for bone fire but we have to wrap up before twelve. No issue as such but manager is saying that it will get too cold in night and we might fall sick and we also have to leave early in the morning for Shimla so that we can spend some time there also." Samarth said to them as he entered.

"OK, let's go outside what are we waiting for?" Jiten said to everyone.

"OK, let's go then, I will ask them to bring tea and toast outside." Rayman says to Riya and Anna.

"What is it Rayman, you are taking only tea. It is time for something else." Samarth is saying to Rayman about hard drinks.

"Yes, time is surely for something else but I will not have it. You guys please enjoy."

"I am with you" Jiten and Avi said to Samarth.

"I will also have a little bit." Ruchi says to Avi under her breathe.

"Yes sure, it's too cold here, this will keep us warm and I think everyone should take little of it."

Very soon everyone is out in the lawn area, where Samarth is working with hotel staff for arrangement of chairs around fire. They placed a table at one side to accommodate snacks and drinks.

"Sir, we have placed tea on the table." One waiter said to Samarth.

"Thanks yaar, please bring some cold drinks and water, and one more thing, do you have ice?"

"Yes sir, we do have ice."

"Bring some ice also and three glasses."

"Sure" Samarth also left with them and brought a bottle of whisky with him and placed on the table. Everyone is in the warm clothes and enjoying warmth from fire as well to keep them warm and safe from surrounding wind and environment which is quiet cold. Samarth is preparing drink and Jiten is arranging snacks.

"What is max time we can have dinner in lawn?" Samarth asked the manager who also came out with waiter to serve water and cold drinks.

"Till eleven o 'clock sir but if you want to have even after that we can place food in dining area, but in that case you have to serve food yourself."

"Can you arrange food here in the lawn?"

"Sure sir, as you wish."

"Samarth, I think it would be better if we have dinner inside, we can drink here and then go inside to have dinner." Ruchi said to Samarth.

"OK." Samarth also instructed manager "we will let you know when we want to have dinner."

Samarth, Jiten and Avi are having drinks glasses in their hands and Rayman and Abhi giving company with cold drink. Anna and Riya are enjoying chips and tea.

"Who wants to play antakshri?" Alan asked to group.

"Let's sing in group." Avi suggested in response.

"OK, you start then." Samarth and Ruchi responded to Avi.

Avi started singing "Ye pyaar humen kis mod pe le aaya" a Bollywood song from one old movie Satte pe Satta and everyone joined him in the song. Everyone is in the party mood in next few minutes, they filled environment with music. People often say that drink can bring artist out of anyone and same effect is visible on Samarth and Avi.

"Let's have dinner." Alan asked first nearly twelve in the night.

"I am also feeling very hungry." Riya and Anna also joined her.

"Let's go inside, we have to serve food ourselves." Jiten, Rayman and Abhi went inside to check arrangement of food. Jiten returned after five minutes and asked rest of them to come inside.

"No chance of hot food, we have to manage with this food." Jiten took food and everyone else also taking food in their plates. Around twelve forty they finished dinner and went back into their room to have some sleep before starting journey back home in the morning. But no one is asleep back in the room except Rayman and Abhi. Samarth and Jiten continued their party in their room, Alan and Samarth's friend discussing office life, and some discussion going on in Anna and Riya's room

"Rayman loves you too much I guess?" Anna asked to Riya while Shilpa is half slept.

"No yaar, you took it all wrong. Actually he thinks that I am his responsibility on this trip and that is the reason he is so caring for me, nothing else. We are just very good friends or rather you can say best friends." Anna is seeing her with surprise; she further added "He will care for you the same way if you are her responsibility." They also went to sleep after gossiping for around one hour about one another's life.

Around eight in the next morning everyone is in the bus and once again bus started after one day halt for their next destination - Shimla. This time environment is entirely different than first time, everyone is very happy and ready for shopping in Shimla. They are singing in the group or gossiping. After around two hour's journey they reached Shimla and parked bus in the parking at main market.

"I am feeling hungry. Let's eat something before exploring market." Anna said to everyone.

"I am also feeling the same." Alan and Riya are also feeling hungry.

"Rayman let's eat something first" Riya says to Rayman and he asked everyone for food.

"I had heavy breakfast in the morning. I am going to other side in the market. You guys can have something and let's meet in half an hour." Samarth said to them.

"I am also not feeling hungry. I am coming with you." Avi also went with Samarth and so Ruchi and rest having something and then met them in committed time. They spent next three hours roaming on mall road in Shimla. They visited nearly every shop in the market without buying anything.

"We should start our journey to back home otherwise we will be late for dropping girls at their homes." Jiten said to Samarth when it is around five in the evening.

"Yes, we should left now. I said to my parent that I will be back before ten o'clock." Alan and Anna are also looking a bit concerned now.

"Yes, I think you guys are right, it will take at least eight hours to reach home and by this equation if we start right now we will at two at our home." Samarth concluded and asked everyone to start moving toward bus and once again bus started moving toward Delhi and next they come out of the bus when bus comes to halt at eleven for dinner at one road side restaurant. Delhi is still hundred kilometers from that place. Around twelve they completed their dinner in half sleep and started their journey once again, and around three Jiten is last to reach his home. Everyone else is already dropped at their home.

So finally this fun filled trip comes to end after two days of fun, food, music, exploration and togetherness and this trip also started journey of few new friendships. Friendships which are going to last long...

Annual party - II

Rayman and Riya are at Dominos at Central market Lajpat Nagar one evening. It is second week of September 2009 and around three months since Narkanda trip.

"Anna called today" Riya said to Rayman.

"Who is Anna?"

"You are saying like you don't know her. Who is Anna?" Riya is mocking Rayman.

"Oh, you are talking about that Anna but why she called you?"

"Why? Can't she call me?"

"Oh she can surely call you. Well, what is it all about?"

"Nothing important, she is telling me about your office's annual party next month, she was asking 'am I coming or not?'"

"Oh yeah, there is actually party in my office next month. So what you said? Are you going with her?"

"Why haven't you told me about it? Now I will not come to party. One more thing she is saying that she is looking for house, she asked me if I can shift with her or she can shift with me. She is looking for PG."

"OK, do you have space in your PG?"

"No yaar, there is no room available and I also can't shift with her as she lives too far."

"OK, so do you want to come to party?"

"It is one whole month for party. I will tell you later if I want to come for party."

"Oh yeah, Party mostly happens around October or November month, so it is more than one month for the party. You take your time to decide but give me at least one week time so that I can make arrangement for your party pass."

It is one Saturday evening Rayman is at 3C's food court at Lajpat Nagar with his friends. They are discussing about their office and personal life.

"How is everything at Noida office?" Rayman asked to Toni and Vishu.

"Everything is good. What specific you want to know, tell me about which girl you want to know?" Vishu replied with mischievous smile on his face.

"Not any specific girl yaar, I am asking about you guys. How are Ram and your boss Baba?"

"Man I am just kidding, we are good and so everybody else. Ram is also fine and you know Baba very well, he is also getting a little better these days."

"Really!! I thought Baba never going to change."

"Yaar, I will also be shifting to Baba's team." Tanu appeared a little upset and angry when she said this.

"Why? What happened?" Rayman asked her.

"Nothing, I think my stars have some fault. They are moving me in some in-house project on which Vicky was working earlier. Now they are moving Vicky into some other project and that is the reason they needs me in place of Vicky." She is really upset and who will not be upset going out of Ram's team and that too in Baba's team.

"Where are you going man?" Rayman asked Vicky.

"Some new project for some Canadian client, some finance related work."

"Oh great news man, it makes perfect occasion for party." Vishu and Toni also supported Rayman for party from Vicky.

"Why aren't they shifting me in new project?" Tanu is crying once again.

"Cause dear they want someone who can work not gossip all the day." Toni commented on Tanu.

"Look who is talking. When do you work in office? It is you my dear who gossip all day not me."

"Leave this nonsense yaar. Who is coming to office's annual party?" Rayman asked to everyone.

"Everyone is coming I guess." Lavanya replied first, she is always very excited for this party.

"I also think nobody has any issue coming for the party." Tanu is second.

"I am also coming" Toni, Vishu and Vicky also confirmed.

"I need one more entry pass. Riya also wants to come in party."

"Only girls can have extra pass, so Tanu or Lavanya can help you on this." Toni suggested.

"I don't have extra pass." Tanu and Lavanya both denied.

"In that case I have to ask someone in my team. What about Diya? Vishu, Is she coming with you or not?"

"I can't confirm right now, but it is still more than a month. Let's see how it shapes up?"

"Hey ask her to come, we haven't met her in so many days, we can meet her on this occasion." Tanu asked Vishu.

"I am not stopping her yaar, she can decide herself if she wants to come for the party." Party continued till ten in the night when Riya asked Rayman to drop her home.

"It is getting late now, we should leave now and don't forget to arrange pass for me. I am coming for party either on extra pass or on your pass." Everyone is laughing on Riya's comment.

"Ask in your team, they might arrange for you." Vishu said to Rayman while bidding him goodnight.

"Yeah, that is a good idea. I will definitely check in my team, but for now I think we should move back home."

One morning in October end Rayman having breakfast at office cafeteria with Alan, Abhi and Samarth. They are discussing about office work, current project and their life outside office, at this time Rayman asked Alan about annual party plans.

"Are you coming for party?"

"What? There is only one major party in whole year and you asking 'Am I coming or not?' I will definitely be coming. Why are you asking? Aren't you coming?"

"No, I am also coming, I am just confirming whether you guys are coming or not."

"Sir, are you coming?" Abhi asked Samarth.

"Not sure but possibly I will also come."

"Alan, Is anyone coming with you?" Rayman asked to Alan.

"No. Why"

"I need your pass for Riya."

"Sure, I will give you my pass." Rayman confirmed to Riya after confirmation from Alan.

"How will you be coming for party? Will you go directly from office by office bus or you come on your own?" Alan asked to Rayman on the way back to his seat from cafeteria.

"Well, I am returning by cab but not sure about going to party. I have to pick Riya first."

"OK, I will also come with you while going to party."

"Sure, it would be better. You and Riya will get company of each other."

"So, it's done then." Later Jay also asked everyone for party and everyone committed that they will be going for the party, Jay is also coming for party, he has some performance also on stage.

It is around seven in the evening Rayman and Riya are waiting for Alan at Ashram chowk. Rayman is no different for the party from any normal day while Riya is dressed in red colored Indian salwar suite with matching Dupatta, her temper going up with time waiting for Alan.

"Why are we waiting for her this long, let's go. Why don't you call her and check when will she be here?"

"Oh ho yaar, I called her few minutes back and she said she will be here in five minutes."

"Oh sorry, I am a bit late yaar. Let's go now." Alan apologizes to Riya and Rayman as she reached at the stop.

"No special preparation for party?" Alan asked Rayman.

"I have left it for you guys." Rayman said to Alan looking at her dress, she is wearing red top with green long length skirt. "One thing I was never able to understand is what makes you girls so strong that you go with so less clothes in this Delhi winter of November. It is so cold out and this chilly wind."

"You will never understand."

Alan and Rayman continued their conversation all the way to party venue about their friends, office and other things, and Riya got angrier sitting in between them listening all the conversation. Around eight thirty they reached at party venue, party is already in full swing. One guy is addressing people from podium on stage. This year party is inside the hall rather than in open area like last year. Rayman's boss Jay is standing on one side of the stage with his friend Harry. Harry and Jay are also dressed very well for party, Harry has very pretty smile on her face. Rayman greeted Jay and introduced Riya to Jay. Jay asked them to take seat near stage and enjoy the snacks and performances. Few people sitting on chairs in front rows and getting bored with the performances. They took chairs in one of the back rows.

"Rayman, Anna is sitting few rows ahead. I am going to her." Riya said to Rayman. Riya and Alan both went to Anna. Anna is also dressed in Salwar Kameez suite like Riya.

"Hi Anna" Riya greeted her.

"Oh hi Riya, how are you? It is so long time since we met last time. It is almost six month since the Shimla trip." Anna is so happy meeting Riya.

"Yeah it is." Riya responded with same joy.

"How is everything?" And series of questions and answers follows from both of them. They haven't noticed Alan and Rayman for next fifteen to twenty minutes until Rayman greeted Anna.

"Hi"

"Oh hi"

"Riya, you stay with Anna and Alan, I will be back in few minutes. Let me check Vishu and others and please have something to eat. Do you want anything to drink?" and he moved out of that area toward drink stall. Anna and Riya are still in their conversation but Alan somehow not able to fit in the conversation.

"Hey man, relax and have patience. We have lot of time for drinks." Rayman greeted Jiten who is in the queue to get his drink.

"Oh hi, I have taken earlier but Samarth sir took that from me and it is just first peg yaar. Do you need anything?"

"No, I will take something later. You carry on." Rayman moved further in search of others.

"Hi sir, why are you drinking alone?" Rayman greeted and asked Samarth at the same time, he is holding peg in one hand while standing in a corner.

"Yeah, I like it quiet while drinking."

"OK then enjoy, see you later."

"Why aren't you drinking? Do you drink naah?"

"Yeah I drink but I usually start late so that I can hold myself till late. Well I am looking for other friends, see you around." Rayman left to search other friends after this comment.

Rayman's friends from old group Vishu, Tanu, Toni, Deepali, Vicky, Utsav and Lavanya all are at snacks stalls. Everyone greeted each other and which followed further gossip.

"Hey Deepali and Lavanya how you guys are here, aren't you guys have any performance this year? You should be behind stage by this time." Rayman asked them.

"That is the reason we are having snacks so quickly and early. We are going behind the stage in few minutes. We have fashion show in few minutes."

"For god's sake keep it short this year, last year you guys have taken all the time we couldn't dance last year." Vishu almost cried with this comment.

"No yaar, we haven't taken all time last year, it is Rayman's boss Jay who took all time in his skate." Lavanya responded with anger in her voice.

"Shit, I noticed Jay by the side of stage few minutes ago. I think he has same plans this year too." Rayman informed them.

"Your manager naah, he always wastes time on stage." Vicky also seems angry this time. "By the way where is your team mate, the one who compared last year's programs?" He further asked to Rayman but this reminds Rayman something else.

"Oh god, Riya is also come with me; I left her with Alan and Anna. She is going to kill me."

"What? Has Riya also come with you? You haven't told us about her. Where is she?" Vishu asked him.

"She is inside the hall. She is with her one friend Anna. She will kill me for sure I have left her there for more than half hour ago."

"You are so stupid. Let me take some snacks for her. I am also coming with you." Vishu said to Rayman.

"That would be great." Vishu and Rayman went inside. Rest of the group also went inside following them except Deepali and Lavanya who is going behind the stage for their performances.

"Do you want anything to drink also?" Rayman asked Vishu when they were passing by drink stall.

"Sure" Vishu replied and Rayman handed snack's plate to Vishu.

"What you want?"

"Whisky"

"OK, I will have beer but I will bring whisky for you." Rayman brought whisky in one hand and beer in other and joined them in few minutes. Vishu handed one plate of snacks to Toni and took his drink and they started moving inside once again.

"Hey what you doing here, where is Riya?" Rayman asked Alan when he noticed her coming toward them.

"I was getting bored there so I decided to look around. Riya is inside sitting with Anna, they are enjoying and gossiping."

"OK. Hey meet my friends. This is Vishu, Vicky, Toni, Tanu, and Lokesh" He introduced each of them one by one and also introduced Alan to them.

"Lokesh, can you please hold my drink?" Rayman handed his glass to Lokesh after seeing Riya coming toward them from distance.

"I have come with you in this party I guess." She commented with anger after reaching near them.

"I was just coming to you, I lost track of time gossiping with Toni and Vishu."

"Don't drag them in this, I know you very well, where is your glass? You must have forgotten me in between drinks. It is my good luck that I met Anna and has someone to talk at least. I am waiting for you for so long and you are nowhere."

"Hi Riya, would you like to have cheela?" Vishu asked her trying to end the argument between them.

"Hi Vishu" and she greeted everyone else after that. "Yeah, I am so hungry. It is more than an hour I am waiting for Rayman and listening bullshit on stage."

"Let's go inside, Vishu please bring one more cheela for Anna also." Rayman asked Riya and Vishu.

"Alan, do you also want to come inside or stay here?" Rayman asked Alan.

"No yaar, I am coming with you."

"Take your glass from Lokesh. I have seen you handing over your drink to him." Riya asked Rayman while moving inside. "I think I need to talk to your mom about it later."

"No yaar, I was not drinking It is for him only. Really I just had only one glass."

"Hmm, you and only one glass, not possible." Everyone moved inside in between conversation.

"Hey Anna, thanks yaar for giving company to Riya" Rayman thanked Anna after reaching to her seat and they also took seats near her seat. "Would you like to have cheela naah? How are you finding party?" Rayman asked Anna after settling down on the chair.

"Nothing exciting yaar, all the performances are boring till now. Rayman, these girls are not from our office." She responded after taking cheela from his plate.

"What!" Rayman asked with surprise looking toward girls performing on stage and this time everyone else has his attention on stage. Before anyone could say anything Anna brought Riya's attention toward Rayman.

"Riya, have you noticed Rayman? He has gone near stage to Jay so that he can watch performance of these girls from closer the stage."

"I know him very well, he is such scoundrel." Vishu responded after seeing him.

"They don't appear from our office. Where they come from?" Rayman asked Jay.

"Why? Do you like someone?"

"No. Just like that"

"I don't know exactly, admin department made all arrangement for this performance."

Performance finished in few minutes and Rayman is back to his seat near Riya and Anna, others moved out of the hall. Alan is not with them, she might have gone to Jiten or Abhi.

"Why did you come back? Why don't you go with these girls? Have you ever thought what people will be thinking about you?"

"You are not eating anything. I am bringing snacks for you." Rayman avoided further conversation on this and moved out to bring something for them.

"So, how was performance and girls?" Vishu asked Rayman when they met on one snacks stall.

"Boring"

"OK, then why you moved closer. By the way our office crowd is better than them."

"I haven't noticed at first."

"Let's drink." They moved toward drink's stall leaving other behind gossiping with each other. Vishu and Rayman are enjoying their drinks and while others are enjoying gossip.

"Let's go inside now, Riya must be getting bored." Vishu said to Rayman.

"Oh my god, I forget once again, but you reminded me on time. She will kill me."

"Don't worry yaar, I am coming with you, I will handle it."

"OK, you go I will take something for them." After that both went inside once again.

"Rayman, please don't drink anymore." Riya said to Rayman.

"I am staying with you here only." He handed paneer tikka and cheela to Anna and Riya.

Riya and Anna are enjoying cold drinks, snacks and gossiping, Rayman and Vishu also sitting with them, Rest of the guys are also came toward stage and enjoying fashion show, Alan is also with Tanu and Vicky. After few minutes all performances comes to end and now D.J. is playing music. Deepali and Lavanya moved to dance floor and few other also followed them.

"I am also going to dance floor." Vishu said to Rayman. "Are you coming? Riya come naah." Vishu asked them.

"No, I can't dance." Riya responded first.

"You go. I will join you later." Rayman responded later.

In the next fifteen minutes nearly everyone is on the dance floor. Vishu asked him once more and then Rayman also went to dance floor but he is not dancing.

"Riya, come on" Vishu once again called her.

"Come on" Rayman also asked her.

"No way" She responded to Rayman. "Please understand."

"Anna, come here on dance floor." Jay called Anna.

"Coming, Riya are you coming?" She also went to D.J. floor.

"No yaar, you carry on"

Anna is dancing with Jay, Samarth, Alan and Jiten at one side of floor and while Deepali, Lavanya, Vishu, Vicky, Toni, and Tanu on opposite side of floor. Riya is sitting in the front row and watching them dance.

"I can't dance anymore." Vishu crashed to one chair near Riya's chair after dancing for around an hour.

"Let's eat then and go back home." Rayman suggested them.

"Anna, are you coming for dinner?" Riya asked her.

"Yeah" She also joined them for dinner. They are now waiting for others to come back from dance floor.

"Rayman, please pass water bottle." Deepali asked him, as he is drinking water at that time.

"Sure" and he passed bottle from which he was drinking.

"Who is that girl, Is she Rayman's girlfriend?" Anna asked Riya.

"I have no idea, but he must have told me if she would."

"Hey Vishu, come on yaar. This is last song. Let's dance naah for few more minutes then we will go for dinner." Lavanya is out of control when she called Vishu on stage.

"Hey come for one more song." Vishu asked Rayman.

"You go, I am too tired yaar."

"Rayman, where were you, come" Jay also asked for him when he noticed him.

"Ok sir." He joined Jay for last song. Jay, her friend, Jiten and Alan are dancing while Abhi and Samarth are standing by their side. Rayman also joined Samarth and Abhi.

D.J. closed after the song and everyone moved toward food stall for dinner. Riya and Anna are having dinner in one plate. Vishu, Toni, Tanu, Vicky and Rayman are also eating together in one or two plates, Deepali and Lavanya are eating together. Alan, Abhi also joined them for dinner and having dinner with them.

Around twelve everyone is at exit gate and waiting for cabs for their homes. Anna, Riya, Alan, Samarth and Rayman left together in Samarth's car as they live on the same route. This time Riya is not getting bore as she also got company of Anna. Samarth dropped Anna near Kalka Ji at her home and then Alan and finally Riya and then Rayman.

Vicky – Alan

*R*ayman, Alan and Abhi are having their breakfast and discussing about annual party events on Monday morning after annual party evening. Rayman is talking about his friends from his old group, Abhi and Alan is commenting on how Rayman got drunk in party.

"How do you guys find my previous group's colleagues? They are enjoying more than our team." Rayman asked to Abhi and Alan.

"Yes, I found your old team much better than our team." Alan replied first.

"Everything looks good from a distance, but from inside they all appears the same." Abhi also added to conversation.

"But I know both of them from inside as well." Rayman said to them and I also agree with Alan.

Rayman noticed a mail from Vicky after returning to his seat from breakfast.

'Hi Rayman,

How are you, how's everything in your new office.

Its only party discussion today in office, same must be at your end. Yaar, I am looking for a house, I want to relocate somewhere near Lajpat Nagar, Vishu told me that you stay near Maharani Bagh which is also near Lajpat Nagar. Tell me, how is locality and everything else there, and how is the rent?

-Vicky'

'What happened now? I think locality and rent is also quite good near my place, that might be reason for his relocation, this locality is not as good as Lajpat Nagar but rent might be a plus point for my place.' Rayman was thinking all these and replied same to Vicky.

'Let's see few houses in this weekend' Vicky's response came quickly.

'Sure' Rayman replied.

A little later Rayman also wrote a mail to Vicky and rest other in his older group.

'Hi Guys

So what is going on there, how is everyone? Tanu, Vishu, Toni and others, you guys haven't sent any mails in so many days.
Is anything new in our group? Has any new girl joined our group in recent past? I didn't come in so many days and I will come soon to see you all.

-Rayman'

'Yes, you scoundrel, you have not seen us from this Friday only. We are all good here, one girl joined Vishu's team, he appears very happy these days.
Rest is good, everyone is discussing about party these days.'

Vicky replied to his mail.

'What! You guys have not told me about that new girl, how does she look?'

Rayman writes mail in response to Vicky's mail.

'She is awesome, milky white, sexy figure and very pretty'. Vicky responded.

'What are you talking about, oh my god, who is that girl, well who cares who is that girl, just introduce to me when I come next time.

Take care'

Response from Rayman says all about his nature. He is known inside his friend for his flirting nature. Saturday came very quickly, whole week gone in between discussion about annual party and pictures of the party. Vicky and Rayman are looking for a house near to Rayman. Vicky is going to stay with his brother and one of his friends. After searching for Saturday and Sunday finally they found one house in Ashram.

"Vicky settled near my home in Ashram. It will be good now we can hang out together." Rayman says to Riya, both were sitting in Dominos outlet in Lajpat Nagar.

"Like you guys not got a chance to meet in ages." Riya made killer comment.

"No yaar, you are taking it in a wrong way, it's not like that. I mean we can be available for each other if there is any urgency, you know." Rayman tries to put his point but it is impossible to convince a girl in any case.

"I know very well, eat pizza." Riya's comment says all about it.

Monday morning Rayman and Vicky running together to catch their office buses for their offices and as usual guys can never be on time for anything especially for bus or train.

"See you in the evening" Rayman say and both start running in opposite direction from Ashram chowk, Rayman running toward Maharani Bagh and Vicky running toward Lajpat Nagar.

"Do you remember Vicky, from annual party? He has shifted to near my house, now I got company to run for bus in the morning." Rayman is talking to Alan and they are sitting on same seat in their office bus.

"Not exactly, but it's good, now you might come on time." Alan responded smiling.

"God knows, this driver purposefully drove bus before time at our stop specially." Rayman tries new excuse for coming late.

"Vicky is one taller guy, with spectacles, very thin, he appears techy geek." Rayman further gives description about Vicky.

"Your all friends are taller." Alan said in return.

"Yes, true. Well, I will try to introduce later with all of them." Rayman responded like she is dyeing to meet his friends.

'Hi, Morning

> I could not catch my bus, are you able to catch your bus?
> How is your teammate? You have not introduced me properly.

-Vicky'

Rayman saw mail from Vicky first thing in morning.

'What? I got my bus, I reached and Alan (My teammate) stopped the bus for me. So how did you reach office? And I will introduce her to you next time for sure.'

Rayman responded to Vicky's mail.

It's January of 2010 and it is still cold environment, which is helping Rayman and Vicky in getting late for bus.

"Your teammate is really good looking, so sexy, so nice figure" Vicky says to Rayman one morning when both running for their bus.

"She is not that good at all. It usually happens that we always tend to fall for girls which are out of our reach. You would not have liked her if she was in your team." Rayman says in response, it's not Rayman's style but he is trying to judge his seriousness for her.

"She looks good to me." Vicky says to Rayman and both bid goodbye to each other before running in opposite direction.

"Hey Alan, One of my friend Vicky, you might met him in annual party, has shifted here, I told you about." Rayman asked to Alan while both travelling in office bus.

"Yes, you told me about it yesterday, how can I forget so early?" Alan's response says that don't make any move now. But Rayman is made of different kind of material all together.

"No, it's good for me that is why I told you, my older group's friends are really nice, and you also lives near our houses so we can met for some outing whenever we want." Rayman is daring too much.

"Yes true, but who is really want to go out with office friends even on weekend after seeing them whole week in office." Alan's responses are making it difficult for Rayman.

"Yes it's also true."

'Hey Bro,

We are coming for Self-Management training at your location tomorrow, and this training as you already know happens once in every month so we will meet every month now.

Toni and Tanu I will also be coming for training.

-Vicky'

'Oh it's really great news, I got to see you all guys. You can come with me in my bus.' Rayman responded next minute.

'Yes, that will be great idea. But bus goes very early and our training will start around 11 AM, hence I will come by own but will return with you.'

'Ok, as you wish.' Rayman replied to Vicky.

"So how is that new girl in your team?" Rayman asked to Vicky, both gossiping at Vicky's home in the evening.

"Don't ask about her, she is so hot, sexy and so fair may be fairer than snow." Vicky's response is saying all about his condition.

"What is her name?"

"What is in the name, see her figure buddy, and you will forget even your name, well you can refer her Priya."

"Nice name, it suits the description which you have just given about her figure. Tell me whom do you prefer, her or the girl from my team?" Rayman asked him.

"Confused on this, I have not seen your team mate that nicely."

"Oh really, I bet you can even tell about her vital stats."

"That is different thing, but seriously it's very tricky to choose one girl from two very sexy girls."

"Hmm, they both are dying for you naah."

"Ohh, you don't know me, Priya is all set, she can die for me even today, and you just introduce me to your team mate and leave rest on me." Vicky is talking like he is down with at least two or three beers.

"You guys are coming tomorrow. I will do my part, But Are you are seriously serious about Alan? I don't think that she is that good."

"What is not good in her? As much I can see her she is awesome and I think you might have seen her in better way since you are closer to her." Vicky says and started laughing.

"You will regret these comments if you got married to her." Rayman's commented.

"May be, but who cares now?" And they both talked and laughed and finally bid good night around mid-night.

"Hello, how are you? Not able to come to meet you in last few days, so much works in office these days, especially after annual party." Rayman is talking to Riya on cell.

"I am good, how are you?"

"I am also good; I want to discuss something with you."

"Sure, tell me."

"You remember Alan."

"Yes I do, arc you fallen for her now? I got call from Anna that you are getting very close to Alan these days. She also told me that she is not very good girl. Anna doesn't like her and so do I. How can I forget that she could not hold my bag for few minutes on Narkanda trip?"

"Yes sure, how could you forget? She abused you, beaten you."

"So Anna was right, I was fool who were advocating you that you are not that kind of guy and you can't fall for a girl who couldn't hold my bag."

"You see, this is the problem with you girl, you drag whole conversation to something else and to most non related topic."

"Yes, only you boys know how to talk, we girls don't know anything. And how dare you talk to me in this tone, and for that girl, if you want to discuss anything be polite. What is it?"

"Nothing, you remember Vicky?" Rayman asked further.

"Yes I know Vicky very well, he is your friend from old group, and He just shifted near to you home. So what is going on, playing any game with me, now you ask, do I remember Vishu, and then Toni, Tanu, what is this all about? Are you drunk?"

"Why can't you listen to me for few minutes?"

"OK"

"I think he likes Alan. should I do something for these guys?"

"Sure, do social service, so what if it will cost you your job."

"Oh ho, I will play safe."

"I sensed it in annual party only, the way Vicky is looking at Alan and I think there is one more girl in their group, he is also constantly looking at her too."

"Yes, he told me about her also, so how was that girl, Vicky told me she is real good looking girl."

"Bullshit, good looking and that girl!"

'Sure she is good then, no girl says another one good' Rayman was thinking about Vicky's team mate.

"Well if he likes Alan then you should help them to know each other, but take good care of you. Good night for now and keep me posted with updates on this, you know maybe I can help you some time." Riya said to Rayman.

"Sure, good night."

"Hey Rayman, we are in your office, Vicky is also with me, come out let's have tea at Ashoka café." Its Toni on phone to Rayman, Toni and Vicky are at Rayman office for SM (Self-Management) training.

"I am coming in two minutes."

"Hey Alan, want to come for Tea." Rayman asked to Alan while going out for Tea.

"Yes, I am coming. Where is Abhi should we ask him also."

"I think he is in meeting."

It's around 12 when both Alan and Rayman went outside, Toni and Vicky got few minutes break in their training. Toni and Vicky are already at Ashoka café and ordered tea and sandwiches.

"Hey Toni, I haven't seen you since party. How are you doing buddy?" Rayman greeted Toni first and then Vicky.

"I am doing well. Tell me about you, How is your work and all." Toni asked in response.

"All is well, meet Alan, she is my team mate. You must have met her in annual party." Rayman introduced Alan to Vicky and Toni.

"And this is Toni, my very good friend and old team mate and this is Vicky my good friend and he has shifted near our homes recently." Rayman also introduced Toni and Vicky to Alan.

"Hey Alan have sandwich." Toni asked Alan.

Rayman and Toni were talking to each other all the time and Vicky and Alan enjoying tea and Sandwich since Toni and Rayman got quite busy in their conversation.

"So, see you guys in evening, Vicky you are coming with us in the evening I guess?" Rayman asked Vicky before returning back to his desk.

"Yes sure, but it depends on time also." Vicky responded and everyone went back to their work.

"Why did you ask me for tea since you already got company?" Alan asked Rayman when they were returning to their seats.

"Since we were also wanted to go for tea, hence I thought better to join them." Rayman handled the situation somehow.

"Come on Alan, let's move, otherwise we will surely miss the bus today and you know our driver also very well, he will never stop bus for us." Rayman says to Alan in the evening.

"Hello, Vicky, are you coming in our bus or not?" Rayman further called Vicky to inform him to come in bus.

"You come outside. I am already waiting at Ashoka café."

"OK, we are coming. You wait for us for two more minutes."

Alan and Rayman met Vicky at Ashoka café and all three started running toward their bus, bus already started moving.

"Hurry Rayman, bus started moving." Alan cried.

Alan reached first and boarded bus, and then Rayman boarded bus. Rayman and Alan occupied one seat of three persons, Rayman signaled Vicky to sit on other seat parallel to his seat.

"So how was training going?" Rayman asked to Vicky.

"Very good and funny, Ma'am asked to draw a picture that can depict our nature, and you would not believe that what and where people imagination could reach. Some people even drew chicken and tiger pictures. My god it was total fun." Vicky replied to Rayman.

"Yeah, same was the seen in my training also last year."

"What tiger and chicken? What tiger and chicken depicts?" Alan asked to Vicky.

"He is saying that he feels like chicken between his senior and his seniors behave like tigers."

"What, It must be so much fun." Alan joined the conversation and no Alan and Vicky talking to each other about training and work in their respective groups and their team member and manager and Rayman also giving them company.

"So, where is your home, how far your house from Rayman's house?" Vicky asked to Alan.

"You know Siddharth Extension, I live there, and it's not too far, around one kilometer from his house."

"No, I haven't gone there."

"OK, it's a DDA flats colony."

After forty minutes discussion they de-boarded bus at Maharani Bagh bus stop, Alan bid good-bye and they started walking for their home.

"So, where were you live?" Rayman mimicked Vicky. "You are going on right track, but a little too fast."

"Oh no, it's just for knowledge nothing serious."

"Better for you, she is not that good."

"What are you saying? Have you even seen her figure closely, she is so sexy and hot?"

"You have gone mad, how many times should I tell you that it's just in your bloody eyes nothing else."

"I am falling in love with her, and it's good if you don't like her, my line is clear."

"Whatever, she is no good at all."

"But I like her, so do something for me at least."

"No way, I said once, she is not good at all and what happened to your team's that girl, which is so sexy, fairer than snow and god know if she is from heaven or what?" Rayman asked Vicky after irritating him.

"Yes, she is also good, and in my team also, I should concentrate on her, you are right. It will be easy for me to meet and hang out with her."

"I said naah, Alan is not good, and you should concentrate on your team mate only."

"Oh, I am not able to decide where should I concentrate now? Leave it yaar, this is getting complicated."

"OK, first decide with calm mind where you want to go, where your heart want you to head?"

"Yeah, that will be good, let's concentrate on golgappa for now." Vicky ended conversation with their favorite snacks.

January 2010 going with confused state of mind for Vicky. Riya also came to Vicky's place few times with Rayman. Riya and Rayman also became good friend of Vicky's brother Raju and their friend Dharmendra also.

"Would you guys have tea?" Vicky asked to Riya and Rayman, both were at Vicky home one weekend.

"Yes, that would be great." Rayman replied.

"Dharmendra, take some time from phone and have tea."

"Off course bro, that would be great." Dharmendra also joins them.

"So buddy, how are you? Riya how is everything with you? I have heard you are leaving your job." Dharmendra is talking to Rayman and Riya.

"Yes, got bored in this job, now either marriage or new job." Riya replied to Dharmendra.

"Yes change will be good."

"How is your love story going bro, how is Manu doing?" Rayman asked Dharmendra about him and his girlfriend Manu. Dharmendra and Manu's story is not less than any movies story, there are lot of complication and twist and turn.

"Everything is going as usual, no positive progress. I will be going Pune this weekend to meet her." Dharmendra love story is not different from other, like all problem and issue from family. I never understand why parent can't take the guys or girl which you choose.

"Has Vicky told you about that girl in his team, he is kind of mad for her, he is singing about her all the day?" Dharmendra asked Rayman and Riya.

"What? I have no information about it. I heard that he is interested in Alan, now who is this girl?" Riya asked to Dharmendra.

"Oh Rayman didn't told you about Priya, she is in my team. But I am really confused between Alan and Riya. Don't knows exactly what I want?" Vicky replied before anyone else could say anything.

"Raju have your tea." Vicky shouted to Raju, who is in other room talking to someone on his cell phone.

Everyone is having tea and Vicky and Riya having conversation about his confused state of mind.

"Well, I have not seen your team's girl, so I can't say anything about her, and as far I know about Alan, She looks good." Riya gives her opinion to Vicky.

"I also like Alan more but Rayman always says she is not that good."

"I doubts Rayman, he must be having his eye on her, which is why he is saying this."

"Oh ho, now you don't start again that crap." Rayman says to Riya.

"I am just kidding, don't take it so seriously."

"Well I don't like her that way, which is why I told you like that. But it will be you, who will say final words on this. So tell me what do you want?"

"Seriously I don't know at all, but I like her. What will you going to lose if you try for me?"

"Probably a friend if you are not serious."

"OK, give me some time."

Everyone enjoyed tea and had conversation about Vicky, Dharmendra and many other things. Rayman and Riya left in the evening. January of year 2010 nearing ends and once again Vicky, Toni and Tanu are coming to Rayman office to attend SM training. Vicky and Rayman discussed their plan to follow the same schedule and plan like last month.

"Vicky and Toni came for training today, I am going to have tea with them would you guys want to come?" Rayman asked Alan and Abhi.

"Sure" Abhi replied and both Alan and Abhi joined them for tea.

Day passed as usual and in evening Vicky and Toni called Rayman on Ashoka café.

"Hey come out yaar, you some time act so much about your work, let's have bread pakoras."

"Hey Alan I am going outside to have bread pakoras, it's nearly bus time so give me a call once you start."

"What pakoras! how can you eat those pakoras, so much oil, how those pakoras tastes?"

"You have to eat once to know the taste, come and have one."

"Really, is it good? Ok, I am also coming with you." Alan also joined Rayman for pakoras.

"Toni, have you ordered pakoras?" Rayman asked Toni.

"Oh yeah, one for each, I might take another one but later. "Ok order one more, we got company today."

"Oh sure, share this plate in the mean time I will order two more, that will be enough I guess."

"Vishu must be missing those pakoras, he loves Ashoka's pakoras." They are missing Vishu's company for pakoras.

Once again Alan boarded bus at first and then Rayman followed by Vicky but today they are sitting on same seat of three persons. Rayman off course sitting in the middle. Alan and Rayman mostly having conversation on the way back home and Vicky joins them some time, but most of the time Vicky is in his thoughts only. Around after forty minutes journey they de-boarded at Maharani Bagh bus stop.

"Can't we go from this side? There must be some way to our home from here as well?" Vicky asked to Rayman pointing toward the direction where Alan is going.

"Actually, there is one way from that route also which goes to our home, let's go from this side today." Rayman knows one alternative way from inside the Bhagwan Nagar, which can give more time to Vicky to be with Alan and make his mind.

"Hey, would you guys like Gulab-Jamun, I love sweets." Vicky offered them treat.

"Sure" Rayman replied and this makes Alan to accept the invitation.

Vicky ordered Gulab-Jamun for everyone on one sweet shop near by bus stop and after having Gulab-Jamun everyone once again they bid good-bye to go their homes but this time they are walking together for a little more distance. Vicky is looking a bit more interested in Alan today.

After few hundred meter Alan and Rayman changes routes to their respective houses, Vicky's inner is not allowing him to come with Rayman but he has no option but to come with Rayman and hence he followed Rayman.

"Rayman do something yaar, I am falling for Alan." Vicky says to Rayman when Alan went to some distance from those guys.

"No. not again"

"No, seriously, I am serious for her."

"OK, I will see what I can do but only if you are serious, I will definitely put some effort to provide you more opportunities to meet and talk and leave rest to you."

"A little more support would be required I guess."

"We will see that later, but we need to work together and with some solid plan."

Riya, Rayman and Vicky, Dharmendra are having tea at Rayman's home. Today's topic for discussion is fielding placement for Alan.

"Ask her for a movie." Dharmendra suggested.

"Yes, and she is dying to watch movie with me, you guys going to get me fired." Rayman not approved it.

"Tell her that I am also coming for movie and I want her company." Riya suggested.

"I can't believe this. You are supporting these guys to get me fired."

"No one is going to get fired, do what I am telling you." Riya as usual started bullying Rayman.

"OK, but I can't promise I might take some time."

14th Fourteen 2010 Sunday, Rayman and Vicky are at Rayman's home and talking about Alan.

"If you have asked her movie then we all might be watching some movie this time. You can't even do one thing for me." Vicky complains to Rayman.

"Hey bro, why don't you understand, it will put my job on risk. We need to play safe."

"Where has Dharmendra gone?" Rayman asked to Vicky.

"Pune, where else he can go. He is gone to his valentine. It is because of you otherwise I might also have my valentine with me as well."

"What happened to your team mate, ask her to be your valentine?"

"I have to ask her, you haven't left any choice to me."

"Let's see in next week. Are you going home on Holi?"

"Yes and are you?"

"I am also going."

On Monday before Holi weekend, when Rayman reached office everyone is discussing something in his team. Alan noticed him first and as he reached there.

"So here he is, congrats Rayman." Alan says to Rayman.

"Why, what happened?"

"You are going onsite. Jay confirmed to us that someone needs to go to Middle East site and everyone suggested your name."

"But it will be you who decide whether you want to go or not, so first you tell me about your wish." Jay asked him.

"Can't say right now, but sure I would love to go but give me some time to talk to my mom then I can confirm."

"Yes, sure take your time but confirm before evening, because travel plan takes time of around one week and we want you to send by next Monday."

"But sir this weekend I need to go home for Holi also."

"Holi is on Saturday and this will take time of one week, so I don't think there will be any problem."

Rayman talked to mom and brother and discussed about his onsite trip. They agreed happily for his trip and Rayman also confirmed to Jay that he is ready to go on trip.

"First I need to start approval process for your travel then you need to provide your Passport for VISA processing, this will surely take some time, I will update you about the progress, just be ready with your Passport and do some shopping for trip. Ask Samarth for required items for trip since he has already gone there several times."

"Sure sir."

Rayman informed everybody from his friends and Riya about his onsite trip. Riya is too concerned about Middle East, as people say it's not very open country, she always saying him to take precaution. Friday evening everyone is leaving early from office as all of the guys need to go home for Holi celebration.

"Rayman give your Passport before going home so your VISA will be processed next week since you are on leave in next week too." Jay says to Rayman when Rayman is about to leave in the evening.

"But sir how I can give my Passport this time, it's at my home, and I have to catch train around nine, I can't bring my passport this late."

"That will be a problem, doesn't anyone lives near your home, give your passport to him or her."

"Yes, that might be a possible solution; I will give my Passport to Alan."

When Rayman and Alan de-boarded at their bus stop Rayman confirmed Alan once again to give her Passport in few minutes at her home, and both left for their home.

"Hey Vicky I am going to Alan's home in a few minutes." Rayman informed Vicky about Passport issue.

"What, oh I asked you to make fielding for me and now I smell something else."

"Riya and I are leaving for our home for Holi celebration around nine before that I have to hand over my Passport to her. Riya already came here so we both are going to Alan's home. Riya is asking if you want to join us for Alan home."

"Look only Riya is my true friend, no one else understands my condition except Riya. But seriously, do you think it will be good if I join you?"

"No way I don't think this even one percent, but it's your friend Riya who thinks it will be OK, you guys are helping me to get fired sooner or later."

"Well if you think it's not safe then you guys should go."

"Oh ho, don't think this much now, come with us, we will see what worse can happen?"

"OK, then let's meet at bus stop, I will reach there in five minutes and from there we will walk to her home."

"OK"

Rayman confirmed Alan's home address from her and in next thirty twenty they are outside her home. Alan's mom opened door for them and they came inside on her request.

"No aunty we will leave now. I just came to give my Passport to her. We are leaving."

"No, not at all, be comfortable, she will be coming. Will you guys like to have tea or cold drink?" Alan's mom asked them and at the same time Alan joined them.

"No aunty it's OK, we are leaving."

"Momma, bring sewainyan for them."

After initial formalities Alan's mom brought sewainyan for them and everyone enjoyed the evening snacks.

"Riya and I are going home tonight, she came at the same time I am coming to you home so I took her with me and when we coming here I met Vicky on the way so I ask him also to join us. I didn't expect to stay this long. Well now I have to leave. Alan, give my Passport to Jay on Monday. See you after Holi."

Rayman tries to justify presence of Vicky and Riya at Alan's home. Alan came down stair to see off Rayman and others, they talked down stair for fifteen more minutes, Alan is talking about her home and her parent.

"It is DDA colony; we are living here even before my birth. We got two and half BHK flat, and you are seeing that are at back of our flat we extended our balcony to provide more space to our balcony garden."

"It's nice." Vicky confirmed. "And I know about extension, that is entirely illegal construction."

"Yeah, you can say so. It's kind of but we are not using that area for our use. We just do gardening there."

"OK, good night for now, see you after Holi." Rayman finally bid good-bye.

"Nothing is going to happen for you my dear friend; you keep on talking this non-sense of illegal construction to her and next time she would not even allow you to enter her that illegally constructed home." Riya commented on Vicky's comment when they are going back to their houses.

"I have not said anything wrong."

"But sometime right thing become wrong if time is not right."

Riya and Rayman boarded their train after one hour to their home. Vicky dropped his plan for going home and decided to stay in Delhi with his brother and friend.

Rayman and everyone else back from Holi celebration and even after ten day his return from home he got no confirmation for departure date from Jay.

It's Friday and everyone is in hurry to go home, Rayman and Alan having discussion in their bus back home.

"What you doing on the weekend, any special plan?" Rayman asked Alan.

"Nothing, I have no special plan for weekend. Why?"

"Nothing special, we might go for movie. I, Riya and Vicky, so if you want and have time then you can also join us."

"Will let you know by tomorrow."

In the evening Rayman and Vicky were having discussion about movie planning, which might take place next day.

"Bro, I have asked her for movie, she will confirm tomorrow, now pray that she say yes. We need to book the tickets and ask Riya to join for movie and your first outing with her is done."

"Oh really, that is great. I will book tickets after her confirmation and you pick-up Riya in mean time and then we can ask her to come to cinema hall. What say?"

"I think plan is all good and should definitely work as well."

Next day Alan called Rayman to confirm that she can join them on Sunday because she needs to go office on Saturday as well. Vicky planned his Saturday with his team mate and off-course that girl in his team. On Sunday morning Vicky booked tickets for movies for the show of three PM, Rayman asked Riya to join movie with Alan and Vicky.

"Hi Riya, Everything is planned now, you need to come for the movie." Rayman asked Riya on cell phone.

"I can't come for the Movie; I have lots of work to get finished this weekend, why did not you tell me earlier about this movie plan so that I could have planned accordingly in advance. If you have done the planning then go alone I am not coming at any cost."

"Oh ho, I thought I will tell you once plan got confirmed, I am not aware about your weekend plan."

"That is the main reason, you are not aware about anything happening in this world except your that team mate Alan, I know all about your gossiping with her all day in office, Anna told me everything, I know what you are doing in the name of Vicky."

"Ok, leave that all today at least, Vicky's plan will go in drain."

"Go to hell, I said once I am not coming, bye now."

"Listen, please come for movie. It's you who always encourages me to do good for others, I am following what you said, Now please don't spoil it, Please come, I know you already getting ready for coming here, you are creating drama nothing else."

"No, now I will not come at any cost, what you just said drama, now I am not coming at any cost."

"Hey look Vicky calling me, I think they already reached there, I am really sorry for whatever I said or did to offend you please come now."

"OK, wait for me at Maharani Bagh stop I will come there, from there we will go together, but this is your last chance, no more mistakes."

"Sure and thanks."

"One more thing, I will not talk to Alan, she has not picked my hand bag on Shimla trip, do you remember?"

"Yeah, I remembered, please come now and do whatever you want to do, just come quick, I will tell Vicky to wait for us."

Everybody went and watched movie Atithi and as Riya said earlier she really did not talked to Alan even a single word. Alan asked Rayman about it and he said that she is upset with him for some personal reason. On way back home Alan agreed to go home by her own while Vicky went home directly from cinema hall, Rayman dropped Riya home and back to Vicky home.

"So how was the outing, have you enjoyed it or not?" Rayman asked Vicky as he reached his home.

"Yeah, it was great, but what happened to Riya, why she seems so upset?"

"Nothing, you will never understand girls."

"OK, leave it then, so what is next?"

"Next is what, we need to plan next step. May be some party, but for party we need some occasion."

First weekend of March 2010, Rayman with whole team having breakfast at breakfast table, Anna also joined them at their table and is sitting near Rayman.

"Where were you, not seen you in so many days." Rayman asked to Anna.

"I was here only doing my work only, I think it's you who were not in your own from few days, I noticed where you concentrating these days, you can see any other girl when you have time from Alan."

"What! Oh no, you are taking it totally wrong, I have nothing to do with her, she is just a team mate nothing else."

"Oh my god, I am kidding, you got so serious." Anna responded but her eyes and body language is suggesting that she is on her words, and not going to believe on Rayman's words at any cost.

"So how is your work going?" Rayman asked to Anna.

"As usual, you know we always work till we drop with load."

"Hey Rayman what happened to your VISA?" Samarth asked in between. And at the same time Anna say bye to Rayman and went to her seat.

"No idea Sir, Jay not updated in last few days about VISA, may be next week I will be able to get any idea."

"OK, it's your first foreign trip that might be reason."

In evening Rayman is talking to Riya on cell phone about his trip and also about Vicky and Alan.

"Yaar, its taking too long now, when will I go? You know foreigner, and maybe I can get some girl there for me."

"Why you want foreigner girl? Are not you able to find any good girl here in India."

"Oh ho, you know foreigner girls are better."

"It's just your mind set."

"Ok tell me, what should we do for Vicky and Alan next?"

"I have nothing to do with Alan. Keep me away from this all."

"Oh ho, you are my partner in my all these plans."

"Don't try your emotional drama once again. Ok tell me what are you expecting from me?"

"Just suggest what should we do next?"

"What is in your mind?"

"Some party."

"Hmm sounds good, go ahead with party plans. It seems good to me as well."

"What should be occasion for party?"

"My birthday is coming this month end we can plan party then. And in party I will tell Alan about Vicky feeling."

"Occasion is prefect but why you want to tell her so early? You will let me fired."

"Oh ho, nothing will happen. I have read this in Alan's eyes."

"Oh my god, now you can read eyes. What else you have read?"

"I have read so many guys' eyes. I will tell you in free time."

"I am free, tell me now."

"OK, do you know about Toni and Tanu?"

"What about Toni and Tanu?"

"Nothing you are a fool."

"Now what with me now, first Toni and Tanu and now me, I think you are fool, go to sleep now, good night."

Next week going as usual until on Wednesday when Jay confirmed Rayman that he need to travel Middle East on Saturday.

"Pack your bag and get ready to go this Saturday."

"What! It is so sudden."

"What is sudden in it? You know about it even before Holi, it's not early but late I guess."

"OK, I will try."

"Flight tickets already booked so you need to hurry."

"Sure sir, I got it. I will leave on Saturday."

"That is good; you will get all important document and required information by Friday."

Rayman is at the park in front of Riya's paying guest and both were sitting on one bench and discussing about Rayman's possible trip.

"I am so much excited now."

"You should be but take precautions there, that is not India and keep in touch with guys in your team in India, and give me few numbers from your team as well."

"You have Samarth and Alan's numbers. You can get in touch with them in case you will not be able to get in touch with me."

"Sure, but you come back soon, you know that I don't know many people here."

"I will, but you know Vicky, Vishu and Alan, I will ask them to visit you on regular intervals."

"Hmm, I will manage you just take care of you."

"One more thing I will not be here on your birthday, so I guess birthday plan can be preponed to get all the things done in place for Vicky before I leave."

"Oh ho, we can do it when you come back."

"No, I think better if we do this week."

"As you wish, Call everyone on Friday may be at your home."

"Sure"

Rayman informed Alan, Vicky Vishu for Riya's birthday as per plan discussed with Riya.

"Hey Vishu, ask Diya as well to come for Riya birthday." Rayman invited Diya as well.

"Ok bro, I can't promise about her but I will try for sure."

"It is weekend buddy; she can stay at Tanu's place if she gets late in return."

"OK, I will try."

Everyone is at Rayman home for Riya's birthday celebration a day before Rayman's departure. Rayman is cooking something at home for everybody, rest of the food and cake ordered from outside. Vicky collected cake and around eight in the evening Alan also showed up at Rayman home. Diya and Vishu are remaining to come at the venue. Alan is talking to Riya in outer room.

"How you find Vicky?" Riya asked Alan.

"What you mean?"

"I mean what you think about him? I am not so sure but I think he likes you."

"I don't knows, I haven't thought this way."

Vishu came around eight thirty and introduced Diya and Alan to each other. Cake formality started in few minutes then they had food and talked till late night. Around ten everyone is about to leave and since it's late so someone need to drop Alan at her home.

"Vishu, can you drop her home by your bike?" Rayman asked Vishu to drop Alan.

"Why don't you drop her, take my bike and drop her, I am here at your home till then."

"I have never driven your bike before, better if you drop her."

On the other hand Vicky's expression saying all about his internal thought. 'Why is no one asking me to drop her?'

"Vicky you go and drop her home." It's Riya who once again helps Vicky.

"Yes I can drop her."

"No way, I don't think it will be safe in night for Vicky to drop her with Vishu's bike, Vishu you go and drop her."

"No man, I am so much tired, I can't go."

Now even Alan is feeling restless.

"Vicky what you waiting for, go and drop her." Riya insisted Vicky to drop Alan home.

"Have you ever driven Vishu's bike earlier?" Rayman asked Vicky.

"No"

"Then how can he drop and in night, Vishu don't take risk bro, drop Alan home."

"I can go by Rickshaw." Alan is getting uneasy with this conversation.

"Vicky I said naah, you go drop her. All bikes are same, Rayman don't you say any other word now." Riya once again insisted.

"Sure, give me the keys of your bike. I will drop her home." Vicky asked Vishu.

Sarfarosi ki tamanna ab hamare dil main hai, dekhna hai jor kitna bajuye katil main hai.

Vicky left with these lines and Vishu and Diya started laughing as he left with Alan, Riya and Rayman also joined them.

"That was too much from you two, why weren't you letting him drop Alan?"

"We are not stopping, just pulling his leg, nothing else" Both replied in one voice, and once again everyone started laughing.

"Vishu, you forget about your bike, he will not come now, he is gone buddy." Rayman says these words and all started laughing.

Vicky came back after around one hour, and started telling about his whole trip.

"Bro, your bike is waste, total waste; it stopped for at least ten times in 2 kilometer stretch." Vicky complains about Vishu's bike.

"I stopped you earlier, why did you go to drop her. Why didn't you let Vishu drop her?" Rayman questioned Vicky.

"Guys lets go to home now, I have to leave tomorrow." Rayman asked them. Then they left for their home, Rayman left Riya her home and checked all document and bags before going to sleep.

Next day morning Vicky and Riya are going with Rayman to drop him Airport.

"I am very nervous now, I can't go, I will miss you all there, and how am I will live without my mom, Vishu and you all?" Rayman says to Riya nearly tears filled eyes.

"What! You were all excited till yesterday and now your emotional drama once again, you always create this scene, I remember when you went to college then you came to Delhi both the time you have created the same drama. Now don't create same scene again." Riya seems angry from outer but internally she is also feeling the same.

"I will remain in touch will you all, and will write regularly."

"Buy mobile connection as soon you reach there and call me on regular intervals." Riya's emotions are now coming out.

"Vicky, Riya doesn't have many friends here; try to keep in touch with her. I will also ask Alan to come and visit Riya frequently." Rayman requested Vicky and at the same time called Alan.

"Hey Alan, I am going yaar. Please try to visit Riya few times, Vicky can give you company to Riya's home." After talking for few more minutes Rayman disconnected and off course he get confirmation from Alan to visit Riya with Vicky.

After around an hour drama Rayman is at airport after creating plot for next few meeting of Alan and Vicky, Rayman called his every friend and family before boarding flight.

Rayman in inside the flight and nervousness in gone now and there is nothing inside his mind now, plain blank without any thought, flight departed with Rayman to gift him a new chapter of his life.

Onsite trip

Rayman reached Riyadh around 5:00 in the evening but migration check took him till late night and after clearing from migration he headed toward his hotel. Rayman got company from few other guys from his Delhi office who already working at this site.

Rayman called his home very first after reaching there and then writes mail to his friends on day morning.

'Hi Friend,

Hope you all are fine. I have reached here safe in the afternoon. How's everything with you guys?

-Rayman'

And very first reply came from Vicky.

'I am good buddy, when you left for flight Riya created a scene on the way back home, She kept on weeping whole way. We all are good. You take good care of you. I am going to meet Riya with Alan in the evening.'

Rayman felt very happy after reading this and knowing the progress in the story of Alan and Vicky.

'Yes, sure keep visiting her and enjoy your evening with Alan. tc'

Later in the evening after mails from all of his other friends, one mail came from Anna.

'Wow, what should I say about Mr. Rayman, you don't even have time to come outside to say Hi to us, writing hello on mail.'

'Hey I have been came out for sure, if I were there'

Anna: 'What are you saying, where you gone, have you been transferred to some other office?'

Rayman: 'No yaar, onsite trip to Riyadh.'

Anna: 'What! Wow, it's really great news, enjoy there to the fullest.'

Rayman: 'What are you saying, people are afraid to come here and you ate saying wow.'

Anna: 'Why? Is not that country good? And it's not even Ramadan; you will get lots of food to taste these days.'

Rayman: 'I also hope the same, by the way, how is your work and how are you?'

Anna: 'Work you knows very well, going as usual, and I am all good.'

Whole day passed in understanding work and conversation with friends through mails, Rayman once called Riya on cell and told her not to worry about him.

"I am very fine here and got very decent company in Riyadh. People are very nice here. Hey Alan and Vicky might come in evening to meet you and if you need anything call Vicky or Vishu; they will be there any time. Take care"

"Sure, you take care of you. I am good, don't worry about me."

Next day when Rayman reached office mails from Riya, Alan and Vicky waiting for him.

'Hi

I hope you are doing well, I am fine, don't worry about me.

Yesterday Vicky and Alan came to meet me in the evening and Alan told me that you are in constant touch with these guys, and all about your experience there, she told me that you have not get your system and it is going to take at least this weekend.

Enjoy there, explore new place.

Riya'

'Hi

I hope you will get your system today; I and Abhi will be coordinating you from our team as per Jay's instruction.

So don't worry about any work from here, we are not going to do anything.

And we went to Riya yesterday, Vicky and I met on the way and then walked to her home.

Vicky is also telling me about you and Riya's drama at airport, he told me that you both nearly in tears, why are you worrying? Everything will be fine yaar.

Take care
Alan'

'So Bro,

Yesterday I met Alan and took her to Riya.

And I got Alan's number from Riya as I need to co-ordinate with her and added her on office messenger as well.

Bro she was looking more beautiful and sexier yesterday.

Yaar do something for me, I will die for her.

By the way how are you and how are girls there?

Don't you dare to stare any girl there, as you do here?

Take care and keep us posted.

Vicky'

Rayman replied Riya's mail and kept Alan and Vicky in same mail also. He further wrote one mail to his entire office friend and one separate mail to Anna only.

(To Riya, Alan and Vicky)

'Hi,

Good to hear that Alan and Vicky came to meet you.

I am also good just missing you all and getting nervous because of this, no worry about work.

You guys keep in touch with each other.

Now let me do some work.

And Vicky I will tell you further steps for your project.

Rayman'

(To all friends)

'Hey Guys

Hope you all are good.

I am all good here, it's very restricted here, but food is good as expected.

No work started as yet, hope I will get system today and may be meeting in second half to understand the work which I am supposed to do here.

Hey Vishu How is Diya? If possible visit Riya sometime.

How is everybody else?

Take care'
(To Anna)

'Hi

How are you, It is just you guys else I am feeling so lonely here? How is your work?

Take care'

Rayman got busy in work and so others but one reply came from Anna.

'Hey

Wow, you are missing me, what a lie, I am not even your that good friend.

Why are you missing us all, enjoy there and explore new place and their culture and specially their food, learn few words of Arabic.

I will remain in touch for sure if I got time from work.

Take care.'

Rayman felt very special upon receiving Anna response and specially the way she wrote everything without caring for anything. He also wrote in response.

'Hey

Really I miss you, so what if you are not very close but you are a friend.

And I learned one sentence in Arabic.

'Arabi Maafi Maloom.' And which means 'I don't know Arabic.'

You too take care.'

Anna also wrote in response.

'It seems you don't have much work there, you have plenty of time to write mails.'

Whole week passed in same conversations, with time conversation got sorter to two or three mails from twenty odd mails. It is Friday morning, Rayman is writing mail to Riya and Vicky.

'Hi

I got system a few minutes ago.

Vicky, it is Alan's birthday on Sunday, you might have seen on Facebook if not then add her there first.

Ask her to come for Party or better arrange party for her take Riya with you to be on safer side.

Or wait for few minutes, I will do invitation part, and from there you guys can carry on.

Take care.'

Rayman wrote a mail to Alan, Abhi, Vicky and Riya with a comment on Alan's birthday.

'Hey Guys

What's up? How's everything going there? I am all set and well here, still missing you all very badly.

@Alan: wishing you very happy birthday in advance. I will call you Sunday as well but can't say for sure.

Abhi, Vicky, and Riya you guys don't leave her without taking grand party from her, and give me party separately when I come back.

Take care'

And as discussed in earlier mail between Rayman and Riya and Vicky, Vicky handled situation from there.

When Rayman reached office on Monday there is a mail from Vicky in his inbox.

'Hey Bro,

Thanks

It went all dramatic. First I mailed her for party and after so many mail exchanges she agreed to come for party on Saturday, she said that she already planned his Sunday. She was saying that she has plans with parent but I doubt seriously about that, she is having someone in her life. Who go with parent these days?

But still I have given party to her and Riya and your other team mate Abhi, he did not showed up, thank god otherwise bill might have gone even higher.

Oh bro I have to pay for her party, she said that she want to pay but I said I will with lots of load on my heart.

Bro how can I check if she has got someone in her life or not?

Riya was also with us whole the time, she managed everything well to keep it safe for me, She hinted Alan about my feelings.

Come soon and we will plan something and party after confirmation.'

Rayman understood Vicky's feeling in one go and written in response to give him a hope.

'Hey

Don't worry yaar, I have never seen her talking to any one, if she have a boyfriend she was surely talk to him but I haven't seen her in office and not even in the bus, so don't worry.

We will surely have a blast on my return.

Bye for now, take care.'

Whole month gone with few more events and Vicky and Alan met few more times especially on all weekends, as Vicky always has this excuse to meet Riya and Vicky also made some progress on his own, like talking to her on mobile and mail conversations. Vicky also told Rayman about SM training session and that he went back in her bus with Alan and on route back home also met Riya and that evening they went out in the evening for snacks party.

On the other hand at Riyadh office Rayman alone working and trying to adjust with new people and environment.

After one month his VISA need to renewed and for that he need to return back, so people there given him two choices to go some other country Bahrain for two day and return back to Riyadh or he can go to India, his home for ten days and come back to finish his work. He chooses to go back to his home and after exactly one month Rayman is back home and in midnight he landed in India and went directly to meet Vicky and Riya at that very odd hour of night and then went home to sleep. Next morning he is in the bus with Alan to office, Alan was also happy to see him.

"Hey thanks very much yaar for helping me from here and also being with Riya in my absence, she doesn't have friends here except me, and hence I worry a little about her."

"This way I got to know Vicky a little, and I think he is good guy."

Rayman is seeing a little positive response for Vicky from her, and in between conversation route to office seem very sorter. In office Jay and Samarth already have knowledge of Rayman's return to India, so they were not much surprised but Abhi and Jiten also very surprised to see him and angry with Jay and Samarth for not informing them. When Rayman looked for his seat Abhi told him that few people moved from outside into their cubicle and all team mates now sitting in one row of their two row cubical and his seat is with people who came from outside, upon enquiring about new people Rayman get to know that a new guy joined in Anna team and Anna are moved inside. Rayman get to know that he will be sitting next to Anna from now, and somehow he is very happy about it due to past communication with Anna when he was in Riyadh.

"So how are you and how was your trip?" Anna asked after entering the cubicle, she is a bit late today. She entered cubicle nearly running as she used to do whenever she is late, I never understood what these two minutes going to change which she covers with her running of some forty to fifty meters while she is already late by an hour.

"I am good and trip was really awesome after few initial hiccups everything went smooth on trip, I might be going back in few days for another round. How are you and what happened, why they shifted you here with our team?"

"Oh don't ask about this whole drama, this new guy joined my team few days back and they were saying that there is no space outside for this guy where I sit earlier, so we shifted here after hundreds of discussion between the bosses. So you tell me about the trip, how was people there and all, have you seen desert there or some other thing, how was food there, I heard they cook awesome non-veg?"

"No yaar, not able to see anything, it is really restricted there, worst thing was that I was not able to see any beautiful girls there, and they don't have any means of entertainment, no cinema, most of the sites are blocked and no drink and finally you can't see any girls, you won't believe bachelors can't even eat with families in the restaurants. But you are right food was awesome, I ate hell lot of non-veg for whole month. How are you finding new company from us?"

"Hmm, you see company is not entirely new, I know every one of you and we met at least twice day. There is no different from outside."

Rayman next writes mail to his friends in his old group while having conversation with Anna whole day long. Especially in first half of the day they are talking like long lost sisters.

'Hey guys,

I am back in India and very eager to see you all, take some time and come to my place to have sweet and chocolates and off course we will be meeting on the weekend, please decide the venue either GIP Noida or 3Cs food court.'

'Hey Bro

How are you and how you feeling coming back to India.
Surely we will be meeting on weekend and we can even plan before that also.

Toni'

First reply came from Toni, followed by Vishu's reply.

'Hey Man,

So they finally released you.
Welcome back, what did you brought for us?
Yes sure weekend will be better option to meet and I guess 3Cs will be better, I have no issue for GIP also but 3Cs will be better to reach for all of us.'

Everyone else also confirmed 3Cs as the venue. Later in the evening while returning home Rayman asked Alan to come home and meet Vicky and Riya also.

Riya, Alan, Vicky and Rayman met at Rayman's home around eight in the evening and gossiping till late in night and then Vicky and Rayman dropped Riya and Alan back to their homes.

Whole week is happening for Rayman as he is seeing India from very different and very own point of view after spending whole month away, and second and especial reason for this is his new neighbor in office and conversation with this new neighbor whole day and bitching, gossiping like girls with each other, so with friendship of Alan and Vicky a new friendship is also in making in background not with the pace of Alan and Vicky but yes there is a progress which is clearly visible to Alan, Abhi and Jay if not to everyone and one major event happened in this series in a little group party. Samarth, Alan, Abhi, Rayman and Anna standing in a circle and having cold drink and samosas and Rayman said something to Anna and addressed her as Alan and Anna made comment on that.

"What is happening? You are seeing Alan in me or you seeing Alan everywhere else also?"

Rayman who is still looking or lost in Anna's beautiful eyes behind those beautiful spectacles and it took him few moments to even realize about his mistake and that he is caught red handed and by the person herself he is staring at, but he handled the situation very well.

"Well I was so much submerged and totally lost in your eyes that I forget everything else in surrounding, can't even remember names of persons."

"Oh ho, Romeo, this is something new, how can you lose in my eyes, how are you even able to see them properly behind these spectacles?"

"Leave this non sense guys. What we noticed is that Rayman has lost in Anna's eyes." Samarth interrupted in between but this is his usual habit of linking team mates with each other, so no one took it seriously even Rayman and Anna. But Rayman understands sensitivity of the conversation and stopped the conversation saying that "There is nothing in between us."

Friday evening 3Cs food court, Rayman and Riya were first to reach there and Vicky, Vishu, Toni, Tanu are expected to come in few minutes.

"Papa was saying about a guy his one friend suggested the guy for me, I think it's time now to get married for me. I will say yes this time. Enough of Job and running around in the city, this all nonsense should end now. What is your opinion?" Riya is talking to Rayman very quietly despite the lot of noise in food court these two are sitting without any activity.

"What can I say, it is your life, see what you want in a guy and say yes if he fulfils all criteria. I am concerned about being alone after your marriage. Who will give me company for all trips and parties and who will go home with me?"

"You can't be so mean, Say something."

"Its decision of your life and you need to take on your own."

"Hey buddy, after so long time, how are you and how was trip? I heard you are going back, actually Vicky told us about it. So when are you going back." Vishu asked him after entering the food court and Diya is following him.

"Oh Hi, Hi Diya, I am all good, you heard right bro. I am not sure about the date but probably on coming weekend I have to fly back to Riyadh." Rayman greeted Vishu and Diya, Tanu also joins them shortly followed by Vicky.

"Is not Toni joining us?" Rayman asked to Vishu and Vicky.

"No yaar, He has gone to his cousin's birthday party, and this is not the first time, he has got some twenty thousand cousins in Delhi and every weekend since he born he has to attend birthday, engagement or marriage of one of his cousin." Vicky replied with anger due to absence of Toni.

"May be his girlfriend name is cousin, and who knows he goes to meet her every weekend." Rayman commented.

"Yes, you have a point." Vishu agreed with Rayman.

"What, girlfriend and his, no way!" Tanu commented after Vishu's comment.

"Let's order honey chili potatoes first then I will have chhole bhatoore next and you guys decide your own order." Vishu as usual ordered chili potatoes and then party continues till ten in the night with lots of gossip and most of the time Rayman sharing his experience of Riyadh. When everyone is leaving for their home, Vishu whispered something in Rayman's ear.

"I have something to discuss with you. Diya and I are thinking of being together. We are planning to talk to our parents and then we will see."

"It's good, I am happy for you guys tell me if you need any help."

Vishu is not in need of any help, but he just wanted to share his feeling or better his planning of future events he has in his mind. Next week went very quickly for everyone, Vicky spent his all week in trying to get a single chance of talking, meeting with Alan, Riya is getting calls from home on regular intervals sometime even twenty calls in a day, everyone from her home putting pressure on her to say yes to marriage, Vishu is busy in arrangement for the meeting of both his and Diya's parent. Tanu and Toni are busy in fighting to kill each other. Tanu was all fired-up on Toni due to some comment Toni made on her in some email conversation, Diya is busy convincing her parent to at least meet Vishu, it is really extremely tough in India for a girl to convince her parent that the guy she is seeing is good and not some gangster or cheap, she is also getting various setbacks from home in form of warning like "come back home we don't want you to work in Delhi." Rayman is busy in office with Abhi and Samarth so that he can get the work completed before he flies again to Riyadh, and again getting goose bump on the name of leaving his entire friends for a month. In these all events no one noticed when Friday came, everyone except Rayman is more concerned about personal life than professional after a very long time. Rayman has to fly on Saturday morning and he came to know about Riya's Friday plans in a call from Riya.

"Hi Rayman, how are you? Papa is coming tomorrow and that guy will also be coming tomorrow evening, I am very nervous."

"What, why are you feeling nervous, and I am sorry yaar, I have to fly in the morning, I won't be able to meet him. You can send me his picture if you say yes to him, and don't worry everything will be all right, say yes if you feel."

"OK, I am coming with you to drop you at airport."

"Sure, Mom is coming Delhi tomorrow, so you and Mom can come with me till airport and she will also get company."

This time Rayman feeling even more nervous because of his new friend in office or because his best friend is getting married very soon and he is not even with her during first meeting with that guy. Rayman talked to Anna whole day and later in the evening to Samarth, Abhi and Alan. Next day as discussed with Riya, Rayman left for Riyadh with lots of worries, Riya with Rayman's mom dropped him at airport. Rayman reached Riyadh by afternoon but it took him till evening to reach his hotel room. After reaching hotel he called Riya to know what happened with that guy who is coming to see her.

"Everybody is fine with the boy and I don't think he is bad for me, so I said yes to Papa." Riya confirmed to Rayman.

"Great, congratulation, have you told Vicky or Alan about it?"

"No, you tell them. I may go back to home for my marriage next month."

"What are you saying? Now who will go for shopping with me, and what about parties with Vicky, Alan and Vishu? You can't leave Vicky in the middle of his love story?"

"Well, it's time for me to set my own story straight, and I will try to take Vicky's story to some conclusion but not any promise."

"OK, as you wish. Bye for now, will talk to you tomorrow."

After putting her phone down Rayman wrote mail to his all friends back in Delhi. And wrote a separate mail to Anna and informed her about Riya's marriage. This one month Rayman enjoyed more in Riyadh as he already know little bit about the place and food ventures which serve good food. While back in Delhi everyone in trying to adjust in new events happing in their lives, Vishu arranged meeting of his parents with Diya parent but as per latest update something went wrong and Vishu and Diya. They are still trying to get things proper. On the other hand Vicky managed to meet Alan on few occasion while visiting Riya or sometime in the evening on their Bus stop as they both de-board their office buses from opposite side of road of a same bus stop. One evening in the beginning of May 2010 a mail came from Vicky.

'Hi Bro,

What is next step now? I can't take it anymore. I want to tell her. Should I go for it?

Vicky'

Rayman replied very next moment.

'Hey Bro,

Have some patience and wait for few more days, how can I tell you from here about the condition of her mind?'

After two days a mail came from Vicky.

'Hey Bro

We went to meet Riya yesterday and on the way I talked to Alan a lot but she is quieter than usual days.
Today I called her and told her about my feeling, she said that I have to tell her in person and then she will decide about it.'

Rayman felt very happy for Vicky at first that at least he did not got beaten. And Rayman wrote a mail to congratulate him and have patience and suggested to meet Alan on weekend and say everything in her front if she wanted to hear. On Monday Vicky confirmed that he told everything to Alan and she said that she need some time to think.

Tanu is shifted in Vishu's team and now she is trying to understand new boss and work and trying to fitting in, Toni whose friends were leaving him one by one first Rayman left for a new group and then Tanu in new team so he is trying to get new friends in his surrounding and his cousins are getting married so he is about to be alone there as well. In the time when nothing good happening around a good news came from Vicky in the end of May that Alan said yes to him after keeping him wait for around two weeks, In the meantime Vicky, Alan and Riya celebrated Vicky's birthday at Lajpat Nagar just two days before the day Rayman is returning back to India but Vicky promised Rayman to give him Party after his return to India.

Rayman worried with all these dramas returned from Riyadh after one month without completion of work and hence might be one more trip of Riyadh. After reaching India Rayman directly went to office and met Jay and Samarth and handed over all the details of project, status and work happened at Riyadh and went to his desk and now time for everyone to gather around him, Oh wait Anna is not on her seat, she is busy in discussion outside with her boss.

"So how was your trip this time?" Alan and Abhi asked Rayman and before Rayman could answer. Samarth and Jiten joined him for more questions.

"So bro, where is the party?" Jiten asked.

"Well, trip went really cool this time and Party, wherever you guys want." Rayman replied.

"OK, so you came with lots of money I guess." Abhi commented.

"Hey Rayman, good to see you, how are you?" Anna also came inside and asked Rayman.

"Good, I am really good, how about you?"

"What about me, I am here as usual and good also. It's you who have stories to tell."

"No stories at all, just the same as last time trip. You tell me how is your work and all?"

"Well then here lot of work must be waiting for you if you have nothing to do there. There is nothing special for me these days, just usual work." Anna went to her seat and start doing her work in between her last sentence. Rayman also switched-on his system after nearly one month and started checking document mails first.

In the evening Rayman went to meet Riya and she seems little nervous. Then he went to meet Vicky who seems very happy in very first glance itself. Vicky goes on telling whole story till late night until both went for sleep. On weekend morning Rayman called Alan, Vishu, Riya, Tanu and Toni one by one.

"Hey Alan Hi, meet me at Vicky's home at eleven fifteen."

"Hey Vishu, meet me at Vicky place at eleven thirty."

Same call like Vishu to Toni, Tanu and Riya, everyone reached at venue on time. When Rayman with Toni, Tanu, Vishu and Riya reached at Vicky home, Alan is already there with Vicky and then Vicky introduced everyone to Alan as her love interest.

"Bro, It's party time now, so where you want to take us all for the party." Vishu said first.

"Off course, I am planning for my birthday party. I was waiting for Rayman to return. Now wherever you guys say we can go."

"We can go to CP or Lajpat Nagar. It is convenient for all of us." Toni suggested first and Tanu supported him and then Vishu and Rayman also.

After little discussion everyone headed for Lajpat nagar. Everyone have great time and after party Rayman dropped Riya, Toni dropped Tanu and went home, Vicky and Alan left together, Rayman came back to Vishu's home after dropping Riya.

"So how is work?" Rayman asked Vishu.

"Same"

"What is happening with Diya, I mean what parents decided?"

"Don't knows yet, just waiting, well no point of discussing that."

"Yes sure, so tell me about work and girls in office."

"Nothing yaar, I am trying to change the job."

"Any offer."

"Yes, I got one from a company in Gurgaon."

"Oh that is great news, congratulation."

"Thanks, we will have party after my joining, but it is going to take around two months."

Both discussed many things in office, Rayman's trips and then conversation turned toward girls of both guys office, later both started abusing their bosses and then both went sentimental for their teams as Rayman already left his old team and Vishu is about to leave.

Jay asked Rayman to go to Riyadh to finish remaining work after three weeks.

"Rayman, you have to fly next Monday to complete remaining work and let's project rolling."

"Sir, I can't go this time, you know Riya, Her marriage in one or two months I can't go Riyadh this time, send someone else and I will provide support from here."

"Yaar, you do not understand pressure from Management, let me see if I can do anything."

"Thanks Sir."

After discussing with everyone in team Abhi confirmed that he will be going in place of Rayman on Jay request, Rayman working closely with Abhi. Jay shifted Abhi's seat near Anna and Rayman's seat with his team, but Rayman still sitting with Abhi to work together and get work done quickly so that Abhi would not take much time in Riyadh.

"What happened these days, you are not going this time and I am also seeing that you are a little upset these days. What happened, you can share with me?" Anna asked one evening to Rayman.

"Nothing, everything is all right."

"OK, you are looking bit tense, hence I asked you. Tell me if there is anything bothering you."

"Nothing serious yaar, something is irritating me for last few days."

"What is it?"

"I don't knows how should I tell you or rather what should I tell you?"

"In that case, start from beginning to end."

Rayman started after taking a deep breathe. "Riya is getting married in few months."

"Hmmm"

"I don't know why? I should be happy about it but I am not feeling happy all about?"

"Why?"

"We studied together and then both came to Delhi; she is my best friend for nearly two decades."

"OK"

"What will happen to our friendship when she got married, can we meet after her marriage, and can we go for shopping together?"

"Why you think so?"

"You are asking this even being a girl, you know girl's life after marriage, and girls can't do few things even if they want to do."

"May be you are right, but you can't do anything for it, Why don't you both get married as far I know you both are very good friends."

"What, we are not just friends, we are relatives first, and it's not like the way you are thinking about it."

"Oh, then what do you want?"

"I really don't know?"

"You should let it go, everything will be all right."

"May be, but why I am dragging you into all this nonsense, you tell me about yourself. How are you?"

"I am good as always. You know I don't take anything much serious so it can't create any problem later. Never attach yourself to anything. But I have this one issue these days, I want to change my job, I am bored here now."

"Why job change, here work, people and salary everything is good, work culture may be an issue and sometimes work load."

"Here bosses don't even have any etiquette to talk to the employees and you are saying that everything is good, you need to take a look outside also to compare things."

"May be you are right. Have you tried anywhere? Or do you have any opportunity?"

"Yes, I tried few but no luck till now."

Rayman and Anna talked till late evening and none of them noticed when office hours got over until when Alan asked Rayman to come for bus. Rayman and Anna talk quite a lot these days since Anna came in his cubicle. She does not have any other friend except Rayman, for some reason she does not like Alan and not prefer to talk with others also except Rayman. Riya and Rayman stopped meeting regularly, meetings became fewer automatically and they got to meet once in a week or even once in fortnight. Riya also told Rayman that Anna told her about his conversation with Anna and she said that he doesn't need to worry about anything. Nothing will change between them and they will always remain friends. But no one knows about it except time. Few months passed and time came for annual party, everyone seems very excited about it once more, Rayman asked Riya to come to his office party for one last time and to meet her friends also.

Lucknow trip

$\mathcal{R}$ayman, Vishu, Vicky and Toni did not met in months. This is first time in years that they didn't meet for months. Vicky is busy in setting his love story straight, trying to arrange a meeting at his home between Alan and his family. Alan also broke news to her mom that she is in love with this guy who came home with Rayman to give Rayman's Passport before Holi, but her mom couldn't recall him and ask her to bring Vicky home someday. Alan's dad is not happy about it as he is planning to search boy for her dear daughter by himself and his daughter destroyed his dream, but he also agreed to meet Vicky when her mom convinced him.

"Why don't you understand, we want the same for her. If she is happy with it then we should also be happy." Alan's mom is trying her best.

"But I don't know that guy and his family background."

"I asked her to bring him home someday, and then you can ask whatever you want to know about him."

"What, you called him without even telling me? So, when is he expected to come over here?"

"This weekend"

"OK, let's see him."

On the other side Vicky is at his sister's place, she lives very near to his place, creating the environment to break news there as well, so later his sister can handle the case of tackling mom and brother. Vicky's brother has a little idea about Alan as he lives with Vicky and overheard few conversations between them. Vicky also have little idea that his brother already broken news for his other family member.

"Di, I want you to meet this girl, she is my friend. You know she works with me." Vicky said to her sister.

"Why? What is special about this girl?"

"Di, why don't you understand?"

"What should I understand, why don't you tell me?"

"I actually like that girl"

"Just like or serious about her"

"Serious"

"OK, bring her here someday then I will tell you about my opinion, but I am happy with yours happiness."

"OK, I will ask her to come here this weekend with me, and I also have to go at her place this weekend."

"Oh ho, Ok bring her here first." Vicky sister trying to tease him but this doesn't left any effect on him.

Vishu resigned from his company after getting job in Gurgaon, he will be joining there next month. Vishu and Diya arranged a meeting between their parents but something went wrong between both parent and some ego clash issue ruined their story and interrupted a story to become a great love story. Vishu took his parent side and so does Diya, no one agreed to disagree with their parent and hence decided to separate and take different path. Vishu kept this to himself only.

Vicky informed Riya and Rayman about whole story of his interview at Alan's place and Alan's interview at his sister's home. They were sitting at Moksha café NFC where Vicky is throwing party to Riya and Rayman for playing supporting role in his story.

"No surprises at Alan place as her mom already setup all the story in our favor, her dad liked me I guess. Anyway he is also in our favor." Vicky is explaining his meeting.

"He likes you I told you so many times. He usually doesn't show emotions but he really liked you." Alan interrupted him.

"May be, and at my place Di handled everything, she already told mom and everyone else and mom liked Alan very much and so does others."

"Oh! Wow, Congratulations to both of you. Now when you guys are planning to tie the knot?" Rayman asked.

"Two years."

"Sure, enjoy."

"Hey, are you guys coming in annual party next month or any other plans?" Rayman asked to Vicky and Alan.

"Why any other plans, we will definitely come for the party and Riya you too come, Alan will arrange for your pass."

"Yes sure, I too want to come for party one last time before my marriage."

"What? You have not us told about it?" Alan asked with surprise.

"Oh I haven't got time, well last month everything got fixed and now I will marry by this year end."

"Oh, congratulation to you, it is party time now, when are you giving party to us? By the way, where does he works?" Alan asked further.

"He works in Delhi. I will definitely give party in some time."

They finished their meal between gossips. Alan and Vicky continued telling various events happened back at their home on each other interview. Vicky broke one other news on the way walking back to home.

"Rayman, do you want to come and shift with me, I am changing my flat and shifting a bit closer to Alan's home." Vicky asked and it brought expression of surprise on everyone's face.

"But why you need me? You already have two guys to share flat with you, your brother and his friend?"

"Oh, didn't I update you guys about their transfers?"

"No!"

"What are you saying bro? I have not given this critical and important information to you all."

"No, I knew about it." Alan replied.

"I know that you knew about it. I am talking about Rayman and Riya."

"No" Riya and Rayman replied in unison.

"OK. Raju is going to Jaipur and Dharmendra to Kolkata. Their work was completed here in Delhi and hence they need to move to new location and I think by October end or November first week they will move there."

"OK, in that case I can come and stay with you, I am also getting bored alone."

"When are you coming then?"

"Let them move and then I will come with you. What you say about mid-November or end of November."

"Great."

Next day in the office Rayman is busy in his work, while Alan is talking to somebody on phone, possibly with Vicky. Abhi is still in Riyadh, Jiten resigned recently and Jay and Samarth talking to Jiten.

"Are you staying till annual party or not?" Jay asked to Jiten.

"It depends on annual party date. You know my last working day, so you can reply it even better."

"Party date is also final in that case you are here even after annual party. Party is next weekend."

"Hey Rayman, how are you? Are you OK now?" Anna asked to Rayman in whisper voice while everyone else is busy in his own business.

"Why, what happened to me? I am all right."

"Oh ho, now you don't act in front of me."

"No, seriously I am ok, by the way what happened to me."

"Weren't you upset because of Riya's marriage?"

"Oh, you are talking about that, well what can I do, so better accept whatever comes in my way, but yes I am really upset about it. It's only you who can read my condition from my face."

"No, it's all written on your face very clearly and anybody can read it, it's just that no one has anything to do with it."

"You may be right." Rayman paused for few moments and Anna went back to her work when he asked her in return.

"Hey Anna, how is your work and all?"

"All is very well. Not much work in last few days so enjoying and giving a little bit training to that new guy joined in my team and preparing for the party, ask Riya to come for the party."

"Yes, I asked her to come, and she is also willing to come, so let's see then." Rayman and Anna both went back to their work.

Rayman sitting with Riya outside Riya's paying guest home a day before the party night and both were arguing over something. Both of them appear very angry over something.

"What can I do about it? It is your marriage so only you have to figure out when you want to go home. I am quite busy in office so I can't go home with you." Rayman said to Riya.

"Yes sure, do whatever you wants to do, you always have time for your office's loafer friends, you must be going in party tomorrow, you have time for that but you can't drop me home." Riya raised her voice a little and soon calmed down a little and continued. "Why don't you understand, how will I take this whole baggage with me, Please come with me?"

"Better ask someone from home to escort you, I really can't come, and we got this new project of some Indian client, so I am too busy this whole month at least."

"As you wish, but you have to come in my marriage."

"I will try but I can't promise."

"It's OK, do whatever is important to you."

"You are coming tomorrow for party?"

"No"

"What now?"

"Nothing, you don't have time for me so do I."

"Oh my god, OK I promise that I will come for your marriage for sure, happy now?"

"Yes, now I am coming for the party. In any case I will be coming for the party." And Riya started giggling after that and both Riya and Rayman went back to their home.

Next morning Rayman, Alan, Abhi are sitting on their seats and doing their work. All the guys are talking about the evening, about the party. Most of the girls are going back home to get ready for the party. Alan asked Rayman.

"I am going back home and on the way to party I can pick Riya."

"What about Vicky?"

"He will meet me at my home, he moved last week to near my home, and from there I am going with him in his new car"

"OK, then I will also come with you if you guys don't mind."

"Sure."

Rayman, Alan and Riya reached at main entrance of party venue in the evening around eight, party is already in full swing. Alan is wearing maroon top with matching skirt. Alan has to host the party event and hence she went to stage very soon after reaching there. Few performances are already completed and Jay is hosting performances alone till Alan joined him on the stage. Vicky followed Alan till very near or in front of stage, from where he can take her pictures. Once again with initial performances stage come to live with speech from top guys. Rayman spotted Anna and ask Riya to join her. After leaving Riya with Anna Rayman went out to find his other friends, first he found Vishu and then Toni.

"Hello brothers" Rayman greeted Vishu and Toni.

"Hi, when you did reach here?" both greeted back and Vishu further asked Rayman.

"Around fifteen minute, I came with Vicky and Alan."

"And Riya, where is she?" Vishu asked back.

"She is inside with one of my friend, Anna."

"Who is Anna now?" Vishu and Toni both asked and their eyes are filled with hundreds of questions.

"Just friend" Rayman responded.

"Really" Vishu asked to confirm.

"Yes really, where are others, Tanu, Deepali and Lavanya?"

"Back stage, Tanu gone few minutes ago and she might be coming back very soon." Toni replied.

"Why?"

"She has nothing to do there. She was gone with Lavanya to give her company."

"OK"

"Hey Vishu want some drink, or snacks."

"Oh I am also feeling hungry, let's have something first." Toni said before Vishu.

"Let's drink. I want to drink a lot today." Vishu also responded.

"Why, what happened bro, any heart breaks?"

"No, this all is bullshit."

"Yeah, let's drink and then we will look around for chicks."

"Wow, this is a perfect plan bro." Toni and Vishu replied in unison. "Let's go" all said in one voice.

"Where is Vicky?" Toni asked.

"Oh Vicky, Alan is hosting event this year, so Vicky is near to the stage and will be there whole evening I guess."

"Oh yes, he is committed, not like us." Toni said in response.

"What are you saying? I and Rayman are also committed." Vishu commented on Toni's remark.

"I am not talking about crime, by the way when you guys got committed?" Toni asked him back.

"We are committed to our drinks."

"Yes." Rayman agreed with Vishu.

Inside the hall on the third row from the stage Anna and Riya gossiping with each other while some guy is boring on the stage with the bullshit speech.

"So are you excited?" Anna asked Riya.

"Why?"

"It is your Marriage!"

"Oh, I really don't know about what I am feeling. I am actually nervous."

"Why?"

"I can't explain really, you only get to know once you will go through same situation."

"May be, but you can share."

"I don't know how it is going to be after marriage."

"And"

"My freedom, these parties, friends, and Rayman, will I be able to even meet him?"

"Off course you can and you will, we will always remain friends and so others."

"I am worried about Rayman also. He is appearing so lonely and worried these days."

"I have seen it, it's visible on his face, he seems quite upset, but you don't worry about him, he will be alright with time. It hurts sometime when some close friend is going away, and you guys are really great friend, how you guys became so good friends?"

"Yeah you are right, it happened with time I guess. We played together in our childhood, grown up together, studied together and then went college together, completed B. Tech from same stream and college. I guess that brought us closer and made us really great friends."

"Since when are you know each other?"

"Childhood and to be precise it's around 15 years."

"Really, it's awesome that you guys kept your friendship for this long, I wish you guys will always remain friend. But for now keep all the worries aside and enjoy your moment, these days will never coming back again in your life. Have you met him?"

"Yes, twice."

"How does he look?"

"Come to my marriage and see by yourself."

"Yes why not?"

Vishu came to them at that moment and Vishu handed over snacks plates to Anna and Riya.

"Hey congratulation, where is the party?" Vishu asked Riya.

"I guess here only we gathered for the party."

"Oh, very funny indeed"

"Where is Diya, Has not she came with you?"

"No"

"Why, what happened?"

"We could not work it out." Vishu murmured under his breath and left Riya and Anna. "Bye, I am going to Rayman."

Riya and Anna continued their discussion and spent their whole evening talking to each other; Rayman and Vishu were sitting just behind them without their notice, Toni and Tanu standing at the back far end with lots of their team mates laughing and gossiping. Vicky is busy taking snaps of his sweetheart who is creating magic on the stage. At around eleven all stage performances completed and all drunkards are now on DJ floor, Tanu, Deepali and Lavanya also dancing there.

"Vishu, come on yaar." Deepali called Vishu, who is sitting quietly.

"I am not in the mood."

"What are you talking about?" Rayman asked "something serous here man, you and saying no to dance, where is your handkerchief, you need to tie it on your forehead and join the mob on dance floor, hey buddy come on."

"No, you carry on."

"Well seriously, I am also not in the mood."

"You always enjoy dancing."

"I know I don't dance but I watch, but this time I am not even feeling for that."

"Then let's go and have one more drink, what says?"

"Sure, let's go."

Anna and Riya are discussing something about Deepali and Rayman.

"Do you remember this girl?" Anna asked Riya.

"Yes, she is the same girl who was dancing with Rayman last year for whole evening and roaming with him all evening. Yes I do remember her."

"Yes, she is the one who is offered him water from her bottle."

"Yes"

Vishu and Rayman returned after thirty more minutes and Riya and Anna still sitting there and enjoying dance and gossiping about some random things.

"Hey Riya, We are quite late now, let's go and eat and then leave, I have enough of party." Rayman asked Riya for dinner.

"Anna, you also come with us." Riya asked Anna as well.

"Sure."

Then they went outside the hall toward buffet arrangement and taken their plates, Vicky is already standing there and having dinner with Alan in same plate. Rayman without taking any further plate started eating with them in their plate, soon Toni and Tanu also joined them in same plate, Vishu came with another plate and Toni and Rayman moved to his plate. Anna and Riya taken food and sat on a table to have their dinner in peace not like these loafers. After dinner everyone left for their homes, Rayman and Riya left with Vicky and Alan, rest of the guys left in office cabs.

One week gone in discussion about the party and event happened in party, on weekend Riya left for her home and Rayman as already said her not accompanying her till her home, but came to station to drop her.

"So, what you decided, Vicky told me about his brother and friend, they moved out from Delhi. Will you shift with him?" Riya asked Rayman while both waiting for her train.

"Yes. Next weekend I will be shifting with him."

"Why in the middle of month, now wait till December."

"It does not matter between the friends."

"OK, as you wish. Don't forget to come for the marriage; you remember it's in the first week of December."

"Yes, I do remember and I will surely come, anything else?"

"No, I am just reminding you."

"How many times"

"Hey lower your voice. First thing you are not coming with me to drop me home and now you are daring to yell at me."

"OK, sorry."

"You better be."

"Now calm down and take care of you in the journey."

"I will, you too take care of you from now."

"I will."

"See you, train has come and it will stop for two minutes only, so bye for now."

"Bye"

Next weekend Rayman is moving to Vicky's flat, it is on the fourth floor with address 7E, it took him around ten minutes to climb to his floor.

"What the hell on this earth inspired you to rent this flat on the top of Himalaya?"

"Love my friend, Love inspired me"

"Oh sure, I once heard from somewhere, what love can really inspire you to do anything and you feel like you did nothing."

"Really, you will never understand."

"Sure, it is you and Alan only, Romeo and Juliet of our time. I am moving in tomorrow only. These days I am quite busy in office somehow got time this weekend. In fortnight I might go home for Riya marriage."

"Sure, I will help you to shift and Raju Bhaiya is also coming so he will also help us in shifting."

"That will be great."

Rayman moved in with Vicky on coming weekend and both spent first day in cleaning and arranging things in their home and then watched television for remaining day. Everything is going normal at office for both of them. Vicky went to Alan's home in evening and then went to roam around in Lajpat Nagar market with Alan. Rayman also joined them late in the evening and they had dinner together. Rayman packing his bag for trip to Riya's marriage on Tuesday evening at the end of November, Riya invited all her and Rayman's friends but no one is able to attend wedding as everyone was busy in his or her work. Wednesday evening Rayman left for Riya's marriage, Vicky came to station to drop Rayman.

"Congratulate her from my and Alan's behalf." Vicky said to Rayman on platform.

"Sure, you take care, see you on Monday, I will stay at home for few days after Riya's marriage. Bye"

Rayman attended Riya wedding on Friday and spent weekend at home. He remains silent most of the time at home but no one asked the reason for his silence and why he appears so upset. Rayman somehow wants someone to hear his voice but he spent whole weekend alone.

On Sunday evening Rayman was back in Delhi and went directly to home but Vicky is not at home. Rayman still looking a bit upset but Delhi has given him a little freshness. Vicky came around eight in the night and awakens Rayman.

"Hey, When did you came, how was your trip?"

"Hi, I came around five and sleeping since then, what time is it?"

"Eight"

"What! I have to reach office and this is the reason I came today, OK see you tomorrow."

"Sure. All the best, by the way, why you need to go office at this odd hour?"

"One new project's work is taking toll on our team."

"You mean Alan also going to be busy, and we will not be able to meet."

"No, only I and Abhi are working with Samarth on this. So you don't need to worry for now, enjoy."

And then Rayman left for office and met Abhi and Samarth, who were already reached office and busy in work. Project work is scheduled for night so Abhi and Rayman planned to stay in office whole night and Samarth left around twelve with promise that he can come at any time in the night if anything required from him. Night passed in work and silence, Rayman and Abhi talked on very few occasion in whole night. Next morning Rayman was sleeping on couch in the reception and Abhi was sleeping in work area on his seat, at 09:00 in the morning people started coming, Anna was first to notice Rayman.

"Hey Rayman, It is morning, awake, people started coming." Anna says to Rayman entering reception area, which make Rayman to wakeup suddenly.

"Oh hi, good morning, thanks for waking me up." Rayman went inside following Anna and ask Abhi to wake up.

After few minutes Rayman and Abhi are working on their systems and talking to each other about the project work. Few moments later Alan came and went for breakfast with Abhi, Rayman stayed back to respond to few mails about progress. After start of this project, Abhi's seat shifted to the side to Rayman seat and Alan still sitting on the seat behind Rayman seat. A few moments later, when Rayman is appearing busy staring on his computer Anna came and sat on Alan's seat to talk to Rayman.

Friendship to Love

"Rayman good morning, how are you?" Anna asked to Rayman after taking Alan's seat. She entered his cubicle and takes Alan's chair and turns toward Rayman and sits on that chair. Rayman was not actually working but staring at PC and lost in his thoughts and hence could not hear her voice at first and she greeted once again.

"I said Hi (stretching I of hi), where have you lost Rayman?"

"Oh Hi" Rayman replied little socked after waking up from his thoughts and he also greeted her in response.

"Oh I was busy in work hence could not hear you voice, How are you? Haven't you gone for breakfast?"

"I am fine, I had breakfast at home." Anna paused for a moment after replying and kept looking at Rayman face, and pulled Alan's chair (on which she is sitting for now) a little closer toward his chair and asked him in whispering voice.

"How are you? How was wedding? Are you all right, you are looking little upset?"

"Who is looking upset? Me!"

"Yes, you"

"No I am fine as always."

"You know Rayman, you can't lie."

"What! Why?"

"Your face reveals everything."

This conversation send shuddering to Rayman body and at the same time given him peace which he was searching from last five days. The same words he was expecting from his close friends and then from his roommate Vicky and then from Abhi, he got those very same words from the person he least expected, and after hearing these words he can't hold his emotions.

"You are right; I don't know why this is happening to me."

"I know because it is always tough to leave your friends."

"May be but I am good now."

"It is good to hear, take care."

Alan and Abhi has come to the floor few minutes ago but none of Rayman and Anna noticed them, Anna noticed Alan and also noticed that she was waiting for Anna to leave her seat so that she can continue her work but Anna stays there and continue her conversation.

"You know I have never seen such friendship in my life, you guys are really great friends."

"You know Anna; I have learned one thing from this whole episode that you should never get attached to anyone, attachment always gives sorrow."

"Oh ho, you will become a saint one day."

"No way"

Now Alan drew herself closure to her seat and this makes Anna to finally leave her seat for Alan and moved back to her seat to continue her work.

"Ahem-Ahem" Alan made taunt on Rayman.

"What!"

"What is going on?"

"What you mean by what is going on?"

"Oh ho, you are acting like you didn't understand my question. I am asking what is going on here between you and Anna."

"Nothing, It is just normal conversation."

"Oh I see normal conversation! Why not, that is why she is not ready to leave my seat."

"You should have asked for your seat from her if you need it so urgently."

"Oh I am just kidding yaar. No need to be serious. OK"

"I am also kidding. I am not serious; we were talking casually and nothing like what you are assuming."

Strangely Rayman is feeling better when Alan linked him with Anna. This might be first sign that he is getting inclined toward Anna. But he turned toward his system without giving any such notion to Alan and started his work where he left it before conversation with Anna. Abhi moved back to his seat near Anna's seat and started his work and soon Rayman joined him on his seat there and both started gossiping there and left for home around eleven as both of them need to come in the evening for today also.

Next morning Rayman and Abhi are at Rayman's seat around quarter to nine in the morning, when Alan came inside to join them.

"So how was yesterday night, is everything went well?" Alan asked to Abhi and Rayman

"Yes. Why?" Abhi responded.

"Nothing, I am confirming whether work is going well or not?"

"Oh manager ma'am, yes everything went well." Rayman responded this time.

"Oh, I am not asking in that way?"

"I know, I am just kidding."

"Let's go for breakfast." Alan asked to both Rayman and Abhi.

"No, I am not feeling like eating, I need to go home first to sleep a bit." Rayman responded.

"I am coming with you." Abhi confirmed with a yes.

"I know why you are not coming, these days you are spending more time with other team's member." Alan chuckled.

"Now you are taking it wrong, she is just a very good friend."

"Oh, why not, since when she became good friend of your?"

"Since the time I came to know her."

"Very well, we are going for breakfast and come with us, if not for breakfast then give us company." Abhi asked this time.

"OK, let's go, I am coming with you."

"So you are not telling me, how was the last night?"

"Nothing exceptional, it was just normal work. Abhi has done everything already few days ago, so we haven't faced any glitch at run time."

"It is really great. Thanks Abhi, you saved even my headache." Alan says to Abhi.

"Oh it's all bullshit, we have done everything together." Abhi said to them.

"Whatever"

They returned from breakfast around nine thirty, everyone came by this time. Alan is at Jay's seat discussing something and after this is time when Anna came to Rayman's seat and sat on Alan's seat and greeted Rayman.

"Hi"

"Hi, how are you?"

"I am good, nothing happened to me. How are you, tell me about you?"

"I am also good what happened to me?"

"Nothing yaar, you guys staying whole night in office."

"Yeah, it was just for two nights only, so from tomorrow once again we shall continue normal routine work."

"Oh great, so how was it?"

"Painful"

"Why? Is it lots of work?

"No, we have to be awake most of the time in night."

"Oh, that is really painful."

"Yes, how is your work these days?"

"They are starting something new on mobile devices. We will be working on some new OS from Google, android I guess."

"Oh, it's really great."

"Can't say, let's see."

"How everything else, are you still looking for change."

"No, not really, I tried few places but nothing worked well, some thing or other went wrong every time. So I am enjoying this new work these days."

"Good"

Alan just like day before waiting for Anna to leave her seat and after few minutes Anna left Alan's seat and went to her to continue work. Abhi and Rayman left office around twelve for home. It is little cold even at twelve outside winter is at peak from December to mid of February and It is just second week of December so it is expected and in few days temperature expected to dip even lower. Abhi and Rayman took DTC bus from Okhla bus stop and Rayman slept all the way to home in bus.

Dec 08 2010 time around nine thirty, Rayman just returned from cafeteria and doing something on his system when Anna came and sat on Alan's seat just like previous two days. She has one cup of tea in her hand which she brought from cafeteria.

"Hi" this time Rayman noticed her and greeted first.

"Hi, how are you?"

"I am good and what about you?"

"I am also good."

"And your work, how is that new android work going?"

"Nice, it's easy, it kind of java."

"OK"

"And they provide various tool and plugins so no such difficulty."

"Oh, that's great."

At that very moment Jay came inside and something made him a little uncomfortable that make him asked Rayman.

"Where is team?"

"They went for breakfast."

"I have noticed these days you guys taking more than one hour to finish breakfast, yaar you should not waste time, I have to give answer to the management."

Rayman just nodded his head in response without uttering even single word and this is time when Abhi and Alan came inside and Jay is about to say something but the he noticed Samarth coming following them so for some reason Jay didn't said anything rather announced news.

"Samarth, most probably today afternoon a girl is joining our team as for Java work."

"Girl, Wow." Abhi, Jiten and Rayman said with wide eyes.

"What, not a girl?" Alan's response is opposite to boys.

"Her name is Naina. Samarth you need to first understand her basic knowledge and then we shall train her accordingly." Jay further continued.

"OK"

In that discussion nobody noticed when Anna moved back to her seat and continued her work, for some reason she does not mingles with Jay and Jiten, sometime she talks with Samarth. Around twelve a very beautiful and sexy girl of around twenty three to twenty four year of age came inside their cubicle with HR representative.

"Where is Jay?" HR rep asked Abhi.

"He is in a meeting." Samarth responded.

"Oh Hi Samarth, how are you?"

"Good and you?"

"Great."

"Good to know this, what you need from Jay, tell me if I can help you." Samarth is like this, he always tries to maintain very good relation with HR Representatives.

"This is Naina. She is joining your team." She responded pointing toward that girl.

"Oh Hi Naina, Jay told us about you in the morning, welcome."

"Hi Samarth" Naina voice is even sexier than she. Rayman, Abhi and Jiten have their eyes fixed on her. This is the usual response of boys when some girl joins their team and this remain for few days and then that girl becomes regular one and no sex appeal visible from the same girl.

"So Naina, come to me if you need anything, this is your team and you will be working with them from now onward." HR Representative left with these words. "All the best"

"So, how are you feeling in this new environment? Have you liked Delhi?" Samarth asked Naina.

"I am from Delhi; I stay in Faridabad."

"Oh nice, where were you working earlier?"

"Bangalore."

"OK, let me introduce you to the team first."

Samarth introduce Naina to everyone from his team and also to Anna and guys from Anna's team. Samarth asked her to sit on seat back to Abhi's and Anna's seat. She had conversation with Abhi, Anna and Alan till lunch time when Jay asked her to join the team for lunch but she refused saying that she will go with her friend. Soon a tall and slim guy came to ask Naina to come for lunch, nobody has seen that guy earlier, later Alan found out that his name is Raman and he also joined with Naina and they use to work together in their previous organization.

Next day around ten in the morning once again Anna is sitting on Alan's seat and talking to Rayman and Alan was sitting on Anna's seat and talking to Naina and letting Naina know about Jay and team culture and work and team members.

"Jay is very strict kind of boss but our team is very much cool."

"And Samarth"

"He is cool."

"How is work pressure?"

"It is too much sometimes and sometimes we have nothing to do for weeks also."

"It is same everywhere."

"Hmm"

On the other hand Anna and Rayman are not talking anything about office.

"How is Riya?" Anna asked.

"No idea, I haven't talk to her after marriage even once."

"Why?"

"Don't knows"

"Wouldn't you talk to her ever?"

"No, I will."

"Then, why not now"

"Giving her space"

"OK, it is also good."

"What is happening with you?"

"I have to shift my room in coming days that is giving pain."

"Where are you going?"

"Dwarka"

"Why?"

"One of my relative's home is there and no one lives there, so it will be better for me."

"Yeah, it might be better."

"Don't know."

"When are you shifting?"

"In one or two months"

"OK"

Alan is back to her seat and then Anna returns to her seat as well and everyone started their work. Jay came and informed Abhi and Rayman that Abhi has to go to client side next month for project work completion and Rayman have to take care from offshore and also about Jiten's resign.

Next day when Rayman reached office he noticed that Rohini bus has already reached office first thing. He knows that Anna comes in this bus. Rayman noticed that Anna is sitting on her seat when he entered work area followed by Alan, Anna was checking her emails. Rayman sat on his seat and Alan put her things and went to washroom to check her makeup.

"Hi" Anna came to Rayman's seat in few minutes and greeted Rayman after taking Alan's seat.

"Hi" Rayman responded and at the same time Naina entered with her friend in the work area and they left after in few minutes for breakfast.

"How are you?" Rayman asked Anna.

"I am great, how are you?"

"I am also good, How is your shifting plans."

"Where Dwarka, nothing finalize now, it's still few months away. How is your work?"

"Good"

"Why are you appearing so dull and why is this beard? Remove it, doesn't suit on you."

"Sure"

Both continued talking until Alan return to her seat, but Anna is still sitting on her seat. Alan placed her bag on her seat when she realized that Anna is not going to leave seat for her she asked Rayman.

"I am going for breakfast, are you coming?" and she started walking toward door with these words.

"Yeah, you carry on, I will be joining you."

"OK"

Abhi also comes in Anna's bus. He joined Alan for breakfast. Few minutes later Anna and Rayman also left for cafeteria. Same trend continues for another week between Anna and Rayman and after few days Anna started completely ignoring Alan on returning to her seat and she leaves Alan's seat only when she wanted to leave. December 2010 last week Rayman's whole team is inside meeting room and they are discussing about team plans.

"Abhi is going Mumbai, Rayman and Alan you guys need to provide him whatever he wants on his visit to Mumbai." Jay said about first plan to Alan and Rayman.

"OK" Rayman responded.

"Samarth you need to guide them."

"Sure" Samarth also nodded.

"Does anybody have any concern?" Jay asked everyone.

"I want to change my seat." Alan raised concern.

"Why?"

"I want to sit near Abhi to understand the work that I need to take care in his absence."

"OK, you can exchange seat with Naina, Naina do you have any concern?" Naina said no in response.

Meeting ended at that point and everyone was back at their seat to continue work. In evening everyone left for their buses Alan and Rayman sitting on same seat in their bus.

"So? You got irritated with Anna?" Rayman asked Alan.

"What? Why should I get irritated with Anna?"

"She takes your seat daily."

"No. Why?"

"You changed your seat today."

"Oh I want to sit with Abhi, nothing else."

"OK, I was just kidding, Is Vicky coming on time today or late as usual?"

"He is busy in some new project these days and he was saying that it will come late for few weeks until they understand new work and new client."

"OK, he is coming quite late around midnight."

"I know."

Rayman was sleeping around ten thirty in night, Vicky still didn't come home, and suddenly he heard some voice.

"Hi" He tried searching here and there but could not find anything.

"Hey why are not you responding?" It's very familiar female voice of some very close person to Rayman. Rayman could not respond. Something is trying to push his emotions and voice down. Rayman further tried to say Hi in response but he is feeling some pressure on his chest which stopping him say any word.

"How are you?" This time Rayman concentrated a little harder and able to recognize the voice. 'Anna?' He muttered under his voice. His heart pounding like anything, he could hear his heartbeat very clearly.

"How are you?" He heard same question twenty times.

Someone entered house switched on light and Vicky face is visible now.

"Rayman" He called Rayman. "Rayman" On the other hand Rayman can only hear that Anna is trying to get his attention by calling his name. When Vicky calls his name he heard that too in Anna's voice. Vicky come closure and shakes Rayman after grabbing his hand.

"What happened?" Rayman asked Vicky after opening his eyes.

"I think you were shivering in your sleep."

"Oh, is it dream?"

"What was it, you are sweating badly and breathing heavily."

"Don't remember anything."

"OK, let's sleep then."

"You had dinner?"

"Yes. I had in office."

"OK, good night"

"Good night"

Vicky went to sleep very quickly but Rayman is completely awake now and thinking about his dream. 'Anna!! Is that really Anna? Why Anna? Am I started liking her? Leave it for now and let's take some sleep.' After few minutes which appears like hours to Rayman, Rayman also slept and trying to return to his that dream to continue conversation with Anna without success.

Next day in morning Rayman was sitting on his seat and Alan was outside in the washroom. Anna and Abhi entered cubicle area and after few minutes Anna came to Rayman seat. She is wearing red colored Salwar kameez suite with her black framed spectacles and black sandals with medium heels height of around two inches, she kept her hair free.

"Hi" Anna greeted Rayman and this send chill down the Rayman spine, Rayman feels like yesterday night's dream continues but with open eyes this time.

"Hi" Rayman replied in trembling voice.

"What happened?"

"Nothing" Rayman controlled himself and looked very carefully on Anna. 'She is appearing more beautiful today, a little slimmer but still chubby, extremely fair skin, little light brown facial hair, rounded nose, a little longer chin and waist length dark brown and little curly hair. And my god, she can smile from her eyes and lips at the same time. Her lips are like petals of roses, she has a very beautiful neck, and her ears are bigger than mine.'

"What?" Rayman asked to Anna when she put her hand on his shoulder and called his name and this took his attention toward her hand and for some reason her hand is looking extremely beautiful today, slim and long fingers with little long nails with partially tampered maroon nail paint, very fair skin and light brown hair and a ring in middle finger with few diamond studded in it. In this whole process Rayman missed to hear even a single word from Anna.

"I asked you three times, how are you? Where have you lost Rayman?" These are first words from Anna which could reach Rayman ear. In response Rayman extended his hand to greet her in sudden urge to touch her hands and responded.

"I am fine, I was thinking about this new project work and that is the reason I could not hear your words." Rayman saved himself somehow but he could not read from Anna's face whether she understood his condition or not.

"OK, You are appearing too busy these days, staying too late in office. You need to take a break. Look, work is never going to end, so why don't do it comfortably. I know work is important and so you are."

"I think you are right, but I believe in complete work early to relax in free time later."

"That free time you are thinking about will never come, the moment that time will come you will be either fired or company will shut down." Anna insisted on her words once again.

"OK, guru ji, I got your point, now let's go for breakfast."

"I had it at my home; you carry on and join Abhi and Alan."

Rest of the day went without any noticeable event and in the evening Rayman once again alone at home waiting for Vicky and went to sleep watching television show F.I.R. It is around eleven thirty in the night when he heard that sweet voice calling his name.

"Rayman, Hey Rayman wake up and talk to me." It is from Anna and today Rayman awake comfortably and trying to listen while Anna continues.

"Why don't you reply me?" Rayman also want to talk but he is not able to speak even a single word for some reason.

"OK, tell me what were you doing?" Rayman want to reply nothing but once again he could not utter a single word and Anna on the other does not care about it and continue talking to him.

"Why do you ignore me in office? You just talk to your friend, I didn't like her at all, and it seems that you can't breathe without talking to her, why are you doing this to me?"

Rayman want to say that "Are you talking about Alan, she is just a friend of mine." But he could not utter this time also.

"I knew it but I didn't like her in any way." Anna's reply suggested that she can hear his thought and he doesn't need to say anything but just think about the answer and she can hear his thought.

"So tell me what you want?" He is thinking again.

"Leave her, don't talk to her." How can she hear my thought? Rayman thought after hearing her answer.

"But she is a friend, try to understand."

"I was giving you suggestion, I am not forcing you." This is girl's response when they really want you to do for sure.

"Hey Rayman" Suddenly Anna's voice converted to boyish one.

"Yes, what happened to your voice?"

"Rayman" voice come a bit launder this time, and that makes Rayman to open his eyes.

"Vicky?" Rayman saw Vicky with surprise and started searching in the room for Anna but she is nowhere.

'Dream once again?' Rayman started thinking but Vicky break this process in between.

"Are you sleeping or awake, your eyes were close but you look like awake." Vicky enquired.

"I was in dream."

"Hmm-Hmm, who else was there?"

"I can't recall."

"OK, then go to sleep, may be you can see her again. Good night."

"Hmm, Good night, turn off the lights before going to sleep."

Next day in office Rayman was at his seat in morning waiting for Anna to come to his seat, since last two weeks Anna hardly missed any day to come to Rayman's seat in morning. Alan and Abhi went for breakfast without Rayman, Rayman put this excuse of reply an urgent mail but in reality he wants to have morning conversation with Anna in morning at first place. After waiting for nearly half hour Anna does not show up and Rayman decided to go for breakfast so he went to cafeteria. After returning from cafeteria he noticed that Anna is still not at her seat. Rayman searched whole floor from his seat but could not find Anna and he started thinking 'what might have happened to her? Is she all right?' This dilemma got broken by an e-mail from Vishu.

'Hi

Where are you?
No mail in last one month, not even replying to our mails.
What happened, Is it work or something else?
We got to know from Vicky that you guys not able to meet or talk at home as Vicky is also staying late in office.

-Vishu'

Rayman wrote in response.

'Hi

Yeah, I have been very busy in these two months.
I will try to come and meet you tonight or tomorrow night.

-Rayman'

Rayman is sitting with Abhi at Abhi's seat. Abhi is sitting on the left side seat of Anna. Abhi and Rayman are discussing work for which Abhi is going to Mumbai. Alan recently shifted near to Abhi's seat and sitting opposite to Abhi's seat. She also joined them in the conversation and discussing about the implementation which is going to take place around two week later in Mumbai. Naina is shifted to near Rayman seat who is trying to understand the shit this team is handling. Jay and Samarth discussing with Jiten about Jiten's handover as Jiten is leaving company in two weeks' time. Other team mates from Anna and Rayman's team busy doing their work on their seats. Anna came around two in the afternoon marching very fast toward her seat. She is trying to cover whole first half time with this quick march toward her seat which can hardly save around thirty second. Anna didn't noticed Rayman, Abhi or Alan. She went straight to her seat without speaking a single word and started working. She didn't noticed anything until tea came at three and she asked tea serving guy to put one cup for her also. Rayman and Abhi also took one each for them. Alan is back to her seat and working on something else now. Rayman turned toward Anna and asked.

"What happened?"

"Nothing"

"Why did you come late?"

"Oh, I had some personal work at home."

"OK, is everything fine?"

"Yes"

Anna turned her seat toward her computer once again and a little later Rayman went back to his seat and continued his work. Naina turned toward Rayman and asked him about the work she was assigned, both discussed for few minutes and this series of the discussion between Rayman and Abhi then Rayman and Naina then Rayman, Jiten, Jay and Rayman, Alan and Abhi continued till the time to leave for home. Abhi and Alan staying till late in office to complete the remaining work, Rayman left and went to Vishu's place that evening. Rayman takes beer cans with him for evening.

"I will not take beer." Vishu said to Rayman after opening door.

"What? What you need then?"

"Whisky would be better, don't worry. I have whisky at home."

"Good"

Vishu made pegs for both of them and brought some snacks too. Vishu created space for two of them to sit in his messy flat and they started drinking and conversation after settling downs a bit. Conversation started a bit formal and went toward personal after few pegs down.

"Where were you? I am sure something fishy." Vishu asked Rayman.

"Nothing yaar, just went a little emotional and work pressure."

"Emotional?"

"Yeah, you remember the day we left college, we felt so nostalgic, and I am feeling same for Riya after her marriage."

"Bullshit, those emotions were due to the fact that we are not sure whether we can see each other and whether we will be able to get such friends and most importantly because we leaving all our friends at one time."

"You are right."

"Then leave this all nonsense and act normal."

"Yeah, you know I am leaving all friends one by one, first college then you all, then Riya got married and you know somehow every guy I make friend he leaves the company. Well leave it and tell me what happened to you, you haven't written a single mail or called even once."

"Yeah" Vishu nodded but that nod is not normal one, this nod saying so many things.

"What happened?"

"Nothing"

"Oh god, now don't act like girls for god sake and tell me what happened."

"Nothing, I told you naah nothing."

"As you wish but it is better to share your burden like I did."

By the time Vishu and Rayman both are four pegs down and not in their senses and that is what make Vishu let his heart speak out.

"You know Rayman I am also feeling same like you these days."

"What? But why?"

"I sometimes think that my decision of taking the relationship with Diya at another level was wrong. We were not able to convince our parent for each other and I have lost my best friend in the process. You know you should never love your best friend and also never consider for marriage not in India at least."

"I agree. How is Diya?"

"Who knows, I haven't seen her since two months." Vishu's face got stoned, no emotion is present there. "I tried my best but I couldn't get her. Somewhere something went wrong, she somehow managed to get her parents' node and I was mine but when both parents' met and they can't agree with each other."

"What went wrong in that meeting?" Rayman cut it in between.

"God knows only, their ego clashes."

"And that is going to ruin a love tail."

"Yes" And with this yes Vishu paused for few moments, Rayman by now emptied two bottles of beer and Vishu is down with at least six pegs, both stopped drinking now, Vishu continues. "I went to her home last week but she doesn't want to see me. I waited for nearly an hour outside her home, she did neither showed-up nor picked my call, she just pickcd my call once and said it's over, don't come after me. Please leave me alone, so I left after one hour." Vishu is saying all this with very straight face, no emotion, no tears, nothing.

"I understand"

"No, you can't, no one can."

Both lost in conversation and went to sleep somewhere around one in the night and next morning Rayman went to office directly from Vishu's home a little late and Vishu also left with Rayman to his office. Rayman reached office around quarter to ten, everyone gone for breakfast except Naina who usually goes for breakfast with her friend Raman and returns earlier than other. Anna is also at her seat reading mails. Few moments later Anna came to Rayman seat and sat beside his seat where a fresher use to sit, he is gone for breakfast with other team members.

"Hi" Anna greeted Rayman without giving attention to Naina.

"Hi, how are you?"

"I am good, how are you, why did you come late today?"

"I went to one friends place last night and could not awake early."

"Party" She smiled mischievously with party word.

"No, not like that, just two friends, but yes we did had party."

"Hmm-Hmm"

"Why you came late yesterday and you are not looking good even when you came in second half. What happened?"

"Nothing yaar, I went Gurgaon for one interview."

"OK, what happened?"

"Nothing yaar, they are not ready to provide cab or bus facility. And then I got call from here saying that why am I not in office, I should have informed them if I am planning for a leave in advance, I said I am not feeling well, they are not ready to listen anything."

"OK, and then that cause mess"

"Yes, you know my boss is great, but these days I am working with her boss for this mobile project."

"Hmm, I know it."

During this conversation everyone is back to his or her seat and then Anna leave the seat and went back to her seat. Naina came to Rayman seat after few minutes for discussion on understanding on some issue she is working on. Later Rayman went to Abhi's seat and Alan, Abhi and Rayman working together on something. One more week gone in this hard work by Abhi especially and on the other hand friendship between Anna and Rayman also growing stronger day by day, Anna is not missing a single day to come to Rayman's seat to have morning conversation and Rayman is not missing any single night without conversation with Anna in dreams. The talks became more casual day by day mostly conversation in night starts from the point it left in the day and feels like continued for whole night. A day before Abhi has to leave for Mumbai its last week of December 2010 around eleven in the night when same voice broke Rayman sleep.

"Hi Rayman" Anna called Rayman with stretched i of Hi. Now Rayman also became familiar with these conversations.

"Oh Hi Anna, How are you?"

"I am good, how are you?"

"Good"

"You seem too busy these days. You are not even coming for breakfast. What is going on?" Last part she said with honey coated I mean with lots of love.

"Yeah, I am quite busy in work these days. Abhi is going Mumbai tomorrow and we have to finish everything before that and we are quite behind schedule."

"You should have planned it well before time naah."

"Yeah"

Rayman tried looking in the surrounding and amazingly everything is black in surrounding, there is nothing visible except Anna glowing like candle in dark night, she is in plain red colored Salwar kameez suite. There were no flowers or garden or fields full of mustard flowers nothing, just black surrounding and in between Anna in red suite, her face is very clear and eyes glued on Rayman. His concentration is broken by a question from Anna.

"How am I looking today?"

"What? Why are you asking this?"

"Say naah, how am I looking today?"

"Beautiful. Very beautiful

"Really"

"Yes, but why are you asking this?"

"I don't know. I just wanted to know."

This conversation continued until Rayman went to sound sleep, next day Rayman reached office at usual time and Abhi and rest of team members already reached office. Abhi came to Rayman's seat and they both started discussion regarding work.

"All set to go tomorrow, we first focus on the things which can stop your travel tomorrow." Rayman said to Abhi.

"OK, most of the things are done. You just need to one thing whenever I call you or mail you respond immediately."

"Sure" Rayman responded but his eyes are searching for someone, and that someone is having her breakfast with her team and entered cubicle after fifteen minutes. Abhi and Rayman are still busy in their discussion, by this time Alan also joined them. Naina is also looking at Abhi and Rayman for some clarification. Anna's entry attracted Rayman's attention until she reached her seat. Anna is in her red suite which she was wearing in last night's dream. When Anna entered in the room Rayman could not move his eyes away from her and when she was walking her dupatta is flying in the air. Rayman is feeling like that he is still in his dream from last night. Rayman is feeling music in the air and not able to listen anything which Abhi or Alan saying to him. Looks like wind in the Anna's surrounding got drunk and flowing in a rhythm which makes leaves fly a bit higher but from where these leaves came inside the cubicle. Anna is smiling with partially opened mouth which makes her upper front teeth visible a little bit. She stopped at Samarth seat before reaching her own seat and started talking something to Samarth. Rayman is not even blinking at this moment. He too wants to join Anna at Samarth's seat but could not move his foot even an inch. Rayman's heart is racing like motor bike. Rayman could not understand why and what is happening to him. This scene continued till Anna went out of Rayman's vision. Rayman was thinking about this incident whole day and when he was having discussion with Abhi in the evening he shared this incidence also.

"Hey Abhi, I want to share something with you."

"Yes, tell me, is anything critical pending for implementation?"

"No, it is something personal."

"OK"

"I am not sure how and where to start and should I really tell you about it?"

"Oh ho, now don't create drama like girls and tell me quickly. I have to leave early and have to finish packing for tomorrow's travel."

"Yaar, I think I am in love."

"What? It's good news. Why you hesitating like a girl then?"

"Don't knows"

"Do I know her?"

"Yes"

"Is any one from office?"

"Yes"

"That basement girl, Samarth is linking you with that girl, Right?"

"No"

"Then"

"What then? Is it some interview going on or what?"

"Oh ho, tell me who is she?"

"What should I say?"

"Her name I guess"

"Hmm"

"What is hmm? Speak up idiot."

"OK" Rayman took a deep breath and continued further "She is your neighbor"

"I have three neighbors"

"It can't be Alan and other one is a boy so who else is left now?"

"Anna! Don't tell me."

"Why?"

"Didn't you found any other girl on this whole planet?"

"Why are you overreacting? What is problem with her?"

"You will get to know soon"

"Why, she is so beautiful and so humble."

"Haven't anybody told you that she is kind of weirdo?"

"Hmm, everyone says this. So what I have no issue with it, she is perfect for me."

"Whatever, have you told her?"

"No"

"Don't even think of it."

"Why?"

"She will kill you for sure."

"How are you so sure?"

"She was in my college, and I know her from there, she does not have any boyfriend even there also and have you seen her getting cozy with anybody here."

"No"

"Then what do you think of yourself, Salman Khan"

"No, Amir Khan, jokes apart I am Rayman and that is enough."

"Bullshit, now stop all these filmy dialogs and listen to me."

"Hmm"

"Maintain a distance from her for few days and concentrate on work. If I got stuck in anything I will kill you when I come back."

"You don't need to worry about work."

"I will see."

"OK, now tell me what should I do?"

"Nothing"

"What"

"Yes, give it sometime and try to realize whether it is love or not."

"OK"

Next day Abhi went to Mumbai and Alan and Rayman got too much busy in their work. Alan doesn't even have time to meet Vicky. Alan and Vicky's meeting limited to weekends only but Alan need to come office on weekends sometimes as well and in that case Vicky just got to see her on the way to office while he drops her and Rayman in his car. In between somewhere end of December 2010 to mid of January 2011 two persons a girl named Anu and a guy named Sky joined Anna's team followed by one more girl Suchi who joined in mid of February 2011. Sky is average looking guy with strange sense of style and with little funky and happy go lucky attitude and Anu is real Indian beauty with few extra inches height then average Indian girls and Suchi is also beautiful but little too chubby.

Abhi is in Mumbai office and Rayman in Delhi office with Jay on new-year eve. They are busy in work and there doesn't seem any possibility of going home that night. Rayman and Jay called Abhi.

"So what is the planning for new-year?" Rayman asked Abhi in conference call.

"I am thinking of staying late and alone in office."

"Why alone? We are giving you company on phone naah." Jay responded from this side.

"Hmm. Very well said sir."

"When are you coming back?" Jay asked to Abhi.

"It is up to you sir."

"It is up to you, finish the work and come back and by the way why you are worried, your home is even nearer to Mumbai, so go home on weekend."

"Sir, FYI it is weekend and we all are in office, and about work, it will take at least two more weeks."

"OK, then finish it and come back, you had dinner or not, it is nearly mid night now. We have ordered Pizza around one and half hour ago and he said he can't commit about time due to new-year eve so we are waiting for it to arrive."

"I already had dinner at cafeteria and my Cab to home has come so I have to leave now and after that you guys have to take care of it from off shore."

"Don't worry yaar, we will finish it."

"OK. Good night Rayman and good night sir."

"Good night" responded both Jay and Rayman.

Pizza arrived around twelve thirty and after having pizza Rayman went to sleep and Jay continued working whole night. Next day is Sunday around eleven in the noon Samarth and Jiten arrived in office. Alan already came at around ten in the morning and brought Parathas for Rayman and Jay. Jiten, Samarth and Alan stayed in office while Jay and Rayman left for home around twelve by the time Abhi also reached Mumbai office.

Next two weeks are very busy for Rayman and his team since they are trying to make Abhi's visit successful. Anna was also appearing busy working with new work and her new colleagues. Anu and Suchi came from some other company and Sky is transferred from some other team and it is rumored that Sky himself asked for this transfer and this busy schedule lessen conversations between Anna and Rayman. Anna is still managing time for morning conversation but time for this conversation reducing day by day. Rayman is trying to avoid conversation with Anna as much as possible since he is in the state of dilemma on Anna and this way he want to be sure on it. When Anna is in front of Rayman he is trying to go away from her but when Anna is not around Rayman put all his effort to search her. Abhi came back in middle of January 2011 and this reduced work load on members of team and it also given opportunity to Rayman to indulge back in conversation with Anna. Vicky is still coming late every night and that is giving Rayman enough quality time to have conversation with Anna in his dreams. Rayman didn't had any conversation with Anna outside office in person or over phone but he is having conversation with her every day in his dreams and this is binding some spell on Rayman which is drawing him closure toward her day by day. A day after Abhi came to Delhi office he is talking to Rayman about Anna.

"What is the progress?" Abhi asked Rayman.

"Everything is done I guess, next month nobody will be required at Mumbai office."

"Oh god, I am talking about Anna."

"What?"

"Now don't create funny faces and tell me, what is the progress?"

"Nothing yaar"

"What you mean by nothing, you told her or not."

"No"

"What do you think, what will be her reaction to it?"

"If somebody can tell me what will be her reaction, my half job will be done. By the way what do you think, should I really tell her or not about it?"

"I think you should forget her, and that will be good for you and for her also."

"But why should I forget her? I really love her.

"Then go and tell her, don't irritate me now."

"But who started this topic by the way?"

"OK, I am sorry, now come back to work for god's sake."

It has been one month since Riya's marriage and Rayman not talked to her ever since her marriage even once for some reason due to too much work in office or may be due to Anna he is not missing her too much.

One evening at the gate of company, Rayman is waiting for Alan to catch the bus. Anna came and Rayman asked her for her cell number. She first teases him and then shared her cell number, when returning from office to home in the bus Rayman started discussion with Alan about Anna.

"Hey Alan, what do you think about Anna?"

"What do you mean by what I think about her? Nothing"

"I mean how do you find her?"

"I didn't found her any way."

"I mean do you like her?"

"Can't you say in direct words?" Alan was not in mood of talking about Anna, she is not very good friends of her so this is expected.

"Nothing" Rayman ended this conversation.

Next day in office Rayman called Riya and they started conversation very formally and asked about wellbeing of each other and how has their life changed in these days? Rayman hinted her about Anna a little.

"Hey Riya, you remember Anna."

"Yes. Why? Has she left company?"

"No, just like that, she is your good friend naah."

"Yeah, but what is so special about her today?"

"Nothing, she became my very good friend these days. We talk every morning."

"You talk with every other girl, there is nothing special about it, you just need a chance nothing else, and don't I know about Alan? You talk to her whole day."

"Oh god, she is committed to Vicky."

"So what"

"Nothing"

At that very moment Naina came to Rayman's seat and asked something about the work she is doing. Rayman put Riya on hold for that duration. Naina asked him few questions and then some gossip about Jay and Samarth followed by formal discussion and then Naina went back to her seat, Rayman again started his conversation with Riya, but before Rayman speak a single word Riya started from where she left.

"I told you, you just need a chance nothing else. Now who is this new girl, I heard her voice for first time."

"So how was the voice, do you liked it or not?"

"It is pretty, do you want me talk to your mother about it. If you like it so much then why not hear it for day night. What says?"

"Nothing yaar, you are right, now I have some work let's talk later, bye."

Jiten final day is in next week but before that Samarth want whole team to go on a memorable trip like Shimla and Narkanda trip they went last year. Samarth talked to everyone including Alan, Abhi, Jiten, Rayman, Jay and Naina and most of the guys got ready for the trip. Two guys and two girls also joined their team in January 2011 Garv, Anish, Shiksha and Sonia. Samarth asked them also to join them in the trip and Samarth also asked Anna to come on the trip but she denied. Rayman also tried convincing Anna to come for the trip but she denied with the excuse of some personal work. Naina also invited her friend Raman for the trip. Samarth with team went to Shimla and Narkanda on weekend of third week of January 2011. Everyone enjoyed the trip. Narkanda and Shimla are full of snow in these months of year. Rayman however was missing Anna's presence all this time on the trip. Monday morning after the trip everyone was talking about the trip at breakfast table.

"So how was the trip?" Jay asked to Jiten.

"Great but we missed you."

"It is Samarth conspiracy once again, he plans trip in such a way so I can't come and keep an eye on his buzz party."

"No sir, we informed you in advance. We planned on short notice because Jiten is leaving this Friday." Samarth could not resist himself from commenting.

"These all are false excuses. Why can't Jiten come on trips after leaving this office?"

No one responded on this one and Jay shows his frustration and anger whole day and this continued for coming few days also. Abhi, Alan and Rayman remained busy in coming weeks also. Friday afternoon at cafeteria farewell is in progress.

"Where is the team, why has not Abhi and Rayman came till now?" Jay asked in anger.

"They are deploying final patch at Mumbai office, you know next week this part will go live." Samarth responded.

"I know everything, only this is the time you guys showing your sincerity, you have time to go on trips but you can't get few minutes time to come here for this little conversation." Jay is still angry with the team. But who really cares about it, Rayman and Abhi joined them in few minutes and in this time Samarth called them twice on Jay's instructions. Jay started with praise of Jiten and then everyone expressed his feelings for Jiten at the end scene became quite emotional especially for Jiten, Jay and Rayman.

Between eleven and twelve in night of February 8th 2011 Rayman was alone at his flat, Vicky is coming late today also like last one month. Rayman heard once again same sweet voice.

"Hi. What are you doing?"

"Nothing"

"Tell me one thing"

"What?"

"Why aren't you telling me?"

"What?"

"That you love me."

"What?"

"Yes"

"I am not sure about it."

"And exactly how much time you need to decide it?" He is thinking hard on her this question but then she called his name but her voice is little hoarse this time.

"Rayman"

"What"

"Rayman" It is voice from Vicky which broke his sweet dream.

"What?" Rayman asked after opening his eyes.

"Have you eaten?"

"No"

"Why"

"I was waiting for you. You said you are coming in half an hour."

"Oh sorry, I forget to update you; I had dinner at sector 58 market."

"Parathas"

"Yes"

"You brought for me or not?"

"No"

"OK, I am not hungry let me sleep. Good night" Rayman again went to sleep in false hope of continuing same dream.

In the morning Vicky got ready for office while Rayman is still inside bathroom taking shower. A Bollywood song "Kaisa ye ishq hai" from movie Mere Brother Ki Dulhan is playing on speakers. Usually both Rayman and Vicky leave at the same time and met Alan on the way to take buses for office. When Rayman getting ready for office one thought is continuously running inside his brain.

'Why she said last night that I should tell her about my feelings, she hasn't told me anything like that earlier. Is it indication that I should propose her or she also feels the same for me?' Rayman could not really understand when he reaches to his bus and boarded it and when he finally reached office. After reaching office Rayman started search for Anna. He wants to share all his feelings with her. Rayman searched her on the floor and then in cafeteria but he could not find her. Rayman noticed that Abhi already reached office that indicates that Anna didn't came today as she also comes in same bus. Rayman asked Alan to find out why she hasn't reached office even now by afternoon. Finally at two in the noon Alan brought news that she is on leave to go back Jammu her home to celebrate something. Rayman felt little sad and remaining day went without any other event.

Thirteen February 2011, a day before valentine day Samarth, Rayman, Sky, Anu, Abhi and Alan are sitting in Anna's cubicle in the area between their seats.

"So who is going on valentine date tomorrow?" Samarth asked an open question which no one responded and then he asked nearly same question from Rayman. "Are you going?"

"No sir, I don't have girlfriend."

"And you Sky?" He then asked to Sky.

"Same story sir, No girlfriend"

"So girls now it is your turn." Samarth asked to all girls at once.

"I am celebrating with my hubby." Anu responded first.

"OK"

"I don't find any boys suitable here." Anna responded after Anu.

"Why? Isn't anybody good in our company?" Samarth asked in response to her answer.

"No" She replied and Alan also supported her in this. This response from Anna made Rayman scared from inside.

'Doesn't she like me?' Rayman thought and left from there and went to his seat and continued his work.

In the evening Rayman got a call from Riya that she need to buy something for her hubby for valentine present and she want him to accompany her to Lajpat nagar market. Rayman didn't notice anything in the evening about Riya or what she bought even this is their first meeting after Riya marriage but he was lost in his thought whole evening. When both were leaving Rayman shared his feelings about Anna with her and somehow that made Riya uncomfortable. I have heard this many times that no girls like that you like or love any of her friend but experienced first time between Rayman and Riya.

14th February 2011 valentine day, Rayman come office on time as usual. Vicky and Alan met on bus stop and exchanged few words there. Vicky has already gifted her bouquet of roses. Rayman wrote a mail to Anna.

'Anna,

Happy Valentine Day, you already rejected me for valentine when you said that no one in office is suitable for you so no point of asking you for the same.'

Within few minutes Rayman received a mail from Anna.

'Hi

Happy valentine day to you too,
And I was just kidding yesterday, and you don't flirt with me or else I will complain against you.'

Response from Anna is not some kind of proposal for love but it still made Rayman feel good that she might have said yesterday because presence of whole team and from her response it seems that she likes me and she didn't denied me. But this is what Rayman thinking about what Anna might be thinking. He doesn't exactly know what she might be thinking when she responded or what she exactly wants to convey.

On February 21 2011 Rayman got an e-mail from Anna inviting him for her birthday party which she was throwing after five months of her birthday and party is on 22nd February at some restaurant in Kalka Ji. Rayman noticed only one thing that he is one of the guys from outside her team who was invited for this party. On 22nd February when everyone is outside office premises Anna's manager Ruchi and Samarth made some comment to link Rayman with Anna and then Anna responded strangely and angrily. She might be thinking that Rayman driving all this non sense or maybe she doesn't like her name gets linked with anybody.

"Rayman must be already committed and I don't have any interest in these nonsense things."

Rayman doesn't react at all but after hearing this comment from Anna Rayman lost in deep thought. Rayman could not sleep properly that night and Next morning when he reached office he noticed that Anna didn't come to his seat and this is first time in two months that she does not come to Rayman seat for morning gossip. Everyone in the both team was working as usual except Rayman, he is trying to observe Anna whenever he got any chance to take sneak a peek of her. When she moves outside work area he follows her till she vanishes from his eye sight and when she enters work area Rayman follows her from the point she comes in his vision to her seat. This behavior continues till twelve o'clock in noon and every time he feels like leaves and flower flowing with her in the air and her scarf is flowing from her shoulder to few feats behind her and few inches above the ground. He can even hear the violin sound in background. Rayman is not noticing anything. Rayman is noticing everyone else also in the team after few months of extreme work while following Anna. He noticed that four newly joined guys are sitting together and talking on some topic and Abhi is giving them some kind of training while Naina is busy in herself and doing her work alone. Samarth and Alan are working together on some issue. Jay is sitting on his seat with one of her friend from other team and gossiping about something. Anna's manager Ruchi is sitting on the seat by the side of Jay's seat and busy in her work. Anna's other team mates, a guy Sky is not doing any work but trying to disturb the girls, a girl Anu is extremely beautiful and extremely fair in complexion, another girl Suchi is looking a bit calm and also lost on her screen and from outside it look like that she is also working but from the reflection in Anna's computer it is visible that she is playing some silly game of bursting bubbles. Around twelve o'clock he wrote an e-mail to Anna.

'Hi

With whom do you think I am committed?
I am in some confusion and want to confess something. I will ask few more questions on the basis of your response.'

And in few minutes he got response from her.

'Hi

Don't waste your time on me.
I am from very strict and traditional Kashmiri family.
I will call you at 9 in the night.'

It is 8:45 in the evening and Rayman waiting for Anna impatiently, Rayman was not able to decide what to do? He is in his bed and then went to terrace for some time but not able to decide where to take call. Rayman didn't notice that clock already ticking ten minutes past nine. His heart is racing faster than motor bike. He is waiting for his phone to ring. Finally he settled in his bed inside the blanket to receive the call and it is good choice also as outside will become chillier with passing time in those February nights.

Love?

"*R*adhe krishna ki jyoti alaukik teeno lok mein chhaye rahi hai, bhakti vivash ek prem pujaran fir bhi deep jalaaye rahi hai, (krishna ko gokul se radhe ko)- 2 barasaane se bulaaye rahi hai…" Rayman's cell started ringing with the song of Vivaah movie at that very moment and Anna picture is visible on the screen, it seems like she is singing song for him.

"Hello" said Rayman after picking-up the cell.

"Hello Rayman, What is this? What you thinks you are you doing?" and this sudden attack of question from Anna awakes Rayman's from her thoughts and he is not in situation to react but Anna does not stopped there and continued bombarding questions in same tone and with same pace.

"Why are you doing this?"

"What am I doing?" Rayman spoke for first time.

"All this" Anna paused after this and now Rayman could hear her increased breath. Rayman first time came in his senses after two and half months.

"I don't know why this is happening to me, I somehow fallen for you."

"Which particular activity or action of mine attracted you toward me, have I ever said anything like that to you?"

"No"

"Then why and how?"

"I don't know but it just happened."

"What you like about me, I know that I am fair is this the reason?"

"No"

"What is it then? Why are not you telling me?" Anna is not giving Rayman any chance, and Rayman is not able to convince his thoughts and love is not something that can be convinced, it is something that just happens.

"You are beautiful for sure but that is not the only reason I fall for you."

"See Rayman, I have always considered you as my great friend but I have never seen you this way and do you think your family will allow all this? By the way what is your caste and community? Doesn't your family have any objection you marrying a girl from other caste?"

"I don't think they will have any issue and I am from schedule caste."

"You know that I am from traditional Kashmiri pundit family, do you think my family will be ready for it?"

"I haven't thought of anything, it just happened to me and I can't control anything." Anna is becoming a bit normal now and that given Rayman a little time to be normal and he further continued.

"I can talk to your father."

"It wouldn't help, and you know what will happen after it, he will warn me but you will never come back." Rayman heard least expected response of a proposal. He was thinking now about 'Is she daughter of some gangster?'

"You know I loved a boy when I was in class seven and I told my mom about him and she told me never ever fall for such thing in life, we will never allow you to do such things so don't give any problems to yourself and us and from that day I never considered any such possibility for me. She told me that dad will kill both me and that boy."

"I understand your point but how can I convince me?"

"One more thing I knows that you had girl friends in past and now you are saying that you loves me, isn't it possible that you fall for someone else some day in future?"

"I don't know about it, I think love can happen at any time with anyone it doesn't care for anything. But I know one thing that I love you for real."

"It is just infatuation and nothing else."

"I am really serious for you."

"My parent will never be agreeing for it and first thing is that even I don't like you that way. You are a great friend and I like you that way only. Have you told everyone in your team about it? These days everyone from your team is linking you with me."

"No, only Abhi knows about it."

"And Alan, She is your best friend you must have told her."

"No, not till now and now no point of telling anyone I guess."

"You are neither Kashmiri and nor pundit. Why don't you understand it is not possible for us to go against the society?"

"I understand"

"Is not your family looking for girls for you for the marriage?"

"What do you think if you will not say yes to me? I will never get married." Rayman said this with little aggression due to rejection.

"I didn't mean that." Anna response is still normal but no girl will say yes after this statement but she further kept her cool and said to Rayman.

"What do you suggest I can do so that you can forget me?"

"I don't think there is anything that can change my mind."

"But this will never happen. The sooner you understand better it will be for you and me."

"I am not forcing you to say yes I am just telling you my point of view."

"But that is not going to work. I can't even remain your friend if you will not stop loving me?"

"What is problem in it, you can remain my friend as it is and I will try to convince you."

"No way, if you will not understand then I can't remain your friend any more. If you can manage to remain a real and good friend then only it is going to work otherwise I will even stop talking to you."

"Why can't it work the way I told you. Try to understand my situation, it is easy to fall in love with someone in no time but it takes a lifetime to forget someone."

"Tell me then how could you forget your previous girlfriends."

"I don't know exactly, those were the circumstances which I could not fight with."

"Then consider same situation this time also. No one dies for anyone, it just happens in movies only."

"I know that very well. No one dies even when their parent dies and I too can live without you." There is pause for few moments and this is second time Rayman could not control his anger in this call but this time he has gone too far but he tries to control situation which is completely out of his hands by now. "I really can't do it Anna, I can't forget you."

"Then I am sorry I could not remain your friend anymore."

"Please try and understand."

"Please, tell me what can I do to help you forget me?"

"I don't know exactly but I think what you can do is." Rayman paused for a moment there and continued.

"Do one thing, whenever you see me in the office tomorrow hit me with a punch with full strength on my nose. It must be hard enough to bleed my nose and try to do it in presence of lots of people."

"And why do you think it going to work and how is it going to work more importantly?"

"I don't know?"

"You didn't know anything, just living in your fantasy world."

"May be you are right but this is what love does to you."

"I don't want to argue on this anymore I told you what I have to say about it. Now it is up to you whether you want to understand or not."

"OK, I will try to remain your good friend and expecting the same from you also."

"Ok tell me one thing, is it true Alan seeing your room mate Vicky?"

"Yes, who told you that?"

"Riya, by the way how is Riya have you met her after her marriage, is she happy after her marriage?" Anna is not in the mood to discuss any further on the topic and hence trying to drag the discussion to something else as soon as possible.

"Yes" And on the other hand Rayman is not in the mood to discuss something else, Rayman voice is shaking now and his eyes filled tears. "Anna" Rayman paused for a moment and composed him to continue further. "Can you do one thing for me?" Rayman is in completely tears but trying to maintain the pitch and texture of voice not to reveal his condition.

"Yes"

"If you ever feel like you started liking me or you think that I am right guy for you. Will you tell me?"

"Yes off course, it is too late now, so good night and please find a girl suitable for you and marry soon. I know you must have told this to your friends but don't tell anyone in the office. It is not like I am scared of anything. No one can even raise a finger on me but what is the point of telling anyone about it."

"Good night"

"Good night"

Rayman and Anna disconnected the call and Rayman sunk in the bed and could not hold the flood which was somehow held inside the eyes till now. Now

Rayman started thinking about the past few hours in between time when he got mail from Anna to this call.

Around eight hour earlier and one hour later Anna's mail:
Rayman in his office wrote a mail to Vicky.

'Hi

I think I have not told you but I am in love with a girl in office, do you remember the girl who was sitting by the side of Alan's seat when you came here to meet us?
I told her a little about it and she said that she will call me around nine at night and then we will discuss about it.'

Rayman then went to Abhi seat and asked him to come for tea outside and told him about the incident happened between Anna and Rayman and that she asked him to wait for her call at nine in the night. When he returned from tea break he already got reply from Vicky.

'Wow, you have not told me about it before, when does this happened, I will come on time today to see what happens on call. All the best'

At four o'clock Rayman wrote a mail to Vishu and informed him that he is in love with a girl who is in other team and who sits near him and she is extremely beautiful and a little weirdo as everybody say about her and that he conveyed her about his intension a little bit over e-mail and she will be calling on his cell to discuss further on this topic. After that Rayman called Riya his best friend and informed her that he said to Anna about what he is feeling about her, not in person but wrote an e-mail to her about it. It was not clear in the mail but she understood somehow and she will be calling him in the evening to discuss further course of relationship. Riya says him to keep his calm and not expect anything out from this conversation if anything good happens that will be great but for now keep the cool and in response Rayman got mad on her and says to shut up and disconnected the call.

"You know Riya I think she is going to say yes."
"I wish you will be right."

"Why do you doubt?"

"I am just asking you not to expect anything, and you always say that expectation always hurts. Why now?"

"Why are you ruining this?"

"I am not ruining anything I am just trying to say that don't get too much excited, it hurt later too much if anything goes wrong."

"OK, OK, bye. I don't have time to listen your bullshit, I have lots of work. Bye"

"Bye"

Rayman got a response from Vishu as he disconnected the call.

'All the best' this response in itself is saying that Vishu is not at all good otherwise he must have discussed this and said so many things but Rayman didn't noticed anything and excepted his well wishes. Rayman is not doing anything in the office and just waiting for the clock to tick the six thirty so that he can go home and wait further till nine to get a call from Anna. On the other hand Anna is not looking any excited and working like any other day, Rayman thought maybe it is not easy for a girl to show her emotions on her face and maybe she might be also excited like Rayman from inside. In between Shiksha and Garv came to his seat to understand and discuss something but he is not in a situation where he could say anything except Anna so he said to those guys to go to Abhi and understand from him. Shiksha and Garv said to him that Abhi is busy doing something and want them to discuss with Rayman but Rayman didn't remembered anything and asked them to discuss tomorrow.

Around six thirty in the evening Abhi asked Rayman to stay a little more than their usual time to help him in one issue but Rayman denied saying that he has to reach home before nine to receive the call from Anna. Abhi reminded him that it is just six thirty and there are around three more hours before it gets nine but Rayman denied to listen anything and went outside to catch bus with Alan ignoring Abhi completely. In the bus a different kind of joy is obviously visible on Rayman face it is same like any child get appraised by elder in his or her childhood and as Anna once said Rayman could not hide anything because his face says all what is running inside his mind.

"What is it?" Alan asked Rayman.

"Nothing"

"There is something for sure, anyone can see it on your face" Rayman already too excited and want to share the news with everyone on the planet, but I think, what Riya says was right, sometime too much excitement and expectation are main reason behind the great deal of pain but Rayman is not in real world anymore to care for these things.

"Yes. There is really this thing I want to tell you about earlier also."

"What"

"I am in love."

"Who is it?"

"Anna"

"What?"

"Yes and there is something more."

"What?" Rayman narrated everything about what is happening with him for last few months and what happened in last week, on valentine eve then valentine day and then yesterday and today morning and what is about to happen after two hours. Alan doesn't react.

Back in current time:

"Rayman" It is Vicky who just came back from office and in a hurry to know what happened on the call and this call from Vicky broke Rayman's journey down the lane from morning to evening. Rayman wiped his tears and take his head out. Vicky is still standing on the gate, in his office clothes which includes tight jeans and slim fit full sleeves shirt but sleeves folded to three fourth lengths and a bag on one shoulder with very big smile on his face.

"What?" Rayman asked.

"What happened?"

"Where"

"What do you mean by where? On your call where else, is she called?"

"Yes, she has called."

"Then"

"She said no."

"What? Why?"

"She has her reasons."

"OK, tell me what happened on the call?" Rayman told whole story in response of this question of Vicky and then Vicky told him what he thought doesn't work out.

"And you think that she is going to say yes, you have to be a little political when talking to girls. You know truth doesn't work always with girls."

"Don't worry yaar I am OK."

"Oh why aren't you going to be OK? Where is she going to get guy better then you?" Vicky is furious on Anna and it is obvious for a friend who really cares, he could not resist abusing her further. "Bitch" this is first time Rayman has seen Vicky abusing someone.

"It is OK, I am going to sleep, I had dinner you can eat if you want to."

"I too had at Alan place. Good night"

"Hmm, Good night"

Vicky chose to sleep in other room while Rayman went back inside the blanket and trying to sleep but tears are not stopping he could not notice when tears stopped and when he slept or he slept with tears.

Next morning Rayman is not feeling to go office but to keep everything as it is so no one else gets worried he went to office on time. Vicky might have updated Alan about the call and hence she didn't ask anything about what happened in last night call on the way to office. After reaching office Rayman directly went to cafeteria for breakfast later Alan and Abhi also joined him, Rayman haven't spilled even a single word to anyone of them and kept eating his breakfast with eyes on the plate only. It seems like Abhi also got news from Alan so he also kept mum. After returning from cafeteria Rayman directly went to his seat without greeting anyone which is against his daily routine but he doesn't felt going to Anna cubicle, on the way to his seat he got a glimpse of Anna from corner of his eyes, she already reached office and started her work and right now she is talking to Sky the only guy in her team.

At eleven o'clock Rayman is moving outside alone to have tea outside. As he went out the development area Anna was coming out of washroom at the same time and as she noticed Rayman, she noticed that Rayman is very nervous and said "Hi" to break the ice. Rayman acted like he doesn't noticed her greeting and kept walking and went out the sight of Anna.

Anna and Rayman came face to face for two more times once when going for lunch and then in the evening when he going out for tea and this time also going alone. Rayman is talking to Anna only in the night in his dream. Ignorance in day and conversation whole night this same story continued for two more days and Rayman ignored Anna completely, his heart want to go after Anna but mind want to go away from her so that he can forget her but this all choking him, it seems like life is going away from him. This is something which he is not able to convey to anyone he called his best friend Riya on second day evening.

"Hi" Rayman greeted Riya in very dull voice.

"Hi, how are you?"

"Good"

"Um hmm, then why isn't it appearing to me from your voice?"

"It may be due to cold."

"Or it might be due to Anna."

"Yeah"

"OK, what happened?"

"She said no"

"I knew that, tell me in detail what happened on call?"

"How do you know, I haven't told you about it, has Vicky told you or Alan?"

"No. Anna told me. But now you tell me in detail."

"What? What she told you?"

"Yes, she told me that you called her and also that you likes her, now will you tell me what happened on call?"

"Yes" and then Rayman told everything to Riya about the call.

"OK, don't worry what if it doesn't work out. There must be someone for you if it's not Anna." Riya is trying to console Rayman.

"Why?"

"Something better is going to happen to you."

"I don't need any better. I just need her."

"If she is in your destiny she will come to you cone day."

"Then why isn't now?"

"We don't have answer for all whys. By the way she called me before she called you."

"What, but why?"

"She told me what you done in office and then she told me that she could not commit and that she can never convince her parent for it then what is the point of considering it. She cares for you and is good friend of your, that is it."

"Why can't she give it a try?"

"She just cares for you and doesn't want you to go under pain when it wouldn't go right later."

"I am already in pain then what will be different in that case."

"If you are feeling so much pain now then it will be even stronger after commitment."

"I don't understand it."

"You have to have patience and need to understand her."

Monday morning in the office Rayman went directly to cafeteria like previous two days and then returned to his seat without talking even single word to anyone and submerged in his computer. Anna has not come to his seat from that day for morning gossip. Rayman is busy in the work when Alan came to his seat.

"Hi"

"Hey hi, what happened?"

"You tell me what happened?"

"What you mean?"

"Why aren't you talking to anyone?"

"What you mean not talking? I am doing my work."

"I know you are working as usual even more than usual but you are not talking to anyone except if it is related to work. You know junior getting scared from you. Abhi said to Shiksha and Garv to ask something to you yesterday they said that you don't look in mood to talk to anyone and they are scared of talking to you."

"What?"

"Yes, Rayman, I understand and Abhi too, it could have happened to anyone, why are you so upset?"

"I don't know what you talking about"

"I have observed that you are not even talking to Anna."

"What is the point? She wants me to forget her. How can I forget if I talk to her?"

"You know, you are making her uncomfortable!"

"What? How"

"By behaving in this way"

"Then what should I do?"

"Think whether is it right, what you doing to her, yourself and others and then decide yourself?" Alan went back to her seat after saying this and Rayman started thinking about the situation.

'What the hell, no one understands that I am in pain, everyone lecturing me to understand her, why doesn't anyone see, what she has done? She can say no to me. She is not even ready to remain my friend if I continue love her and people expecting me to behave usual.' Rayman paused for a moment and continued thinking. 'But what am I expecting from me? Am I being too mean now? I am just thinking about me I guess. She must be also in dilemma. Who knows she might love me also. I know she likes me, maybe she denied because of her parent or society. But how does it matter to me. I know just one thing that I am in pain and I need only this one thing in my life nothing else and still I am not getting her. Oh god why? Please give me Anna and I will never ask for anything from you again. But she might be also in pain, I haven't talked to her not even looked at her since that day.'

"Rayman" Rayman dream broken by Jay, he is calling him inside meeting room. Samarth is also inside the room.

Rayman started thinking. 'Has Alan or Abhi told them about Anna and me? I don't think so, what happened then?' Rayman sat on a chair after going inside the room.

"Friday is last day of Samarth." Jay said to Rayman.

"What!"

"Yes"

"Why didn't you tell me earlier about it?"

"So that work doesn't get affected"

"And even you didn't tell me about it." Rayman is furious on Samarth now.

"Jay asked me to keep it to myself only."

"Why now then?"

"What has happened Rayman? Why are you so furious? I called you so that you can arrange farewell for Samarth and understand work from him. If you don't want to do it then you can leave and I will ask Abhi for it." Jay also responded in same tone, Rayman realizes that Anna is taking toll on him and he has to make peace with himself.

"I am sorry sir. I will do the necessary arrangements." Rayman left after saying that.

"What you think about Rayman, will he be able to handle the work, I seriously doubt it." Jay asked to Samarth as Rayman left.

"He just lack right attitude otherwise he is just perfect."

Rayman is at his seat and thinking about what he needs to do to make everything all right for everyone especially for Anna and himself. 'I need to continue talking to her as usual but I have to take care also to control my emotions for her. It is also possible that she might also fall in love with me with time, let's give time a little more time. What should I do next then, I have this whole week for Samarth's farewell, what if I can plan in such a way so that her team can also come for this farewell too, what can be issues?...

One is that we can't go out. OK.

We can't spend too much time also.

I have to take her boss in confidence for it.

No other team must know about it.

And most importantly there was no such event happened in past where two teams participated except company's annual party and it will be difficult specially for a farewell party, people never want to glorify farewell because it will encourage others also to leave. What the hell, they will not ensure that all facilities should be provided to retain employee and rather keeping an eye on all bullshit.'

Next day Rayman went straight to Sky's seat in the morning, Rayman and Anna's teams were sitting at the same area in different cubicles. Area has two rectangle cubicles where six people can sit in each cubicle the area can also be viewed as four rows, Rayman is sitting in first row from entrance at the far corner from entrance. There is a glass wall at upper half area on Rayman's row which shows reflection of all other three rows. Shiksha and Garv are sitting in the same row with Rayman and Sonia, Anis, and Naina are sitting on the other row in Rayman cubicle. Naina is sitting behind Rayman while Sonia at near the entrance. Anna's has seat on the fourth row from entrance in the middle. Abhi is sitting at one end toward entrance in her row and Sky on the other side. Alan, Suchi, and Anu are sitting on other row of Anna's cubicle. Alan is sitting behind Abhi, Suchi behind Anna and Anu behind Sky. Samarth and Jay sit in separate small cubicle in the same room by the side of meeting room.

"Hi buddy, good morning" Rayman greeted Sky and shake hand with him and then moved to Anu, Suchi, Alan, Abhi seat and in the last to Anna seat.

"Good morning" Rayman extended his hand after greeting Anna.

"Good morning" no expression on her face. Rayman went for breakfast with Alan and Abhi, while Anna went for breakfast with Sky, Anu and Suchi and sat on different tables.

Rayman has not talked to Anna in the whole first half but he can see her in the reflection on glass wall above his seat, sometime he can see the reflection of her computer monitor and sometime her face. Rayman went to Sky seat just before lunch.

"In which team you were working before transfer?"

"I am in the phase 2 office." Sky replied but not looking interested in conversation, and it is obvious as Rayman is not in his team and doesn't share any work with him.

"I was also in different team in Noida office before coming here, how many years here in this company?"

"Four and half"

"Wow"

"It doesn't look like I have this much experience naah."

"Yes" They talked casually for few more minutes and then Rayman went to Abhi's seat to discuss about work.

Rayman later went for lunch with his whole team and Anna went with her team and they sat on different tables this time too. Rayman went to Abhi and Alan seat in the evening at snacks time and had a little conversation with Sky, Anu and Suchi. Anna is not looking interested in any conversation. She is also taking precautions now. Same story continues till Friday morning.

Friday morning after breakfast Rayman and Abhi went out to make arrangements for the evening party for Samarth farewell. Rayman suggested buying a white color t-shirt and different color markers and a clock with twelve mini picture on each hour mark. Abhi arranged pictures from everyone in team and put those pictures on the frames in the clock. Rayman and Alan asked all team members one by one to write message on that white t-shirt. When this all done Rayman asked Abhi to ask all team member of Anna's team also to come and write message on that t-shirt. First half passed in this activity.

Around five in the evening Rayman went to Jay seat and asks him that it is suitable time to go up stair to cafeteria for Samarth farewell. Jay asked Rayman and Abhi to continue with the arrangement in response. Abhi and other team mates started moving to cafeteria. Rayman went to Anna's manager Ruchi and asks her for coming to cafeteria for Samarth farewell.

"Hello Ma'am, It is Samarth's last day today and you are his good friend so I think it would be great if you can come to cafeteria for his farewell. It is not some big event just little party."

"Oh, sure, I would really love to come."

"One more thing"

"Yes"

"It will be great if you can allow your team for few moments. It will not take much time."

"You mean for farewell?"

"Yes"

"Why not, you can take them with you."

"Thanks ma'am"

Around fifteen minutes later Ruchi arrived followed by her team for farewell. Everybody went emotional when Jay started event with praising Samarth and then Ruchi also said few words about him followed by comments from everyone from Ruchi's team and then from Jay team, finally Samarth also thanked everyone and this concluded event.

Rayman and Alan are going back home from office in the bus when Alan asked Rayman.

"What happened back there?" Alan asked Rayman.

"Where"

"At Samarth's farewell"

"What you mean?"

"I mean you called Anna."

"You said naah that I should remain normal with Anna that is why I am behaving like this and I am also thinking that I should give it some more time."

"OK, and?"

"How could I call only her? So I planned this whole thing."

"Well executed, what is next?"

"Well right now nothing, but it would be better if I can make friend with all of her team mates."

Rayman was at home alone as Vicky in at Alan's home. Vicky was coming home a little late and hence not able to meet Alan in last whole week, so he decided to go her home to meet her and her parent. Rayman is thinking about Anna and what went wrong, why she said no.

'What went wrong and what should I do to overcome?

Was I rude in the call, yes I was, I shouldn't had argued with her.

I know that I am not very good looking but I am not bad. And I am a good guy, and I guess even she thinks the same about me. What can I do now? I can't live without her.'

Rayman went to sleep in those thoughts and at the same time he heard one sweet voice.

"How are you?" Anna asked to Rayman.

"What you doing here at this time?"

"How are you?" She completely ignored his question.

"Good and you"

"I am also good"

"Why you did this to me?"

"What have I done?"

"Don't you love me?"

"Yes, I do"

"Then why did you denied?"

"Oh ho, don't be so impatient."

"I am dying you know and you are saying to have patience."

"How you lived without me till now, hold for some more time, I understand your urge but sweet heart wait a little more."

"That is because I wasn't in love with you at that time."

"Why are you doing like this? We meet every day and you know we might be from one of the few lucky couples who can spend around ten hours together on five out of seven days. What else you want?"

"I want to see in your eyes while holding your hands in my hands and you watch me doing all this."

"Oh ho! So romantic! What else?"

"I want to talk to you whole day and night."

"And"

"I want you to sit idle doing nothing. I will do everything for you. I want you to eat with me."

"Impressive, you are quite romantic"

"I want to hold you in my hands"

"Um hmm"

"Don't take it otherwise"

"Hey Rayman, wake up, Rayman-Rayman" suddenly Anna's voice change.

"What happened" Rayman opened his eyes and sees that Vicky is standing in front of him. Television in on and one song is playing on it from movie New York.

"Tune jo na kaha mein woh sunta raha"

"Khamakha bewajah khwaab bunta raha…"

"Why haven't you eaten?" and Vicky switched off TV after asking this to Rayman.

"Oh, I am not hungry."

"OK, I had eaten at Alan's place. I need to go office early tomorrow, Good night."

"Good Night"

Next day in office Rayman repeated the same behavior, went to Sky seat and greeted Anu, Suchi and Sky. He came to these guys seat just before lunch time and then at evening snacks time. Rayman is trying to spend maximum time with Anna's team. One day when he is doing some work at his seat Naina come to discuss something.

"I think we can do it by this way also." Naina said to Rayman.

"Yeah"

"But there is one issue…." Naina voice started fading as Rayman saw Anna rose from her seat to go outside. Rayman fixed his gaze on her and that remain fixed on her till she moved out of the cabin. Rayman followed Anna with his eyes from her seat to out of cabin and until she went out of his sight.

"Rayman, are you listening what I am saying to you?" It is Naina once again.

"Yes, I was thinking about something else, can you say once more?"

"Yes, I was talking about that issue, but let me try first then we can discuss later." And she went to her seat.

Next few days are no different, Rayman greets everyone in the both team in the morning then gossiping at lunch time and little work in between and then talking to Anna whole night in his dreams. It continued till March 9 2011 when he went to Anna near the exit gate of office in the evening when she is going out to catch her bus to home.

"Hi Anna"

"Hi" Anna got scared when she saw Rayman approaching her.

"Can we talk for few minutes?"

"What is it?"

"Can you come here?" Rayman asks Anna to come a little far from others who were standing near the gate.

Anna came near him thinking. 'I swear to god I am going to kill him today. Why doesn't he understand? What he has to say now? Oh God, Please save me. I am going to kill somebody.'

On the other hand Rayman also thinking.

'For some reason she is looking a bit scared. I am not going to eat her. Why this security guy trying to listen this conversation? Is it safe and good to talk to her here?'

"Anna" Rayman once again called her name.

"Yes" She replied with irritation.

"I don't think it is good to talk here, Can I call you sometime?"

"Yes sure"

"Thanks"

"But not today, I am going to my aunt's place tonight. You can call me tomorrow."

"Sure"

"Anything else, I have to catch my bus."

"No, bye, take care"

"Bye" and Anna left with irritation.

"What is going on?" Alan just come out and joined Rayman who is approaching bus.

"Nothing, just wishing her good bye"

"OK"

Next day is pretty normal without any exception just Anna could not come in first half as she was at her aunt's place in Gurgaon and due to this no conversation took place between Anna and Rayman. Rayman is thinking whole day in office.

'I have to analyze, what went wrong last time? Should I call her? I know I am giving her lots of troubles but I love her. It is affecting me badly. I don't know when did I done any work in office last time? I have to do something, what can bring peace to me? It is only a yes from her. In that case I have to think what went wrong for me. First thing is that I was rude a bit last time, I have to control my aggression. At least my response when she asked that "Is not my family looking for a girl for me?" was very rude. Second she mentioned about caste difference and being her a Kashmiri. Can I do anything on it? No. But I should look for the details on it. Third she seems scared of me, I need to know the reason and work on it. Oh god, please help me.'

In the evening around nine Rayman was alone at home and thinking whether he should call her or not.

'I have asked her for one more chance and she gave it to me then why shouldn't I call her. Let me first tell her about my condition and then leave everything on her. I think it is good time to call, she also called at this time only.' Rayman dialed her number thinking all this and she picked on first ring.

"Hello" Response came in sweet voice of Anna.

"Hello, how are you?"

"I am good but what is it, why are not understanding?" Anna is too much angry and that is visible in her voice too.

"Anna, listen one thing first, you know I am really nervous and I know that you are also feeling the same but please try to understand that this time is tough for me. Please don't be angry otherwise I will not be able to even say why I called you today. Please just listen to me first."

"What is this Rayman?" Her voice is much normal compared to previous statement. "I feel that only I am best at drama, talk a lot, can handle any situation and I am big drama queen, but you are even better at it. OK, tell me what you have to say, I am listening."

"Why do you appear nervous talking to me at the gate that day?"

"I am afraid of you."

"Why?"

"I know you have feeling for me and I am scared that you might not to take my rejection in good sense."

"Anna, please don't be afraid of me. Believe me I will be last person on earth who can hurt you. I love you and that love is real. I can never even think of hurting you. So first thing I want to tell you is that don't be afraid of me."

"OK, I get your point, I am just taking precaution otherwise I know that you are a good person."

"Thanks for believing me." Rayman paused for a moment and then continued. "Anna, I tried to go away from you forget you, even you might have noticed that I have stopped talking to you for this period, but you can't even imagine what I am going through. I can't live without you. You are always in front of me in days and nights, you can't believe that you talk to me even in nights in my dreams."

"Rayman please try to understand and control your emotions. It is just infatuation nothing else, it will hurt more if you give it motivation. There is nothing like love, it is just happens in book and movie, you will be able to forget me with time."

"Please listen to me first"

"OK" she seems frustrated a little this time.

"My love is real for you, I want to marry you, I am not able to work for last two months at least, you are always on my mind, I have not taken even a single breathe without your name on my mind, I am just asking you to consider if it possible for you in any way, I can do anything whatever can make you say yes."

"Nothing, really nothing can change my decision or my mind. You should understand it, I really respect your feelings but it is not possible, I can never think about anything which can give my parent any trouble and I can never hurt them."

"I understand it Anna but what can I do about my feelings?"

"If it were America I might have married you but you can understand it not possible in India. You know here in India we don't live just for ourselves but we also live for our family, relatives and society."

"Then come elope with me."

"From whom, my parent, where would we go? I can't."

"Really, even I can't, OK, just tell me one thing."

"What?" she is once again a bit normal.

"Have you ever able to notice that I like you?"

"Yes, the way you stare at me anybody can know that you have feeling for me."

"Anna, No one can ever love you more than me." Desperation is showing in Rayman's pleading.

"Everyone says the same."

"Has anyone else said this to you?"

"Yes, many, I remembered one, he is my flat mate's friend and he was in army, he was good looking also and he once proposed me, I said I can't love you, you can be my fried if you want to, but he is not ready for that, he used to call me for few days, I ignored him completely and stopped picking his calls and then even stopped replying his messages, he use to wish me on birthday and all, I didn't even responded to that and in few months he forgot me. You see that is how boy loves, they forget with time."

"But what could he have done? It is only you who want him to forget you. He has done the same and now you saying that this is how boy loves. Well not all boys are same."

"Hmm-hmm, you will be saying this only because you are also a boy no different."

"Believe me, I will never forget you, and whatever happen in future I will always love you."

"Do you know this one thing?"

"What"

"You live in fantasy world only, nothing practical in it."

"Whatever"

"Rayman"

"Yes"

"Tell me one thing, why you love me?"

"I don't know exactly, it just happens."

"Is it because that I am fair? Or you find me beautiful."

"I don't know, I think you are very good person, very honest and direct and beautiful of course."

"Why me, can't you love somebody else, so many girls joined last month, love someone from these girls, so many beautiful girls joined, they are even friend of your team members."

"Love does not work that way, it just happen with someone special not for everyone."

"Then what do you think I can do to help you?"

"Say yes to me."

"That is not possible for me. I really want to remain your friend but if you don't change your mind I don't think I will be able to continue this friendship. It is up to you whether you want to continue your madness or you want to remain my friend."

"If you want, I or rather we can talk to your dad."

"No chance I told you last time also he is going to kill you for sure."

"Why are you so afraid of him?"

"Because my mom told me in my childhood that I can't love anyone and I was brought up with that thought in my mind."

"That was childhood and things have changed from then why can't we try now?"

"I know my mom and dad better than you."

"You are not ready to anything for our love. You have to give it a try only then you can decide it is good or bad."

"I don't want to be facing more pain later and hence taking precautions now. I am not the kind of girl who wants to take advantage of you and roam with you for few day and take gifts from you and then tell you that my parent are not ready for it and then leave you in pain. I want you to face the reality."

"I am also not asking for that kind of love. I want to continue it for forever."

"You started again, why can't you be just a friend?"

"Why can't be my forever?"

"OK, I will be your sister forever."

"What?"

"Yes, I can think you as my brother and if you ever say anything like this to me I will bring rakhi (a bracelet sister ties to brother) for you in office and tie to you and who knows that might change your mind."

"Please don't say this. At least respect my feelings."

"I am doing the same for last few days and that is not helping."

"If you bring rakhi than I will bring sindur (vermilion) for you and we can decide by fighting and if you win you can tie rakhi and if I win I will put sindur on your forehead."

"Oh god, I can't tolerate your nuisance now."

"OK, I will try from my side to control my feeling, it really is like suicide for me but I will try for you."

Call got disconnected at around eleven in night. We were talking over one and half hours. Rayman could not wish her good night before call got disconnected and Rayman is thinking about this one thing only.

'I should call her to say good night at least. What will she be thinking? What kind of love is it? I could not call her again to wish her good night. Is it really good to call her again as she is already irritated by me. What should I do? Think about both the options.

Well If I don't call her, she might even didn't notice it or she might be happy that I finally not annoying her or she might be a bit sad that I don't love her or what kind of love is it. And what can happen if I call her, she might get irritated with my call that I am already doing to her so that will make no difference. She might think that I thought about wishing her good night. I think calling her is better.' And so Rayman called Anna after two and half minutes.

"Hello" It is Anna once again and this time also she picked on first ring but she is looking a bit angry from her hello only. "What is it now? I already told you whatever I have to say. Now it is up to you whether you want to understand or not. Why are you troubling me again?"

"Anna, I just called to wish you good night. Last call got disconnected somehow. Good night. Bye"

"OK Good night" and long killing silence followed the call and now only sound coming is of Rayman's sobbing.

Love and Friendship

A week later Abhi, Alan and Rayman are having breakfast at the office cafeteria, a little later Anna also came with Sky, Anu and Suchi for breakfast, Sky asked all them to join Rayman's team on their table. Sonia and Shiksha also joined them on the same table, Naina with her friend Raman sitting on other table.

"Next week is my last week in the company and then I am going back home Pune." Abhi says to Alan and Rayman.

"We will miss you so much." Shiksha said these words with heavy voice.

"Yeah, I am also feeling the same at this time but I am happy at the same time because I am going home."

"I understand, and now tell me what you want to tell me earlier." Rayman responded this time.

"I want to spend last few days with you and Vicky, so I am thinking of shifting to your home."

"It's a Great idea."

Vicky and Rayman help Abhi to bring his baggage to their home and now all three friends enjoying to the fullest. They are riding bikes to Noida office, having Parathas at sector 58 - Noida, watching movies and gossiping till late night. One night after gossiping when they went to sleep Abhi heard voice of sobbing from Rayman's bed but he didn't said anything at that time rather he talked to Rayman next morning at breakfast table.

"What is this going on?" Abhi asked Rayman.

"Where"

"I noticed that you are creating trouble for you and your future."

"Hey don't you go round and round just tell me straight what you want to say."

"I was awake last night till late."

"Oh, leave that."

"Why leave that. It is serious, Rayman you have to move on now, you have tried from your side and I know that your feelings are real for her but somewhere down the line you have to decide that it is limit and only you are going to decide that limit. I will only say that be wise and do what is good for you and your future."

"Who and what need to be chosen?" Alan just joined them and asked same question.

"Nothing" Rayman replied but Abhi told Alan everything.

"What can be done now? She can't say yes to you and you know that and why are you so adamant on it?" Abhi further said.

"It is not me. It is just my feelings for her which I am unable to control, you would not understand leave it please. It will take some time."

Abhi and Alan both tried from their side to make Rayman realize that he has to forget Anna and move on in his life for his life, family and career but he is not ready to listen anything on this topic. Whole week passed in the same manner and Rayman is going crazier for Anna day by day, when on the desk Rayman always trying to take a look at Anna desk and sometime he just uses glass wall above his seat to see her reflection. Abhi and Alan always trying from their side to make Rayman understand that he needs to live in real world and he has to understand from his own that what he is dreaming is not possible.

Friday morning Rayman is at his desk and humming one song from movie Tanu weds Manu.

"Vaise to teri na mein bhi, maine dhondh li apni khushi" "Tu jo gar haan kahe to baat hogi aur hi…"

And then he received call from Vishu.

"Hello" Rayman responded as he picked the call.

"Hello, what is your and Vicky plan for tomorrow?"

"Mine is nothing but Vicky might go to his office."

"OK, I will come to your place and then we will also go with Vicky."

"Why?"

"I will tell you tomorrow."

"OK"

Next morning is Saturday and it is normally a holiday but Vicky have to go office for some important project work, Vishu also joined them and they reached office around eleven. Vishu left Vicky and Rayman at Vicky office and left with Vicky's car to go and meet some of his friend and told Vicky and Rayman that he will be back in around one and half hour. Vishu returned around twelve with a girl with him.

"She is Raina, we met last month and will be marrying in one or two month time." Vishu introduces Raina to Rayman and Vicky.

"Hello Raina, I am Rayman."

"Hello and I am Vicky."

"Hello" comes from a very sweet voice of Raina who is sooner going to be member of this gang.

"When will you guys leave for home?" Vishu asked Rayman and Vicky.

"It all depends on Vicky." Rayman responded first.

"Around in an hour"

"We will also come with you in that case, leave us at Spice Mall, we are going to watch movie."

"Sure" Vicky responded and left rest of them at reception and went inside to complete remaining work.

"You guys can also come with us for movie." Raina asked Rayman.

"Well, Vicky is going with Alan in the evening and what I will do alone with you guys. So better you guys enjoy the movie."

"Aren't you going with anyone?" Raina asked to Rayman.

"No actually I am staying at home." So many thoughts running inside Rayman mind at the time when he responded to Raina.

'Was Vishu and Diya's journey ended? Is Vishu really happy or just showing from outside? What is the hurry to get married so early, who knows everything can turn out to fine later? But who am I to decide these things for Vishu, It is his life and whatever he does I should be with him as his friend.'

Raina and Vishu looking great together, Raina is a beautiful girl with very fair complexion, beautiful nice long hair and average height and a little chubby and she is looking perfect with Vishu. Vicky came out before committed time and all four left for Spice mall at twelve thirty and after dropping Vishu and Raina at mall Vicky and Rayman left for home and then Vicky dropped

Rayman at home and finally left with Alan for movie. Rayman and Abhi spent day together at home.

Monday morning and it is last day for Abhi. Rayman planned with Naina and Jay for the farewell party of Abhi. Jay and Rayman having conversation in meeting room around eleven on Monday morning.

"Rayman, why don't you ask Abhi to stop and work here? I am not feeling good leaving him. I just want him in my team."

"But sir, you have to understand that he is going back his home."

"We can give him option to work from home. He can work from Pune or can work in Mumbai office and go Pune on weekends."

"I can't ask him to stay back, I could have asked Samarth but you said that time that he has all valid reasons so I hadn't said anything to him, now I think that Abhi also got valid reason so please let him go."

"It is your wish and understand one thing that now you have to take greater responsibilities."

"I will try my best and why worry when you are with me."

Later in the evening Rayman asked Alan to ask Ruchi and her team to join in Abhi's farewell party. Alan first said that it would not look good.

"Is it just because you want Anna in every event of our team or something else?"

"I don't know exactly but I think it will also not look good if we don't ask then after all they sit with us from last three months."

"OK, I will ask Ruchi but not anyone else."

"OK, but can you ask her to send her team."

"I will do that too but I am sure Anna will not come for this."

"That is upon my luck."

Alan and Rayman are at Abhi's seat around three afternoon and they are discussing about how Abhi feeling going home and all. Alan turned her seat toward Abhi seat who is sitting just behind Abhi seat and Rayman is standing in between Abhi and Anna seat.

"So how are you feeling man?" Rayman asked.

"I will tell everything in the evening event."

"And why do you think that we are giving you farewell anyway?"

"I know you might not want to give me any party but I also know that my juniors Shiksha, Sonia, Garv and my friend Alan will definitely planning one for me."

"May be but tell us, will you going to miss us?

"Definitely"

"Who is going to help me now on my client issues?" Alan asked with heavy voice.

"You can always call me on my cell number."

"Don't give your cell number to anyone here or they will make your life hell." Anna said to Abhi.

"No yaar, friends don't make life hell."

"If you don't give me your number I will come to Pune." Alan is looking very sad as Abhi is like brother to her.

"Run away from here, or she will go to Pune chasing you." Anna is pulling Alan leg and possibly this is the reason why these two girls are not friend because they never leave any chance to pull each other's leg.

"Anyone wants to come for tea at Ashoka's café." Rayman asked Abhi and Alan for tea.

"No yaar I am not in the mood." Abhi responded.

"This might be your last tea at Ashoka's, come naah."

"OK" Abhi nodded and Alan also joined them and then Rayman asked Anna.

"Coming?" He knows that she will never say yes to his any proposal but he asked somehow.

"You guys carryon, I have lot of work and I don't take tea from outside also so you carry on." Anna's response is exactly as per Rayman's expectation but he further continued.

"This might be last tea with Abhi and tea is not bad outside."

"OK, you go I will be coming in five minutes." This is really unexpected for Rayman. She hasn't talked to him since that day he proposed her second time and now she is coming for tea. Rayman left, Abhi and Alan already reached outside.

"Have you guys ordered tea?" Rayman asked Abhi and Alan.

"Yes"

"How many"

"Three of course"

"Make it four"

"Why, who is coming?"

"Anna"

"What?" Abhi and Alan both are surprised, in few minutes Anna is coming outside but she is not alone rather coming with Sky. She came near Abhi and stayed there while Rayman asked guy from café to bring tea for Sky and Anna.

In the evening at Abhi's farewell party everyone assembled in the cafeteria at the terrace from Rayman team. Ruchi is in a meeting so she could not come for the event, Rayman is worried now, there is already rare possibility of coming her for the event, now when her bosses is not coming, this is making her possibility of coming even less. Everyone is talking about Abhi and how good he is as a person and how good he is as a worker and everyone is praising him. But Rayman has his eyes fixed on cafeteria entrance waiting for Anna to enter from that gate but she is nowhere. Nearly half hour passed and now Rayman also left hope for Anna to come and started speaking for Abhi at that very moment Anna entered cafeteria followed by Anu, Suchi and Sky. Rayman stuck in the middle of what he was speaking and could not remember what he was saying, Rayman could not took his eyes away from Anna and followed her from the gate till the table where they are sitting.

"Sir" Naina called Rayman to continue but he is not listening to anything from anybody. "Rayman" She tried further without making any impact on Rayman.

"Rayman" this time Abhi called and shake him by his hand.

"Oh, sorry I was thinking about the past few days we spent together on last project." Rayman somehow handled situation and at that moment Ruchi also came to cafeteria after finishing her meeting.

"Sorry, I got late." Ruchi said after entering cafeteria. "Rayman, you carry on."

"Yeah, I was talking about the past project on which I was working with Abhi for last five months, initially I haven't got any chance to work with him and then I got chance to work with him for this last project for around six months."

"Yeah" Abhi commented on Rayman remark and then Rayman continued further.

"And in those six months I got to know this one thing that if we are working together than we can do anything." Rayman further said few things followed by words from Alan, Jay, and then Shiksha, Sonia, Naina and Garv shared their views on Abhi as a person, friend and colleague. Naina went too much emotional.

"I worked with him for just two months and in those two months I noticed and can say with assurance that no one can make you understand anything better than Abhi, he is a good friend, colleague and mentor. I will always miss you. Thanks for being such support."

"Thanks, I didn't know that I have created such impact."

"I am too worried how am I going to work and who is going to help me. You are always there whenever anybody need any help from you." Alan is also broken and now it is turn for Anna.

"We are from same college but I think you joined later than me I noticed you when I came in Ruchi team."

"Anna, we had joined on same day." Abhi responded on her remark.

"Are you sure we joined same day?"

"Yes"

"Oh, I haven't noticed, well I know you are a good friend and person, and you are always ready for help other. I just want to tell you this thing that people in this world always trying to take advantage and most of person will not be as good as you got here in your team, so take care of yourself. Help others but take care of yourself first. It was nice knowing you. If I ever come to college I mean Pune I will definitely call you."

"Sure you are always welcome."

After that everyone from Anna and Rayman team said something whether they worked with Abhi or not but they are able to notice good characteristics of Abhi as a friend and as a person. Rayman and Naina arranged snacks and cold drink for everyone.

In the evening at Rayman's home Vicky and Abhi are already at the home and Alan joined them around eight in the evening as next morning Abhi has to catch his train and Vicky and Rayman is dropping him at station before the departure hence this is final meeting of friends. They gossiped till late and then all went to Alan home, Abhi went emotional while meeting Alan's parent. Next morning Abhi left on time for Pune and before leaving he once again said to

Rayman to forget Anna and concentrate on work and try to find and marry some other good girl and then he said to Vicky to take care of Alan and marry soon and call him in the marriage. Vicky and Rayman promised him to visit him in Pune someday but everyone from them knows that neither Vicky nor Rayman is going to Pune to visit Abhi. Next morning Alan informed Rayman that she has also resigned from the company and moving out of the company in May end and going to join some government organization.

Next day one guy a little chubby, with short and curly hair sitting on the desk where Abhi use to sit, Jay introduced him to Rayman saying that "This is Vivek and he is working with other team in our group and is in installer team, he will be working on sharing basis with us from now and you can take his help if you need on any of the installer work and he is also good in Java so you can also take his help on that too." Rayman and Vivek had conversation later in the day regarding the work and personal life. Vivek already knows Sky, so sooner Vivek became friend with everyone in Sky team including Anna.

One day in April second last week Anna's team and Rayman decided to go out for contri lunch and everybody left in an Auto for a restaurant named Khidmat at Kalka Ji and in the Auto Anna and Sky arguing over something and Rayman took Anna's side everyone in the Auto know that Anna is wrong and this made everyone notice that Rayman always takes Anna's side whatever is the situation. Sky pulled his leg for this but Rayman never cared for this. While returning Anna strangely asked Rayman to come in her Auto but Rayman denied as her Auto is already full and can't accommodate him.

On return everyone asked Rayman for the contribution they need to pay back to Rayman as Rayman paid bill at the restaurant for this party. In response Rayman replied everyone with the amount. Neither Anna came to Rayman to enquire for the amount and nor Rayman informed her about it. Next day Rayman got a mail from Anna with a warning in it which came in response of an old good morning mail from Rayman.

'Hi

Why haven't told me about the lunch amount. Sky told me the amount which is three fifty. I will give you the money. Take it quietly. Otherwise it will not be good for you. ☺

Anna.'

Rayman missed the smiley which is present at the end of those deadly words in that mail from Anna and that is the reason he took the mail a little aggressive but replied very politely.

'Hey Anna

I really don't mean to pay your contribution or giving you a treat by not telling you the amount, everyone else asked me the amount so I told them about it. But you haven't asked for it so I haven't told you. You can fairly understand my situation since I am already nervous when anything comes between you and me and now you are saying that it will not be good for me, what worse can happen to me than denial from you.

Rayman'

Anna responded next morning.

'Hey

Why are you taking it all wrong and so seriously, I also don't mean anything by saying that 'it will not be good for you', I was just kidding yaar there was smiley after this line, haven't you noticed that. I just want to pay you the money as soon as possible. Just take it from me.'

Rayman laughed at first after seeing reply from Anna and checked smiley in original mail and was shocked that how could he miss smiley at first place. He also replied on the mail.

'Hey

I really didn't noticed smiley, I just read that deadly line from you and could not notice the smiley. You can't imagine how important you are for me? And I really got scared seeing that mail from you. I just don't want to lose you at any cost. You can understand my condition.'

Anna got very much angry seeing this response from Rayman and responded with anger.

'Hi

Look Rayman, I told you so many time that please don't talk to me like this, I really don't like these kinds of mails. Please don't write me further mails.

Thanks'

Rayman went to Sky's seat for some conversation before lunch that day, while he is returning from Sky's seat Anna stopped him for a moment and that scared Rayman but she just returned Rayman the amount for party contribution without saying any word to Rayman. This story between Rayman and Anna continued and at the same time everyone from Rayman team observed Rayman's situation. One day Naina asked Rayman to help her on some issue.

"Rayman I got stuck on this issue, I tried several approaches but I am not able to figure out anything."

"Hey Naina, I am not good at Java." Rayman inspected code at her system and further said. "You know Anna? She is very good at java, why don't you and ask her if she can help us out."

"OK"

Naina went to Anna's seat and as Rayman expected Anna listened Naina very carefully and suggested her few approaches and asked her that she can come at any time if these things don't work. One day after lunch Rayman was at Sky's seat and by now Rayman has become good friend with Sky, Vivek, Suchi and Anu. Sky got some news from somewhere.

"Hey Anna, Anu, Suchi, have you guys heard?"

"What?" Anu asked curiously.

"Our team getting transferred to Noida office, company got a new building on lease and few teams will be transferred from here also." These words gave shock to everyone from Anna's team but Rayman felt these words like nails being hammered on his chest.

"Is my team also getting transferred?" Rayman asked with fear.

"I think only my team is getting transferred from here at first, then may be later few other team will join us there."

"When"

"In a week time or so"

"How am I supposed to reach Noida office from my home, I live at Dwarka, it's too far from Noida, it will take too much time for me." Anna also looking worried.

"They will provide cab or bus, but travel time will increase for you for sure." Rayman responded to Anna.

"I don't want to go?" Anna nearly cried.

"Who cares?" Sky said to her and she hit Sky on his shoulder when he said these words.

From that day onward on alternate day news kept coming for transfer and that is making Rayman nervous with time, till now he was happy thinking that at least he can spend his whole day near Anna. What if she didn't accepted his proposal but still they spent most of the time together at the distance of few yards. April passed in between these stories, some people saying that every team will be transferred to new office while some saying that some particular team going new place.

In between all those events one day Vishu called Rayman to inform him that he is getting married in the end of May possibly on 29 May 2011 and he has to come for the wedding, this is not a formal invitation rather just informative invitation from Vishu to Rayman but he promised Rayman to invite him formally with invitation letter also. Later in the day Rayman called Toni and Vicky to confirm from them whether they got call from Vishu about his marriage and he got positive response from them. Rayman booked tickets for himself and Vicky on the same day to attend Vishu wedding ceremony. April and most of the May passed without any major event except one lunch party on which everyone from Anna and Rayman team went out. Party is thrown by Jay's one friend from some other team but she invited everyone from both the teams. Rayman spent all day in office working and thinking about Anna and whole night talking to her in his dream for last five months, and with moving time Rayman losing concentration in work. Rayman got lot of work after Abhi's departure and made good relationship with everyone in new team. As May nearing Rayman was thinking about Alan's last day as she is last of his friend to leave the team rest of the guys already left company and afterward he will be alone until he makes new friends. He became quite friendly with everyone in the team but real friendship going to take some time. In second last week of May Rayman made all arrangement for Alan farewell and like previous two occasion he called Ruchi and her team for the event, but unlike previous two events this time he need to call Ruchi and her team by himself as Abhi is already gone and event is for Alan hence can't ask her to invite. So he asked Ruchi to join and also if she can allow her team to come. Everything went well and everybody as expected said good thing about Alan, Rayman only concentrating on Anna, Jay got the situation and hence asked Naina to arrange snacks and drinks for the event and left Rayman to sit there in the farewell event. Naina went to counter of cafeteria to order snacks and cold drinks for all while Anna is speaking on Alan.

"I have noticed this one thing that she always wears beautiful and matching earrings and she changes those earrings daily. She is a good friend and we will miss her." Rayman knows from inside that she just said last line to make everyone feel good, if she was asked to say from her heart, she would have never said those words.

Next Sunday morning 29 May 2011 Vicky and Rayman left together for Vishu's wedding. Rayman is meeting other after five months. He was not able to meet other due to work and Anna while Lokesh is meeting them after one year time. All friends enjoying each other's company a lot and then Vishu showed up for arranging their lunch.

"Hey Rayman, Vicky when did you guys came?" Vishu asked entering their room in hotel, where Rayman and Toni already laying on the floor in front of AC hardly two feet away from the AC and rest are laying on the bed.

"We have reached around half an hour ago" Vicky replied to Vishu and Rayman barely opened his eyes.

"How come Dulhe Raja (Groom) came here?" Rayman asked.

"Have you guys had lunch?"

"Except me and Rayman rest had lunch in the market, they came in the morning and explored whole Lucknow." Vicky responded.

"I send food for you guys but my college friends ate whole of it so now you guys need to go out and have lunch somewhere."

"Don't worry yaar, we will take care of that and we will never forget that you didn't even offer lunch to us on your wedding, now go and concentrate on your preparations." Rayman responded.

Vishu left and Rayman and Vicky forget about lunch rather spent whole afternoon lying on the floor. In the evening everyone including Vishu danced a lot with processing of Groom toward stage. In return journey everybody have to catch same train at around one thirty on next day early morning and hence everybody reached station around twelve thirty.

Next month passed without any major event in Rayman's life, Alan moved to Pune in some company as Anna amazingly predicted when Abhi left for Pune, Vicky started looking for jobs in Pune as he want to go to Alan, Toni and Tanu both are busy in work on some in-house project which is in lime light for few months, news for Anna team shifting to Noida office came at least three times just to upset Rayman and no shifting happened, Sky and Vivek became good friends, Shiksha, Sonia, Naina somehow got to know about Rayman and Anna, a new guy Rahul joined Rayman team in May end and Jay informed team that a new guy Upen is going to join the team in the end of July. One fine day Rayman called Jay in meeting room in the end of June.

"Sir, I need to share something." Rayman said to Jay looking very upset that day.

"What happened? I know you have lot of work these days but most the critical work nearly done and you and team doing great. Everyone in team performing quite well and I told you already about the new guy Upen and that will further decrease load on you."

"It is something else."

"Tell me then"

"I was not able to concentrate on work fully from last few weeks due to some personal problem."

"I noticed that but you are still doing well. I have no issue with your work."

"Thanks for understanding me."

"Tell me one thing if you consider me your friend."

"Sure sir whatever"

"Who is she?"

"Nobody"

"You know every child thinks that his parent doesn't know what is he up to but they forget that their parent had also experienced childhood."

"I said naah sir, nobody"

"OK, just tell me is she in our office, I can help you." help word made Rayman think about telling him everything as he is not seeing any other hope from anywhere else.

"Yes"

"Now I know who she is." Discussion comes to end with this Jay's comment and both left the room. Rayman knows that yes it is very easy to guess his love interest, first due to their changed behavior with each other second their strong friendship suddenly ended, third Rayman doesn't have any other female friend outside his team and Anna doesn't have any other male friend outside her team.

One day Rayman went to Anna's seat around two in the afternoon and asked her about how is she? And how is her work and all? As they are not communicating from two months now so Rayman thought of go and talk to her on her desk. But she didn't responded at all and ignored Rayman completely and this response upset Rayman a lot and on returning to his seat he couldn't control his emotions and tears come out of his eyes and at that very moment Sky noticed him and asked him about it through e-mail.

'Hi Rayman

I just noticed that you are crying, it might be and I hope it should be some illusion but I know it is not.

I know you have lot of work but don't be upset. You are inspiration to many including me. Please tell me what happened if you think that I am your friend'

Rayman responded on Sky mail.

'Hey Sky

Nothing in office, it is something personal.
I just can't control emotions for few second and you noticed at that moment only. Well, I am all right now, thanks'

Sky replied another mail asking for the reason followed by series of mail in form of conversation.

Sky - 'Is it love?'

Rayman - 'Yes'

Sky - 'Do I know her?'

Rayman - 'It is tricky and I don't want to share it with anyone'

Sky - 'Oh ho, I am not going to tell anyone, Is it Anna?'

Rayman - 'Yes, but how you noticed?'

Sky - 'From behavior of you both and how she reacts when you come to my desk. Have you told her about it?'

Rayman - 'Yes, I told her'

Sky - 'Then what she said?'

Rayman - 'She said No'

Sky - 'Why?'

Rayman - 'She has some personal and valid reasons'

Vishu returned Delhi with Raina after their honeymoon and Vicky and Rayman planning with Tanu, Toni and Lavanya to visit them as they reach Delhi. Vishu called and updated Rayman that they are reaching their home around five in the evening and so Rayman reached Vishu home around six in the evening.

"Hello bhabhiji (sister in law). How are you?" Rayman greeted Raina first.

"I am fine and you can call me by my name - Raina." Raina responded to Rayman greeting.

"Don't be so formal yaar. You can call her by name." Vishu also supported Raina.

"I will prefer bhabhiji."

"OK, as you wish" Raina responded. Raina and Vishu went inside to bring snacks and drink for Rayman and a little later Tanu, Toni, Vicky and Lavanya also joined them and they gossiped till nine or ten in the night. Rayman and Vicky left together while Toni, Tanu and Lavanya left together after that. Rayman directly went to sleep after reaching home but sweet voice of Anna broke his sleep sooner.

"Hi, where were you gone?"

"Hi, Oh I went to meet my best friend Vishu and his wife they just returned Delhi after their wedding, I want you to come with me someday to meet them."

"I would love to, how are you? You are not talking to me since last few days except in the morning and that too just for wishing me morning."

"I am all right"

"You seem very happy today."

"You see I visited Vishu today and I always feel better meeting him."

"Why"

"He is like brother to me"

"OK and how you feel after meeting me?"

"You can't imagine. I feel like I have achieved everything and there is just joy and satisfaction."

"Oh ho, I didn't know that you love me this much."

Conversation continued till late and same or related conversation happening each night in the dreams. One day in July month it is some celebration is going on in the company on women empowerment and that time Anu and Suchi suggested Rayman to bring chocolate for all girls in his and their team on this occasion and so Rayman and Vivek went to bring chocolate for everybody in both team. Vivek gave chocolate to everyone in both team but Anna refused to take chocolate and returned chocolate back to Rayman. Whole scene is quite dramatic when Anna refused and Rayman is about to throw chocolate in the dust bin but he stopped himself in between and gave that chocolate to Sky as he don't want to make Anna upset in any way.

Month passed in same way of friendships, fights, work and love. In the end of the month Upen joined the team, he is tall, little dark, handsome with slimmer body and perfect height of around six feet. Jay is not in office the day Upen is joining the team so Rayman introduced him to all members of his and Anna's team. When Rayman introduced Upen to Anna, she just said a very dry and rude Hi in response due to the fact that Rayman introduced him to her. Upen given seat on the left side of Anna's seat where Vivek is sitting now and Vivek shifted to other area outside this area. When Rayman introducing Upen to everyone he went to Ruchi seat, and Ruchi informed them that she is moving Europe for few months and now someone else will lead her team and which make Rayman worried as new manager might want team to move outside the area, will he or she allow the team to go with his team?

Love?

$\mathcal{R}$ayman came home in the evening around eight and to his surprise Vicky has already at home, and it is first time in three months and second thing which amazed him even more is that he has book in his hand and he is serious in study.

"What happened bro?"

"I want to change job."

"What happened? Is everything all right back in office?"

"Yes"

"Then what"

"I want to go to Pune."

"OK, you enjoy your study, I had dinner and going to sleep."

"OK, good night"

"Tell me one thing"

"Yes"

"Why she said no to me?"

"Please, not this time, and if possible then please forget that witch, she has done some spell on you, what you like in her? She doesn't even look well."

"She looks good to me and that is what matters to me."

"She is never going to say yes, and for god sake forget her now and please don't bug me with her now, let me study."

"OK, good night."

"She will never say yes to you and don't go after her, search some other good girl this time."

"Good night"

"One more thing I noticed that her nose is not straight."

"Good night"

"Alan told me that she doesn't have any other friends in office."

"Good night"

Around a week later in office Upen, Jay and Rayman are having a discussion in the meeting room.

"So how are you finding this place?" Jay asked Upen.

"It is quite early to comment anything on it."

"How do you find girls here?"

"Not too many girls and I am not kind of person who have eyes on team mates."

"I am not asking in that sense ok tell me how is Anna, she sits by your right side only."

"She is weird, we talked only few times and she asks everyday same question 'how much sugar in tea today?' and whatever I reply she takes tea. I don't know why she asks me if that is not going to change her decision?"

"Weird?" Jay asked in response.

"Why? Don't you guys find her weird?"

"She is my good friend and I don't find her weird but I have no issues with your opinion." This time Rayman responded to Upen.

"OK"

Later discussion turned toward work related thing and meeting continued for more than one hour. Later in the evening Rayman and Garv working together for some project, Garv fiddling with Rayman mobile while Rayman is doing something on his computer.

"Sir, Can I see pictures on your mobile?" Garv asked Rayman.

"Why not but be careful I have every type of media in my cell"

"Sure"

While exploring pictures on Rayman mobile Garv noticed something that Rayman might not want to share with him but those pictures make Garv ask this question.

"Sir, do you like Anna?"

"What, what make you ask this question in between the work?"

"Sir, it is only you who is working I am looking at the pictures on your cell phone."

"Shit, I forgot this" Rayman murmured and then said to Garv. "Why you think so?"

"You have hundreds of her pictures in your cell."

"Those pictures are from some function held in office."

"And you noticed only her in the festival."

"OK, I like her nothing else, she is just a good friend nothing else, now can we continue work?"

"Sure sir, but I think there is something more than just friendship."

"Whatever"

Garv is not a kid who can be tricked with these excuses and he understood the situation. Rayman on the other hand is not actually able to concentrate on work since Garv mentioned Anna and hence he went out to Ashok café to have tea and after one hour Rayman left for home and went directly to bed but sleep in nowhere near him. Vicky came around eleven in the night and he went to other room and started studying. Little later Vicky went in kitchen to have some water and he noticed that gas stove is on, He called Rayman to check.

"Rayman, have you cooked something?"

"No. Why"

"Stove in on"

"What"

"Have you cooked something in morning?"

"Yeah, Tea"

"By god, that girl is going to kill us both."

"Which girl you are talking about? Who is going to kill us?"

"I am talking about that mare, the love interest of yours. When will you forget her? Now she is a risk on our lives. It is too much now. You left gas stove on for whole day."

"It just happened by mistake. It is not intentional."

"You will kill us both by mistake one day, come out of the thought of that girl."

"Leave it yaar, nothing bad happened naah."

"What you want then, it is just god's grace that I noticed it."

"Now don't create scene and let me sleep."

"So you can dream about that witch."

Friday in office around eleven o'clock Shiksha is sitting at Rayman seat and having discussion on something when Anna came inside the cubicle from somewhere, and Rayman couldn't resist and followed her to her seat with his eyes.

"Isn't she looking too beautiful today?" Rayman murmured.

"What?" Shiksha heard something.

"Nothing, I was thinking about this issue only."

"Haven't you said something else?"

"I guess no"

"But I heard something else and one more thing Garv is good friend of mine too."

"So"

"Nothing, we discuss many things on breakfast table"

"I said naah I haven't said anything."

"OK"

Rayman and Shiksha have no further conversation on this topic. But Rayman knows now that Garv had told Shiksha about that night incident when Garv sneaked a peek of Anna pictures in his cell phone but there is no point of discussion on it.

Later in the evening Rayman is at Vishu home, Vishu and Raina are already at home when Rayman reached there and Raina opened door for him.

"Hello, bhabhiji"

"Hello Rayman, how are you?"

"Oh, I am good bhabhiji, how are you?"

"I am also good."

"And you bro?"

"I am good just relaxing yaar. Tell me what is the planning for weekend?"

"Nothing, I will just relax at home."

"Same here buddy."

"Bhabhiji what is your planning?"

"No plans. Where can I go alone without my dear husband? I am also at home. But why are you at home? Go somewhere; watch some movie with your girlfriend."

"I am not that lucky to have girlfriend."

"Why? Vishu told me that you are after some of your colleague. What happened with her?"

"Nothing bhabhiji, my bad luck"

"Why your bad luck, it's her good luck."

"Bhabhiji"

"What bhabhiji. Hey Vishu go make some tea for him and me. What are you doing on your laptop all the day?"

"Nothing yaar just checking emails. Hey Raina Why don't you make tea? or Give me five minutes"

"No leave this laptop now, he is here to meet you not me."

"OK, going" Vishu left laptop on the table and standup from bean bag to go inside to make tea at that very moment Raina grabbed his hand and stopped him.

"What now" Vishu asked her.

"Nothing you sit here, I was just asking so you leave you laptop, now you sit here with Rayman and I will make tea."

"In that case bring bhujia also."

"OK" Raina went inside after that and Vishu and Rayman are having conversation now.

"So what happened with that your colleague? You haven't updated me since months."

"Nothing"

"Oh speak up and share with me."

"Nothing yaar, she said no" Rayman is nearly in tears.

"Why"

"This is India buddy. And here just two hearts are not responsible for commitment in love. You need to take care of so many things."

"Caste issue"

"Yes caste is also an issue"

"What else"

"She is a Kashmiri"

"Oh ho, so she is a Kashmiri, must be very beautiful then. That is the reason you are not able to take her out of your mind."

"No, this is not the only reason for my love for her. Yes she is beautiful of course especially if you see her from my eyes. She appears most beautiful girl on earth to me but what is more important to me is her heart, she is so straight forward and transparent from her heart, she is extremely honest and innocent. You know you just need to see her eyes once and I assure you that you can't save yourself from falling in love with her. You need to look on the innocence on her face. She is so fair yaar what else can I say? Her smile can even give life to dead people and when she speaks…"

"Hey Rayman, do you want my husband to fall for her also?" Raina came in the hall at that very moment and cut Rayman's statement in between.

"No, not at all bhabhiji"

"Your voice is clearly audible in kitchen also and I heard everything." Raina handed over tea to Rayman and Vishu and took one cup for her and then offered bhujia to Rayman and Rayman passed bhujia to Vishu after taking some.

"No bhabhiji, it's not like that."

"Then, tell me also"

"Leave it bhabhiji. There is nothing to share about"

"As you wish, I just want to know what went wrong, what I want is just that you get married to someone so that I can also get a company."

"I am ready even today. It is just that she is not ready for it."

"Then why are you after her, look some other girl naah, tell me what kind of girl you want, I will see if can get someone suitable for you."

"Oh no bhabhiji, I just need her only."

"Yeah, he is crazy for her." Vishu is also pulling Rayman's leg now.

"As Vishu told me and from your description I don't think there is any of your chance with her."

"I have left everything on god these days."

After having tea and snacks Rayman is leaving for home, Vishu asked him if he can come for movie tomorrow and he confirmed for the movie and next evening these three with Vicky went for movie at GIP Noida. Vishu in return dropped Vicky and Rayman at their home and then went to his home.

September 16 2011 Friday, Vicky called Rayman in office to inform him about the plan Vicky made with Vishu and Raina to go on a trip to Massourie and asked him to come on the trip and also said that this might be his last trip in Delhi as he will be moving to Pune after fifteen days, Rayman also has nothing to do except wishing Anna on her birthday which is also on this weekend.

Next morning around five o'clock in the morning Vishu, Raina, Vicky and Rayman left for massourie in Vicky's car. Around eleven they crossed Dehradun and stopped on some road side restaurant to freshen up and at that time Rayman wished Anna her birthday with fear inside as he is not sure about

Anna response, but a little later a normal response came from Anna and he got a little relieved after the response.

One Friday evening Sky came to Rayman and asked him whether he is coming office on Saturday? Rayman responded that he has no work in office for Saturday and then Sky told him that Anna is coming on Saturday due to some work and He is also coming to give her company and asked Rayman if he can also come. It would be really an opportunity to have conversation with Anna. Next morning Rayman come office even earlier than normal days. Rayman is quite impatient now while waiting for Anna to come office. Sky also came around ten o'clock but Anna is nowhere.

"If you say I can check when she will be coming?" Sky said to Rayman.

"No, no need of it, she will doubt you."

"As you say" and Rayman and Sky went outside for tea at that moment.

Anna came around twelve o'clock and went to her seat, Rayman is at his seat at that time and singing some song (Ishq-Risk from the movie mere brother ki dulhan) under his breath. Anna started working as she reached at her seat.

"Why you came so late?" Sky asked her.

"Isn't it enough that I came on weekend, what else you expect? I have other stuffs to do. I cleaned house and then cooked for me then only I came office, not like you guys"

"OK ma'am, now concentrate on work."

No conversation between Anna and Sky until lunch time and then Rayman asked Sky what they would like for lunch and everybody agreed on having Pizza and When Pizza arrived Anna spoke first time to Rayman when she asked him to have Pizza and Pizza worked as ice breaker in between Anna and Rayman. Around two o'clock Anna is partially done with her work and she is little free and now she moved her attention from work to Sky and Rayman.

"When did you come?" Anna asked Sky.

"Around ten thirty, Rayman was already here by then"

"He doesn't seem to have any life outside this office." She doesn't realize what she said.

"I think you know that better than me." Sky has naughty smile on his face when he said those words.

"What! Shut up."

"Why shut up?"

Rayman came in their cubicle at that time and sat on Suchi's seat which is behind Anna's seat and joined the conversation, obviously topic is changed now.

"Rayman is that chain you wearing made of gold?" Anna asked Rayman with surprise.

"Yeah. Why?"

"Don't you have any fear if someone snatch it or may harm you in the process?"

"No, I remain alert and if somebody will try to take it from me I will rather handover it than fight with him and get my bones fractured. By the way you also wearing lot of gold, aren't you scared of snatching?"

"No, I take precautions. You chain design is good, heavy chains like goons."

Sky and Rayman laughed on her remark and at that moment Rayman's feet came in her eyesight.

"Your foot is so dirty"

"What" Rayman asked her with surprise and then she brought her foot forward and placed parallel to his foot.

"Look, can you see the difference?" Sky also placed his foot with Anna and Rayman feet and that make Anna comment further on Rayman foot.

"See, Sky's foot is better but your foot is really dirty."

"Hey, it is skin color, he is fairer than me and you are not even comparable to me, you are of snowy color." That comment of Rayman made Anna smile and after a little while all three went outside for tea at Ashok cafeteria.

By this time few people noticed that Rayman like Anna and few of them doesn't like this much but few decided to help Rayman. Other guys from both the teams also knew about whole situation but they are not discussing this with Rayman or Anna and reason for this is probably that Anna and Rayman are not even on talking terms. Shiksha, Sonia and Naina especially tried few times to take this topic with Rayman but Rayman ignored any possibility of such conversation.

One evening around eight o'clock in the office Jay, Anna and Rayman are only guys in the office and Jay and Anna is having chit chat on Anna seat while Rayman is working on his seat and in that conversation with Anna Jay asked her 'Is he is a good singer?' To this Anna responded that she never noticed his singing and then Jay said that she can decide at that time only that who can sing better in between Jay and Rayman and So Rayman and Jay both sung one by one.

"Kehna hai –kehna hai SSS, aaj tumse ye pehli baar.

Ho SSS tum hi to laaye ho jeevan main mere pyaar-pyaar-pyaar"

From the movie Padosan (Neighbor) and now Anna has to decide who is better between Rayman and Jay.

"I think you both sung well, while you sung very similar to original voice but Rayman has his own style and unique voice, so I think you both were great." Anna said to Jay after listening to both.

"No, No, You have to decide who was better in between us." Jay insisted a review from Anna.

"I think you both are good at singing." After that Jay asked her why is she staying so late in office and that too alone in the team to which she replied that she had some work but that work already got completed but she has to wait for office cab till nine. Jay asked Rayman "how has you came office?"

"I came by bike"

"Then you can drop her home."

"No sir, it is ok, I will go by cab" Anna refused to go, while Rayman on other hand want to drop her home but he also knows from inside that Anna will never like this and in between this dilemma he chose not to ask her to drop her.

"Sir, I have lot of pending work to complete before I leave, so I can't drop her."

Next morning around eleven in the office everyone from Rayman's team is in the meeting room having some conversation when Jay called Anna inside meeting room and once again troubled her asking about last night incidence and once again raised question about who is better in term of singing in between Rayman and him. Anna once again responded what she said last night and that response once again made Jay a little uncomfortable and he asked again to consider a review to her decision and made her wait in the meeting room just to answer that who is better and now even Anna is getting irritated with this question again and again. Anna knows from inside that this torture can be stop only when she says that Jay is better but she is not sure how Rayman is going to take it, he might relate it to the troubled friendship or love or whatever between them and in between Rayman also got hint how he can help Anna in resolution of this little issue.

"Anna, just say it to him that he is better than me and only then he is going to leave you."

"Yeah I guess so, OK sir, you sung better last night." Anna left after saying that but after that everyone able to notice that how little trouble to Anna made Rayman uncomfortable. Jay tried to pull his leg on this but Rayman turned discussion toward work and ignored his comment.

One day in last week of September around eleven o'clock Rayman got call from his mom.

"Hello, how are you? Are you all right?" Mom asked him.

"Yeah mummy, I am all good, what happened, why you called?"

"When did you called last time, it has been four months neither you came home nor you called us, what is going on there, I know you might be busy in work but what kind of work is it that you didn't even have time to call."

"No mummy it is not like that, I was too much busy in work." Rayman voice got heavier with that and his mom got to know that there is something wrong which he is not telling him.

"Baua (Rayman's nickname), is everything all right? Tell me what happened?"

"Yeah mom" Rayman controlled himself a little now.

"Are you crying?"

"No"

"Why don't you take few days leave and come home."

"No mom, I can't, I have too much work."

"OK, take care and come home and keep calling. At least call us once in a week."

"Hmm, sure"

Later in the day Rayman got call from his sister and she also shows concern for the same thing.

"What has happened Baua? Mummy called me and told me that you are crying while talking to mummy, what happened, tell me now?"

Rayman first tried to give her false excuses but finally he has to tell her everything.

"There is this girl in my office, she isn't in my team but I love her and she just said no when I proposed her."

"Is she sits near you?"

"Yes, she sits in my cubicle and we meet daily"

"Why she said no?"

"She is from very higher caste, she is Kashmiri Brahmin."

"Haven't you noticed it before?"

"I couldn't control my emotions for her even after knowing it."

"She sits with you naah. Give her some time if she is in your destiny she will come to you, be strong and if she isn't in your destiny even then what is the point of crying? You have to understand, it is not possible any way."

"I will try"

First Monday of October 2011 it was Rayman birthday on weekend and he waited whole day for wishes from Anna, everyone called or messaged him except Anna, Rayman knows from inside that she is not going to call him but some part of his inclination continuously telling him that she will call him at some point of time but his all hope faded as with passing time. Naina, Sonia and Shiksha arranged cake for Rayman birthday on Monday in the office and by now everyone in team got to know what is cooking between Rayman and Anna and hence Naina called everyone from Anna's team. Everyone comes to cafeteria except Anna and Rayman still waiting for her to come before cutting cake she came around fifteen minutes later and as she entered cafeteria she ask for apologies from Naina. Rayman cut cake and everyone put cake on Rayman's face. Anna initially hesitated a little but later put a lot of cake on Rayman face and that is best gift of birthday for Rayman. Anna still not wished him birthday.

October 9 2011, Vicky and Rayman are standing on a platform on Delhi railway station. Rayman has come to drop Vicky for train to Pune. Vicky is joining new company in Pune on coming Monday, Vicky and Rayman both got very emotional at parting time. Rayman got alone after that, most of his friends already left team, first Jiten then Samarth followed by Alan and Abhi and now his roomie Vicky also leaving him and this made him even more emotional.

One morning in next week in office Rayman, Vivek, Sky and Anna at Anna seat having morning tea and Anna is asking about contact details of some mover and packer service who can help her to shift her home from her old place to new place at Dwarka.

"Hey Vivek, do you have any contact of anyone who can shift my goods."

"Yeah, I need to check, I will message you in the evening. When are you shifting?"

"On weekend" at this moment Jay also joined conversation and asked Anna.

"What happened? Where are you shifting?"

"Dwarka"

"Why are you shifting so far from office, you are living near to office then what is the need to shift so far?"

"Some personal reasons"

"OK, I also lives near that place, it is really good place by the way. How are you shifting?"

"Don't know at this time, I am looking for some transport guy."

"Do you live alone here?"

"Yes"

"Aren't you scared of living alone? I am also living alone and I have to keep light switched on whole night otherwise I could not sleep." Rayman asked Anna after hearing their conversation.

"What is to fear in it? I just take sheet over my head and sleep. But as far I know you live with Vicky naah, the guy who is dating Alan."

"Yeah I use too but he is shifted to Pune now."

"What! Hasn't Alan also gone to Pune?"

"Yeah"

"Has he gone due to Alan?"

"Off course"

"I can't believe that even these days everyone is becoming Romeo. Oh god"

"What is big deal in it? By the way don't you fear from ghost?"

"Ghost, there is no such thing."

"There is. When someone dies with any of his desire unfulfilled he becomes ghost." Vivek responded to Anna's comment.

"Then I will surely become ghost one day." Rayman commented and Anna smiled on this comment.

"What kind of guy you will marry?" Jay suddenly changed the topic of discussion and asked Anna.

"What! Why are you asking this?"

"I too got a daughter and I want to know a girl's opinion."

"Good looking and well settled."

"What you mean by well settled? Money, home and car"

"Off course, don't you want same for your daughter?" Anna is talking realistic. "And I am not demanding BMW or Mercedes but any normal car will do"

"I will look for a genuine guy and that will be enough for me."

Conversation continued a little more and then Rayman and Jay moved back to their seats.

Once again news for Anna team shifting to Noida office is in lime light and this time everyone is saying that shifting is sure and they will be shifting on coming Monday on October 17.

With passing time Rayman is going crazier for Anna, he is dreaming her whole night and this doesn't seem to stop in near future for him. On the other hand in real life rift between Anna and Rayman growing day by day and news is spreading between both the teams, everyone from both the team know everything about this story and everyone is trying from their side to help Rayman but at the same time people also listening Anna's point of view. Sky tried convincing Anna directly since he has become very good friend of Anna but Anna is not listening anything on this topic while Anu and Suchi trying to convince Rayman to forget her but Rayman is also not listening anything. Both Rayman and Anna are rigid to their point and they don't want to listen or understand anything.

Distances
(Dooriyan bhi hain jaroori)

*R*ayman notices that Anna is not on her seat when he reaches office on Monday morning. Rayman is thinking that either she is not coming or she might be adjusting her makeup in washroom. Few moments later she entered cubicle and has a different hair style, her original hair had curls like Julia Roberts had in pretty women and now she has done a little change in curls like drew Barrymore had in Lucky you. She has broad smile on her face, everyone is surprised after seeing her new look, everyone is commenting on her new hair styling. Sky made some comment saying 'it is not looking good and previous one was better', and at that moment Rayman stood from his seat to have a look on her hairdo, Rayman is able to read the question from her eyes "What you think, is Sky right?".

"Earlier one is great and this is even better." Rayman commented on her new hair style and in response she thanked him with a smile on her pretty lips.

On Wednesday Sky, Vivek, Rayman and Garv planned to have tattoo and left for Lajpat Nagar market to get tattoo done. They visited few parlors and then decided to get tattoo done in one parlor and Sky and Vivek got same OM symbol on their hands while Rayman tattooed letter '**A**' on right arm for Anna. Next day Sky shows his tattoo to Anna and told her about Rayman's 'A' tattoo and told her that this 'A' stand for Anna.

"That would be for some Anarkali not for Anna." She responded on Sky's remark.

One day Rayman cell is ringing on his seat and he is not at his seat so cell rang for some time and that too with old fashioned tring-tring ringtone.

"Whose cell is this, how irritating is this ringtone." Anna asked to Sky who is looking toward Rayman seat.

"It is coming from your Rayman's cell"

"Shut-up"

"Why shut-up"

"Ask him to change this irritating ringtone."

"Why don't you ask him, he can even change his cell, by the way his last ringtone was good."

"That irritating devotional song" Rayman came inside and received the call to end their conversation.

One day in first week of October around twelve thirty in afternoon Sky is going onsite to some country in middle eastern region in few days and he asked Rayman to tell him something about his trip as Rayman already went to same site earlier, Sky and Anna are having conversation on something at their seat when Rayman reached their seat having a cup of tea in his one hand.

"Why aren't you saying yes to him?" Sky is talking about Rayman to Anna.

"It is between me and him, you wouldn't understand."

"Try me"

"He is not that smart yaar"

"What kind of guy you like?" by that time Rayman reached their seat and standing with support from Sky desk.

"Like John Abraham" Anna responded to Sky question and hinted with eyes to Sky that don't disclose conversation topic to Rayman as it might hurt him.

"Oh ho John Abraham, and what do you think of yourself, Bipasha Basu?"

"No. I am better than her."

"Really, OK than tell me what you like in John Abraham?"

"His height and muscles, Isn't he sexy?"

"Yeah" This time Rayman replied to take Anna side and that make Anna look at Rayman in strange manner, she somehow never wanted Rayman to take her side, or in public at least and especially when she thinks she can handle the matter by herself.

October 14 2011 Friday, It is Rayman sister birthday and around eleven o'clock he called his sister to wish her birthday.

"Hello. Happy birthday"

"Thanks. How are you?"

"I am good, what is your planning for today?"

"Nothing, are you coming home?"

"Naah"

"So what is going between you and that girl? Any progress"

"Naah, but a bad news in this event, she is moving to other office on Monday."

"But I think it is better. It will help you forget her."

"God knows only, where is Brother and how is he? How is bhabhi and mom?"

"Everyone is great, Brother has gone to school"

"Where is he teaching?"

"Same school, we teachers are not like you guys who changes job every other year"

"But I am in same company for last five years"

"Hmm, my brother is exception"

"OK, bye for now, take care, I will call you later and then talk to mom as well."

"Bye, you too take care and forget that girl I will search someone better than her."

"Impossible"

"In that case you will surely get her"

Rayman hanged that call and sunk in the thought and came back to reality when Naina told him that Anna and Anu team is shifting to Noida office possibly on Monday and they should do something today and Rayman went to Anu and Anna seat and asked them.

"Is your team's transfer news confirmed?" Rayman asked Anna.

"Yes, we are going on Monday, you guys should give us farewell." Anu replied to Rayman.

"Nice idea, let's go out for lunch, we guys will give you treat." Rayman asked his team mates to go out for lunch with Anna's team before they move to new location and everyone from his team supported this idea.

Around quarter to one everyone started moving for a restaurant in neighborhood named Khidmat. Anna with other girls from her team gone with Rahul and Rayman and other followed them. Jay and his friends have not come for the party due to some meeting back in the office and no one in the party is really caring for their presence. Group is divided in two sections one is ordering only vegetarian food while other interested in non-vegetarian food, Rayman is in non-vegetarian section and Anna even being non-vegetarian chose vegetarian section but during lunch when everyone is half done Anna asked Rayman if she can take non-veg from his plate and Rayman nodded his head in yes. Rayman has his eyes on Anna all the time and everyone else there are able to notice this time but no one from Anna or Rayman seems to be concerned this time as Anna is in Delhi office for one more day only. In return Upen given ride to Rayman till office on his bike while Rahul somehow managed all the girls from both the teams Anna, Anu, Suchi from Anna team and Shiksha, Naina and Sonia from Rayman team in his car. Everyone reached office around three o'clock, Rayman met jay at the entrance and Jay is seems unhappy with this party event but Rayman told him that Anna moving on Monday morning to Noida office and it might be last party with her and Rayman's comment make Jay understand the situation and he cooled down but Jay said to Rayman that he should always inform him about his moves in advance so that he can manage situation back in office.

Around six in the evening Upen, Rahul, Sonia, Shiksha and Naina are enjoying their tea and bread pakoras at Ashoka café. Naina and Shiksha are the first to take this topic up for conversation.

"Upen sir, you must be aware about it." Naina asked.

"What?" Upen also asked a question in response.

"Rayman doesn't appear in good shape these days. He seems very upset, is it due to other team going to Noida? Some time I feel like he likes Anna but I am not sure, I have seen him staring at her few times."

"I have also observed it." Shiksha also said same thing.

"Rahul, do you have any clue?" Sonia is next to throw question on Rahul.

"I have no clue on it, he might have told something to Upen only. Upen sir, has he said something to you?"

"Yes, he told me many things but I can't share anything with you guys, he is a friend and he has faith in me, I don't want to break that trust."

"We are just concerned for him."

"I understand it very well but I am confused yaar"

"What is confusion in this? Just tell us what he told you."

"OK, I can tell only that he is upset due to that team transfer nothing else."

"We will find the rest." Sonia and Shiksha responded like some detective and at that very moment Rayman also came outside to join this tea party and they change the topic of conversation. Rayman went back inside after finishing his tea and left other to enjoy the bread pakoras and continue their previous conversation. Shiksha started conversation with an incidence her one friend shared with her other day.

"You guys know my friend Pooja from other group?"

"Yes" Sonia replied.

"She was telling me about one incidence she observed at cafeteria over lunch one day"

"What?" Naina and Sonia asked.

"One day Rayman with our team having lunch at one table and Anna with her team at other table and Rayman adjusted his chair at least three four times just to sneak a peek of Anna. Whenever someone comes in between his line of vision, he adjusts his chair to see Anna."

"Hmm, you know I have to discuss many things with him during day and sometime I was discussing something with him and if Anna pass from alley at the same time, Rayman forget everything in that duration. He doesn't even speak a work in that duration." Naina shared her observation.

"I have also observed this. He just stops in middle of conversation when she comes in his sight." Sonia is next to complete the puzzle.

"I am not sure but he is probably upset due to Anna's transfer and I can understand this I have also gone through this kind of experience." Naina is concerned for Rayman.

"But we can't do anything." Girls said in one voice.

"Forget it. He will be all right in few days. You guys are over reacting." Upen and Rahul are unmoved by all this drama created by girls and it is visible in this Upen statement.

On the other hand Rayman is busy in his work and in between trying to spend as much as possible time with Suchi and Anu and trying to have little conversation with Anna as well.

"Anu, how are you feeling going to new office from Monday." Rayman asked to Anu.

"If you ask me, I really don't want to go new office, I am much comfortable here."

"Why? What is the problem in new office? That office is better than this office. I have friends there and they told me that office is better. Suchi what is your take on transfer?"

"It makes no difference for me, I am equally happy for both places, new place will give chance to make new friends."

"Why? Aren't old friend good enough?"

"You want me to tell the truth." She paused after that taunt and then further said after few moments "It's not like that, we will miss you all for sure."

"OK, good to know that. I think distance of new office will not be any issue for you and Anu."

"Yup"

"But Anna will have to travel double the distance." This is at least five months since he said something about her in public, Anna is busy doing some work on her system, she is able to hear this comment but she is unmoved.

"No idea" Suchi commented and Anna responded after that.

"I don't want to go, I am happy here, distance is a factor but I also like this office. I am already wasting around three hours a day in travelling and now I don't know how many more hours will be wasted every day."

"They will provide you cab to your home. They are already providing cab on few routes and I think they should provide cab to you also as your home is really very far from Noida office."

"I already talked to admin guy Anand and he said that cab can't be provided, I have to commute via Metro." Anna and Rayman talking like this in months and now Anna will be going to different office in one day.

"Oh God, is there any direct Metro or you have to change?"

"Direct Metro from office to my home and you don't worry about it this much, I can manage yaar." And this is one of the best qualities of Anna that even after rift between them whenever there is a chance of conversation she is always normal with Rayman.

Around six thirty in the evening everybody is leaving from the office and everyone from Anna team is bidding good bye to everyone on the floor including Rayman's team members. They are bidding good bye to person who are not going with them or discussing how it is going to be in new office with guys who is going with them. Suchi and Anu came in Rayman cubicle to have last words with Rayman, Shiksha and Sonia. Anna is just behind them but she doesn't enter the cubicle rather stayed just outside cubicle and talking to Shiksha and Sonia from there only. Rayman knows from inside that Anna will come to his seat and he has to go there before she leaves area. Rayman went near Anna in between those thought and wished her good bye with shaking hand with her. Rayman got to know from Anu that they will be coming to office Monday morning and then office bus will take them from this office to Noida office around ten o'clock. Weekend went in dilemma for Rayman, he was thinking about Anna whole the time and never able to get the answer of the question which is continuously running in his mind. "How am I going to live when she is nowhere near me? What will I do without her? How am I going to control my emotions on Monday? How am I going to remain in touch with her? Will she remain in contact with me or not? At least I am spending nine hours daily with her in the office and now even that is snatched from me. This is not right, where is justice in it? I will die without you Anna. Please stay with me. Please."

15 October 2011 Saturday around nine in the evening Rayman is at Vishu home and Vishu and Raina having discussion with Rayman about office work and personal life.

"Why aren't you marrying? I will also get company for gossiping." Raina asked Rayman.

"I am ready from ages but she is not saying yes."

"Rayman please leave her yaar and stop harassing that poor girl. By the way how does she look? I haven't even seen her picture, Vicky told me last time that her behavior is abnormal, is it so? I am sure you must be having her picture in your cell phone." As Raina expected Rayman does have her picture on his cell.

"I don't know if she is abnormal, she appear normal or even you can say best girl I have ever met."

"Hmm, Hmm" Raina mimicked Rayman. "Why will she appear abnormal to you?" Raina looks at Anna picture and further continued. "She isn't bad. By the way how is she?"

"She is fine, what will happen to her, she is just giving pain to me and enjoying. Well she is being transferred to Noida office with her team."

"And you?"

"No"

"Why? What will happen to your love story?"

"Who cares about me?"

"I think" Raina made face like she is in deep thought and Rayman looking at her face very carefully while Vishu enjoying this whole conversation between his friend and wife and then Raina continued "She must be happy about thinking of transfer at least she will not be irritated there by you now."

"Bhabhi, are you at my side or her? By the way she wasn't appearing happy yesterday?"

"What is the twist in tale now? Has she started liking you?"

"No, nothing like that, it is just that Noida office too much far from her home."

"OK, I see, you should gift her car."

"She just needs to ask once."

"Hey Romeo, stop it now, why aren't you understanding yaar. What you want, why you irritating that girl, I think she must have asked for this transfer. I wish she just ask once me for help her and I swear I will break your neck. Stop yaar please otherwise she will report in police against you very soon." Vishu also joined conversation now.

"Vishu stop yaar, he is already disturbed due to her transfer and you are adding up in his problems. Why don't you help him? Why not kidnap that girl?" Raina scolded Vishu but she surely pulling Rayman's leg in this.

"Bhabhi please drop this idea."

"And what do you thinking of me, I am not some gangster, I will never kidnap anybody. If you take my opinion, you should forget her, this will be good for you and her and me and my wife as well or else every time you will bore us with this story." Vishu is feeling hungry now and asked Raina and Rayman to start dinner and this conversation continued after dinner too, later Vishu bring playing cards from other room and they played till early morning. Rayman stayed at Vishu home for rest of night.

Rest of Sunday went without any event except in the evening Rayman thought about a plan and called Vivek around eight thirty in night keeping in mind that Vivek can give him a hand of help in his plan.

"Hello, is it Vivek?" Rayman confirmed after calling him.

"Hello, yes Vivek. Who is it?"

"Rayman"

"Oh hi Rayman, what is it? Where did you get my number?"

"From Sky, yaar I need some information."

"Yeah, tell me"

"I need to board Dwarka bus tomorrow. Can you help me finding the stop?"

"Have you shifted to Dwarka?"

"Nope, I am at friends place."

"OK, yaar I really don't know about it but I can give you my friends contact number he can help you, he is actually coming from Dwarka in office bus."

"OK, that will do."

"Hey, why didn't you ask Anna? I think she is your friend and she also comes in Dwarka bus."

"No, give me your friend's number."

"Why? What happened?"

"Something personal, leave it for now. Please."

"OK"

Rayman called Vivek's friend to get details of Dwarka stop for boarding office bus in the morning. He provided him location of a bus stop in sector ten of Dwarka. 17 October 2011 Monday: Rayman wakes up around five in the early morning and got ready for office. It is quite early to leave for office but Rayman left around six thirty in search of auto rickshaw for Dwarka and reached Dwarka sector ten around seven forty but it is just his plain bad luck that he is standing on wrong one of the two bus stops of Dwarka sector ten. Around seven fifty he called Vivek's friend once again to confirm about bus location and got to know that bus already reached at sector ten bus stop and he is not able to see Rayman at bus stop, Rayman responded that he is at sector ten bus stop only and he hasn't also seen the bus. Then he told him that he might be on other bus stop and asked him to come toward airport road bus stop and from there he can catch bus if he can reach there in five minutes as bus is standing at signal. Rayman reached at suggested bus stop somehow and now waiting for bus. Rayman noticed office bus with office logo on it and nearly came in front of the bus to signal to stop the bus. Bus came to halt with screeching breaks and Rayman boarded bus after roaming from one stop to another in Dwarka for last fifteen minutes and driver stared Rayman with the look of rage but Rayman is unnoticed about that and the reason for this behavior is person sitting on the seat in front of the entry gate, yes it is Anna.

It is a seat capable to hold three people but she is sitting in one corner and her hand bag occupying the rest of the seat. Rayman forgets about everything on seeing her and hit his head at something above the seats. Rayman sat on seat near the entry gate by the side of Anna's seat. When Rayman is sitting on the seat Anna looked at him from corner of the eyes and acted like she hasn't seen him and ignored him completely. Rayman is looking at Anna from corner of his eyes and Anna is also looking at Rayman in the same way. Rayman could not notice when office arrived. Around nine o'clock at breakfast table in the cafeteria Rayman is having breakfast with team members from both the team including Suchi, Anu, Vivek, Shiksha, Sonia and Rahul leaving Naina and Anna and Upen usually comes a little late around ten after breakfast time since he usually doesn't eat breakfast in office cafeteria. Everyone on the table is talking to Anu and Suchi about their feelings on transfer to new location and Rayman has eyes on entrance for Anna. On the other hand in the work station area Anna and Naina are sitting on their seats and Anna asked Naina.

"Hey Naina, will you tell me this one thing?"

"Yes, what is it?"

"Has Rayman shifted to Dwarka, have you heard anything like this."

"I have no idea, not heard anything like this."

"Why?"

"I have seen him there today actually he came in my bus."

"If you don't mind can I ask you one thing?"

"Yes"

"Is there anything between you and Rayman?"

"Why?"

"Just like that"

"No, there is no such thing, it is just him I don't know why is he behind me. He is now irritating me."

"What do you mean?" after that Anna started telling Naina everything under her breath.

"Nothing yaar, we were just friends and one day out of blue he proposed me, I tried many times to make him understand that it is not possible for me. But he does not understand anything."

"Tell me in detail."

"There is nothing to share, he proposed me, and I said no to him many times. He often stares me in office like that can change my mind. I said so many times that we can either stay only friends or no connection at all but he does not understand anything, and continuing his foolishness."

"So you must be happy now by this transfer."

"Yes, you can say this. I am worried about the distance only, but for sure I am relieved from him now. I am just worried about is he shifted to Dwarka?"

"I don't think so, otherwise he must have told us about it."

"I wish"

"By the way, why aren't you accepting his proposal?"

"Personal reasons and what he thinks of himself John Abraham, Why should I say yes?"

"Hmm, everyone has his own wish and one should respect it, no one can force for it."

"He has girlfriend in past, how can he love someone again?"

"I can't say anything on it. Do you want to come for breakfast?"

"Yeah, let's go. Last breakfast God save me from that freak."

Anna and Naina joined everyone else at breakfast table, Anna greeted everyone except Rayman and everyone return same response including Rayman. Everyone had breakfast in between discussion.

"When is your bus coming to pick you?" Rayman asked to Anu while looking at Anna from corner at his eyes.

"Admin guys are saying that bus will come around ten o'clock."

"It's nine fifty, we need to hurry now." Anna said in between.

"How will you be managing from Dwarka, have you talked to Admin about it?"

"I can manage. There is Metro directly from Dwarka to Noida and from there office will take us to office. It will be little hectic but I think I can manage. By the way Dwarka is growing these days, I am seeing lots of guys roaming in Dwarka these days." As she made last comment about roaming guys in Dwarka she is looking at Rayman will naughty smile on her lips. Rayman knows that last comment is for him but he didn't respond at all.

Bus reached office at given time of ten o'clock and people started moving out of the office, few other teams from other groups also moving to Noida office with Anna's team. Rayman, Vivek and few other members from his team are already standing at the office gate with Jay and her friend. Anu came out very first and everyone including Vivek and Rayman wished her good luck for transfer to new office and then came Suchi followed by members from other teams and then came Anna with the guys from other teams but she stayed at the gate near Vivek and Rayman. All the other guys standing with Rayman moved toward bus to bid them farewell.

"All the best and keep mailing us" Vivek said to Anna, Rayman is still in shock and could not utter a single word out of his mouth. He was standing like a statue.

"Sure" Anna responded to Vivek while Rayman is still standing in shock. Anna is now moving out of the gate and suddenly she turned back and said one line of a song to Vivek and Rayman from the movie "Break Ke baad"

"Dooriyan bhi hai jaroori, Jarrori hain ye dooriya (Distances are also necessary.)" and then moved toward the bus.

Everyone is settled in the bus. Jay, Vivek and others bid good bye one final time inside the bus and get off the bus and then they joined Rayman at the gate of office. He is still standing in the same pose. Bus started moving around ten thirty and goes out of the vision of Rayman.

Food festival

$\mathcal{R}$ayman came inside with dropped shoulders. On reaching he noticed Naina, Shiksha and Sonia are sitting in his cubicle near Naina's seat and colloguing about the discussion happened between Naina and Anna. Upen and Rahul are also standing near them, Rahul informed Naina that Rayman is coming and that make them quiet. Rayman went to his seat and sat there with both of his closed and then drunk water. He is trying to hide his all emotions and at that moment he heard something from the discussion between Shiksha and Naina.

"Now four places are vacant in this cubicle, I want to come in this cubicle." Shiksha said to Naina.

"Well I am taking Anu seat and you guys choose from other vacant seats." Naina responded.

"I too wanted that seat but after now I will take Suchi's seat." Shiksha responded on Naina's comment.

"I will take your seat" Sonia also want to come in that cubicle and for the simple reason, this cubicle is quiet compared to outer one.

"I also want to come in that cubicle." Rayman cut in between.

"Where" and Rayman sunk into his thoughts after hearing this question from Naina.

"Rayman" Upen asked again.

"Yeah, yeah I want to come to this seat." Rayman pointed toward Anna's seat.

"But that table is very rough." Naina commented.

"No issue I will manage."

"Why don't you bring your table here and I guess your system's display is better, are you bringing that here?"

"No, I want everything to remain as it is on this desk."

"In that case I will be going to your seat. You know one senior guy in each cubicle should be good for team. What you say?" Upen asked to Rayman.

"OK, I agree with you."

Later in the day everyone moved to their new seat after confirming with Jay. Now Upen moved at Rayman's seat and sitting with Garv, Rahul and few other guys from the team and Rayman is sitting on Anna seat and Naina is sitting in a corner in the row behind him, Shiksha is sitting on other corner, a new guy in the team Sahil is sitting in between Naina and Shiksha, Sonia is sitting on right side of Rayman and a new girl to team Pooja is sitting on left side of Rayman. Naina asked Rayman one question under her breathe but that question took everyone's attention toward this conversation only.

"Rayman, may I ask one question?"

"Yes, what is it?"

"Do you love Anna?" this question shocked Rayman.

"What! Why are you asking this?"

"Tell me naah, do you love Anna?"

"Who have told you?"

"First tell me than I will tell you everything, do you love Anna or not?"

"Yes I do, but who told you?" By now even Shiksha and Sonia are also looking at both of them.

"Anna"

"What!"

"Yes, in the morning when you guys were gone for breakfast. She told me everything about it and also that you came in her bus today."

"Why she told you about it now? Well it doesn't matter now as she has gone from here."

"What now?"

"Nothing, she anyways will never say yes."

"How are you so sure? You might not have tried your best."

"You tell me than what should have I done?"

"How can I tell you? Tell me whole story first than maybe I can help."

"Yes tell us, maybe we can help." Sonia and Shiksha also joined them in conversation. Rahul and Upen is not participating actively but they are listening whole conversation.

"You also know about it." Rayman asked Sonia and Shiksha.

"Yes, who can't guess from the way you look or rather stare at her?"

After that Rayman narrated whole story to all of them and asked for promise from all of them that this story should remain in between those guys of his team only. After listening story Naina and Shiksha suggested that Rayman should leave her for some time alone to give her a little room to make her realize his absence.

And days passed without any news from Anna's side to Rayman but she is in constant touch with Shiksha and other girls. Rayman tried few time contacting her through mails but she never responded. It is expected since she told Naina a day before going to Noida office how much relieved she will be feeling after moving away from Rayman.

In Rayman's old group, Vicky is not in touch with any one since he shifted to Pune. Tanu recently updated everyone that she is looking for change in job. Toni as usual busy in work or functions of his cousins. Lavanya is shifting to Australia in few months possibly in end of December. Vishu and Raina are learning about marriage life. One evening Vishu called Rayman and invited him to his home for evening snacks and asked him to bring bread pakoras from Ashoka stall from his office, and also asked him to call Tanu also. Rayman called Tanu when he left office and updated her with the plan and she is also joining them in the snacks party. Rayman reached around seven thirty and by the time no one reached home. Rayman called Vishu and asked 'when is he coming' to which he replied that 'he will reach in twenty minutes and Raina is already reached and on the stairs.' Rayman called Tanu and she informed that she will be reaching in twenty minutes too and as Rayman hung the call Raina already reached and unlocking the door to let him enter the home. Few minutes later Raina and Rayman are sitting in the room.
"So how is life going?" Raina asked Rayman.
"Fine, just missing Vicky otherwise everything else is fine."
"Work"
"Work is also good. By the way I called Vishu he will be reaching in twenty minutes and Tanu also said twenty minutes."
"I knew about Vishu, when are you marrying?"
"No idea"
"Marry soon. I will get one company for outing and shopping."

"I told you that I am ready but she is not ready."

"But you said that she can't then why don't move on?"

"It is not that easy bhabhiji."

"That I understand, but you are stuck try to forget her."

"I tried but she is not going out of my mind for even a second. Why don't we talk something else?"

"Why? This is also important issue and we should discuss it. You must be known about Vishu's girlfriend."

"Yeah"

"He told me everything and also that he tried from his side but later when he has committed for marriage he forgot everything with time and I know he might not be able to forget her in one day, but he forgot everything with time and one thing I can say for sure that we are happy now." At that moment Vishu and Tanu entered home together.

"Where you got her?" Raina asked Vishu.

"She is coming in Rickshaw when my cab dropped me out of our block's gate."

"Don't make excuses now? I know now where you are going after office, hmm" Raina pulled Vishu leg.

"Raina" Tanu commented on her remark.

"Just kidding yaar"

"So bro, has she shifted?" Vishu asked Rayman.

"Who is she?" Tanu asked Vishu.

"Haven't you told her about it?" Vishu asked Rayman.

"What is this whole story?" Tanu further asked them.

"Nothing, I must have told you about Anna, she and her team transferred to Noida office."

"Yeah, I knew about Anna, when was she shifted to my office? I haven't seen her, tell me how she looks like?"

"She is in a team of four members. Three girls and a guy, in that team you can notice her very easily, she is extremely fair, about my height, not thin and not fat just perfect, very much beautiful, long black hairs and a little stylish curl and what else, Oh yeah one more thing she wears glasses usually with black frame and gold ear rings, two gold rings in right hand, usually keep medium length nails around 2 mm and most of the time nail paint is partially removed from nails."

"I am not some painting artist Rayman. By the way don't you have any of her pictures?"

"Yes I do."

"Then show me"

Raina came with bread pakoras in a plate and Vishu brought tea for them while Rayman is showing Anna's pictures to Tanu on his cell phone.

"I have met her, she is in Sky team."

"How do you know Sky?"

"I met Sky for annual party events preparation, we were preparing together for our performances."

"OK"

"Yeah, and she is weird."

"What you mean weird?"

"We were having breakfast in cafeteria and then Sky and his team joined us. She was seated all the time without any expression, no smile, and no hi or hello, there were three other girls they greeted us but she said nothing."

"So what she doesn't knows you that is the reason for her silence."

"It's all bullshit"

"Leave this nonsense yaar, let's enjoy tea and bread pakoras" Rayman avoided further discussion on Anna, so they are discussing other things like work at office, Tanu's desire to change her job etc. After around two and half hours discussion Rayman is dropping Tanu at her PG and on the way to his home.

"What do you feel? Has Vishu done right to Diya?" Tanu asked to Rayman.

"I don't know everything and can't say anything but I know one thing that he tried everything with Diya and when nothing worked he is giving his hundred percent in this relationship."

"What about Diya?"

"She is good friend and will always remain, and I am really upset for what happened between them. I only know that she didn't let her parent down and so Vishu, they both done great thing and I respect them for it. I don't even know whether their parent or anybody else will care about it but they will always remain above all for me."

"She doesn't talk to me anymore."

"Why?"

"Not sure about it."

"OK, We reached your PG, let's talk about it sometime else. Bye."

"Rayman" Tanu paused after calling him.

"What"

"I want to share something with you but don't ask any questions in between."

"What is it?"

"You know I am going through tough phase of my life these days"

"Not exactly"

"Hmm. It is because I kept it secret all the time."

"So what is it, tell me."

"I had a boy in my life, don't ask who?"

"What you mean by you had?"

"We have to break up, his family is not agreeing."

"Go on"

"You know we both tried and tried our best"

"I have no doubt about that"

"I am hopeless only God can do anything now, well I am trying to forget him and to move on in life but you can understand that it is not that easy."

"Agree"

"Now here is one twist in the tail. When I am trying to move on in the meantime one of our friend"

"You mean friend of your and that boy's"

"Yes and don't ask anything further, please listen quietly"

"Sure, I will keep my mouth shut now"

"That guy is really good friend of mine and I know him for more than five years now, one day he said to me that he likes me. How can a friend who even knows my past can say this to me, I have never seen him that way"

"So what"

"What you mean, it doesn't work this way, suppose even if I accept his proposal, he will always remind me my past."

"You will forget everything with time and if he loves you even after knowing about your past, I think it will be best if you accept his proposal."

"I don't think so; friendship and love are two different things and should be treated like that."

"You are not giving him fare chance"

"I don't want to create trouble in his and my life in future, and you know what is worse we aren't not even good friends now"

"Do I know him?"

"I said to you in beginning don't ask anything"

"OK, I will suggest that you should listen to your heart"

And after that Rayman left for his home and after reaching he went directly to sleep.

"How are you?" It is around two o'clock one sweet female voice broke his sleep.

"Anna! Where were you? I was looking for you everywhere."

"I am with you always but you didn't reply my question 'how are you?'"

"I am very much fine now after seeing you. How are you?"

"I am also good. Where were you?"

"Oh, I was at Vishu home, we were having tea and bread pakoras at his place."

"Why haven't you called me?"

"Ha! I forgot to call you and you are saying like you would have joined us if I called you."

"It was secondary but first you should have called me."

"OK, I swear I will always call you in everything. OK?"

"Hmm, good, now tell me why you love me or first tell me what love is?"

"I love you because I love you there is no reason behind it. And love is something that I can't describe or rather I don't know."

"Try at least or tell me what you think about it."

"Love is when two people find themselves compatible to each other in all means and I said compatible not equal."

"But I think friendship is also the same thing."

"May be but I think friendship is when two people need not be compatible to each other but still they understand and support each other and both try to be compatible to each other."

"Don't get it."

"OK, what people say? That we make friends and god makes lovers. Agree?"

"Yes"

"So try to get the catch in this saying. We make friends means we make ourselves compatible to each other to continue the friendship and now second part that god makes lovers means lovers are already compatible to each other and they were created by god in such a way so they don't have to make any changes in them to be compatible to each other or maybe you can say that is the reason they fall for each other. So whenever you have to change yourself to continue the relationship it is not love."

"Then why friendship is considered above to love?"

"Because love is selfish and friendship is selfless."

"What! How"

"Because in love you are not making any compromises to yourself while in friendship you have to make many changes in yourself and compromises to fulfill commitment you made with your friends, in love you both already agreed for something but in friendship you don't need to agree but support other. In love you have to agree on something and do that thing while in friendship you don't need to agree all the time with what you have to support. Friendship and Love are two emotions which no one can clearly comment which one is great sometime friendship appear above and sometime love appears above. Krishna has a great friend in Sudama and all-time great lover in Radha."

"Does Meera also love Krishna?"

"Yes she surely does but here is a little difference in her love and that difference made it devotion."

"Ok, so what is devotion?"

"Devotion when you don't care about whether person is compatible with you and you just make changes in yourself or compromise or do whatever it takes to be compatible with other. What matters to you is that you just love other person you don't even need anything in return."

"OK, so I can say that for me you are just a friend and I think you put me somewhere in between love and devotion."

"I can't say that for sure." At that moment alarm clock on Rayman's cell start playing Rocky movie theme song to awake him. Rayman is still laying for next few minutes thinking about the dream and then got up to get ready for office, after getting ready he has to run alone for the bus now as there is no Alan or Vicky to give him company.

Around ten o'clock Rayman is at his seat working and then Shiksha told him about Anna and that she was not able to arrange office cab to his home and struggling on Metro train every day to reach her office and returning from office. Rayman thought for a while and wrote a mail to Anna.

'Hi Anna,

Hope you are doing great. I am also good here just missing your presence. I have heard that you are facing trouble in getting cab from office. Few guys from my old group already availing this facility, you can talk to Tanu or Lavanya in my old group, they will help you in getting cab.

Weather is getting colder and you usually pick cold too early so take precautions.

Take care and write back whenever you need to talk to me.

Bye'

On the way home thought came in Rayman mind in form of poem while he travelling alone in that auto rickshaw.

"Jab dekhta hoon apne in hathon ko bade gaur se,
Lagta hai yahin kahin ik lakir teri bhi hogi.
Ye hawa, ye ghata, ye fiza, ye baharen,
Sab hain bemani gar tu jo sath na hogi.
mere lye ik tu hi sari duniya hai,
aur tere liye shayad main is duniya main hi nahin hoon.
Dil toh ye chahta hai kit u kabhi to aaye,
Aur mujhko bataye ki main sahi nahin hoon.
Yahan wahan idhar udhar hain na jaane kitne chehre,
Bas ik tu hi nazar nahin aati hain,
Dhoondhta hoon har chehre main ek tera chehra,
Na pakar tumko na jaane aankh kyun nam ho jati hai.
Jabse tumne mujhse yun munh mod liya,
Mujhko yun tanha chhod diya.
Main kya batlayun tumko ai priye,
Maine is duniya se naata tod liya.
Har pal, har ghadi, har lamha teri yaad aati hai,

Ye jaan jakar bhi na jaane kyun nahin jaati hai,
Ek bas tu hi hai jo mujhko itna satati hai,
Kabhi teri yaad mujhe hasati hai, kabhi tu mujhe rulati hai."
(Whenever I see my hands with concentration,
Appears there will be a line of yours.
This wind, these clouds, this atmosphere, and this spring,
Everything is meaningless if there is no compliance of yours…)

As expected no response came from Anna but this doesn't make any impact on Rayman and he kept writing greeting mails to Anna once or twice in week. Whole November went the same way. Shiksha and Sonia are constantly in touch with Anna during this whole time and also keeping Rayman informed with Anna's where about. Anna is not able to get office cab as no one else is on that route and office decided not to provide cab for single person. Rayman is in touch with Sky, Anu and Suchi and he is in touch with his friends Tanu, Toni and Lavanya like earlier days. Lavanya is a good friend of Sky so she gets chances to meet Anna often.

In mid of November one day Sky mailed Rayman in a reply of mail and informed him that his team is reporting now to a new manager Dee Pee in place of Ruchi as she is moved to onsite few months before and it is becoming inconvenient to coordinate due to difference in time zone. Sky told him that Anna is working with Dee Pee on regular basis and having lots of meeting with him and she is facing trouble working with this new manager. He often shouts on her, sometimes even in public also and treating her very badly. Rayman wrote a mail to Anna.

'Hi Anna

How are you? I am good and everything is fine here.
I talked to Sky and he told me that Dee Pee has some issue with you and your work and he is not behaving properly. You are very upset with him and appear very tense these days. Hey don't worry and have faith in you. It happens sometime that it takes some time to understand each other in a team. I know you are great at what you do and I want you to believe in yourself.

People said so many things about me too in past. I was even transferred from my old group because few people thought that I am not good at work. You don't care about all foolish thing Dee Pee is saying. These days are not very good for me as well as there are rumors that Jay is leaving and his manager is always bossing round with me, once again I have to prove myself. In my view you know more about work than Dee Pee. So please be happy.

Take care'

Anna replied first time after moving to Noida office next day around twelve o'clock.

'Hi Rayman,

I am not tensed at all yeah I am upset though. But I made up my mind that I will change this job very soon. I asked them so many times that this place is far from my home but nobody is listening and I don't really care about Dee Pee. Although you are right about that he lacks professional attitude.

I am fine and I am advising you also that there is nothing to prove for you also, why you hear anything from anybody, if things are not going great than search new job and change.

Take care'

Coming weeks are no different for anyone Anna is experiencing same behavior from her manager and this is reason she is looking for new job and giving interviews on every weekend. Rayman is not having too much work since Upen joined the team but he has still not able to cope with rejection from Anna and his pursuit for getting acceptance from Anna is still on and he is in constant touch with Anna through girls of his team. Anna is also facing the issue of travelling from Dwarka to Noida every day. Rayman is looking for a new home as he is fade up living alone from last two months after Vicky shifted to Pune, and in this pursuit he talked to Vivek, Sky and Upen but he is not able to get any success.

One ray of hope came in first week of December when girls from Rayman's team planned to go for food festival which is going on in Connaught Place. Upen, Rahul, Sonia, Shiksha, Rayman and Naina are going for this outing and Naina suggested that she with Shiksha can try and ask Anna also to join them in this weekend outing. Naina asked Anna on Friday on cell if she can join them for this trip and Anna says she can join them if she is not going office and someone from her team is joining them Around nine o'clock in the evening Rayman called Naina to get confirmation whether Anna is coming tomorrow and Naina said that she possibly not going to office but she said that she can come only if someone from her team also join her. Rayman is tensed for moment and then he decided to call Suchi and Sky but none of them is available tomorrow due to personal commitments but Sky promised that he will try from his side to come. Rayman once again called Naina and conveyed her that Sky might come and he will confirm about it tomorrow morning. Naina conveyed same message to Anna and in return she also confirmed that she will be joining them as and when Sky confirm about his availability. Rayman went to bed praying that Sky must come tomorrow with them but before that he again called Suchi if she can manage to come but she said that it is not possible for her as some of her relatives coming to visit her. He then called Upen and narrated everything, Upen suggested him to drop a message to Suchi saying 'Plz' and emphasized on writing plz rather than writing whole word and he ensured that this will definitely make impact.

Saturday morning around nine o'clock Rayman made his first call to Sky about the confirmation for outing, Sky said that he is going out with someone else and he will not be able to make it, 'what the fuck!' are the first words come in Rayman's mind. But he manages his emotions and called Naina to inform her about it. Naina called him back in about twenty minutes and updated him that she called Anna and Anna said first she might have to work from home or it is also possible that she need to go office and second if no one comes from her team she is afraid that she can't come. Rayman slumped in his thoughts for few minutes and then called Suchi once again even after knowing that she already denied that she can't join them, her cell rung for quite some time but no response, he tried two more times without any success and then he called Shiksha and narrated every detail to her and asked her to talk to Suchi and ask her to come. When he is waiting for call from Naina and Shiksha on any update, he called Sonia and discussed his pain with her and second setback came from Sonia when she said that she can't come either and wished that Anna will definitely come for outing. Upen and Rahul also not able to make it for the outing. At ten fifty Rayman left home after waiting for around half hour without success for Shiksha and Naina's call and just before leaving home he informed Naina that he is leaving from his home and will meet him at Sarita Vihar metro station in around half an hour and when he is locking his door at that very moment he got call from Shiksha.

"Sir, I called Suchi, and good news is that her business with her relative or friend has finished and she is coming with us, we have to wait for few more minutes for that."

"Oh really, I can't ever forget this favor from you and her thank you Shiksha. Well, I am leaving right now and I and Naina will meet you at Sarita Vihar metro station in approximately thirty minutes."

"Done"

Rayman then called Naina to confirm her about availability of Suchi and Naina informed him in return that she is also leaving home and she will update Anna about Suchi's availability for outing. Fifteen minutes later Rayman is heading toward metro station when he got call from Naina.

"Anna can come but she is busy in office work right now and she said that around two she will be free and it is up to us whether we want to wait for her but she has suggested that we should carry on without her, what you say sir?"

"We shall wait for her?"

"OK, I also said the same thing to her. Don't worry let's meet at metro station."

"Sure" And as Rayman ended the call, he got another call from Sky.

"Rayman, how are you doing? Are you still on for that food festival trip?"

"Yes"

"I can also join you yaar. I am at Lajpat Nagar right now and my business is done. Tell me where can you meet me?"

"Thanks yaar, Suchi is also coming and possibly Anna too. I am near Sarita Vihar and will be going toward C.P. with Suchi, Shiksha and Naina so we can meet at Lajpat Nagar metro station."

"Let's see you then."

Eleven thirty Rayman reached Sarita Vihar metro station and called Naina and Shiksha and informed them that he has reached and waiting for them. Naina came first around fifteen minutes later and Shiksha came five minutes after that and they started journey to C.P. at twelve thirty. Shiksha informed them that Suchi will be meeting them at next station and they called and sync up with Suchi to let her board the train and then they reached at Lajpat Nagar station and now waiting for Sky to join them. Sky came around after one hour at one thirty with two of his friends from the office. Naina in mean time called Anna to update her that Sky and Suchi both are coming and also get her status about when can she come at C.P.? Anna said that she will be reaching around three. Quarter to three they reached Rajiv chowk metro station and after reaching there Naina once again called Anna to check whether she left and she get to know that Anna will be leaving in ten more minutes and around one hour after leaving she will reach Rajiv chowk. Sky and his two friends want to go out of Rajiv chowk and Suchi also said that they can wait outside metro station. Rayman is adamant to wait for her at station premises and Naina and Shiksha also want to remain with him at station and that make Suchi and Sky also to wait at the station against their wish. First thirty minutes passed without any problem but after that people started boring except Rayman. Suchi is singing song to tease Rayman, after fifteen more minutes now everyone got bored and want to move out of station and trying to convince Rayman also to go out of metro station but Rayman still adamant to stay at station.

"Let's go outside we can wait there and explore things around" Sky is getting irritated now.

"Bahut der se dar pe, aankhe lagi thi"

"huzur aate aate bahut der kar di, huzur aate aate bahut der kar di" Suchi is singing song and Naina and Shiksha joined her.

"Sky and anyone who want to go can go outside but I am not going anywhere, I will wait here." And that comment from Rayman once again makes everyone to wait there. They are sitting in groups of three at different places at metro station and now people started noticing them. At around four o'clock Naina screamed suddenly to informed everyone about the arrival of Anna. Rayman noticed her when Shiksha and Sonia greeted her. Anna then met everyone and greeted one by one. Everyone is out of the metro station in ten minutes. After roaming in various alleys in C.P. they finally entered in one alley where food festival is going on in form of various foods' stalls.

There are lots of stalls carrying various kinds of Indian foods from all parts of India. Everyone is talking to each other while walking toward stalls, Shiksha and Naina talking to Anna and Suchi is also walking with them, Sky and his two friends walking few feet ahead of them and Rayman is behind everyone and near to Anna. Rayman is looking only at Anna during this time. She is looking even more beautiful today. He is not able to decide what made her more beautiful this distance or her simplicity today, she isn't wearing any makeup, purple striped t-shirt, plain blue jeans, carbon black color hoody jacket, light gray slipper with small green flower on strips, hair tied in a little pony style, black color framed glasses and finally her trademark smile on her face making her most beautiful in whole world. Rayman is not letting distance go beyond five meters between him and Anna, his concentration broke when Anna suddenly started running behind Sky when he made some comment on coming late and she followed him few blocks and finally caught him and hit him on his back with her hand. Rayman could not even breathe properly all that time fearing that Anna might lose balance and slip. Next he noticed when a car stopped with screeching breaks near him and he noticed that Anna ran while crossing road in middle of traffic and managed to cross road successfully but Rayman is following her without looking anything around and that left him in middle of the road stranded in front of car which is about to hit him. He murmured "She will let me killed one day for sure."

After roaming for fifteen minutes they finally reached at the destination and then Rayman asked everyone.
"Golgappa"
"Yeah, I will also have golgappa." Naina and Anna also nodded.

After having golgappa they moved ahead and exploring few more shops then Sky asked everyone to have Kulche and Bhatoore. Anna is having Bhatoore while Rayman is having Kulche, Sky and Suchi eating in Anna plate while Shiksha and Naina in Rayman's plate. Rayman and Anna noticed that they are not eating from each other plate and hence first Rayman handed his plate to Sky and then Anna handed her plate to Naina so both can have food from each other plate. Rayman is still not moving more than five feet away from Anna. Everyone is enjoying the outing to the fullest, Rayman is looking happy after seeing Anna after so many days, Anna is also seems very happy. They further moved to next stall of chuski or gola, Rayman asked everyone at chuski stall.

"Kaala khatta (a flavor of gola which mean black and sour)"

"I too" Anna want the same flavor as Rayman. Naina, Suchi and Shiksha also took chuski but some other flavor. Anna exchanged her chuski glass with Naina to taste her flavor also and Naina showed gesture of kindness when she exchanged that glass with Rayman voluntarily.

At next stall Anna asked everyone for bhelpuri and then she turned toward Rayman and asked.

"Rayman bhelpuri?" and these were first words from Anna for Rayman, he could not understand what to react or say. He just nodded his head in a definite yes. She brought two plates of bhelpuri and this time Anna and Rayman having in one plate and Suchi, Naina and Shiksha in other plate, Sky, and his friends moved little ahead of these guys.

"Has anyone know, where gurudwara balasaheb is?" Shiksha asked to others.

"No" came common response.

"I visited once but not sure about the location."

"I know where gurudwara is." Sky returned to them and his friends left for their home.

"Let's go gurudwara." Shiksha asked everyone.

"Let's go" response came from everyone.

"Let's take auto rickshaw till gurudwara" Suchi suggested and she got support from everyone.

"No yaar, let's walk, we can also have chit chat on the way" Anna said to them.

"Let's walk sir" Naina said to Rayman "We can have chit chat hmm-hmm."

"No yaar, let's go by auto rickshaw, I am tired now." Suchi said making sad face.

"You can go by auto if you want to and if anyone else also feeling tired he can go with her." Rayman suggested a way keeping both opinions.

"Hey Suchi, let's walk naah yaar, you are not some oldie." Anna asked to Suchi.

"OK, let's walk"

Everyone started walking toward balasaheb gurudwara around six in the evening and this time everyone walking in one group. Rayman not left Anna alone since he saw her today and maintaining consistent distance of five feet from her. Naina, Shiksha acting at mediator between Rayman and Anna most of the time. They reached gurudwara talking whole way and after reaching there everyone took cloth for covering head from gurudwara, Anna and Rayman entered at very same moment while rest already entered the premises. Rayman, Suchi and Anna stayed behind to offer prayer while other moved little forward. Suchi is taking her time while Rayman and Anna came a little away from her and sat in a corner.

"She has gone in very deep prayer of god" Rayman broken the silence.

"Yeah"

"How is everything with you?"

"Good, Isn't Suchi crying?"

"What?"

"Let's come and see her"

"Sure"

"What happened?" Anna asked to Suchi after reaching to her.

"Nothing, I was never able to control my emotions in temples or gurudwara."

"Oh, I thought something is wrong." Anna wiped her tear and placed her hand on Suchi' shoulder. Anna and Suchi sitting together Suchi placed her head on Anna shoulder and Rayman sitting nearby and then some loud bang came which scared them.

"BANGGGG"

"What was that?" Anna asked to Rayman "Bomb"

"It looked like one" and then sound came once again and this time both Rayman and Anna looked toward source of sound at first floor.

"Oh! It's that drum's sound. They are signaling others for prayer time."

"Yeah" and then these three also stood up with other who lined up for prayer and after prayer Anna and Rayman were first to move out and they sat on a mat which was laid on floor in open area outside main building and waiting for others to come out.

"What else is going in your team?" Rayman asked Anna.

"Nothing specific, Ruchi might come back in one month or so."

"Why? Is her work is done there?"

"I think she is also leaving company."

"What? I haven't heard of it."

"I am also not sure but heard from someone else"

"OK, how is work? Is Dee Pee behaving same like earlier time?"

"Yeah, he is such a rascal. How is everything in your team, everyone seems so happy working under you? You have so many girls in your team. You are team lead naah."

"Yeah"

"You are giving much freedom to your team, I usually talk to them and they always say good things about you."

"Maybe" rest of guys came outside at that moment and everyone offered Prasadam to each other. Shiksha suggested that they should go to pond to sprinkle water on their head and wash eyes and feed fishes. Rayman is leading other toward pond. Sky and Suchi are coming in the end and Naina and Shiksha in the middle. Rayman reached first and submerged tip of his foot in water after sprinkling water on his head and face and that make a fish come near his foot and as that fish is about to kiss Rayman foot a scream came from his behind.

"Rayman SSS, That fish will give you electric shock." Rayman could not understand the situation and pulled his foot out immediately to turn backward in fear to know the source of that scream. Anna is still is awe and looking very innocent in that pose and then Rayman realizes situation that Anna mistaken these fishes with eel fish and after realizing exact situation he drew himself closure to her.

"These are not eel fishes. This pool is not to kill people, see people are bathing in the pond, what are you thinking yaar?"

"Are you sure?"

"Yeah, OK, Let's go nearer and you also dip your hand and touch fishes, they just touch and go away, it feels great."

Shiksha, Naina are few feet away on right side to them and already sprinkling water on their head and face on the other hand Suchi and Sky are behind them and staying on the stairs of pond. Rayman glanced over Naina and Shiksha when Anna shouted and they are still laughing and Anna dipped her hand and right foot tip and took out very quickly.

"Come and let's sit here and click some pics." Suchi called everyone to stairs.

"Let's go" Naina asked Rayman and Anna. Shiksha and Sky already reached at stairs, Rayman followed them and Naina and Anna coming behind him.

Suchi handed her phone to Rayman to click pictures and she sat with Anna on her left side and Shiksha on right, Naina sitting on lower stair in front of Anna and Sky and Rayman are clicking pictures. When Rayman focused to take a snap Anna intentionally hid behind Naina, Rayman waited for few minutes and finally asked her to show up. Rayman clicked a picture and then Shiksha took the camera and asked Rayman to sit. Rayman sat on right side of Naina and Shiksha clicked few snaps and everyone stood up after photo session to go out.

"What now?" Sky asked to everyone.

"I think time to leave for home, what time is it?" Naina asked in response.

"Eight"

"I want to see hand bags on some shops at CP" Anna said to Suchi and other girls. "Can we stay at C.P. for some time, I can check at hi-design store."

"This time" Suchi asked in awe. "It's too late yaar, I will be late to reach PG, and same issue will be with others."

"Yeah, I too have to reach my PG before ten" Shiksha also raise her concern.

"Me too, I also committed ten at home" Naina also said the same thing and that made Anna's face go down.

"OK, let's go home then" Anna said with her head down and that nearly killed Rayman, Rayman requested Shiksha and Naina if they can give her company.

After looking for bags in few stores Anna decided not to buy any bag and decide to check come other day and in the process they reached to metro station where everyone has to catch metro to their destination. Sky asked everyone if they can come for movie.

"Let's go for some movie yaar"

"Movie this time, you lost your mind" Suchi is first to comment.

"Why, Anna can come with you to your PG and Naina can stay at Shiksha PG, and I live near your PG so we will drop you your PG. Rayman can come to my place."

"Sky if anyone of you or Rayman had car I would have definitely come with you for movie, in that case you guys could drop us all at our home after movie, but I am afraid it is not possible right now" Anna responded to Sky suggestion"

"Anna, I am not sure about movie, but you will definitely see a car in a week time or so. Somebody will definitely buying a new car."

Anna bid good bye to everyone after that, Sky decided to go for movie, Rayman Shiksha, Suchi and Naina came with Anna to metro station, Anna boarded train toward Dwarka and at the same time rest boarded train toward Sarita Vihar and memorable trip came to end.

For next few days discussion of food festival trip is happening in Rayman cubicle and as Sky guessed rightly Rayman is searching for car this whole time and Upen and Rahul are also helping him in this task. Two weeks later Jay gave him good news that annual party is on coming Friday and that give him hope of meeting Anna in annual party. On annual party day Upen and Rayman is busy in the office while everyone left for the venue at 3:00 in the afternoon, Rahul has also gone with Naina, Sonia and Shiksha and with other team mates leaving only Upen and Rayman behind to finish task before leaving.

Around four o'clock Shiksha called Rayman to inform him that she met Anna at party venue and that make Rayman even more eager to reach venue. He is not able to work anymore and now he is not doing anything and creating hindrance in Upen's work. Rayman marching up and down in the work area and creating havoc in front of Upen and asking him in every five minute to wrap up the work and go to party. Around five o'clock Rayman and Upen finally left for party.

On reaching venue, Rayman nearly ran inside talking to Shiksha on cell phone and he turn back to shout toward Upen.

"See you inside, I am going"

"You carry on and search her, I am right behind you" Rayman hasn't cared to respond and moved inside.

"Where is she?" Rayman asked Shiksha on reaching her seat.

"She was just here five minutes ago. She might have gone behind stage or maybe washroom to check her makeup?"

"Makeup" Rayman mocked up to Shiksha knowing that Anna is not in to makeup.

"Yeah, Naina tell him about her makeup, she is wearing quite a lot today"

"Really" Rayman asked to Naina and Shiksha.

"Just wait for two minutes and see yourself" Naina said to him.

"She is not like you thought of her, she wears makeup even in office sometimes, and it is just that you could not see it." Shiksha is not far behind in making taunt. Upen came by this time.

"Bro, Where is she?"

"I don't know, Naina and Shiksha saying she was here few minutes ago and then she went somewhere just moment before I came inside."

"She must had seen you"

"How is she looking today?" Rayman ignored Upen's comment completely and asked Sonia, Shiksha and Naina about Anna.

"You see by yourself, in my view she is looking flawless and more beautiful than usual." Sonia responded first.

"Where she went?" Rayman murmured with head down.

"She will be coming soon, don't be so impatient" Raman said to Rayman and Rayman now noticed him for first time since he entered. He is sitting with Naina on her right side. Shiksha and Sonia sitting a row ahead of Naina and Raman and Upen sat on right side chair to Shiksha's chair. Shiksha, Naina, and Sonia are looking no different from office, they directly came from office but Anna might have taken her time on her makeup. At this moment Rayman could not move his eyes away from the entrance after noticing Anna coming toward them, not even able to blink his eyes. She is in light blue colored salwar suit with dupatta on her left shoulder, and wow! She is looking awesome without spectacles, her beautiful eyes now made whole surrounding lively. She is wearing contact lenses and what! She is wearing makeup on her eyelids and that too of sky blue color, hmm-hmm matching with color of her suit, Wow! And nice nail paint and that's incredible. She definitely has given time to her makeup, otherwise nail paint that too nicely done as she usually has messed up nail paint. She is wearing high heels that are also different from normal days; she usually wears nearly two inches heels.

"Hello" Rayman said to Anna but he still not blinked even once since he saw her today.

"Hello" she replied and sat on left side of Shiksha, between Shiksha and Sonia. Naina and Raman talking to each other in whispering pitch, someone performing dance on the stage on some Bollywood number. Anna is talking to Sonia and Shiksha while Upen and Rayman are sitting silently.

"Hey, want something to drink?" Upen asked to Rayman.

"No, I have left drinking completely."

"You take cold drink yaar."

"OK, let's go" Upen and Rayman went to take drink. Upen return with one large peg of whisky while Rayman with cold drink and first thing he noticed after returning to his seat is that Anna is not there.

"Where has she gone?" Rayman asked to Sonia and Shiksha in complete awe.

"No idea" Shiksha replied. Rayman sat on his seat and Upen sat after leaving few seats due to whisky peg in his hand. Rayman is trying to look all over place and his eyes constantly searching for Anna everywhere but not able to locate her. Everyone is watching dance performance as Suchi and Mansi are also performing in this dance but Rayman still searching for her, and he finally noticed her few rows behind Naina's row. Upen, Sonia and Shiksha moved forward to see the performance while Rayman moved back toward Naina's seat to go a little closure to Anna seat. Shiksha and Sonia also came near Anna after dance performance.

"Where was she gone?" Rayman asked to Shiksha.

"She got scared from Upen, she is shivering."

"Why?"

"Because he is drinking, you also stay away from him or she will not talk to you too."

"Why?"

"She is saying that you must also be drinking."

"God, Phew, but I'm not drinking yaar."

"I told her but she didn't believe me."

"OK, I will sit with you guys and I will tell her that she doesn't need scare of Upen also. He is a friend and a very good guy. Upen is with Rahul and they are drinking at this moment too."

"I think she will be all right in few moments, you don't worry"

"Hmm" Rayman is thinking of not leaving her at all for rest of the evening. He switched chair with Shiksha on returning to his seat to keep Anna in his vision. Raman and Naina are laughing at his this action.

On the stage award are being distributed for various events and in between one award is given to Rayman's group too and anchor called everyone from the group on the stage. Sonia, Shiksha, Naina, Upen and Anna are also going to stage but Rayman stayed behind and then Anna turned back and said first words to Rayman.

"Come, why aren't you coming? Let's come." Rayman as usual could not reply anything and just nodded his head in yes and followed her to the stage.

After few hours of fun, watching performances on stage and then dancing on D.J. floor they decided to have dinner. Anna and Rayman occupied one table with other friends for dinner, Rahul and Upen said that they will eat later.

"Are you crying?" Shiksha asked to Anna, her nose is red and eyes are wet.

"No, I have cold."

"You nose is so red" Naina teased her.

"Hmm" It is already eleven thirty when they finished their dinner and now everyone is in hurry to go back home.

"I am going to take dessert, do you want?" Anna asked to Rayman, everyone else already gone to take sweets.

"Yeah"

"Jalebi" She further asked Rayman.

"Sure" Anna brought Jalebi and passed to everyone including Rayman.

Sonia and Shiksha are going to take cab, Rahul and Upen are still drinking, Suchi and Mansi are gathered around a guy who has over drunk and creating havoc in mid of party and people saying that the guy is Sky. Rayman said to Shiksha and Sonia to wait and said that he will be coming to help them get the cab to home. Anna is standing near an electric heater when Rayman left her to let Shiksha and Sonia get cab.

Anna is constantly looking at Rayman and her eyes are saying that don't go away, please stay with me, tears rolling down from her eyes. She wants to say something to Rayman and he is trying to locate Rahul, Upen or Sahil but he could search anyone of them and then Shiksha called his name from behind. "Let's go sir". Rayman went after Shiksha and Sonia with a stone on his heart and returned quickly to find Anna nowhere near that electric heater. He searched her everywhere but couldn't find her. He just missed the chance of his life. She wanted to say something and he left at that moment. What can be done now? After searching for rest of the evening he failed find her. She has possibly already gone to her home. Around twelve thirty in mid night Upen, Rahul and Rayman left together for their homes.

"Radhe krishna ki jyoti alaukik tino lok mein chhaaye rahi hai bhakti vivash ek prem pujaarin phir bhi deep jalaaye rahi hai" Rayman's cell is ringing.

"Hello" Rayman greeted Sky after picking up the phone early morning on Saturday.

"Hello, how are you?"

"Can't be better, how are you? You was over drunk last night so tell me about you."

"I am fine, do you know?"

"What?"

"Anna" and he paused after that.

"Don't create suspense after taking her name or I will die"

"She resigned"

"You must be kidding"

"Nope, I am serious bro, she resigned on twenty first."

"She can't do this, I mean why?"

"She was facing too much trouble in last few days, especially from her manager."

"Hmm, I understand"

"Are you all right?"

"Yeah, I guess so. Ok, bye. I will come to your place in the evening."

"Sure, bye, but call me before coming here"

"Hmm, bye"

"And take care"

"I will" Rayman was not able to digest it and still thinking that it might be some kind of joke and decided to go his home to confirm from Suchi also.

Around seven in the evening Rayman went to Sky's home and they together went to Suchi's apartment. She lives few blocks away from Sky's apartment. Suchi also confirmed that Anna resigned and possibly sometime in march she will leave office. Rayman is quite upset but he is controlling his emotions. Around nine Rayman and Sky decided to go back to Sky's home and way back home Rayman could not control anymore and started crying like a child.

"What happened?" Sky asked Rayman.

"I am dead sure that she will not remain in touch after leaving."

"How can be you so sure?"

"I know her very well"

"She will, believe me" Sky tried to console him but tears still rolling down from both of his eyes. Sky trying hard to console him but he continued crying in the middle of the street. Sky took him his home and tried consoling him till he fall sleep with tears and sobbing.

On Monday Rayman broke news in his team and Shiksha and Naina called Anna, they also got the same confirmation but she asked them not to spread this news and keep it to them, especially news should not go to Rayman. Shiksha told her that he already knew about it. Rayman decided to buy car, he wants to give ride to Anna in his car before she leave the office. Upen and Rahul suggested Rayman to learn driving before buying new car but work is not allowing him to learn. New Year came without any major news and Rayman is all alone in the office on New Year eve and suddenly Vishu and Raina came to his office to pick him.

"Let's go to my place, you are celebrating New Year with us my friend." Vishu said to Rayman after reaching to his seat, there is no one else in whole office.

"Is there any party?"

"Sure, you can cook for us."

"My pleasure"

"Don't worry, we will order from somewhere, you just need to pack your bag."

"Let's go" Vishu, Raina and Rayman going toward Vishu home in his car and having chit chat about personal and professional life, Rayman broke Anna's resignation news to them. Raina read from Rayman's face that he is upset and narrated few of her friends story to console him that how people meets even after going away for some time if they meant to meet someday. After reaching home Raina made tea for everyone and in that duration Vishu also tried to console him and asked him to forget her.

"But people rightly say that 'you can't influence someone to love and even not to love' and here both of cases exist in this story.

Rayman spent his New Year eve at Vishu home playing cards with Raina and Vishu till 2:00 AM. Rayman also informed Vishu and Raina that he is planning to buy car in one or two week. Vishu said that this might divert his mind away from Anna for some time so he must go for it and advised him to join some good driving classes before buying new car so it can remain new for some time.

Anna's comment about car is still in Rayman's mind and finally in mid of January after one and half month of that trip Rayman bought car on January 18, 2012 but even after suggestion from Rahul and Upen he didn't learn to drive. And hence Jay dropped him till Vishu's home and Vishu drove his car to his home. Next day he got mails from everyone including everyone from Anna's team congratulating him on his new car and asked him to send sweets to them and also asked him to drive his car to their office to give them a test ride in his car. Rayman responded saying that he will be sending sweets in one or two day time but he can't drive car to their office even if he wants to as he doesn't knows driving. Next day Rayman sent chocolates in an envelope through office internal courier and wrote Anna's name as recipient.

Final days

*A*nna screamed on highest pitch "Chocolates came for me" as soon as she received a package through internal courier. Anna screamed so loud that even Raman is able to hear her voice from two cubicles away from her cubicle. Sky, Suchi and Anu are already at her seat.

"Who sent these chocolates" Sky asked her even after knowing that Rayman sent those chocolates.

"Rayman, for his new car"

"Why is only his car? It is your car too" Sky whispered in her ears

"Shut up and have chocolate"

"Why not"

"What is the reason for these chocolates" Raman is standing next to Sky now.

"Hey Raman, have chocolate, Rayman has bought car and he sent chocolates for us" Anna is very happy and distributing chocolates. So many things running in her mind about why he sent chocolates, will he be coming to office also? In between all these thoughts she is going to all her friends and distributing chocolates and no one noticed whether she is able to eat any or not.

On the other hand Rayman discussing with Shiksha and Naina about Anna's resignation and a new girl Jiya who recently joined their team is trying to understand what kind of discussion these guys are in to?

"What you think sir, will she revoke her resignation?" Shiksha asked Rayman.

"I don't think so and I am dead sure for one more thing that when she will leave this office she will not remain in my touch."

"Why? May be she might even come closure, she might be scared of being noticed but when she move away she might miss you." Naina commented.

"I wish you are right but if that was the case she should have noticed my absence in last two months."

"Yeah"

"Suggest me one thing"

"Yeah"

"What should I give her as farewell memento?"

"Something she can keep with her."

"In that case I can stay with her forever."

"Sir, control"

"OK, seriously suggest something, what she usually keeps with her every time"

"She keeps only her cell phone with her all the time, you can also give her something that she can keep on her desk.

"Like"

"Table clock, pen stand, quotes book"

"Hmm, can think of these, well what about cell phone?"

"She will hit with that phone on your nose" Shiksha commented in between Naina and Rayman.

"Shiksha, can't you say anything in my favor?"

"I am saying truth."

"Whatever, what about cell phone, her cell phone is waste. It's always plugged in for charging."

"No doubt about that" Naina commented laughing.

"She is planning to buy Samsung Ace" Shiksha said to Rayman.

"OK, why not I buy the same phone for her?"

"She will never accept it from you?"

"Maybe but I should try."

"As you wish, sir you should fast on Monday and Lord Shiva will surely give her to you"

"I am great believer of Lord Shiva, but I don't think these fast and prayer really work for selfish purpose"

"Sir, give your hundred percent with belief and he will definitely listen you."

"I will try with my hundred percent."

In the evening when Naina came at her seat from outside, she is looking very upset, tear nearly falling out of her eyes.

"What happened?" Rayman asked Naina.

"Nothing Why"

"Has Jay said anything?"

"No"

"Why you looking so upset? It never happens to you."

"No I am ok" and she is again looking same with this comment, she is so tough girl. Really

"Tell us naah" Shiksha asked this time.

"Nothing yaar" she said and paused for a moment and then continued "Yaar Papa yesterday came to me in evening around nine, I was talking to Raman at that time. He asked to hang the phone and asked me to talk to him."

"What? Did he know that you are talking to Raman?"

"I don't know but that is not the issue. He started after I hung up, he said that he don't want me to think about love marriage, he also said that he know everything about Raman and if we do anything against his wish it will not be good for both of us. He has also threatened me to kill us both."

"He must be just bluffing" Rayman said to her.

"No, he was serious"

"Really, tell me why he is so against your love marriage? Is he against inter-caste marriage?"

"Maybe but there is something else"

"Then what"

"It is his false stubbornness, he always taunt when any of our known or relative does any love marriage, now I think he is scared of facing the same in his home. He doesn't want to taste his own medicine I guess."

"What are you saying? Is it just his false stubbornness which is superseding over his child's joy and happiness?"

"I don't know, I only know that I am also his daughter, if he determined I will also not back off from my commitment."

"All the best"

January went without any other major events, Rayman as discussed with Naina and Shiksha actually bought cell phone as farewell gift for Anna. Rayman started taking driving classes and he progressed well. Rayman started Monday fasts in belief that only god can help him now, Vicky and Alan mailed everyone that they are getting married on February 10th. Tanu is still looking for new job and she is busy in interviews. Vishu and Rayman have decided to go to Vicky marriage and booked their tickets. Rayman learned a little driving and on January 26 and he decided to go on a long drive as it is holiday, but where to go on his first drive. He decided to go to Anna's office on his first drive. It might be a little too much for first drive but what could be better than Anna's office for his first drive and he found that she has written quote which matches Rayman's dare 'Nothing is impossible even the word says I'm possible'.

One fine day in Noida office Anna and Sky are arguing over something and argument turned toward interesting one.

"Why don't you get married?" Sky asked Anna.

"I want true love."

"So fall in true love with someone"

"There is no true love these days."

"I know someone who loves someone truly." And she left argument staring at Sky after this comment from Sky.

"What happened? I really know someone." Sky taunted her from behind.

"I don't want to talk about him, please shut-up or I wouldn't talk to you also." She turned to answer very angrily.

February 1st, Friday Rayman once again went to Noida office with hope that this time he will be able to see her. He reached Noida office around five o'clock in the evening. She is not at her seat when he walked inside to her cubicle. Anu, Suchi and Sky are sitting in the same cubicle and he sat near Anu's seat and they are talking about the work, personal life and his car. Rayman promised to give them test ride in his car. Anna came after twenty minutes and went directly to her seat without saying any word to anyone. She remained busy rest of the day. Rayman left office with Sky and Tanu at six thirty and Anna also left at the same time but no word at that time also. Rayman dropped Sky and Tanu on the way to his home and on the way Sky and Tanu started conversation about Anna and that turned his concentration away from driving and he hit his car to someone else's car and that created a scene on the road.

First week of February ended with a very good news to Rayman when Shiksha and Naina informed him that Anna is coming back to their office in next week possibly on February tenth but there is little problem in it as he already committed to go to Vicky marriage on same day. Rayman and Vishu left for Indore for Vicky marriage on February 9th, Thursday with dual mind whether he should stay to meet Anna after so many days or he should go to Vicky marriage, Upen suggested that marriage will not be canceled without him and Vishu asking him to come for the marriage as he can meet Anna later too but Vicky marriage will not happen again. He finally left with Vishu with heavy heart but before leaving he asked Shiksha to welcome her and left chocolates for Anna with Shiksha and Naina.

Everyone is enjoying at Vicky wedding, Abhi also came from Pune to attend marriage. Abhi and Vishu have their attention toward Vicky marriage while Rayman is still thinking about Anna. He called Shiksha to get all information about her at nine fifteen but she informed him that she hasn't come yet. Shiksha asked Rayman to have a little patience and also informed him that she called her in the morning and she will be coming around twelve. Shiksha called Rayman at two thirty and informed him that Anna has come to their office and she seems very happy returning to our office. She is looking very beautiful and she has little cold so she is wearing a scarf and that is making her even more beautiful. Her seat initially decided one floor below to our floor but something went wrong and they arranged her seat in our cubicle. Rayman could only utter Thanks god.

Rayman returned on Sunday night and on the way his mind is full of Anna's thoughts.

'What should I do? Is she in my destiny? She could have gone from that office only but she came back, there must be some reason behind it. She was with me when I need someone to hold me and I am becoming too selfish, thinking about only me so mean of me. Then what? I should think about her not just me. I will try to make her happy. She must enjoy rest of her days here.'

Monday morning when Rayman reached office Anna is already in the office, Rayman learned driving a little by now and is coming by his car. Anna is sitting at Shiksha seat.

"Who is sitting at my old seat?" Anna asked to Shiksha.

"Rayman"

"But it still has my monitor, he has better monitor than this"

"Yeah, he has given his monitor to Upen sir and took yours"

"He is mad and I have no doubt about it"

"Good morning" Rayman extended his hand to greet her.

"Good Morning" She replied with anger thinking why he kept my system to create drama in front of everybody. But Rayman responded with smile and that made her smile in return.

"You guys have not gone for breakfast" Rayman asked to Shiksha.

"We were waiting for you."

"It is Monday so I am on fast."

"Come naah sir, have tea" Naina also came to their seat and she greeted Anna and Shiksha.

"OK, let's go. Has Upen came or not?"

"He will not come before ten as usual."

"Rahul"

"He already came and talking to someone outside on his cell phone, possibly to his girlfriend"

"OK, we will ask him on the way"

Naina called Rahul for breakfast and they reached cafeteria. Everyone took Parathas and tea while Rayman took just tea due to his fast. Anna talking very less on the breakfast table she might be missing her team from Noida office as it is her second day in this office but Shiksha, Naina and Sonia included her in their conversation and asking her how is her notice period going, Is Dee Pee still behaving badly with her, Jiya, Sahil, Pooja not having proper idea about Rayman's story and they are curious why she is getting so much attention from everybody in the team. Jiya and Pooja got little hint as it is not difficult for girls to read such situation. They finished breakfast in between gossip. Upen is at his desk when they came back to their seat and asked Rahul and Rayman for tea at outside Ashoka's stall. Rayman asked Shiksha, Sonia and Naina and Sonia asked Anna to join them. She initially refused saying that she had lot of work and she need to report Dee Pee about the progress but came on promise from Naina that they will return in ten minutes. Upen taunted on Rayman when they returning inside office.

"Go my Simran, live your life for one month." Comment is similar to one famous dialog from movie Dilwaale dulhaniya le jayenge (DDLJ).

"Amen"

At lunch time Rayman asked Shiksha and Sonia to ask Anna to come with them for lunch as she seems too busy in her work. Upen is already at Rayman's seat with Rahul.

"Bro, Let's go" Upen insisted one more time.

"Just one minute, Shiksha has gone to ask Anna."

"Let's go bro, they will bring her don't worry."

"Just one minute"

"OK"

"You guys carry on I will join you in few minutes, it is really urgent." Anna said to Shiksha and then everyone except Anna went to cafeteria.

Anna came after twenty minutes and by that time everyone done with their lunch and Rayman was not eating due to fast. Anna came to their seat with her plate for lunch.

"You guys can go back to your desk if you are done." Anna asked everyone as everyone looking like they are done few minutes ago.

"No, we have nothing very urgent. You can take your time." It was from Rayman.

"I am feeling like drinking something. Upen, Rahul, Does anyone wants cold drink?" Rayman asked everyone.

"No" voice came from everyone and Shiksha, Sonia and Naina are laughing for Rayman's this behavior.

"And you, do you want cold drink?" Rayman asked to Anna.

"No, I had already taken everything."

"OK" Rayman brought cold drink and giving company to Anna for her lunch.

Rayman went to Upen's cubicle to ask him for tea around four thirty in the evening. Upen and Rahul went outside with Rayman. Rayman asked Sonia and Shiksha too that they can come if they want to join them. Naina from behind asked Rayman with blinking her eyes, should they ask Anna also to come outside and Rayman also responded a yes from his eyes. Rahul and Upen are having their tea while Rayman has his eyes on the path to Ashoka café waiting for someone.

"He is not here with us" Rahul said to Upen comment on Rayman.

"I know that, Rayman you have tea, she will be coming. I don't understand why?"

"You would not understand"

"Hmm-Hmm, You have enlightened by god naah." Naina and Sonia came outside before Upen could complete his statement.

"Isn't she coming?"

"Nope, she said she can't come outside, she has too much work, but she said it will be good if we can bring tea inside"

"OK" Rayman kept in mind to take tea for her and Sonia did the rest to hand tea to Anna at her seat.

Next day is Tuesday and Rayman cooked Poori with potatoes curry and brought for team too. Everyone is at Rayman's seat in the office and discussing what he has brought for breakfast and then they went to cafeteria for breakfast and on the way Rayman stopped at Anna seat and extended his hand to shake with her, she showed no emotions in return, Rayman asked her to come for the breakfast and she followed him.

On breakfast table Rayman gave Poori and curry to everyone, except Anna everyone has taken Poori. But she said that she will take later. Everyone is busy in their breakfast but Rayman has his one eye on his tiffin and he is waiting for Anna to eat from it. When everyone is nearly done with breakfast, she finally took Poori and curry from his tiffin and asked in return.

"Have you cooked your breakfast?"

"Yes"

"Do you cook daily?"

"No only on Tuesday"

"Why only on Tuesday?"

"Because I am on fast on Monday and hence eat Curry and Poori on Monday evening and I prepare things for next day also."

"But usually girls use to do Monday fast for good husband." Anna laughed after commenting on Rayman.

"Girls use to do for husband and boys for good wife" Shiksha said to Anna.

"Why are you doing these fasts?" Anna asked to Rayman and he just stared in return and his eyes saying 'Are you really asking this?' in disbelief.

At lunch time Anna once again came twenty minutes later today and by that time everyone done with their lunch and Rayman is still eating rice and slower than his usual pace in wait of Anna. Anna came to their table with her plate for lunch.

"I will eat more. Will anyone want rice?" Rayman asked everyone.

"No" voice came from anyone while Shiksha, Sonia and Naina are laughing at Rayman's behavior as they and other at that table know very well this is all to give her company for lunch.

"And you, do you want?" Rayman asked to Anna.

"No" She did also understand everything.

"OK" Rayman brought rice and giving company to Anna.

Story is same for whole week in Breakfast, Lunch and evening snacks and tea. Rayman is trying from his side to keep Anna happy all the time, talking to her about her work and trouble with Dee Pee. Everyone is going together for breakfast, lunch, tea and snacks. These forty days are going to be some different than usual days, after lunch everyone goes for walk outside and then enjoying ice-creams on one ice-cream stall and they are paying for it one by one in round robin fashion. His team mates pampering her like princess. Shiksha, Sonia, Naina, Jiya and Pooja are always with her. They sometime ask her about personal life like where she going after leaving here? When will she marrying? What is she doing on weekend? How is she feeling leaving this office? Even boys from Rayman's team Upen and Rahul are treating her very well for his friend Rayman. One thing is also common in all those days that Anna always joins them a little late at lunch table sometimes due to meeting with Dee Pee and sometimes due to work and till that time everyone is nearly finish with their lunch but Rayman every day overeating rice to give her company for lunch and Anna made her habit to pull Rayman's leg on every occasion with some witty comment. Sometimes Anna got time for evening tea and sometimes they took tea inside for her.

Next Tuesday morning came with a surprise for Rayman, everyone is at breakfast table and Rayman similar to last Tuesday brought Poori and potatoes curry and like last time this time also Rayman asked Anna to have Poori and she also responded the same that she will take later. When everyone finished their breakfast, Anna took last Poori and potatoes curry from his tiffin while Rayman is talking something to Sonia and Shiksha. Rayman is sitting in front of Shiksha and Anna is on right side of Shiksha after Jiya. There is no other boy except Rayman on the table.

"What do you feel Sonia when someone stares at you?" Anna suddenly fired one question to Sonia which took everyone's attention to this conversation.

"I feel like slapping him" Sonia answered to Anna.

"What you think Shiksha, are you thinking the same?"

"Umm" Shiksha choked for a moment and said yes a second later without understanding anything.

"What happened?" Naina asked to Anna.

"Nothing" she paused for a moment and then asked to Rayman next "Rayman what do you think?" by now Rayman understood that she is talking about him and he does not responded at all but Anna didn't stop there.

"Rayman, do you feel the same?" Anna called his name one more time to ask him the same question.

"Yes" and he collected his tiffin and said to Naina that he is going down stair.

"She wasn't talking about you, why don't you understand?" Shiksha and Sonia are saying to Rayman when everyone came back to their seats. Naina and Jiya are also trying to understand. Jiya by now got to know about Anna from Upen and Naina.

"I think she was talking about someone from cafeteria staff." Naina said next.

"I also think the same" Jiya also supported Naina's opinion.

"Give me some time I will ask her" Sonia said to them and then everyone went back to their seats.

Around half an hour later Sonia went to Anna to ask about incident happened at breakfast table. Sonia came to her seat after fifteen minutes and her expression less face is saying that something is wrong for sure. She didn't say anything rather wrote mail to Rayman which says.

'You were right. She was talking about you at table.

When I asked her why she made such comment? She couldn't control her emotions and burst out that it's your team lead who continuously staring at me. She also said that someone from seniors noticed you staring at her and said to her that your behavior bringing her in everyone's attention.'

For next few hours everything is quiet in cubicle. No one is talking to one another until Upen came to Rayman's seat at lunch time.

"What happened bro? This place is looking like some library. Has Jay said something? Let's go for lunch."

"You guys carry on. I will be joining you later."

"Why, what is so urgent?"

"Sir, let's go." Sonia asked Rayman. Naina and Jiya also came to their cubicle. Rayman is still working on his system and not looking at anyone. Sonia told Upen about breakfast drama and what Anna told her.

"OK, tell me, am I really staring her on breakfast table?" Rayman asked to girls.

"No" answer came in unison.

"Do you feel that I stare at her all the time?"

"Sometimes but that was before she went to Noida office, I haven't observed this since she came back from Noida office" Shiksha said this time.

"Yeah, I also observed sometimes but when we were all talking to each other and I think this is normal." Jiya also shared her view.

"Oh bro, leave it and let's go for lunch." Upen said to him once again and insisting to join on lunch.

"It's not what you are thinking. You guys go and I will be joining you at lunch table."

"OK"

"Sonia, ask Anna for lunch. Naina take her with you for lunch." Rayman said to Sonia when they are going to cafeteria.

"We shall. There is no difference for us. She was upset because some senior said something to her. She will be all right and you too come soon." Naina assured him.

"I am staying with you and I will go with you." Upen said to Rayman.

"No bro, you also go with them, I am coming in few minutes."

"OK bro, come soon."

Everyone went to lunch, Anna also went with them and everything is normal at lunch. Everyone is talking to each other normally, no discussion about morning incidence. After thirty minutes Upen is again at Rayman seat.

"You are not treating me as friend."

"Why?"

"Why did you lie to me?"

"Yaar, I was busy, I will go later for lunch."

"As you wish" Upen went to his seat. Rayman has not gone for lunch even later in the day and when in evening Jiya and Naina asked him for tea. He said that 'take her with you. I am not feeling like going out.' Going home he was thinking all the way about morning incident.

'I must be wrong. I must have done something which hurt her. I was thinking about giving her smiles during her remaining days and now I am reason behind all the trouble to her. What can I do? Should I stop talking to her? How much I talk to her in whole day hardly for ten minutes? Whatever I shouldn't come in front of her, be it breakfast or lunch or anything else. I will not go for lunch and breakfast with her also but I should ask others to give her company. I can go alone or may be with someone else.'

Same thing is running in his mind all the time even after reaching home and even when he laid on bed to sleep but when he slept a sweet voice awakes him.

"Rayman" voice is from Anna and he is in his dream as usual.

"Yes, what is it? What you want now, you scolded in front of everyone, why were they thinking about me?"

"Darling, you should understand my situation. I was upset. You didn't know what people talking about us. Forgive me."

"It is ok, I understand. What you want to talk about?"

"Tell me what after love? What you want after that?"

"I want to marry you."

"Then"

"We will have kids"

"So you love me just for kids, we can adopt kids"

"No my dear, not just for kids"

"Then"

"I will take you to my mom. You will love talking to my brother, his wife, my mom, my younger sister and her son. You know she has a four years old son. He is so cute."

"Really, I love to come with you. What else?"

"I want you to meet my friends Vishu and her wife Raina."

"But they are your friend naah"

"Yes but they are really good and when you meet them you also become their friend"

"Really, OK what else?"

"I want to care you, love you for rest of my life."

"Hmm-Hmm. Anything else?"

"I will cook for you and I will do all the work with you always"

"Hmm"

"I want you to come with me for parties and meet my all friends."

"Hmm"

"I want you to stay awake with me all night and talk to me."

"My parent will never permit for it."

"What? Talking to me entire night?"

"No yaar, marrying you"

"Really, but why?"

"Because it is India and here love and emotions come after caste region and religion"

"I understand but we can try to make them understand and if they don't agree than we will elope to marry. I promise I will remain as their own son my whole life. I will try to persuade them my whole life and take care of them"

"What if they don't change their minds?"

"I will also not change my mind of persuade them."

"Really, what will you do if I get angry?"

"I will do whatever you want. I will take you out for dinner and if you like I will cook at home and we will go for shopping and I will hear everything you want to say. I will not say anything when you will scold me. I will hear your every threat like songs and I will sing for you."

"OK-OK my dear darling."

"And I promise I will never get angry with you, I want to grow old with you, we will have kids and in our old age I want to sit with you in our balcony and we will talk to each other all the time." Rest of the night has gone in conversation between them.

Next morning Rayman reached office an hour late and by that time everyone is back from breakfast. He went directly to his seat without saying anything to anyone.

"You came late intentionally." Shiksha asked him.

"No, I was not able to awake"

"Sir, forget it now" Sonia said next.

"Go back to work" His voice is so intense in response that no one dared to say anything further.

Lunch time is also no different, one again Rayman denied to for lunch and this time Upen insisted to stay with him for lunch but Rayman convinced him to go with others. Anna went with everyone for lunch. There is no difference for other at lunch. Everyone is talking as usual about their work and daily life. Jiya is sharing some incidence from her PG, Shiksha is not happy in her PG, Sonia is also saying the same but about her home, how she is not feeling free living at home. Upen and Rahul are not talking much. Anna is discussing about her work and she is happy now coming to this office since it is saving her one hour of travel in morning and one in evening.

Ice-cream treat and evening snacks are no different than lunch, Rayman stayed at his desk and Thursday is no different from Tuesday and Wednesday. Thursday evening Shiksha and Rayman are having conversation at Rayman's seat.

"Sir, for how many days will you fast?"

"I am not fasting except Monday"

"I know you are not eating anything"

"Off course I am eating after you guys, and I am eating dinner at home too."

"Anna was asking today"

"What?"

"Why aren't you coming for lunch or breakfast?"

"I am doing what she wanted earlier and now she has problem in it too."

"She has no problem in anything. She was saying that she stopped you from staring not coming on lunch or breakfast."

"Whatever, she doesn't want me to be with her and I am doing this for her happiness."

"Why are you doing this sir? She doesn't really want it. She already told Sonia that someone provoked her against you. She said in anger and she doesn't mean to insult you. Why are you creating scene in her last days? You were saying that you will give her happiness in these days."

"I am doing the same"

"You are giving her guilt nothing else"

"Leave it, we will see it later. She can also say it to me"

"You want her to apologize to you"

"No, she just needs to talk to me and that will do"

"You two are weird"

"Thanks"

Friday is also no different even after everyone tried to convince him to come out but he is rigid on his words. In evening Shiksha came at is seat to inform him.

"Anna has to come on Saturday"

"Who else is coming from her team?"

"Dee Pee is coming to make sure that she will remain busy in work and rest of her team is in Noida so no one is coming."

"Is anybody coming from our team?"

"No, nothing is pending in our team."

"She will get bore alone and Dee Pee also going to trouble her" Rayman is concerned even after no conversation with her last whole week.

"I guess you are right. So are you coming?"

"I can't say anything now."

"Come. That might help you two to clear misunderstanding"

"Yeah, it is a good suggestion"

Saturday morning Rayman reached office at ten thirty. He brought self-cooked stuffed Parathas from his home and tea from Ashoka café and went directly to his seat. Anna is already at her seat and Dee Pee is at her seat too. They are discussing something. Rayman started his work on his system. Few minutes later he went to Anna's seat and offered Parathas to her and Dee Pee. Dee Pee rejected Parathas but Anna took few bites from his tiffin and this is after five days that they again came face to face with each other. Anna in response thanked him and smiled.

At lunch time Rayman came to Anna's seat and asked her for lunch and she as usual said that she will join him in few minutes. I was really never able to understand that what she will change in those few minutes. Well she came after thirty minutes and by that time Rayman finished his lunch and waiting for Anna with his eyes on cafeteria entrance but she entered cafeteria when he is leaving thinking that she will not be coming. She finished her lunch in very quick time and returned to her seat. Rayman is doing something on his system since he has nothing to work but Anna is busy on her seat in work. Around three o'clock Rayman asked her for tea at Ashoka's stall she said that she wants to come but she can't come due to work. OK is only word in response from Rayman. He returned with two cup of tea in his both hands from outside and handed one to Anna. Dee Pee is still sitting at her seat and discussing something. He stares at Rayman like he is not giving tea to Anna rather giving roses to his daughter.

It is somewhere between three thirty to four o'clock when she came to Rayman's seat. Rayman is doing something on his system and hence could not see her coming.

"Is something urgent pending which makes you come?" she asked him.

"Honestly, not really"

"Tell me one thing" She asked with her pretty voice.

"Is your work finished?" He asked question in response to her question.

"No, some issue at server and Dee Pee asking someone to check at Noida office"

"OK ask what you want to know"

"Why you stare at me?"

"I don't stare at you really, my eyes are big which give the impression that I am staring even when I am looking at someone normally. You know when I came here initially Jay use to think that I stares him and asked me in one meeting about it."

"Really, but I am warning you if you stare at me I am really going to slap you." she said with smile on her face.

"What!" Rayman is in shock that in spite of saying sorry she is repeating her words 'what kind of girl is she?'

"And why have you stopped coming with us, I stopped you for staring, not talking to me or coming with me"

"I will come, Promise" and at that moment Dee Pee came to inform her that issue will not resolve and she can go home. She said that she will be leaving in thirty minutes as there is something pending which she can do at his system also. She came to Rayman seat once again at 5:00 in the evening.

"I am leaving"

"I am also going and I will drop you on the way."

"No it's ok. You continue your work I will go"

"Nothing is so important"

"No you continue your work"

"Oh yaar, my work is done and I am also going, come with me."

"OK, when are you leaving?"

"Right now"

"Wait for me for five minutes, I will be coming out"

"OK" Rayman responded thinking 'earlier she was saying that she is going and when I said I will drop her, now she wants five minutes. She must be checking pepper spray in her hang bag.'

Rayman is outside office, no other car is parked except his car and he is standing near his car waiting for Anna. She came exactly in five minutes and Rayman opened car door for her and then he sat on driver's seat.

"You must be very happy." These were Anna's first words after sitting in car.

"Why?" Rayman asked even after knowing answer from inside and thinking 'Yes, I am very happy and why shouldn't I be? The girl I love most in my life, one for which I bought this car is sitting in this car'

"You bought new car" she answered cleverly.

"Yeah, I am happy, very much happy. Put the seat belt"

"You learned driving" she asked with putting seat belt.

"Yeah little bit and improving with time"

"You mean you are not good at it."

"It is just one month yaar. I will improve with time but you don't worry I know enough to drop you safe"

"OK"

"How is your wok going these days? You seem too much busy in work, Isn't Dee Pee behaving properly?"

"Everything is fine. It's for one more month only then I will be gone, then they will torture someone else." She is very happy saying this.

"Hmm"

"I know that you love me so much that you forget everything when you see me and you lost in your thoughts"

"Hmm"

"I know you don't do ti intentionally but it happens by chance."

"Hmm, you are right"

"But please don't come to Gurgaon after me."

"What if come to your company?"

"I am going to through you out after beating you"

"Really, I will not come after you. I care for you and I know what you want."

"Leave me at this metro station, I will take metro from here to Dwarka" Anna said to Rayman when they are crossing Govind Puri metro station. They were talking to each other all the way and it took them around twenty minutes to reach there since Rayman doesn't let car cross the speed of thirty KMs per hour.

"Are you sure? I can drop you wherever you want"

"Yeah, drop me here" Rayman dropped her at Govind Puri metro station as per her wish and against his wish. He wants that this journey to last forever but how can he dares to go against her wish. After dropping her he informed everyone in her team about it and also that misunderstanding is sorted out between them and what they talked all the time.

Monday morning is once again become same. Everyone is at the breakfast table. Rayman is once again looking happy and everyone in team also happy with him. Tuesday morning Rayman once again brought Poori with curry like last week which everyone enjoyed including Anna. Wednesday Upen, Naina and Jiya asked for treat from Rayman for his car and he promised that not today but someday he will definitely give party and for that he will need to consider first whether Anna can make it. Days are passing without any major incident. Anna is feeling happier with passing days due to satisfaction of leaving this office. Her last few months are not so great due to her new boss and she was not able to create the comfort zone which can help her in working. On the other hand Rayman's anxiety is increasing with passing days thinking 'how will he remain in touch with love of his life? She will never want to remain in touch with her past.' Next week's Monday and Tuesday were also same as earlier two weeks, on Tuesday it is Anna's turn to pay for ice-cream after lunch and when she is trying to pay for the treat Rayman stopped her saying that she is a guest and here for just two more weeks and he will be happy to pay on her side and out of blues she agrees to it. Around four in the evening Shiksha, Naina, Jiya, Anna and Sonia are at Rayman desk having discussion about Naina. She is facing some problem in her love life.

"What is the problem in it?" Shiksha asked Naina, she has special interest in those things.

"Dad is not allowing"

"Why, what is the problem?"

"No one can understand the problem of parents." Rayman replied Shiksha's query.

"And they knows that we can't ignore them and hence they torture us" Naina said in response.

"So when will you getting married?" Anna asked Naina.

"May be after three years, Someone please suggest me some good name for my kid which can contain name from me and Raman." Naina asked to Rayman.

"One minute." Rayman thought for a moment and then said "Raina".

"Oh wow, what a nice name"

"Actually my friend Vishu's wife name is Raina." And then Rayman realized that Anna and Rayman can also form this name.

Next day is Wednesday in breakfast everything is normal and till twelve there is no difference from past few days. Rayman went to Anna' seat at twelve o'clock and asks her.

"Is it ok if we will take half hour extra in lunch time? Will there be any problem for you?"

"No, it is ok"

"OK, I will let you know details in five minutes" He then went first to Upen and then to all other team mates to confirm about their availability for party.

Everyone is out of the office at quarter to one and girls are going with Rahul to go in his car but it is Rayman's luck that Rahul couldn't find his car in parking or maybe it's Upen and Rahul's plan as they are searching his car on wrong side so that Anna can go in Rayman's car. Naina took the front seat with Rayman in his car and Anna is sitting with Pooja, Shiksha and Sonia at back seat and Jiya has to go in Rahul's car.

"Kabhi Kabhi Hum Ek Doosre Ko Kho Kar Bhi Toh
Pyaar Ko Ooncha Darjaa Dete Hain
Juda Reh Kar Pyaar Ki Oonchaaiyon ko Praapt Karte
Har Pyaar Milan Toh Nahin, Judaai Bhi Toh Ek Pyaar Hain
Hum Hain Iss Pal Yahan, Jaane Ho Kal Kahan ..."

First song played on car's stereo and dialog before song made environment real quite inside car because this described exact situation between Anna and Rayman. It is looking like Rayman saying these words to Anna. Destination for this group is Suruchi restaurant at Faridabad road and they took toll road from Okhla to Faridabad to reach their destination. Rayman reached first and Rahul reached a few minutes later and they returned after one and half hour having lunch and capturing these wonderful moments in pictures and everyone is returning in same car on which they came to restaurant.

Music on one song played on stereo and this is time when Anna screamed.
"It song is Rafta-Rafta from Hulchul movie"
"Yeah" Rayman answered.
"How you recognized so early?" Shiksha asked with surprise.
"I have heard it many times, I love this song." Anna responded to Shiksha and then she drew herself closure to front seat and next line said to Rayman. "I love your collection, it's really amazing."
"Thanks" Rayman thanked her first for liking his collection and second for coming in his car for second time.

Anna is for only two more weeks in this office and Rayman wants to give something to her as farewell memento so he discussed ideas with everyone in the team and after getting few suggestion he decided to buy a diary similar to slam book and decided to go each of Anna's friend and collect their thoughts for Anna from all of them. Second he bought a cell phone as Shiksha informed him that she is planning to buy one so why not as a farewell gift, third a top of light sky blue color but something is still missing so after thinking for few days he started writing best moments from the day he first saw her to her last forty days with him in a diary. He also wrote few poems in that diary. Rayman went to all her friends to get their thoughts on slam book and for that he went to Suchi's home. She was living with her one friend Mansi at that time and they were first two people to write in that diary. Then he went to Sky's home to get his thought and Suchi suggested him that he should go to Meena's home to get her thought on this diary as she is Anna's close friend and they together joined this company but next name on his mind is Anu but Anu is married and living with her husband and his parent and he is not sure how to approach her as he never met her husband, so he called Shiksha and told her to company him for Anu's home.

"Shiksha, I am coming to your PG, please come with me to Anu home, please. I know her house but I am not confident going her home alone"

"What you saying sir, don't you know that she is married?"

"I know it and that's why I am afraid going there alone."

"I am not feeling that it is right."

"OK, I am taking responsibility of whatever happens at her home"

"It is not going to make any difference for me"

"Please"

"Sir, please try to understand"

"Please, come."

"OK, give me a call when you reach here"

"Come, I am outside of your PG"

"What! Give me five minutes to get ready. I am coming in few minutes"

"OK" Shiksha as promised came out in five minutes and both went to Anu's home, Anu is in total awe after seeing Rayman and Shiksha at her door.

"What is it?" she asked without even welcoming them inside.

"Shiksha told her everything"

"You could have sent it to my office"

"I don't want to leave it to anybody"

"OK, give me few minutes"

"Sure, you can take your time. I have lot of time."

"Tea or cold drink"

"Whatever"

"OK, you guys sit here and give me just fifteen minutes" Anu came after ten minutes with her thought penned down in diary.

"Thanks"

"Why are you thanking, we are from her team and we should be doing this, thanks you are taking so much pain but one thing I will say one more time, she doesn't worth you wait."

"Leave this to me, bye and take care, and sorry for this trouble"

"It is nothing, bye"

"Now I have to go Meena's home on the weekend" Rayman said to Shiksha when they are back in his car and going toward her PG.

"Meena, you mean Anna's friend" Shiksha asked in surprise.

"Yes. Why?"

"Do you know her home?"

"I will get to know from someone, don't you worry about that."

"This is love"

"Yup, and here come your PG, let's meet tomorrow. Good bye" Rayman reached home after dropping her home and when he reached home he started writing in second diary in which he use to write about his best moments with Anna and then went to sleep at mid-night and then there is no difference in his dream, Anna came in his dream to discuss their romantic life.

Next day is also same in all respects. Rayman is appearing in sleep since he was busy writing his thoughts and poems in diary all night. Naina and Rayman stayed till late due to work and around nine thirty Rayman said that he will drop her home when they are going Naina home they were talking about Anna.

"Sir, what do you think?"

"About what"

"Will she remain in your touch?"

"I don't think so"

"I too doubt"

"Why don't you try again?"

"What?"

"Propose her one more time, this time she has seen you in better way. You know my inclination always says that she loves you."

"No chance. I am not going to hurt her this time in anyway. I don't want to give her any trouble"

"On her last day"

"She will never say yes"

"Last times you haven't proposed her on face, this time try face to face, she will definitely say yes"

"Let's see"

"You know, I have told everything to my mom and you know what she said?"

"What"

"That you are really a very good person"

"Hmm" Rayman dropped her home and after reaching his home he again started writing his diary.

Next day is also same in all respects. Today Shiksha and Rayman stayed till late due to work and around nine thirty Rayman said that he will drop her home when they are going her home they were talking about Anna.

"Sir, she will not remain in your touch?"

"Hmm"

"Why don't you try again?"

"What?"

"Propose her one more time, this time she has seen your better side. You know my inclination always says that she loves you."

"You know Naina also said same thing to me last night when I was dropping her home"

"Really, so are you proposing her again?"

"I haven't decided yet."

He is thinking about suggestion given by Naina and Shiksha after reaching home.

'Should I really try one more time? What if she gets angrier? But what do I have to lose? I know there is a risk but bet on this risk is also really important for me. Where will I get chance to say something face to face? I should be ready for it, how should I propose her? What about a ring? Hmm it is a good idea.' He couldn't remember when he went to sleep in those thoughts.

Next day is also same in all respects and similar to previous two days today Sonia, Shiksha and Rayman stayed till late due to work and around nine thirty Rayman said that he will drop Sonia home and Shiksha can take cab to her home and they are talking about Anna all the way to her home.

"Sir, this week and she will be gone?"

"I know that"

"Sir, what are plans for her last day? How will you manage your emotions?"

"I don't know, I am asking god to give me strength"

"Sir, you bought cell phone for her"

"Yes"

"What else is in the plan?"

"I bought a top for her and one slam book and one diary which I am writing with poems and best moments."

"OK, who will be writing slam book?"

"All her friend, team mates"

"Are not we writing in it?"

"I will give you all on last day. I want it to remains surprise"

"All right sir."

Seventeen March 2012 Saturday, Rayman called Meena after taking her contact number from Suchi to get her address. He informed her that he will be coming to her home for some work in one hour. Rayman reaches her home after one hour drive from his home and he gets her thoughts on diary. Now everyone wrote in the diary except his team members. Meena was surprised to see Rayman on her door since he is not very close friend to her and as far she knows he is not even close friend of Anna. She asked many questions to which he replied that his team has decided it and he is executing plan since he owns a car.

Eighteen March 2012 is Sunday and Rayman is at Vishu home with Tanu, Vishu and Raina and once again they are discussing about Anna and Rayman. Everybody knows that she will be going two days and everyone consoling Rayman. On the other hand Rayman is not sure about Anna's last day whether it is nineteen or twenty March as HR rep has not confirmed her any date. He was thinking about completing his diary and getting remaining people's thoughts on the slam book next morning. Time passed really fast having fun at Vishu home. Around eleven thirty Rayman said to Tanu that he need to go home to pack few things for tomorrow so they need to hurry to their homes. Rayman dropped Tanu at her home going back to his home and Tanu told him to take care on one turn as it is very sharp but he is in hurry and thinking about Anna and her last day's preparation and then.

"BANGGG" he hit his car to some car at that sharp turn. He came out of his car and noticed that his car's front right head lamp is completely damaged. He walked to other car to see a guy in mid forty on driving seat.

"Are you all right?" Rayman asked to that man.

"Yeah, and you, are you all right?"

"Yeah" Rayman reversed his car a little bit to let the other car pass and then started his journey to home once again. After reaching home he parked his car. Then wrote last few pages in poem's diary and packed that diary with cell phone and kept slam book opened.

Nineteen March 2012 Monday, Everyone is at breakfast table and they were having breakfast and Rayman is not able to speak anything thinking that this is Anna's last day and everyone from his team also feeling for him.

"Why are you so upset?" Anna broke the silence with this question to Rayman and as usual she never forgets to pull his leg on breakfast. She made it her habit since she came back to throws one liner on Rayman and in response he always smile but today is little different so he replied with blank face.

"No, I am not upset"

"When will you going, Is today your last day?" Shiksha asked her.

"No, tomorrow, I told you earlier also"

"You said earlier that date can be 19 or 20 march."

"Oh, HR rep confirmed twenty." And this brought little life to Rayman's face.

"Hey bro, what happened to your car?" Upen came a little early today and he asked Rayman.

"It got hit last night"

"Are you driving?"

"Yeah"

"Oh bro, learn properly first"

"Are you all right?" Shiksha, Sonia, Naina and Jiya all asked him one by one.

"Yeah"

"What happened?" Rahul asked about accident.

"I think I was thinking about something and couldn't see other car coming from other side."

"Drive carefully with attention on road or you will die soon." It is Anna's comment which stunned everyone.

"I will" he murmured under his breath and they came back to their seats after lunch.

Rayman handed slam book to Naina and Shiksha to get everyone's thought on it. Naina started with Upen but he said that he will write at last, and then she went to Vivek and got same response from him too. Rahul also gave him same response, nobody wants to write first. Girls wrote in first half followed by Upen and Rahul. Naina and Vivek were last to write. Naina noticed that

Rayman has not written anything on it so she asked him 'why hasn't he written anything?'

"I don't want that she has to read anything from me when she doesn't want to remember me, and hence I have written separate diary for her."

"Sir, you should write something in it."

"I am not feeling it would be good idea"

"I think you should write at very first place as a friend, you were her friend even before this happened."

"Hmm you are right; I should write at least 'all the best' to her."

Rayman returned to his seat leaving responsibility of diary to Naina. Rest of the day passed as usual, same lunch, same ice-cream party followed by evening snack and then tea. In evening everyone gathered around Anna's seat including Rayman. Rayman is standing a little far compared to other and everyone talking about 'how is she feeling?' She is appearing very happy telling her feelings. Everyone went home with questions in mind about what will happen tomorrow.

"Will Rayman be able to control his emotions?"

"Will he be proposing her again on her last day?"

"Will it be any normal farewell or some drama will happen?"

"Is there any possibility of yes from Anna's side?"

"What is plan for her farewell and who is planning for it?"

"Will she give time to celebrate her farewell?"

"What will be Rayman gifting her? Will he really gift her cell phone as he said earlier? And more importantly will she accept it?"

The Last Conversation

20th March 2012, Tuesday Rayman came office very early at around eight thirty in the morning. No one has reached office yet but he wants to see Anna as soon as possible and waiting for her impatiently. He is feeling butterflies in his stomach. He is very nervous and heart beat is already matching with the speed of supersonic plane. Rayman is at his seat trying to work but he is not able to concentrate. Upen came second around fifteen minutes later and it is earlier than his usual time.

"What is it? You came so early, has anything stuck?" Upen asked with surprise as he entered cubicle to see Rayman.

"I couldn't sleep properly in night hence I came office early."

"When did you come and why can't you sleep?"

"I came half an hour ago. I don't know something was running inside my brain all the time."

"Anna?"

"Yes"

"Just one more day brother, when she will go from this office you will also forger her."

"God knows"

"It is just your madness nothing else, how many time should I tell you that she is a weirdo."

"It is her last day so leave it for today."

"OK bro, it is your life and your wish. I am always with you whatever you decide. Have you guys planned anything for her farewell?"

"No plan as of now."

"Who is planning?"

"No one I think I will decide the course"

"You must"

"What should we do?"

"Whatever you want to do"

"Hmm, let me think, let others come then I will discuss with them also to finalize something."

"Sure, let go to cafeteria for breakfast"

"Let others come and it might be my last breakfast with her so let's wait"

"Yeah sure, as you wish. I am at my desk and checking mails, let me know when you are ready"

"Sure"

Everyone came in between 9:00 to 9:15 and then they decided to go up stair for break-fast.

"How are you feeling today?" Naina asked Anna and this question created fear inside Rayman's heart, he doesn't want to hear that she is happy going away from him and he also doesn't want to hear that she is feeling sad, some unknown fear haunting him from inside, but this is her day and she should say whatever she is feeling.

"Honestly, I have mix feelings. You all know that last few days I have lot of work and frustrated me and hence I am happy that I am going to some new and better place."

"Will you ever consider coming back?" Shiksha asked her.

"Not until something went wrong and it is really necessary for me, so you can consider a no."

"Hmm, who want to be here?" Shiksha said in response.

"You will come to get you final settlement and relieving letter. We will meet then." Naina said to Anna.

"Definitely"

"Have you got NOC from all departments?" Rayman asked her.

"Yeah, most of things are ready, just need to check with HR rep in second half."

"Will you need to go to other office for clearing things?"

"No, I think HR rep has done everything."

"Great" Pain is clearly visible in Rayman eyes but he is somehow holding his emotions.

"Please refer my CV in your company" Jiya and Shiksha asked her.

"Mine too" Sonia also said the same thing to her.

"Let me settle first in that company and then I will call you all there." She said to them but everyone knows that she will never refer Rayman.

Everyone returned to their seat after breakfast and now everyone from this group except Anna discussing her farewell and at that moment Jiya came to his seat.

"Sir, may I ask you something?"

"Definitely"

"It is not related to work"

"No issue"

"Do you love Anna?"

"What kind of question is it?"

"Please tell me naah"

"Why do you want to know?"

"Everyone in group knows about it except me."

"Hmm, I do love her but equally important thing you should also know that she doesn't."

"What? Why?"

"She has her reasons"

"Have you tried resolving those reasons? You might have not tried in right way."

"Maybe, but it's my request don't do anything that can hurt her."

"I understand it better than you sir."

Around twelve Rayman mailed everyone in his team except Anna and asked them 'They should go out for lunch for her farewell?' But he has to cancel this plan as no one in favor of it Most of them suggested in response that 'it will high light this and Anna possibly will not like it.' At lunch time Upen and Rahul came to Rayman's seat, and Rayman asked Sonia and Shiksha to ask her for lunch and today even after having so much work and formalities for relieving she said that she will be coming with them. No one is saying anything on table then Upen started the conversation.

"When shall be getting party?" he asked to Anna and this is one of the few conversations he ever had with Anna.

"Let me join and then I will invite you all."

"Who gives party after going?" He commented on her response.

"I promise I will give you party. Let me join then I will call you all for sure."

"We will wait for your invite."

"When are you joining?" Naina asked Anna.

"Possibly I will join on next Monday or April first."

"April fool"

"No yaar"

They returned from lunch after one hour and Rayman asked them for ice-cream party, and he volunteered for ice-cream party.

"Are you guys coming for walk, let's have ice-cream?"

"Sure" Shiksha and Sonia responded but Anna is not looking in the mood.

"I have to go to HR department to complete some formalities."

"It will not take more than ten minutes" Rayman asked her.

"OK" she said yes this time.

Anna went to HR department and rest of guys went to their respective seat after having ice-cream. Everyone is busy in his or her work when Rayman sent them a mail asking about what they should plan for farewell in form of options.

"Pizza party or just cake will do?" Everyone suggested that pizza will be not be good as everyone had lunch few hour ago and they are also not sure about Anna's reaction to it. Rayman also agreed after hearing their point of view.

Around half hour later Rayman is at Upen's seat and ask him to come out with him, Upen is busy in his work but he could not say him no today.

"Hey, come with me, I have some work."

"Tea" Upen asked in surprise.

"No, going out to the market."

"Is anything still pending? Slam book is ready, you bought card also, something else?"

"Nope, Will tell you on the way?"

"Where are we going?"

"New friend's colony"

"Let's go, are you taking car or should I take my bike?"

"Car" after fifteen minutes both reached NFC market and searching for flowers shop. Rayman already told Upen that they are going to get bouquet for Anna.

"I had never given any bouquet to any one before in my life, you should have called Rahul, he must be better person for this job." Upen said to Rayman.

"I have given once before"

"To whom"

"I have given to Vishu and his wife when they returned to Delhi after their honeymoon."

"OK, brother. I noticed one shop there. Take whatever you want for her."

"Roses"

"As you wish"

"We have to put it at Rahul desk till evening"

"I will do that, don't worry"

Rayman and Upen came back to office in half an hour and they stopped at Ashoka café to have tea and Rayman put bouquet at Rahul desk in mean time and Upen called Shiksha for tea and also asked her to bring everyone else and told her that try to bring Anna also as this might be last tea for Rayman with her. Shiksha came followed by Naina, Jiya and Sonia but Anna is nowhere.

"Isn't Anna coming for tea?" Rayman asked when he saw everyone except Anna.

"I called her she is with HR rep, she said that she might come but not sure, she asked to wait for her for few minutes."

"No issue"

Anna didn't came for fifteen minutes but Rayman is in no mood to go inside, he asked others that it would be favor to him if they can give few minutes since it is for just one last day but he knows that he didn't even need to say this to his friends. Everyone else is feeling the same today for him. After nearly half an hour later she came nearly running out of the office building and it is her habit to walk very fast or run when she is late for something and even today she is no different. Rayman is holding his tears in his eyes when she came panting with full smile of her face.

"Everything is done finally." She said to others.

"Congratulation" Shiksha said and other followed except Rayman because now he is in no condition of spilling any word out of his mouth and he don't want to create scene by crying out so he kept mum and brought tea for her.

"You guys had tea?" She asked Rayman and then turned toward Shiksha to ask them the same question. Rayman again just nodded without saying even a single word.

"Yeah, we had few minutes earlier." Shiksha said to Anna but to everyone's surprise Rayman once again having tea in his hand to give her company still standing quite.

"Only exit interview is pending"

"So you will be free in one hour at max." Shiksha and Naina are talking to Anna. Rayman is looking at her and trying to capture this moment in his heart forever. She is wearing red color Salwar kameez suite. She looks even more beautiful in red color with matching red color high heal sandals, and hand bag of same color.

Around 3:00, Rayman wrote mail to Shiksha, Sonia, Jiya and Naina asking about which cake he should order for evening party. In response everyone teased him with suggestions like 'girl in my life' or 'hello kitty' cakes and finally agreed for some 'chocolate fruit wild forest' cake. Sonia ordered cake and asked them to deliver around five thirty. Rayman is no mood of work entire day and he is dragging others also from their work.

Around four thirty Anna came back to her seat after finishing with her exit interview, she has no work so she was sitting at her system and checking e-mails and wrapping up her things.

"Shiksha" Rayman called her.

"Yes"

"Please go and check with Anna if she is done with all her work and also ask her when is she leaving office and also ask her to meet us before leaving."

"Hmm, I think she is free now."

Shiksha went to her seat and came back after ten minute followed by her. She came and sat near Shiksha and Sonia's seat. Sahil and Pooja are working on their system while Jiya, Rahul and Upen also busy on their systems in their cubicle. Rayman and Naina turned their seat toward Anna and this is the time when Garv and Vivek who were shifted to some other cubicles few days back came in Rayman's cubicle to have conversation with Anna one last time before her departure.

"When are you giving party to us?" Garv asked her.

"After joining and you can come to meet me anytime you want, you are a good friend." Anna always considered Garv a good friend.

"Sure, you need to send a mail and we all will be there whenever you want to give us party."

"Sonia, I have given your name in HR to handover my relieving latter and final settlement papers."

"No issue"

"You can handover those papers to your friend who lives near my home and I can collect from her."

"No issue, whenever we meet I will give it to you or if you want I can handover to her as well." Sonia confirmed to her. Rayman is looking at her at this time, but he is still not saying anything but thinking about discussion between Anna and Sonia.

'You don't need to worry about any of your work till I am here, I have handled such matters in past for many of my friends why wouldn't I do it for you. I will drive Sonia to your home to handover your documents if I have to.'

Rayman asked Jiya if cake has come when everyone else is busy in his cubicle, and Jiya confirmed that cake will come around five fifteen. Rayman asked Jiya and Upen if he need to call anyone else for the farewell. Upen suggested that Jay is not in the office but her friend is close to Anna so it would be better if they call her and Vivek. Upen asked Rayman in return to confirm 'Is someone coming from her team from Noida office?' Rayman said that no one has said anything, Sky called yesterday saying that they want to come but it will be difficult for them and they will call her in the evening on her cell. We don't have to wait for them to which Upen chuckled 'Who is waiting for them I am just confirming.' Rayman is back to his seat with Jiya and Upen and at that time Rahul also came to join them.

"Rayman let me know when I have to bring the bouquet." Rahul whispered to Rayman as he entered area.

"Sure, not now may be around five thirty."

Anna is discussing those last moments with everyone with a broader smile on her face. Garv is talking to her with her hand in his hand and that took Rayman's attention toward conversation.

"Your life will be happy and it will be arranged marriage. You will have a daughter as your first child." Garv said to Anna, he is actually saying this after reading her palm and that gave Rayman sigh of relief.

"This is all bullshit. Everything will be decided by our deeds." Rayman said to them.

"No sir, it really matters." Garv said to him

"Then tell me, what is in my hands?" Rayman placed his hand in front of his face.

"You will also have a daughter as first child."

"Is there any further study?"

"No chance"

"What about marriage?"

"It will take some time and an arranged marriage."

"How can you say so? What if kidnap someone to marry me?"

"Sir, I can bet nothing can change it."

"Sir, come here" Jiya called Rayman from her cubicle at around five twenty.

"What is it?" Rayman asked her after reaching her seat.

"Sir, cake has arrived and we have put it at cafeteria. When are we planning to go there?"

"In ten minutes, you guys carry on and I will be coming with all other things. Naina has slam book. She will be bringing that and I will ask Rahul to bring the bouquet."

"What about phone and diary?"

"I will give her in private after the party."

"That will be better."

"OK sir you ask Rahul and I will be calling Naina and others, and one more thing."

"What"

"Should we take Anna with us or you will be calling her?"

"It is the same thing, you guys take her with you, and I am coming with Rahul and Upen, rest of you go to cafeteria."

"OK, Naina come here for a moment." Jiya called Naina and narrated everything to her.

"She is very happy today and looking even more beautiful." Naina said to Rayman as she came to Jiya seat.

"Yeah, thanks for compliment."

"Why aren't you talking to her? It might be your last chance. I am sure she will try to go as far from as possible from you after going from here."

"No, where, why shouldn't I talk to her." Nervousness is quite visible on his face. He is not able form sentences.

"Sir, everything will be all right" Sonia said from behind "All the best"

"Hmm, thanks" Rayman said to her thinking 'Why can't I breathe properly, what is this trying to kill me, why am I choking?'

"Hey Rahul, It's time." Rayman said to Rahul to indicate that he will need to bring the bouquet.

"Done sir" and that signal is enough for him.

"Shiksha, Sonia, Jiya, and Garv you guys take Anna upstairs to cafeteria."

"Sure sir." Shiksha responded. "And you?"

"I am coming with Upen and Rahul. I am going to call Harry ma'am."

"Jay sir's friend"

"Yeah"

"Come soon"

"Sure, Vivek you too go upstairs" Rayman said to Vivek who were talking to Anna at that time.

"Sure brother" and then everyone went to cafeteria.

"Sir, you too go upstairs, I will bring the bouquet, don't worry about that." Rahul gave confirmation to Rayman while moving toward his seat. "Upen sir you also go with him."

"Are you sure?" Upen asked in return.

"Hundred percent"

"OK, let's go Rayman."

Jiya is getting cake and Shiksha and Sonia deciding where to sit after reaching cafeteria. Anna is standing with Naina and Garv, and Garv and Anna still talking about something. Vivek is helping Sonia and Shiksha in deciding where to sit. Rahul came in less than two minutes time and tried handing over bouquet to Rayman but he denied saying that it might not look good and he should put it at table. By that time Sonia, Shiksha and Vivek joined two tables to create ample space for all the people. Anna sat on left side of the table. Jiya, Naina, Shiksha and Sonia are sitting by her left side and in the same order and Garv, Vivek, Upen and Rahul sitting by her right side. Harry ma'am came and pulled a chair near Anna to sit by her side. Jiya and Naina placed cake on the table and Rahul placed bouquet in the center of second table and Rayman is sitting right side of table across Anna but hide himself behind the bouquet so that at least Anna can't see anything from his face.

"Why are you sitting so far, there are so many vacant chairs in between?" Anna said to Rayman, who is stealing his eyes from her since after noon.

"I am ok here."

"Come here and sit on this chair." She pointed toward a chair to her right side and adjacent to her chair. Garv immediately vacated his chair to give him seat, and pulled one for him from another table and sat behind Rayman and little later Harry started conversation.

"Hmm, nice cake"

"Yeah it is" Anna also complimented.

"Let's cut the cake first" Jiya and Shiksha said to them. Upen and Rahul sitting quietly and Rayman still not saying anything and still looking at Anna.

Anna cut the cake and Jiya offered her first piece of cake and put second piece on her face, and Naina and Shiksha also joined Jiya in this while Sonia is capturing those moments through her cell phone camera and this is the time when Garv got carried away while putting cake on her face and Rayman for a moment shifted his concentration from Anna to Garv. Anna is trying to hide herself and trying to get away from Garv but he is following her with cake in his both hands. Rayman is watching from distance thinking that he might kill him for his this deed but controlling his emotions and watching all the drama and god listened Rayman voice and Vivek out of blue helped Anna and held Garv and this give Anna a chance to put cake back on Garv face, but she didn't stopped there and she went freak after that and ran after everyone to put cake on their face, started with Jiya followed by Sonia, Shiksha, Naina, Rahul and Vivek everyone is resisting at first but other helping her. Finally she is coming toward Rayman and Rayman draw himself forward rather than resisting and she put cake like face pack on his right cheek. Harry went back to work area due to some meeting after cake Holi and everyone once again settled around table at the place where they were sitting earlier after cleaning their faces.

"So Anna, share your experience at office." Sonia said to Anna.

"You guys start, I will follow you" she responded.

Sonia started and as per custom she praised her and said so many things, same followed by Shiksha, Jiya and Naina then Pooja and Sahil are also no different. Everyone said that she is good person and a good friend and they enjoyed her stay with them. Garv this time also got carried away and put her to his sister place and so many things, everyone promised that they will stay in touch forever. Then Vivek, Upen and Rahul just completed formality, Rayman since morning not said anything and even now not ready to open his mouth and he knows that even Anna will be nervous thinking 'what he will say?' Naina and Sonia once again insisted Rayman to say something.

"Anna, I know her from the day I shifted from Noida office to this office or in this team and she is always a great friend and an inspiration for me and my team." He paused for a moment and then thinks for a moment and preparing what he want to say further 'I know that you will never want to remain in my touch for sure. You know Anna I can never explain this in words, you are one of the best friends, or it would be even better if I say that you are the best friend because you know I had a time in my life when I was about to broke and I need a hand to support and a shoulder to cry and which I am expecting from my friends especially from Vishu and Vicky but that is the time when I found a shoulder a hand from you, you held me together.' But he doesn't want to embarrass Anna with these word so he prefers to say something else "We shall always remain in touch with each other" and waited for few moment and looking at her for her reply.

"Yeah, definitely" she nodded but not as commitment rather taunt.

"Sir, it is getting late, we have to catch our buses, gift her other things." Naina said to Rayman.

"Yeah, Vivek you give her gift pack." Rayman pointed toward the slam book.

"Sir, you gift her" Rahul and Shiksha insisted.

"It is same."

"Everyone can place hand on diary" Sonia suggested better alternative.

Rahul, Upen, Rayman, Vivek gifted her slam book together and then Sonia, Shiksha, Jiya and Sonia gifted her bouquet. It is six fifteen now and now everyone is in hurry to catch bus for their home. Everyone moving out of cafeteria, Sonia, Shiksha and Naina stayed there to clean the mess. Rayman is just behind Anna and he stopped Anna at the exit gate.

"I have something for you."

"What else? You guys have given me everything."

"I want to gift you something from my side."

"I can't take anything."

"First take it and then it is your decision you want to keep it or not."

"What other people will think about it?"

"I don't know."

"OK, I will let you know."

Six thirty half of the guys left for their buses and suddenly Rayman's cell phone started ringing.

"Pyaar to hona hi tha, pyaar to hona hi tha." This is custom ringtone for Anna's call only.

"Hello"

"Hello, give it to me, now no one is here to see it." She said to Rayman about his gift.

"Sure" Rayman said nothing else and went to Anna seat with a gift pack and she put packet in her hand bag.

"What is in it?"

"You check yourself"

"Huh" she exhaled angrily.

Rayman went to his seat and came back to her seat once again after two minutes to ask her.

"If you don't mind may I drop you home?"

"No, I will go by bus." Rayman submerged in his thought when she denied 'How will I gift her ring? I bought ring thinking that I will gift her in person. Naina and Shiksha also said that I should propose her on last day. How can I propose her now when I will not get any chance to meet her in person?' He is going back to his seat in between thoughts. 'May be she want to go with her friends in bus, she might want to say good bye to them also. Should I ask her one more time, I will not say anything to her on the way, but I should drop her home today, It's her wish if she don't want to talk but I have to drop her.' Rayman could not think anything else except Anna, he stood from his seat and looking toward her seat, Anna also stood up to go out of office.

'Anna, please take me with you. Anna, please listen to me, take me with you.' Rayman is looking at her trying to say from his eyes and he without even noticing moved toward Anna.

"Hey Anna, If you don't mind I really love to drop you home."

"No, I will go by bus, you don't worry. You don't need to take any trouble for it."

"Not any problem at all."

"It is OK Rayman, I will go by bus."

"As you wish"

Rayman went back to his seat and wrapping up his things to go home. Everyone in the team also wrapped up their things. Shiksha and Jiya already went out to catch their bus and Sonia is working on something and hence stayed back.

"Hey bro, are you coming out for tea?" Upen and Rahul came to Rayman and asked him for the tea.

"Sure. Wait for me for few minutes."

Upen and Rahul going out ahead of Rayman and Anna is following them followed by Rayman. Rayman still thinking that he should at least drop Anna to her bus. Naina is following Rayman and she whispered in his ear.

"Sir, have you given her your diary and other things?"

"Yup"

"Now wait for her call. She will not spare you this time without at least thousands of curses."

"Naina, speak good"

"All the best, bye"

"Thanks, bye" Rayman continued following Anna with thoughts in his mind.

'She must be very uncomfortable carrying all these things, and how can she carry these many things in her two hands?'

"Upen, should we drop her to her bus?" Rayman asks Upen.

"Rayman please leave her now. She doesn't want you to drop her otherwise she must have come with you."

"How will she carry these many things to bus?"

"Bro, she isn't carrying gas cylinders. She is carrying just a bouquet and a diary and I am sure she can take this much weight."

"Hmm, but"

"What but? Have tea and let her go."

"Sure brother"

Rayman is watching Anna going away from him and possibly for forever with tea in his hand and plea in his mind 'Please take me with you'. She is managing hand bag on her right shoulder and bouquet in her left hand and walked toward bus. After half an hour Rayman and Upen are at their seat. Sonia is working on her system.

"Sonia, have you done with your work?"

"Yes sir, I am done and now waiting for cab, I have to wait till nine."

"Come with me, I will drop you home. Upen when are you leaving?"

"I am waiting for you guys."

"Let's go then"

"Sure" Sonia and Upen picked their things to move out.

Sonia and Rayman started conversation about incidents happened in the day on the way to her home.

"Sir, have you given her your diary?"

"Yes"

"Let's hope for best now."

"Yeah"

"But I am really proud of you"

"Why?"

"I thought for once that you will break down but you managed to control your emotions. We all were sure that you will cry aloud today."

"Honestly, I was also not sure about how will I handle it and that is the reason why I hid behind bouquet but then she called me near her. She is so unpredictable sometime."

"Hmm, but she was happy with everything."

"And this is what I really wanted."

"Farewell and everything went well"

"Yeah, let's hope that my gifts also go well with her."

"Hmm"

Rayman dropped Sonia home and reached his home around 08:15 and at the same time Shiksha called him.

"Hello"

"Hello Shiksha, have you reached home?"

"Yeah, how are you feeling now? Have you gifted her diary?"

"Yeah and I am fine."

"Then wait for her call. She will be calling you in few minutes."

"Don't know?"

"She will definitely call and be ready for curses."

"Why someone going to abuse for gifts?"

"She will tell you in detail."

"OK, I think Naina is calling, I will call you back."

"OK, bye"

"Hello Naina"

"Hello sir, whom are you talking to, is it Anna?"

"No, Shiksha, Anna will never call me."

"Sir, I am sure she will call either today or tomorrow."

"Naina, she is calling. I will call you back."

"No, wait sir. Let her wait for some time."

"Why should I let her wait?"

"Sir, please let her wait for some time."

"Oh, she hanged. Naina I am going to call her and then I will call you in few minutes."

"Sir, please. She will call you again. Let her call you."

"Why are you doing this? I am calling her."

"Sir"

"Naina, she is calling again, bye for now, I will call you in few minutes."

"No"

"Why?"

"Wait for some time. You know this is the reason why she never said yes to you. You didn't let her realize your importance."

"OK, she disconnected again."

"Now don't call her back and wait for her call."

"As you say, but I will wait for fifteen minutes only and then I will call her."

"You don't have to wait even five minutes, she will call you soon"

"Let's see"

Rayman disconnected the call and switched-on television after freshen up and watching some romantic songs and as Naina told him Anna called him in few minutes and he went to terrace after picking the call.

"Hello Rayman"

"Hello"

"Are you driving or reached home?"

"I have reached home. Why"

"I asked because of your habit of banging your car. What is this?"

"What is what?"

"Who give so expensive cell phone as a gift? I can't take that cell phone."

"I have gifted as a friend, please accept it."

"Who gives a friend a cell phone and that too so expensive?"

"People give even more expensive things in friendship. Friends don't care about the price."

"But I can't accept it. Please understand and take it back. If you don't take it back I will never talk to you, if you want to remain in touch with me then take it back."

"As you wish, I have never forced you for anything. I have always accepted whatever you wished or expected from me."

"I will send your cell phone back to you with Shiksha or Sonia and please take it back."

"I told you naah, as you wish"

"Your diary is far more valuable for me than this"

"Thanks"

"Rayman, you are mature enough to understand that I can never commit for this relationship. I already told you that I am from traditional Kashmiri Brahmin family. How can you think that I can marry a lower non-Kashmiri Brahmin guy? My parent will never permit and I can't even imagine going against their wish. I am not like Naina, she is really a wild girl and she can do anything for her love but I can't. Tell me why you love me so much, because I am beautiful and fair?" she is very calm and composed during conversation.

"Why do you think so?"

"Hmm, you have written so much in that diary."

"Yeah, you are beautiful no doubts about it but there are other things which brought me closure to you."

"I have read little bit, I really like the poems" She said that she read little bit but from conversation it is quite obvious that she read whole diary before calling "And why have you written that you bought car for me?" She said last sentence with little anger in her voice. "Keep your car for your wife only. And now you have gifted your diary and pen to me so stop writing poems for me. Write everything for your wife from now. You know this make me really happy that you love me and love me so much and which girl would not be happy to have a lover like this? But I am saying this for you, I care for you, and I never want my friend troubled. So please forget me and move on in your life. You have no future with me." She started this time with aggression but sooner she is back to her previous pitch. "Where you had bought top from? You have wasted so much money. I can take diaries and top but you have to take your cell phone back."

"I will"

"You use that phone; it will suit you. Live a grand life, new car, and new cell phone."

"I don't believe in show off. Anna, I bought one more thing for you and I want to give that you in person while dropping you home but I couldn't get a chance to give you that thing."

"What is that?"

"I can't tell you, you will get angry."

"I wouldn't"

"I know you will definitely get angry and then you will start scolding me."

"I promise you that I will not scold you, really. Now please tell me what is it?" She said this line with so much love that this is enough for Rayman to give even his life.

"I bought a ring for you, a diamond ring."

"I already have two diamond rings."

"That doesn't make it a non-diamond ring."

"Why did you buy a diamond ring for me? You should buy for your wife."

"I can't describe that but really I have not purchased it to propose you with that ring."

"Why don't you get married and gift that ring to your wife?"

"Even everyone at my home wants me to marry but I said no to them."

"I noticed in your resume that your dad is not alive then why you troubling your mom, get married for her at least."

"I will but after sometime."

"I know you love me and I respect your feelings but at the same time I don't want you to waste your life after me. I want you to be happy always. Marry some good girl. All the best and be happy. Good night."

"Good night and take care" She hanged the call and Rayman is in tears now. He knows that there is no further hope. He will not be able to see her any more. He falls on his knee on the terrace and crying uncontrollably.

'Dear God, why is it me? But thank you for giving me these forty days to live my life' tears rolling down from both of his eyes. 'Why this discrimination plays so important role in any one's love story. I know that I belong to lower caste, I am not like Anna in anyways but how is it my fault? It is god's decision to send me to particular caste. Anna, I can't live without you, please come and hold my hand, take me with you. I want to die right now.' Rayman stood with feeling of jumping off the terrace and closed his eyes thinking that he will be on ground in few seconds but as he closed his eyes with heavy breathes to see his mother in front of him. 'I can never give trouble to my mother, no way.'

'Anna, I loved you, I love you and I will always love you.'

This dialog automatically came in my mind "I suppose in the end, the whole of life becomes an act of letting go. But what always hurts the most is not taking a moment to say goodbye." from the movie Life of Pi and I think Anna wished perfect good bye to Rayman in the end.

-udayman singh

Epilogue

Finally let me introduce myself, I am Raina, Vishu's wife and very good friend of Rayman, Tanu and Toni. I was with Rayman and witnessed how he went crazy in love for a girl who could not commit for him. Unfortunately I never got a chance to meet her to know the actual reasons from her side. I, Tanu and Vishu always said to him to forget her and move on in life but I know that it is not that easy for him. I am fed-up listening about Anna all the time, she is like this or that, she is so beautiful, she is like angel, her smile, her face, her nature and you just need to see her once smiling to fall in love with her. Tanu, Toni and Vishu are also fed-up like me and once we went for Murthal trip with Rayman's team mates then I realized that even Upen, Shiksha, Naina and his other team mates also fed-up listening about Anna all the time. I pray and wish that Anna will be with him someday to end our torture.

Frankly I want him to marry someone who can become my good friend and can give me company. But as a friend and his bhabhi I also want and wish that he get girl of his dreams.

Glossary

Rayman - (pronounced as Ray (as in blue ray) Mon (as in Monday))

Anna – (pronounced as Aena)

Didi/Di – Elder sister

Parathas – Indian fried bread can be stuffed with veggies.

Yaar – Friend

Tc – take care

Salwar (Kameez) suit – Salwar are loose pajama-like trousers. The legs are wide at the top, and narrow at the ankle. The kameez is a long shirt or tunic, often with a western-style collar or collarless or Mandarin collar. The sides left open below the waist-line, give the wearer greater freedom of movement.